*Acclaim for Toni Morrison's*

# SONG OF SOLOMON

"It places Toni Morrison in the front rank of contemporary American writers. She has written a novel that will endure."
—*The Washington Post*

"Lovely. . . . A delight, full of lyrical variety and allusiveness. . . . [An] exceptionally diverse novel."
—*The Atlantic Monthly*

"A rich, full novel. . . . It lifts us up [and] impresses itself upon us like a love affair."
—*The New York Times Book Review*

"Morrison dazzles. . . . She creates a black community strangely unto itself yet never out of touch with the white world. . . . With an ear as sharp as glass she has listened to the music of black talk and uses it as a palette knife to create black lives and to provide some of the best fictional dialogue around today."
—*The Nation*

"A marvelous novel, the most moving I have read in ten years of reviewing."
—*The Plain Dealer*

"Toni Morrison has created a fanciful world here. . . . She has an impeccable sense of emotional detail. She's the most sensible lyrical writer around today."
—*The Philadelphia Inquirer*

"A fine novel exuberantly constructed. . . . So rich in its use of common speech, so sophisticated in its use of literary traditions and language from the Bible to Faulkner . . . it is also extremely funny."
—*The Hudson Review*

"Toni Morrison is an extraordinarily good writer. Two pages into anything she writes one feels the power of her language and the emotional authority behind that language. . . . One closes the book warmed through by the richness of its sympathy, and by its breathtaking feel for the nature of sexual sorrow."
—*The Village Voice*

"Morrison moves easily in and out of the lives and thoughts of her characters, luxuriating in the diversity of circumstances and personality, and revelling in the sound of their voices and of her own, which echoes and elaborates theirs."
—*The New Yorker*

*Also by Toni Morrison*

**FICTION**

*Love*

*Paradise*

*Jazz*

*Beloved*

*Tar Baby*

*Sula*

*The Bluest Eye*

**NONFICTION**

*The Dancing Mind*

*Playing in the Dark:
Whiteness and the Literary Imagination*

*Toni Morrison*

# SONG OF SOLOMON

Toni Morrison is the Robert F. Goheen Professor of Humanities, Emeritus at Princeton University. She has received the National Book Critics Circle Award and the Pulitzer Prize. In 1993 she was awarded the Nobel Prize in Literature. She lives in Rockland County, New York, and Princeton, New Jersey.

INTERNATIONAL

# SONG OF

# SOLOMON

*Toni Morrison*

**VINTAGE INTERNATIONAL**

*Vintage Books • A Division of Random House, Inc. • New York*

**FIRST VINTAGE INTERNATIONAL EDITION, JUNE 2004**

*Copyright © 1977, 2004 by Toni Morrison*

All rights reserved under International and Pan-American
Copyright Conventions. Published in the United States by
Vintage Books, a division of Random House, Inc., New York,
and simultaneously in Canada by Random House of Canada
Limited, Toronto. Originally published in slightly different form
in hardcover in the United States by Alfred A. Knopf, a division
of Random House, Inc., New York, in 1977.

Vintage is a registered trademark and Vintage International
and colophon are trademarks of Random House, Inc.

The Library of Congress has cataloged the Knopf edition
as follows:
Morrison, Toni.
Song of Solomon.
I. Title.
PZ4.M883So [PS3563.08749]
813'.5'4
77-874

**Vintage ISBN: 1-4000-3342-X**

*Book design by Gwen Townsend*

www.vintagebooks.com

Printed in the United States of America
30  29

*Daddy*

*The fathers may soar*
*And the children may know their names*

# Foreword

I have long despised artists' chatter about muses—"voices" that speak to them and enable a vision, the source of which they could not otherwise name. I thought of muses as inventions to protect one's insight, to avoid questions like "Where do your ideas come from?" Or to escape inquiry into the fuzzy area between autobiography and fiction. I regarded the "mystery" of creativity as a shield erected by artists to avoid articulating, analyzing, or even knowing the details of their creative process—for fear it would fade away.

Writing *Song of Solomon* destroyed all that. I had no access to what I planned to write about until my father died. In the unmanageable sadness that followed, there was none of the sibling wrangling, guilt or missed opportunities, or fights for this or that memento. Each of his four children was convinced that he loved her or him best. He had sacrificed greatly for one, risking his house and his job; he took another to baseball games over whole summers where they lay in the grass listening to a portable radio, talking, evaluating the players on the field. In the company of one, his firstborn, he always beamed and preferred her cooking over everyone else's, including his wife's. He carried a letter from me in his coat pocket for years and years, and drove through blinding snowstorms to help me. Most important, he talked to each of us in language cut to our different understandings. He had a flattering view of me as someone interesting, capable, witty, smart, high-spirited. I did not share that view of myself, and wondered why he held it. But it was the death of that girl—the one who lived in his head— that I mourned when he died. Even more than I mourned him, I suffered the loss of the person he thought I was. I think it was because I felt closer to him than to myself that, after his death, I deliberately sought his advice for writing the novel that continued to elude me. "What are the men you have known really like?"

He answered.

Whatever it is called—muse, insight, inspiration, "the dark finger that guides," "bright angel"—it exists and, in many forms, I have trusted it ever since.

The challenge of *Song of Solomon* was to manage what was for me a radical shift in imagination from a female locus to a male one. To get out of the house, to de-domesticate the landscape that had so far been the site of my work. To travel. To fly. In such an overtly, stereotypically male narrative, I thought that straightforward chronology would be more suitable than the kind of play with sequence and time I had employed in my previous novels. A journey, then, with the accomplishment of flight, the triumphant end of a trip through earth, to its surface, on into water, and finally into air. All very saga-like. Old-school heroic, but with other meanings. Opening the novel with the suicidal leap of the insurance agent, ending it with the protagonist's confrontational soar into danger, was meant to enclose the mystical but problematic one taken by the Solomon of the title.

I have written, elsewhere and at some length, details of how certain sentences get written and the work I hope they do. Let me extrapolate an example here.

"The North Carolina Mutual Life Insurance agent promised to fly from Mercy to the other side of Lake Superior at 3:00."

This declarative sentence is designed to mock a journalistic style. With a minor alteration it could be the opening of an item in a small town newspaper. It has the tone of an everyday event of minimal local interest, yet I wanted it to contain important signs and crucial information. The name of the insurance company is that of a well-known black-owned company dependent on black clients, and in its corporate name are "life" and "mutual." The sentence starts with "North Carolina" and closes with "Lake Superior"—geographical locations that suggest a journey from south to north—a direction common for black immigration and in the literature about it, but which is reversed here since the protagonist has to go south to mature. Two other words of significance are "fly" and "mercy." Both terms are central to the narrative: flight as escape or confrontation; mercy the unspoken wish of the novel's population. Some grant it; some despise it; one makes it the sole cry of her extemporaneous sermon upon the death of her granddaughter. Mercy touches, turns, and returns to Guitar at the end of the book, and moves him to make it his own final gift to his former friend. Mercy is what one wishes for Hagar; what is unavailable to and unsought by Macon Dead, senior; what his wife learns to demand from him, and what the townsfolk believe can never come from the white world, as is signified by the inversion of the name of the hospital from Mercy to "No-Mercy." But the sentence turns, as all sentences do, on its verb. "Promise." The insurance agent does not declare, announce, or threaten his act; he promises, as though a contract is being executed between himself and others. He hopes his flight, like that of the character in the title, toward asylum (Canada, or freedom, or the company of the welcoming dead), or home, is interpreted as a radical gesture demanding change, an alternative way, a cessation of things as they are. He does not want it understood as a simple desperate act, the end of a fruitless life, a life without examination, but as a deep commitment to his people. And in their response to his decision there is a tenderness, some contrition, and mounting respect ("They didn't know he had it in him"), an awareness that his suicide enclosed, rather than repudiated them. The note he leaves asks for forgiveness. It is tacked on his door as a modest invitation to whoever might pass by.

Of the flights in the novel, Solomon's is the most magical, the most theatrical, and, for Milkman, the most satisfying. Unlike most mythical flights, which clearly imply triumph, in the attempt if not the success, Solomon's escape, the insurance man's jump, and Milkman's leap are ambiguous, disturbing. Solomon's escape from slavery is also the abandonment of his family; the insurance man leaves a message saying his suicide is a gesture of love, but guilt and despair also inform his decision. Milkman believes he is risking his life in return for Pilate's, yet he knows his enemy has disarmed himself. These flights, these erstwhile heroics, are viewed rather differently by the women left behind. Both the quotation and the song of the title fairly shout that different understanding. To praise a woman whose attention was focused solely on family and domestic responsibilities, Milkman summons a conundrum: that without ever leaving the ground she could fly. My father laughed.

*Part I*

# Chapter 1

The North Carolina Mutual Life Insurance agent promised to fly from Mercy to the other side of Lake Superior at three o'clock. Two days before the event was to take place he tacked a note on the door of his little yellow house:

> At 3:00 p.m. on Wednesday the 18th of February, 1931, I will take off from Mercy and fly away on my own wings. Please forgive me. I loved you all.
> (signed) Robert Smith,
> Ins. agent

Mr. Smith didn't draw as big a crowd as Lindbergh had four years earlier—not more than forty or fifty people showed up—because it was already eleven o'clock in the morning, on the very Wednesday he had chosen for his flight, before anybody read the note. At that time of day, during the middle of the week, word-of-mouth news just lumbered along. Children were in school; men were at work; and most of the women were fastening their corsets and getting ready to go see what tails or entrails the butcher might be giving away. Only the unemployed, the self-employed, and the very young were available—deliberately available because they'd heard about it, or accidentally available because they happened to be walking at that exact moment in the shore end of Not Doctor Street, a name the post office did not recognize. Town maps registered the street as Mains Avenue, but the only colored doctor in the city had lived and died on that street, and when he moved there in 1896 his patients took to calling the street, which none of them lived in or near, Doctor Street. Later, when other Negroes moved there, and when the postal service became a popular means of transferring messages among them, envelopes from Louisiana, Virginia, Alabama, and Georgia began to arrive addressed to people at house numbers on Doctor Street. The post office workers returned these envelopes or passed them on to the Dead Letter Office. Then in 1918, when colored men were being drafted, a few gave their address at the recruitment office as Doctor Street. In that way, the name acquired a quasi-official status. But not for long. Some of the city legislators, whose concern for appropriate names and the maintenance of the city's landmarks was the principal part of their political life, saw to it that "Doctor Street" was never used in any official capacity. And since they knew that only Southside residents kept it up, they had notices posted in the stores, barbershops, and restaurants in that part of the city saying that the avenue running northerly and southerly from Shore Road fronting the lake to the junction of routes 6 and 2 leading to Pennsylvania, and also running parallel to and between Rutherford Avenue and Broadway, had always been and would always be known as Mains Avenue and not Doctor Street.

It was a genuinely clarifying public notice because it gave Southside residents a way to keep their memories alive and please the city legislators as well. They called it Not Doctor Street, and were inclined to call the charity hospital at its northern end No Mercy Hospital since it was 1931, on the day following Mr. Smith's leap from its cupola, before the first colored expectant mother was allowed to give birth inside its wards and not on its steps. The reason for the hospital's generosity to that particular woman was not the fact that she was the only child of this Negro doctor, for during his entire professional life he had never been granted hospital privileges and only two of his patients were ever admitted to Mercy, both white. Besides, the doctor had been dead a long time by 1931. It must have been Mr. Smith's leap from the roof over their heads that made them admit her. In any case, whether or not the little insurance agent's conviction that he could fly contributed to the place of her delivery, it certainly contributed to its time.

When the dead doctor's daughter saw Mr. Smith emerge as promptly as he had promised from behind the cupola, his wide blue silk wings curved forward around his chest, she dropped her covered peck basket, spilling red velvet rose petals. The wind blew them about, up, down, and into small mounds of snow. Her half-grown daughters scrambled about trying to catch them, while their mother moaned and held the underside of her stomach. The rose-petal scramble got a lot of attention, but the pregnant lady's moans did not. Everyone knew the girls had spent hour after hour tracing, cutting, and stitching the costly velvet, and that Gerhardt's Department Store would be quick to reject any that were soiled.

It was nice and gay there for a while. The men joined in trying to collect the scraps before the snow soaked through them—snatching them from a gust of wind or plucking them delicately from the snow. And the very young children couldn't make up their minds whether to watch the man circled in blue on the roof or the bits of red flashing around on the ground. Their dilemma was solved when a woman suddenly burst into song. The singer, standing at the back of the crowd, was as poorly dressed as the doctor's daughter was well dressed. The latter had on a neat gray coat with the traditional pregnant-woman bow at her navel, a black cloche, and a pair of four-button ladies' galoshes. The singing woman wore a knitted navy cap pulled far down over her forehead. She had wrapped herself up in an old quilt instead of a winter coat. Her head cocked to one side, her eyes fixed on Mr. Robert Smith, she sang in a powerful contralto:

> *O Sugarman done fly away*
> *Sugarman done gone*
> *Sugarman cut across the sky*
> *Sugarman gone home. . . .*

A few of the half a hundred or so people gathered there nudged each other and sniggered. Others listened as though it were the helpful and defining piano music in a silent movie. They stood this way for some time, none of them crying out to Mr. Smith, all of them preoccupied with one or the other of the minor events about them, until the hospital people came.

They had been watching from the windows—at first with mild curiosity, then, as the crowd seemed to swell to the very walls of the hospital, they watched with apprehension. They wondered if one of those things that racial-uplift groups were always organizing was taking place. But when they saw neither placards nor speakers, they ventured outside into the cold: white-coated surgeons, dark-jacketed business and personnel clerks, and three nurses in starched jumpers.

The sight of Mr. Smith and his wide blue wings transfixed them for a few seconds, as did the woman's singing and the roses strewn about. Some of them thought briefly that this was probably some form of worship. Philadelphia, where Father Divine reigned, wasn't all that far away. Perhaps the young girls holding baskets of flowers were two of his virgins. But the laughter of a gold-toothed man brought them back to their senses. They stopped daydreaming and swiftly got down to business, giving orders. Their shouts and bustling caused great confusion where before there had been only a few men and some girls playing with pieces of velvet and a woman singing.

One of the nurses, hoping to bring some efficiency into the disorder, searched the faces around her until she saw a stout woman who looked as though she might move the earth if she wanted to.

"You," she said, moving toward the stout woman. "Are these your children?"

The stout woman turned her head slowly, her eyebrows lifted at the carelessness of the address. Then, seeing where the voice came from, she lowered her brows and veiled her eyes.

"Ma'am?"

"Send one around back to the emergency office. Tell him to tell the guard to get over here quick. That boy there can go. That one." She pointed to a cat-eyed boy about five or six years old.

The stout woman slid her eyes down the nurse's finger and looked at the child she was pointing to.

"Guitar, ma'am."

"What?"

"Guitar."

The nurse gazed at the stout woman as though she had spoken Welsh. Then she closed her mouth, looked again at the cat-eyed boy, and lacing her fingers, spoke her next words very slowly to him.

"Listen. Go around to the back of the hospital to the guard's office. It will say 'Emergency Admissions' on the door. A-D-M-I-S-I-O-N 8. But the guard will be there. Tell him to get over here—on the double. Move now. Move!" She unlaced her fingers and made scooping motions with her hands, the palms pushing against the wintry air.

A man in a brown suit came toward her, puffing little white clouds of breath. "Fire truck's on its way. Get back inside. You'll freeze to death."

The nurse nodded.

"You left out a s, ma'am," the boy said. The North was new to him and he had just begun to learn he could speak up to white people. But she'd already gone, rubbing her arms against the cold.

"Granny, she left out a s."

"And a 'please.' "

"You reckon he'll jump?"

"A nutwagon do anything."

"Who is he?"

"Collects insurance. A nutwagon."

"Who is that lady singing?"

"That, baby, is the very last thing in pea-time." But she smiled when she looked at the singing woman, so the cat-eyed boy listened to the musical performance with at least as much interest as he devoted to the man flapping his wings on top of the hospital.

The crowd was beginning to be a little nervous now that the law was being called in. They each knew Mr. Smith. He came to their houses twice a month to collect one dollar and sixty-eight cents and write down on a little yellow card both the date and their eighty-four cents a week payment. They were always half a month or so behind, and talked endlessly to him about paying ahead—after they had a preliminary discussion about what he was doing back so soon anyway.

"You back in here already? Look like I just got rid of you."

"I'm tired of seeing your face. Really tired."

"I knew it. Soon's I get two dimes back to back, here you come. More regular than the reaper. Do Hoover know about you?"

They kidded him, abused him, told their children to tell him they were out or sick or gone to Pittsburgh. But they held on to those little yellow cards as though they meant something—laid them gently in the shoe box along with the rent receipts, marriage licenses, and expired factory identification badges. Mr. Smith smiled through it all, managing to keep his eyes focused almost the whole time on his customers' feet. He wore a business suit for his work, but his house was no better than theirs. He never had a woman that any of them knew about and said nothing in church but an occasional "Amen." He never beat anybody up and he wasn't seen after dark, so they thought he was probably a nice man. But he was heavily associated with illness and death, neither of which was distinguishable from the brown picture of the North Carolina Mutual Life Building on the back of their yellow cards. Jumping from the roof of Mercy was the most interesting thing he had done. None of them had suspected he had it in him. Just goes to show, they murmured to each other, you never really do know about people.

The singing woman quieted down and, humming the tune, walked through the crowd toward the rose-petal lady, who was still cradling her stomach.

"You should make yourself warm," she whispered to her, touching her lightly on the elbow. "A little bird'll be here with the morning."

"Oh?" said the rose-petal lady. "Tomorrow morning?"

"That's the only morning coming."

"It can't be," the rose-petal lady said. "It's too soon."

"No it ain't. Right on time."

The women were looking deep into each other's eyes when a loud roar went up from the crowd—a kind of wavy *oo* sound. Mr. Smith had lost his balance for a second, and was trying gallantly to hold on to a triangle of wood that jutted from the cupola. Immediately the singing woman began again:

> O Sugarman done fly
> O Sugarman done gone . . .

Downtown the firemen pulled on their greatcoats, but when they arrived at Mercy, Mr. Smith had seen the rose petals, heard the music, and leaped on into the air.


The next day a colored baby was born inside Mercy for the first time. Mr. Smith's blue silk wings must have left their mark, because when the little boy discovered, at four, the same thing Mr. Smith had learned earlier—that only birds and airplanes could fly—he lost all interest in himself. To have to live without that single gift saddened him and left his imagination so bereft that he appeared dull even to the women who did not hate his mother. The ones who did, who accepted her invitations to tea and envied the doctor's big dark house of twelve rooms and the green sedan, called him "peculiar." The others, who knew that the house was more prison than palace, and that the Dodge sedan was for Sunday drives only, felt sorry for Ruth Foster and her dry daughters, and called her son "deep." Even mysterious.

"Did he come with a caul?"

"You should have dried it and made him some tea from it to drink. If you don't he'll see ghosts."

"You believe that?"

"I don't, but that's what the old people say."

"Well, he's a deep one anyway. Look at his eyes."

And they pried pieces of baked-too-fast sunshine cake from the roofs of their mouths and looked once more into the boy's eyes. He met their gaze as best he could until, after a pleading glance toward his mother, he was allowed to leave the room.

It took some planning to walk out of the parlor, his back washed with the hum of their voices, open the heavy double doors leading to the dining room, slip up the stairs past all those bedrooms, and not arouse the attention of Lena and Corinthians sitting like big baby dolls before a table heaped with scraps of red velvet. His sisters made roses in the afternoon. Bright, lifeless roses that lay in peck baskets for months until the specialty buyer at Gerhardt's sent Freddie the janitor over to tell the girls that they could use another gross. If he did manage to slip by his sisters and avoid their casual malice, he knelt in his room at the window sill and wondered again and again why he had to stay level on the ground. The quiet that suffused the doctor's house then, broken only by the murmur of the women eating sunshine cake, was only that: quiet. It was not peaceful, for it was preceded by and would soon be terminated by the presence of Macon Dead.

Solid, rumbling, likely to erupt without prior notice, Macon kept each member of his family awkward with fear. His hatred of his wife glittered and sparked in every word he spoke to her. The disappointment he felt in his daughters sifted down on them like ash, dulling their buttery complexions and choking the lilt out of what should have been girlish voices. Under the frozen heat of his glance they tripped over doorsills and dropped the salt cellar into the yolks of their poached eggs. The way he mangled their grace, wit, and self-esteem was the single excitement of their days. Without the tension and drama he ignited, they might not have known what to do with themselves. In his absence his daughters bent their necks over blood-red squares of velvet and waited eagerly for any hint of him, and his wife, Ruth, began her days stunned into stillness by her husband's contempt and ended them wholly animated by it.

When she closed the door behind her afternoon guests, and let the quiet smile die from her lips, she began the preparation of food her husband found impossible to eat. She did not try to make her meals nauseating; she simply didn't know how not to. She would notice that the sunshine cake was too haggled to put before him and decide on a rennet dessert. But the grinding of the veal and beef for a meat loaf took so long she not only forgot the pork, settling for bacon drippings poured over the meat, she had no time to make a dessert at all. Hurriedly, then, she began to set the table. As she unfolded the white linen and let it billow over the fine mahogany table, she would look once more at the large water mark. She never set the table or passed through the dining room without looking at it. Like a lighthouse keeper drawn to his window to gaze once again at the sea, or a prisoner automatically searching out the sun as he steps into the yard for his hour of exercise, Ruth looked for the water mark several times during the day. She knew it was there, would always be there, but she needed to confirm its presence. Like the keeper of the lighthouse and the prisoner, she regarded it as a mooring, a checkpoint, some stable visual object that assured her that the world was still there; that this was life and not a dream. That she was alive somewhere, inside, which she acknowledged to be true only because a thing she knew intimately was out there, outside herself.

Even in the cave of sleep, without dreaming of it or thinking of it at all, she felt its presence. Oh, she talked endlessly to her daughters and her guests about how to get rid of it—what might hide this single flaw on the splendid wood: Vaseline, tobacco juice, iodine, a sanding followed by linseed oil. She had tried them all. But her glance was nutritious; the spot became, if anything, more pronounced as the years passed.

The cloudy gray circle identified the place where the bowl filled every day during the doctor's life with fresh flowers had stood. Every day. And when there were no flowers, it held a leaf arrangement, a gathering of twigs and berries, pussy willow, Scotch pine. . . . But always something to grace the dinner table in the evening.

It was for her father a touch that distinguished his own family from the people among whom they lived. For Ruth it was the summation of the affectionate elegance with which she believed her childhood had been surrounded. When Macon married her and moved into Doctor's house, she kept up the centerpiece-arranging. Then came the time she walked down to the shore through the roughest part of the city to get some driftwood. She had seen an arrangement of driftwood and dried seaweed in the homemakers section of the newspaper. It was a damp November day, and Doctor was paralyzed even then and taking liquid food in his bedroom. The wind had lifted her skirt from around her ankles and cut through her laced shoes. She'd had to rub her feet down with warm olive oil when she got back. At dinner, where just the two of them sat, she turned toward her husband and asked him how he liked the centerpiece. "Most people overlook things like that. They see it, but they don't see anything beautiful in it. They don't see that nature has already made it as perfect as it can be. Look at it from the side. It is pretty, isn't it?"

Her husband looked at the driftwood with its lacy beige seaweed, and without moving his head, said, "Your chicken is red at the bone. And there is probably a potato dish that is supposed to have lumps in it. Mashed ain't the dish."

Ruth let the seaweed disintegrate, and later, when its veins and stems dropped and curled into brown scabs on the table, she removed the bowl and brushed away the scabs. But the water mark, hidden by the bowl all these years, was exposed. And once exposed, it behaved as though it were itself a plant and flourished into a huge suede-gray flower that throbbed like fever, and sighed like the shift of sand dunes. But it could also be still. Patient, restful, and still.

But there was nothing you could do with a mooring except acknowledge it, use it for the verification of some idea you wanted to keep alive. Something else is needed to get from sunup to sundown: a balm, a gentle touch or nuzzling of some sort. So Ruth rose up and out of her guileless inefficiency to claim her bit of balm right after the preparation of dinner and just before the return of her husband from his office. It was one of her two secret indulgences—the one that involved her son— and part of the pleasure it gave her came from the room in which she did it. A damp greenness lived there, made by the evergreen that pressed against the window and filtered the light. It was just a little room that Doctor had called a study, and aside from a sewing machine that stood in the corner along with a dress form, there was only a rocker and tiny footstool. She sat in this room holding her son on her lap, staring at his closed eyelids and listening to the sound of his sucking. Staring not so much from maternal joy as from a wish to avoid seeing his legs dangling almost to the floor.

In late afternoon, before her husband closed his office and came home, she called her son to her. When he came into the little room she unbuttoned her blouse and smiled. He was too young to be dazzled by her nipples, but he was old enough to be bored by the flat taste of mother's milk, so he came reluctantly, as to a chore, and lay as he had at least once each day of his life in his mother's arms, and tried to pull the thin, faintly sweet milk from her flesh without hurting her with his teeth.

She felt him. His restraint, his courtesy, his indifference, all of which pushed her into fantasy. She had the distinct impression that his lips were pulling from her a thread of light. It was as though she were a cauldron issuing spinning gold. Like the miller's daughter—the one who sat at night in a straw-filled room, thrilled with the secret power Rumpelstiltskin had given her: to see golden thread stream from her very own shuttle. And that was the other part of her pleasure, a pleasure she hated to give up. So when Freddie the janitor, who liked to pretend he was a friend of the family and not just their flunky as well as their tenant, brought his rent to the doctor's house late one day and looked in the window past the evergreen, the terror that sprang to Ruth's eyes came from the quick realization that she was to lose fully half of what made her daily life bearable. Freddie, however, interpreted her look as simple shame, but that didn't stop him from grinning.

"Have mercy. I be damn."

He fought the evergreen for a better look, hampered more by his laughter than by the branches. Ruth jumped up as quickly as she could and covered her breast, dropping her son on the floor and confirming for him what he had begun to suspect—that these afternoons were strange and wrong.

Before either mother or son could speak, rearrange themselves properly, or even exchange looks, Freddie had run around the house, climbed the porch steps, and was calling them between gulps of laughter.

"Miss Rufie. Miss Rufie. Where you? Where you all at?" He opened the door to the green room as though it were his now.

"I be damn, Miss Rufie. When the last time I seen that? I don't even know the last time I seen that. I mean, ain't nothing wrong with it. I mean, old folks swear by it. It's just, you know, you don't see it up here much. . . ." But his eyes were on the boy. Appreciative eyes that communicated some complicity she was excluded from. Freddie looked the boy up and down, taking in the steady but secretive eyes and the startling contrast between Ruth's lemony skin and the boy's black skin. "Used to be a lot of womenfolk nurse they kids a long time down South. Lot of 'em. But you don't see it much no more. I knew a family—the mother wasn't too quick, though—nursed hers till the boy, I reckon, was near 'bout thirteen. But that's a bit much, ain't it?" All the time he chattered, he rubbed his chin and looked at the boy. Finally he stopped, and gave a long low chuckle. He'd found the phrase he'd been searching for. "A milkman. That's what you got here, Miss Rufie. A natural milkman if ever I seen one. Look out, womens. Here he come. Huh!"

Freddie carried his discovery not only into the homes in Ruth's neighborhood, but to Southside, where he lived and where Macon Dead owned rent houses. So Ruth kept close to home and had no afternoon guests for the better part of two months, to keep from hearing that her son had been rechristened with a name he was never able to shake and that did nothing to improve either one's relationship with his father.

Macon Dead never knew how it came about—how his only son acquired the nickname that stuck in spite of his own refusal to use it or acknowledge it. It was a matter that concerned him a good deal, for the giving of names in his family was always surrounded by what he believed to be monumental foolishness. No one mentioned to him the incident out of which the nickname grew because he was a difficult man to approach—a hard man, with a manner so cool it discouraged casual or spontaneous conversation. Only Freddie the janitor took liberties with Macon Dead, liberties he purchased with the services he rendered, and Freddie was the last person on earth to tell him. So Macon Dead neither heard of nor visualized Ruth's sudden terror, her awkward jump from the rocking chair, the boy's fall broken by the tiny footstool, or Freddie's amused, admiring summation of the situation.

Without knowing any of the details, however, he guessed, with the accuracy of a mind sharpened by hatred, that the name he heard schoolchildren call his son, the name he overheard the ragman use when he paid the boy three cents for a bundle of old clothes—he guessed that this name was not clean. Milkman. It certainly didn't sound like the honest job of a dairyman, or bring to his mind cold bright cans standing on the back porch, glittering like captains on guard. It sounded dirty, intimate, and hot. He knew that wherever the name came from, it had something to do with his wife and was, like the emotion he always felt when thinking of her, coated with disgust.

This disgust and the uneasiness with which he regarded his son affected everything he did in that city. If he could have felt sad, simply sad, it would have relieved him. Fifteen years of regret at not having a son had become the bitterness of finally having one in the most revolting circumstances.

There had been a time when he had a head full of hair and when Ruth wore lovely complicated underwear that he deliberately took a long time to undo. When all of his foreplay was untying, unclasping, unbuckling the snaps and strings of what must have been the most beautiful, the most delicate, the whitest and softest underwear on earth. Each eye of her corset he toyed with (and there were forty—twenty on each side); each grosgrain ribbon that threaded its pale-blue way through the snowy top of her bodice he unlaced. He not only undid the blue bow; he pulled it all the way out of the hem, so she had to rethread it afterward with a safety pin. The elastic bands that connected her perspiration shields to her slip he unsnapped and snapped again, teasing her and himself with the sound of the snaps and the thrill of his fingertips on her shoulders. They never spoke during these undressings. But they giggled occasionally, and as when children play "doctor," undressing of course was the best part.

When Ruth was naked and lying there as moist and crumbly as unbleached sugar, he bent to unlace her shoes. That was the final delight, for once he had undressed her feet, had peeled her stockings down over her ankles and toes, he entered her and ejaculated quickly. She liked it that way. So did he. And in almost twenty years during which he had not laid eyes on her naked feet, he missed only the underwear.

Once he believed that the sight of her mouth on the dead man's fingers would be the thing he would remember always. He was wrong. Little by little he remembered fewer and fewer of the details, until finally he had to imagine them, even fabricate them, guess what they must have been. The image left him, but the odiousness never did. For the nourishment of his outrage he depended on the memory of her underwear; those round, inno- cent corset eyes now lost to him forever.

So if the people were calling his son Milkman, and if she was lowering her eyelids and dabbing at the sweat on her top lip when she heard it, there was definitely some filthy connection and it did not matter at all to Macon Dead whether anyone gave him the details or not.

And they didn't. Nobody both dared enough and cared enough to tell him. The ones who cared enough, Lena and Corinthians, the living proof of those years of undressing his wife, did not dare. And the one person who dared to but didn't care to was the one person in the world he hated more than his wife in spite of the fact that she was his sister. He had not crossed the tracks to see her since his son was born and he had no intention of renewing their relationship now.

Macon Dead dug in his pocket for his keys, and curled his fingers around them, letting their bunchy solidity calm him. They were the keys to all the doors of his houses (only four true houses; the rest were really shacks), and he fondled them from time to time as he walked down Not Doctor Street to his office. At least he thought of it as his office, had even painted the word OFFICE on the door. But the plate-glass window contra- dicted him. In peeling gold letters arranged in a semicircle, his business establishment was declared to be Sonny's Shop. Scrap- ing the previous owner's name off was hardly worth the trouble since he couldn't scrape it from anybody's mind. His storefront office was never called anything but Sonny's Shop, although nobody now could remember thirty years back, when, presum- ably, Sonny did something or other there.

He walked there now—strutted is the better word, for he had a high behind and an athlete's stride—thinking of names. Surely, he thought, he and his sister had some ancestor, some lithe young man with onyx skin and legs as straight as cane stalks, who had a name that was real. A name given to him at birth with love and seriousness. A name that was not a joke, nor a disguise, nor a brand name. But who this lithe young man was, and where his cane-stalk legs carried him from or to, could never be known. No. Nor his name. His own parents, in some mood of perverseness or resignation, had agreed to abide by a naming done to them by somebody who couldn't have cared less. Agreed to take and pass on to all their issue this heavy name scrawled in perfect thoughtlessness by a drunken Yankee in the Union Army. A literal slip of the pen handed to his father on a piece of paper and which he handed on to his only son, and his son likewise handed on to his; Macon Dead who begat a second Macon Dead who married Ruth Foster (Dead) and begat Magdalene called Lena Dead and First Corinthians Dead and (when he least expected it) another Macon Dead, now known to the part of the world that mattered as Milkman Dead. And as if that were not enough, a sister named Pilate Dead, who would never mention to her brother the circumstances or the details of this foolish misnaming of his son because the whole thing would have delighted her. She would savor it, maybe fold it too in a brass box and hang it from her other ear.

He had cooperated as a young father with the blind selection of names from the Bible for every child other than the first male. And abided by whatever the finger pointed to, for he knew every configuration of the naming of his sister. How his father, confused and melancholy over his wife's death in childbirth, had thumbed through the Bible, and since he could not read a word, chose a group of letters that seemed to him strong and handsome; saw in them a large figure that looked like a tree hanging in some princely but protective way over a row of smaller trees. How he had copied the group of letters out on a piece of brown paper; copied, as illiterate people do, every curlicue, arch, and bend in the letters, and presented it to the midwife.

"That's the baby's name."

"You want this for the baby's name?"

"I want that for the baby's name. Say it."

"You can't name the baby this."

"Say it."

"It's a man's name."

"Say it."

"Pilate."

"What?"

"Pilate. You wrote down Pilate."

"Like a riverboat pilot?"

"No. Not like no riverboat pilot. Like a Christ-killing Pilate. You can't get much worse than that for a name. And a baby girl at that."

"That's where my finger went down at."

"Well, your brain ain't got to follow it. You don't want to give this motherless child the name of the man that killed Jesus, do you?"

"I asked Jesus to save me my wife."

"Careful, Macon."

"I asked him all night long."

"He give you your baby."

"Yes. He did. Baby name Pilate."

"Jesus, have mercy."

"Where you going with that piece of paper?"

"It's going back where it came from. Right in the Devil's flames."

"Give it here. It come from the Bible. It stays in the Bible."

And it did stay there, until the baby girl turned twelve and took it out, folded it up into a tiny knot and put it in a little brass box, and strung the entire contraption through her left earlobe. Fluky about her own name at twelve, how much more fluky she'd become since then Macon could only guess. But he knew for certain that she would treat the naming of the third Macon Dead with the same respect and awe she had treated the boy's birth.

Macon Dead remembered when his son was born, how she seemed to be more interested in this first nephew of hers than she was in her own daughter, and even that daughter's daughter. Long after Ruth was up and about, as capable as she ever would be—and that wasn't much—of running the house again, Pilate continued to visit, her shoelaces undone, a knitted cap pulled down over her forehead, bringing her foolish earring and sickening smell into the kitchen. He had not seen her since he was sixteen years old, until a year before the birth of his son, when she appeared in his city. Now she was acting like an in-law, like an aunt, dabbling at helping Ruth and the girls, but having no interest in or knowledge of decent housekeeping, she got in the way. Finally she just sat in a chair near the crib, singing to the baby. That wasn't so bad, but what Macon Dead remembered most was the expression on her face. Surprise, it looked like, and eagerness. But so intense it made him uneasy. Or perhaps it was more than that. Perhaps it was seeing her all those years after they had separated outside that cave, and remembering his anger and her betrayal. How far down she had slid since then. She had cut the last thread of propriety. At one time she had been the dearest thing in the world to him. Now she was odd, murky, and worst of all, unkempt. A regular source of embarrassment, if he would allow it. But he would not allow it.

Finally he had told her not to come again until she could show some respect for herself. Could get a real job instead of running a wine house.

"Why can't you dress like a woman?" He was standing by the stove. "What's that sailor's cap doing on your head? Don't you have stockings? What are you trying to make me look like in this town?" He trembled with the thought of the white men in the bank—the men who helped him buy and mortgage houses—discovering that this raggedy bootlegger was his sister. That the propertied Negro who handled his business so well and who lived in the big house on Not Doctor Street had a sister who had a daughter but no husband, and that daughter had a daughter but no husband. A collection of lunatics who made wine and sang in the streets "like common street women! Just like common street women!"

Pilate had sat there listening to him, her wondering eyes resting on his face. Then she said, "I been worried sick about you too, Macon."

Exasperated, he had gone to the kitchen door. "Go 'head,

Pilate. Go on now. I'm on the thin side of evil and trying not to break through."

Pilate stood up, wrapped her quilt around her, and with a last fond look at the baby, left through the kitchen door. She never came back.

When Macon Dead got to the front door of his office he saw a stout woman and two young boys standing a few feet away. Macon unlocked his door, walked over to his desk, and settled himself behind it. As he was thumbing through his accounts book, the stout woman entered, alone.

"Afternoon Mr. Dead, sir. I'm Mrs. Bains. Live over at number three on Fifteenth Street."

Macon Dead remembered—not the woman, but the circumstances at number three. His tenant's grandmother or aunt or something had moved in there and the rent was long overdue.

"Yes, Mrs. Bains. You got something for me?"

"Well, that's what I come to talk to you about. You know Cency left all them babies with me. And my relief check ain't no more'n it take to keep a well-grown yard dog alive—half alive, I should say."

"Your rent is four dollars a month, Mrs. Bains. You two months behind already."

"I do know that, Mr. Dead, sir, but babies can't make it with nothing to put in they stomach."

Their voices were low, polite, without any hint of conflict.

"Can they make it in the street, Mrs. Bains? That's where they gonna be if you don't figure out some way to get me my money."

"No, sir. They can't make it in the street. We need both, I reckon. Same as yours does."

"Then you better rustle it up, Mrs. Bains. You got till"—he swiveled around to consult the calendar on the wall—"till Saturday coming. Saturday, Mrs. Bains. Not Sunday. Not Monday. Saturday."

If she had been younger and had more juice, the glitter in her eyes would have washed down onto her cheeks. Now, at her time of life, it simply gleamed. She pressed the flat of her hand on Macon Dead's desk and, holding the gleam steady in her eyes, pushed herself up from the chair. She turned her head a little to look out the plate-glass window, and then back at him.

"What's it gonna profit you, Mr. Dead, sir, to put me and them children out?"

"Saturday, Mrs. Bains."

Lowering her head, Mrs. Bains whispered something and walked slowly and heavily from the office. As she closed the door to Sonny's Shop, her grandchildren moved out of the sunlight into the shadow where she stood.

"What he say, Granny?"

Mrs. Bains put a hand on the taller boy's hair and fingered it lightly, absently searching with her nails for tetter spots.

"He must've told her no," said the other boy.

"Do we got to move?" The tall boy tossed his head free of her fingers and looked at her sideways. His cat eyes were gashes of gold.

Mrs. Bains let her hand fall to her side. "A nigger in business is a terrible thing to see. A terrible, terrible thing to see."

The boys looked at each other and back at their grandmother. Their lips were parted as though they had heard something important.

When Mrs. Bains closed the door, Macon Dead went back to the pages of his accounts book, running his fingertips over the figures and thinking with the unoccupied part of his mind about the first time he called on Ruth Foster's father. He had only two keys in his pocket then, and if he had let people like the woman who just left have their way, he wouldn't have had any keys at all. It was because of those keys that he could dare to walk over to that part of Not Doctor Street (it was still Doctor Street then) and approach the most important Negro in the city. To lift the lion's paw knocker, to entertain thoughts of marrying the doctor's daughter was possible because each key represented a house which he owned at the time. Without those keys he would have floated away at the doctor's first word: "Yes?" Or he would have melted like new wax under the heat of that pale eye. Instead he was able to say that he had been introduced to his daughter, Miss Ruth Foster, and would appreciate having the doctor's permission to keep her company now and then. That his intentions were honorable and that he himself was certainly worthy of the doctor's consideration as a gentleman friend for Miss Foster since, at twenty-five, he was already a colored man of property.

"I don't know anything about you," the doctor said, "other than your name, which I don't like, but I will abide by my daughter's preference."

In fact the doctor knew a good deal about him and was more grateful to this tall young man than he ever allowed himself to show. Fond as he was of his only child, useful as she was in his house since his wife had died, lately he had begun to chafe under her devotion. Her steady beam of love was unsettling, and she had never dropped those expressions of affection that had been so lovable in her childhood. The good-night kiss was itself a masterpiece of slow-wittedness on her part and discomfort on his. At sixteen, she still insisted on having him come to her at night, sit on her bed, exchange a few pleasantries, and plant a kiss on her lips. Perhaps it was the loud silence of his dead wife, perhaps it was Ruth's disturbing resemblance to her mother. More probably it was the ecstasy that always seemed to be shining in Ruth's face when he bent to kiss her—an ecstasy he felt inappropriate to the occasion.

None of that, of course, did he describe to the young man who came to call. Which is why Macon Dead still believed the magic had lain in the two keys.

In the middle of his reverie, Macon was interrupted by rapid tapping on the window. He looked up, saw Freddie peeping through the gold lettering, and nodded for him to enter. A gold-toothed bantamweight, Freddie was as much of a town crier as Southside had. It was this same rapid tapping on the window-pane, the same flash-of-gold smile that had preceded his now-famous scream to Macon: "Mr. Smith went splat!" It was obvious to Macon that Freddie now had news of another calamity.

"Porter gone crazy drunk again! Got his shotgun!"

"Who's he out for?" Macon began closing books and opening desk drawers. Porter was a tenant and tomorrow was collection day.

"Ain't out for nobody in particular. Just perched himself up in the attic window and commenced to waving a shotgun. Say he gotta kill him somebody before morning."

"He go to work today?"

"Yep. Caught the eagle too."

"Drunk it all up?"

"Not all of it. He only got one bottle, and he still got a fist fulla money."

"Who's crazy enough to sell him any liquor?"

Freddie showed a few gold teeth but said nothing, so Macon knew it was Pilate. He locked all his drawers save one—the one he unlocked and took a small .32 from.

"Police warn every bootlegger in the county, and he still gets it somehow." Macon went on with the charade, pretending he didn't know his sister was the one Porter and anybody else—adult, child, or beast—could buy wine from. He thought for the hundredth time that she needed to be in jail and that he would be willing to put her there if he could be sure she wouldn't loudmouth him and make him seem trashy in the eyes of the law—and the banks.

"You know how to use that thing, Mr. Dead, sir?"

"I know how."

"Porter's crazy when he drunk."

"I know what he is."

"How you aiming to get him down?"

"I ain't aiming to get him down. I'm aiming to get my money down. He can go on and die up there if he wants to. But if he don't toss me my rent, I'm going to blow him out of that window."

Freddie's giggle was soft, but his teeth strengthened its impact. A born flunky, he loved gossip and the telling of it. He was the ear that heard every murmur of complaint, every name-calling; and his was the eye that saw everything: the secret loving glances, the fights, the new dresses.

Macon knew Freddie as a fool and a liar, but a reliable liar. He was always right about his facts and always wrong about the motives that produced the facts. Just as now he was right about Porter having a shotgun, being in the attic window, and being drunk. But Porter was not waiting to kill somebody, meaning anybody, before morning. In fact he was very specific about whom he wanted to kill—himself. However, he did have a precondition which he shouted down, loud and clear, from the attic. "I want to fuck! Send me up somebody to fuck! Hear me? Send me up somebody, I tell ya, or I'ma blow my brains out!"

As Macon and Freddie approached the yard, the women from the rooming house were hollering answers to Porter's plea.

"What kinda bargain is that?"

"Kill yourself first and then we'll send you somebody."

"Do it have to be a woman?"

"Do it got to be human?"

"Do it got to be alive?"

"Can it be a piece of liver?"

"Put that thing down and throw me my goddam money!" Macon's voice cut through the women's fun. "Float those dollars down here, nigger, then blow yourself up!"

Porter turned and aimed his shotgun at Macon.

"If you pull that trigger," shouted Macon, "you better not miss. If you take a shot you better make sure I'm dead, cause if you don't I'm gonna shoot your balls up in your throat!" He pulled out his own weapon. "Now get the hell outta that window!"

Porter hesitated for only a second, before turning the barrel of the shotgun toward himself—or trying to. Its length made it difficult; his drunkenness made it impossible. Struggling to get the right angle, he was suddenly distracted. He leaned his shotgun on the window sill, pulled out his penis and in a high arc, peed over the heads of the women, making them scream and run in a panic that the shotgun had not been able to create. Macon rubbed the back of his head while Freddie bent double with laughter.

For more than an hour Porter held them at bay: cowering, screaming, threatening, urinating, and interspersing all of it with pleas for a woman.

He would cry great shoulder-heaving sobs, followed by more screams.

"I love ya! I love ya all. Don't act like that. You women. Stop it. Don't act like that. Don't you see I love ya? I'd die for ya, kill for ya. I'm saying I love ya. I'm telling ya. Oh, God have mercy. What I'm gonna do? What in this fuckin world am I gonna dooooo?"

Tears streamed down his face and he cradled the barrel of the shotgun in his arms as though it were the woman he had been begging for, searching for, all his life. "Gimme hate, Lord," he whimpered. "I'll take hate any day. But don't give me love. I can't take no more love, Lord. I can't carry it. Just like Mr. Smith. He couldn't carry it. It's too heavy. Jesus, *you* know. You know all about it. Ain't it heavy? Jesus? Ain't love heavy? Don't you see, Lord? You own son couldn't carry it. If it killed Him, what You think it's gonna do to me? Huh? Huh?" He was getting angry again.

"Come down outta there, nigger!" Macon's voice was still loud, but it was getting weary.

"And you, you baby-dicked baboon"—he tried to point at Macon—"you the worst. You need killin, you really *need* killin. You know why? Well, I'm gonna tell you why. I *know* why. Everybody . . ."

Porter slumped down in the window, muttering, "Everybody know why," and fell fast asleep. As he sank deeper into it, the shotgun slipped from his hand, rattled down the roof, and hit the ground with a loud explosion. The shot zipped past a bystander's shoe and blew a hole in the tire of a stripped Dodge parked in the road.

"Go get my money," Macon said.

"Me?" Freddie asked. "Suppose he . . ."

"Go get me my money."

Porter was snoring. Through the blast of the gun and the picking of his pocket he slept like a baby.

When Macon walked out of the yard, the sun had disappeared behind the bread company. Tired, irritable, he walked down Fifteenth Street, glancing up as he passed one of his other houses, its silhouette melting in the light that trembled between dusk and twilight. Scattered here and there, his houses stretched up beyond him like squat ghosts with hooded eyes. He didn't like to look at them in this light. During the day they were reassuring to see; now they did not seem to belong to him at all—in fact he felt as though the houses were in league with one another to make him feel like the outsider, the propertyless, landless wanderer. It was this feeling of loneliness that made him decide to take a shortcut back to Not Doctor Street, even though to do so would lead him past his sister's house. In the gathering darkness, he was sure his passing would be unnoticed by her. He crossed a yard and followed a fence that led into Darling Street where Pilate lived in a narrow single-story house whose basement seemed to be rising from rather than settling into the ground. She had no electricity because she would not pay for the service. Nor for gas. At night she and her daughter lit the house with candles and kerosene lamps; they warmed themselves and cooked with wood and coal, pumped kitchen water into a dry sink through a pipeline from a well and lived pretty much as though progress was a word that meant walking a little farther on down the road.

Her house sat eighty feet from the sidewalk and was backed by four huge pine trees, from which she got the needles she stuck into her mattress. Seeing the pine trees started him think-ing about her mouth; how she loved, as a girl, to chew pine needles and as a result smelled even then like a forest. For a dozen years she had been like his own child. After their mother died, she had come struggling out of the womb without help from throbbing muscles or the pressure of swift womb water. As a result, for all the years he knew her, her stomach was as smooth and sturdy as her back, at no place interrupted by a navel. It was the absence of a navel that convinced people that she had not come into this world through normal channels; had never lain, floated, or grown in some warm and liquid place connected by a tissue-thin tube to a reliable source of human nourishment. Macon knew otherwise, because he was there and had seen the eyes of the midwife as his mother's legs collapsed. And heard as well her shouts when the baby, who they had believed was dead also, inched its way headfirst out of a still, silent, and indifferent cave of flesh, dragging her own cord and her own afterbirth behind her. But the rest was true. Once the new baby's lifeline was cut, the cord stump shriveled, fell off, and left no trace of having ever existed, which, as a young boy taking care of his baby sister, he thought no more strange than a bald head. He was seventeen years old, irreparably separated from her and already pressing forward in his drive for wealth, when he learned that there was probably not another stomach like hers on earth.

Now, nearing her yard, he trusted that the dark would keep anyone in her house from seeing him. He did not even look to his left as he walked by it. But then he heard the music. They were singing. All of them. Pilate, Reba, and Reba's daughter, Hagar. There was no one on the street that he could see; people were at supper, licking their fingers, blowing into saucers of coffee, and no doubt chattering about Porter's escapade and Macon's fearless confrontation of the wild man in the attic. There were no street lights in this part of town; only the moon directed the way of a pedestrian. Macon walked on, resisting as best he could the sound of the voices that followed him. He was rapidly approaching a part of the road where the music could not follow, when he saw, like a scene on the back of a postcard, a picture of where he was headed—his own home; his wife's narrow unyielding back; his daughters, boiled dry from years of yearning; his son, to whom he could speak only if his words held some command or criticism. "Hello, Daddy." "Hello, son, tuck your shirt in." "I found a dead bird, Daddy." "Don't bring that mess in this house. . . ." There was no music there, and tonight he wanted just a bit of music—from the person who had been his first caring for.

He turned back and walked slowly toward Pilate's house. They were singing some melody that Pilate was leading. A phrase that the other two were taking up and building on. Her powerful contralto, Reba's piercing soprano in counterpoint, and the soft voice of the girl, Hagar, who must be about ten or eleven now, pulled him like a carpet tack under the influence of a magnet.

Surrendering to the sound, Macon moved closer. He wanted no conversation, no witness, only to listen and perhaps to see the three of them, the source of that music that made him think of fields and wild turkey and calico. Treading as lightly as he could, he crept up to the side window where the candlelight flickered lowest, and peeped in. Reba was cutting her toenails with a kitchen knife or a switchblade, her long neck bent almost to her knees. The girl, Hagar, was braiding her hair, while Pilate, whose face he could not see because her back was to the window, was stirring something in a pot. Wine pulp, perhaps. Macon knew it was not food she was stirring, for she and her daughters ate like children. Whatever they had a taste for. No meal was ever planned or balanced or served. Nor was there any gathering at the table. Pilate might bake hot bread and each one of them would eat it with butter whenever she felt like it. Or there might be grapes, left over from the winemaking, or peaches for days on end. If one of them bought a gallon of milk they drank it until it was gone. If another got a half bushel of tomatoes or a dozen ears of corn, they ate them until they were gone too. They ate what they had or came across or had a craving for. Profits from their wine-selling evaporated like sea water in a hot wind—going for junk jewelry for Hagar, Reba's gifts to men, and he didn't know what all.

Near the window, hidden by the dark, he felt the irritability of the day drain from him and relished the effortless beauty of the women singing in the candlelight. Reba's soft profile, Hagar's hands moving, moving in her heavy hair, and Pilate. He knew her face better than he knew his own. Singing now, her face would be a mask; all emotion and passion would have left her features and entered her voice. But he knew that when she was neither singing nor talking, her face was animated by her constantly moving lips. She chewed things. As a baby, as a very young girl, she kept things in her mouth—straw from brooms, gristle, buttons, seeds, leaves, string, and her favorite, when he could find some for her, rubber bands and India rubber erasers. Her lips were alive with small movements. If you were close to her, you wondered if she was about to smile or was she merely shifting a straw from the baseline of her gums to her tongue. Perhaps she was dislodging a curl of rubber band from inside her cheek, or was she really smiling? From a distance she appeared to be whispering to herself, when she was only nibbling or splitting tiny seeds with her front teeth. Her lips were darker than her skin, wine-stained, blueberry-dyed, so her face had a cosmetic look—as though she had applied a very dark lipstick neatly and blotted away its shine on a scrap of newspaper.

As Macon felt himself softening under the weight of memory and music, the song died down. The air was quiet and yet Macon Dead could not leave. He liked looking at them freely this way. They didn't move. They simply stopped singing and Reba went on paring her toenails, Hagar threaded and unthreaded her hair, and Pilate swayed like a willow over her stirring.

# Chapter 2

Only Magdalene called Lena and First Corinthians were genuinely happy when the big Packard rolled evenly and silently out of the driveway. They alone had a sense of adventure and were flagrant in their enjoyment of the automobile's plushness. Each had a window to herself and commanded an unobstructed view of the summer day flying past them. And each was both old enough and young enough to actually believe she was a princess riding in a regal chariot driven by a powerful coachman. In the back seat, away from the notice of Macon and Ruth, they slipped off their patent leather pumps, rolled their stockings down over their knees, and watched the men walking down the streets.

These rides that the family took on Sunday afternoons had become rituals and much too important for Macon to enjoy. For him it was a way to satisfy himself that he was indeed a successful man. It was a less ambitious ritual for Ruth, but a way, nevertheless, for her to display her family. For the little boy it was simply a burden. Pressed in the front seat between his parents, he could see only the winged woman careening off the nose of the car. He was not allowed to sit on his mother's lap during the drive—not because she wouldn't have it, but because his father objected to it. So it was only by kneeling on the dove gray seat and looking out the back window that he could see anything other than the laps, feet, and hands of his parents, the dashboard, or the silver winged woman poised at the tip of the Packard. But riding backward made him uneasy. It was like flying blind, and not knowing where he was going—just where he had been—troubled him. He did not want to see trees that he had passed, or houses and children slipping into the space the automobile had left behind.

Macon Dead's Packard rolled slowly down Not Doctor Street, through the rough part of town (later known as the Blood Bank because blood flowed so freely there), over the bypass downtown, and headed for the wealthy white neighborhoods. Some of the black people who saw the car passing by sighed with good-humored envy at the classiness, the dignity of it. In 1936 there were very few among them who lived as well as Macon Dead. Others watched the family gliding by with a tiny bit of jealousy and a whole lot of amusement, for Macon's wide green Packard belied what they thought a car was for. He never went over twenty miles an hour, never gunned his engine, never stayed in first gear for a block or two to give pedestrians a thrill. He never had a blown tire, never ran out of gas and needed twelve grinning raggle-tailed boys to help him push it up a hill or over to a curb. No rope ever held the door to its frame, and no teen-agers leaped on his running board for a lift down the street. He hailed no one and no one hailed him. There was never a sudden braking and backing up to shout or laugh with a friend. No beer bottles or ice cream cones poked from the open windows. Nor did a baby boy stand up to pee out of them. He never let rain fall on it if he could help it and he walked to Sonny's Shop—taking the car out only on these occasions. What's more, they doubted that he had ever taken a woman into the back seat, because rumor was that he went to "bad houses" or lay, sometimes, with a slack or lonely female tenant. Other than the bright and roving eyes of Magdalene called Lena and First Corinthians, the Packard had no real lived life at all. So they called it Macon Dead's hearse.

First Corinthians pulled her fingers through her hair. It was long, lightweight hair, the color of wet sand. "Are you going anyplace special, or are we just driving around?" She kept her eyes on the street, watching the men and women walking by.

"Careful, Macon. You always take the wrong turn here." Ruth spoke softly from the right side of the car.

"Do you want to drive?" Macon asked her.

"You know I don't drive," she answered.

"Then let me do it."

"All right, but don't blame me if . . . ."

Macon pulled smoothly into the left fork of the road that led through downtown and into a residential area.

"Daddy? Are we going any special place?"

"Honoré," Macon said.

Magdalene called Lena pushed her stockings farther down on her legs. "On the lake? What's out there? There's nothing out there, nobody."

"There's a beach community out there, Lena. Your father wants to look at it." Ruth reasserted herself into the conversation.

"What for? Those are white people's houses," said Lena.

"All of it's not white people's houses. Some of it's nothing. Just land. Way over on the other side. It could be a nice summer place for colored people. Beach houses. You understand what I mean?" Macon glanced at his daughter through the rear-view mirror.

"Who's going to live in them? There's no colored people who can afford to have two houses," Lena said.

"Reverend Coles can, and Dr. Singleton," Corinthians corrected her.

"And that lawyer—what's his name?" Ruth looked around at Corinthians, who ignored her.

"And Mary, I suppose." Lena laughed.

Corinthians stared coldly at her sister. "Daddy wouldn't sell property to a barmaid. Daddy, would you let us live next to a barmaid?"

"She owns that place, Corinthians," Ruth said.

"I don't care what she owns. I care about what she is. Daddy?" Corinthians leaned toward her father for confirmation.

"You're going too fast, Macon." Ruth pressed the toe of her shoe against the floorboard.

"If you say one more thing to me about the way I drive, you're going to walk back home. I mean it."

Magdalene called Lena sat forward and put her hand on her mother's shoulder. Ruth was quiet. The little boy kicked his feet against the underside of the dashboard.

"Stop that!" Macon told him.

"I have to go to the bathroom," said his son.

Corinthians held her head. "Oh, Lord."

"But you went before we left," said Ruth.

"I have to *go!*" He was beginning to whine.

"Are you sure?" his mother asked him. He looked at her. "I guess we better stop," Ruth said to nobody in particular. Her eyes grazed the countryside they were entering.

Macon didn't alter his speed.

"Are *we* going to have a summer place, or are you just selling property?"

"I'm not selling anything. I'm thinking of buying and then renting," Macon answered her.

"But are *we*—"

"I have to go," said the little boy.

"—going to live there too?"

"Maybe."

"By ourselves? Who else?" Corinthians was very interested.

"I can't tell you that. But in a few years—five or ten—a whole lot of coloreds will have enough to afford it. A whole lot. Take my word for it."

Magdalene called Lena took a deep breath. "Up ahead you could pull over, Daddy. He might mess up the seat."

Macon glanced at her in the mirror and slowed down. "Who's going to take him?" Ruth fiddled with the door handle. "Not you," Macon said to her.

Ruth looked at her husband. She parted her lips but didn't say anything.

"Not me," said Corinthians. "I have on high heels."

"Come on," Lena sighed. They left the car, little boy and big sister, and disappeared into the trees that reared up off the shoulder of the road.

"You really think there'll be enough colored people—I mean nice colored people—in this city to live there?"

"They don't have to be from this city, Corinthians. People will drive to a summer house. White people do it all the time." Macon drummed his fingers on the steering wheel, which trembled a little as the car idled.

"Negroes don't like the water." Corinthians giggled.

"They'll like it if they own it," said Macon. He looked out the window and saw Magdalene called Lena coming out of the trees. A large colorful bouquet of flowers was in her hand, but her face was crumpled in anger. Over her pale-blue dress dark wet stains spread like fingers.

"He wet on me," she said. "He wet me, Mama." She was close to tears.

Ruth clucked her tongue.

Corinthians laughed. "I told you Negroes didn't like water."

He didn't mean it. It happened before he was through. She'd stepped away from him to pick flowers, returned, and at the sound of her footsteps behind him, he'd turned around before he was through. It was becoming a habit—this concentration on things behind him. Almost as though there were no future to be had.

But if the future did not arrive, the present did extend itself, and the uncomfortable little boy in the Packard went to school and at twelve met the boy who not only could liberate him, but could take him to the woman who had as much to do with his future as she had his past.

Guitar said he knew her. Had even been inside her house.

"What's it like in there?" Milkman asked him.

"Shiny," Guitar answered. "Shiny and brown. With a smell."

"A bad smell?"

"I don't know. Her smell. You'll see."

All those unbelievable but entirely possible stories about his father's sister—the woman his father had forbidden him to go near—had both of them spellbound. Neither wished to live one more day without finding out the truth, and they believed they were the legitimate and natural ones to do so. After all, Guitar already knew her, and Milkman was her nephew.

They found her on the front steps sitting wide-legged in a long-sleeved, long-skirted black dress. Her hair was wrapped in black too, and from a distance, all they could really see beneath her face was the bright orange she was peeling. She was all angles, he remembered later, knees, mostly, and elbows. One foot pointed east and one pointed west.

As they came closer and saw the brass box dangling from her ear, Milkman knew that what with the earring, the orange, and the angled black cloth, nothing—not the wisdom of his father nor the caution of the world—could keep him from her.

Guitar, being older and already in high school, had none of the reluctance that his young buddy still struggled with, and was the first one to speak.

"Hi."

The woman looked up. First at Guitar and then at Milkman.

"What kind of word is that?" Her voice was light but gravel-sprinkled. Milkman kept on staring at her fingers, manipulating the orange. Guitar grinned and shrugged. "It means hello."

"Then say what you mean."

"Okay. Hello."

"That's better. What you want?"

"Nothin. We just passin by."

"Look like you standin by."

"If you don't want us here, Miss Pilate, we'll go." Guitar spoke softly.

"I ain't the one with the wants. You the one want something."

"We wanna ask you something." Guitar stopped feigning indifference. She was too direct, and to keep up with her he had to pay careful attention to his language.

"Ask it."

"Somebody said you ain't got no navel."

"That the question?"

"Yes."

"Don't sound like a question. Sound like an answer. Gimme the question."

"Do you?"

"Do I what?"

"Do you have a navel?"

"No."

"What happened to it?"

"Beats me." She dropped a bright peeling into her lap and separated an orange section slowly. "Now do I get to ask a question?"

"Sure."

"Who's your little friend?"

"This here's Milkman."

"Do he talk?" Pilate swallowed a piece of the fruit.

"Yeah. He talk. Say something." Guitar shoved an elbow at Milkman without taking his eyes off Pilate.

Milkman took a breath, held it, and said, "Hi."

Pilate laughed. "You all must be the dumbest unhung Negroes on earth. What they telling you in them schools? You say 'Hi' to pigs and sheep when you want 'em to move. When you tell a human being 'Hi,' he ought to get up and knock you down."

Shame had flooded him. He had expected to feel it, but not that kind; to be embarrassed, yes, but not that way. She was the one who was ugly, dirty, poor, and drunk. The queer aunt whom his sixth-grade schoolmates teased him about and whom he hated because he felt personally responsible for her ugliness, her poverty, her dirt, and her wine.

Instead she was making fun of his school, of his teachers, of him. And while she looked as poor as everyone said she was, something was missing from her eyes that should have confirmed it. Nor was she dirty; unkempt, yes, but not dirty. The whites of her fingernails were like ivory. And unless he knew absolutely nothing, this woman was definitely not drunk. Of course she was anything but pretty, yet he knew he could have watched her all day: the fingers pulling thread veins from the orange sections, the berry-black lips that made her look as though she wore make-up, the earring. . . . And when she stood up, he all but gasped. She was as tall as his father, head and shoulders taller than himself. Her dress wasn't as long as he had thought; it came to just below her calf and now he could see her unlaced men's shoes and the silvery-brown skin of her ankles.

She held the peelings precisely as they had fallen in her lap, and as she walked up the steps she looked as though she were holding her crotch.

"Your daddy wouldn't like that. He don't like dumb peoples." Then she looked right at Milkman, one hand holding the peelings, the other on the doorknob. "I know your daddy. I know you too."

Again Guitar spoke up. "You his daddy's sister?"

"The only one he got. Ain't but three Deads alive."

Milkman, who had been unable to get one word out of his mouth after the foolish "Hi," heard himself shouting: "I'm a Dead! My mother's a Dead! My sisters. You and him ain't the only ones!"

Even while he was screaming he wondered why he was suddenly so defensive—so possessive about his name. He had always hated that name, all of it, and until he and Guitar became friends, he had hated his nickname too. But in Guitar's mouth it sounded clever, grown up. Now he was behaving with this strange woman as though having the name was a matter of deep personal pride, as though she had tried to expel him from a very special group, in which he not only belonged, but had exclusive rights.

In the heartbeat of silence that followed his shouts, Pilate laughed.

"You all want a soft-boiled egg?" she asked.

The boys looked at each other. She'd changed rhythm on them. They didn't want an egg, but they did want to be with her, to go inside the wine house of this lady who had one earring, no navel, and looked like a tall black tree.

"No, thanks, but we'd like a drink of water." Guitar smiled back at her.

"Well. Step right in." She opened the door and they followed her into a large sunny room that looked both barren and cluttered. A moss-green sack hung from the ceiling. Candles were stuck in bottles everywhere; newspaper articles and magazine pictures were nailed to the walls. But other than a rocking chair, two straight-backed chairs, a large table, a sink and stove, there was no furniture. Pervading everything was the odor of pine and fermenting fruit.

"You ought to try one. I know how to do them just right. I don't like my whites to move, you know. The yolk I want soft, but not runny. Want it like wet velvet. How come you don't just try one?"

She had dumped the peelings in a large crock, which like most everything in the house had been made for some other purpose. Now she stood before the dry sink, pumping water into a blue-and-white wash basin which she used for a saucepan.

"Now, the water and the egg have to meet each other on a kind of equal standing. One can't get the upper hand over the other. So the temperature has to be the same for both. I knock the chill off the water first. Just the chill. I don't let it get warm because the egg is room temperature, you see. Now then, the real secret is right here in the boiling. When the tiny bubbles come to the surface, when they as big as peas and just before they get big as marbles. Well, right then you take the pot off the fire. You don't just put the fire out; you take the pot off. Then you put a folded newspaper over the pot and do one small obligation. Like answering the door or emptying the bucket and bringing it in off the front porch. I generally go to the toilet. Not for a long stay, mind you. Just a short one. If you do all that, you got yourself a perfect soft-boiled egg.

"I remember the messes I used to make for my father when I cooked. Your father"—she directed a thumb at Milkman—"he couldn't cook worth poot. Once I made a cherry pie for him, or tried to. Macon was a nice boy and awful good to me. Be nice if you could have known him then. He would have been a real good friend to you too, like he was to me."

Her voice made Milkman think of pebbles. Little round pebbles that bumped up against each other. Maybe she was hoarse, or maybe it was the way she said her words, with both a drawl and a clip. The piny-winy smell was narcotic, and so was the sun streaming in, strong and unfettered because there were no curtains or shades at the windows that were all around the room, two in each of three walls, one on each side of the door, one on either side of the sink and the stove, and two on the farther wall. The fourth wall must back on the bedrooms, Milkman thought. The pebbly voice, the sun, and the narcotic wine smell weakened both the boys, and they sat in a pleasant semi-stupor, listening to her go on and on. . . .

"Hadn't been for your daddy, I wouldn't be here today. I would have died in the womb. And died again in the woods. Those woods and the dark would have surely killed me. But he saved me and here I am boiling eggs. Our papa was dead, you see. They blew him five feet up into the air. He was sitting on his fence waiting for 'em, and they snuck up from behind and blew him five feet into the air. So when we left Circe's big house we didn't have no place to go, so we just walked around and lived in them woods. Farm country. But Papa came back one day. We didn't know it was him at first, cause we both saw him blowed five feet into the air. We were lost then. And talking about dark! You think dark is just one color, but it ain't. There're five or six kinds of black. Some silky, some woolly.

Some just empty. Some like fingers. And it don't stay still. It moves and changes from one kind of black to another. Saying something is pitch black is like saying something is green. What kind of green? Green like my bottles? Green like a grasshopper? Green like a cucumber, lettuce, or green like the sky is just before it breaks loose to storm? Well, night black is the same way. May as well be a rainbow.

"Now, we lost and there was this wind and in front of us was the back of our daddy. We were some scared children. Macon kept telling me that the things we was scared of wasn't real. What difference do it make if the thing you scared of is real or not? I remember doing laundry for a man and his wife once, down in Virginia. The husband came into the kitchen one afternoon shivering and saying did I have any coffee made. I asked him what was it that had grabbed hold of him, he looked so bad. He said he couldn't figure it out, but he felt like he was about to fall off a cliff. Standing right there on that yellow and white and red linoleum, as level as a flatiron. He was holding on to the door first, then the chair, trying his best not to fall down. I opened my mouth to tell him wasn't no cliff in that kitchen. Then I remembered how it was being in those woods. I felt it all over again. So I told the man did he want me to hold on to him so he couldn't fall. He looked at me with the most grateful look in the world. 'Would you?' he said. I walked around back of him and locked my fingers in front of his chest and held on to him. His heart was kicking under his vest like a mule in heat. But little by little it calmed down."

"You saved his life," said Guitar.

"No such thing. His wife come in before it was time to let go. She asked me what I was doing and I told her."

"Told her what? What'd you say?"

"The truth. That I was trying to keep him from falling off a cliff."

"I bet he wished he had jumped off then. She believe you? Don't tell me she believed you."

"Not right away she didn't. But soon's I let go he fell dead-weight to the floor. Smashed his glasses and everything. Fell right on his face. And you know what? He went down so slow. I swear it took three minutes, three whole minutes to go from a standing upright position to when he mashed his face on the floor. I don't know if the cliff was real or not, but it took him three minutes to fall down it."

"Was he dead?" asked Guitar.

"Stone dead."

"Who shot your daddy? Did you say somebody shot him?" Guitar was fascinated, his eyes glittering with lights.

"Five feet into the air . . ."

"Who?"

"I don't know who and I don't know why. I just know what I'm telling you: what, when, and where."

"You didn't say where." He was insistent.

"I did too. Off a fence."

"Where was the fence?"

"On our farm."

Guitar laughed, but his eyes were too shiny to convey much humor. "Where was the farm?"

"Montour County."

He gave up on "where." "Well, when then?"

"When he sat there—on the fence."

Guitar felt like a frustrated detective. "What year?"

"The year they shot them Irish people down in the streets. Was a good year for guns and gravediggers, I know that." Pilate put a barrel lid on the table. Then she lifted the eggs from the wash basin and began to peel them. Her lips moved as she played an orange seed around in her mouth. Only after the eggs were split open, revealing moist reddish-yellow centers, did she return to her story. "One morning we woke up when the sun was nearly a quarter way cross the sky. Bright as anything. And blue. Blue like the ribbons on my mother's bonnet. See that streak of sky?" She pointed out the window. "Right behind them hickories. See? Right over there." 

They looked and saw the sky stretching back behind the houses and the trees. "That's the same color," she said, as if she had discovered something important. "Same color as my mama's ribbons. I'd know her ribbon color anywhere, but I don't know her name. After she died Papa wouldn't let anybody say it. Well, before we could get the sand rubbed out of our eyes and take a good look around, we saw him sitting there on a stump. Right in the sunlight. We started to call him but he looked on off, like he was lookin at us and not lookin at us at the same time. Something in his face scared us. It was like looking at a face under water. Papa got up after a while and moved out of the sun on back into the woods. We just stood there looking at the stump. Shaking like leaves."

Pilate scraped the eggshells together into a little heap, her fingers fanning out over and over again in a gentle sweeping. The boys watched, afraid to say anything lest they ruin the next part of her story, and afraid to remain silent lest she not go on with its telling.

"Shaking like leaves," she murmured, "just like leaves."

Suddenly she lifted her head and made a sound like a hoot owl. "Ooo! Here I come!"

Neither Milkman nor Guitar saw or heard anyone approaching, but Pilate jumped up and ran toward the door. Before she reached it, a foot kicked it open and Milkman saw the bent back of a girl. She was dragging a large five-bushel basket of what looked like brambles, and a woman was pushing the other side of it, saying, "Watch the doorsill, baby."

"I got it," the girl answered. "Push."

"About time," said Pilate. "The light be gone before you know it."

"Tommy's truck broke down," the girl said, panting. When the two had managed to get the basket into the room, the girl stretched her back and turned around, facing them. But Milkman had no need to see her face; he had already fallen in love with her behind.

"Hagar." Pilate looked around the room. "This here's your brother, Milkman. And this is his friend. What's your name again, pretty?"

"Guitar."

"Guitar? You play any?" she asked.

"That ain't her brother, Mama. They cousins." The older woman spoke.

"Same thing."

"No it ain't. Is it, baby?"

"No," said Hagar. "It's different."

"See there. It's different."

"Well, what is the difference, Reba? You know so much."

Reba looked at the ceiling. "A brother is a brother if you both got the same mother or if you both—"

Pilate interrupted her. "I mean what's the difference in the way you act toward 'em? Don't you have to act the same way to both?"

"That's not the point, Mama."

"Shut up, Reba. I'm talking to Hagar."

"Yes, Mama. You treat them both the same."

"Then why they got two words for it 'stead of one, if they ain't no difference?" Reba put her hands on her hips and opened her eyes wide.

"Pull that rocker over here," said Pilate. "You boys have to give up your seats unless you gonna help."

The women circled the basket, which was full of blackberries still on their short, thorny branches.

"What we have to do?" Guitar asked.

"Get them little berries off them hateful branches without popping 'em. Reba, get that other crock."

Hagar looked around, all eyes and hair. "Why don't we pull a bed out the back room? Then we can all sit down."

"Floor's good enough for me," said Pilate, and she squatted down on her haunches and lifted a branch gently from the basket. "This all you got?"

"No." Reba was side-rolling a huge crock. "Two more outside."

"Better bring them in. Draw too many flies out there."

Hagar started for the door and motioned to Milkman. "Come on, brother. You can help."

Milkman jumped up, knocking his chair backward, and trotted after Hagar. She was, it seemed to him, as pretty a girl as he'd ever seen. She was much much older than he was. She must be as old as Guitar, maybe even seventeen. He seemed to be floating. More alive than he'd ever been, and floating. Together he and Hagar dragged two baskets up the porch stairs and into the house. She was as strong and muscular as he was.

"Careful, Guitar. Go slow. You keep on busting 'em."

"Leave him alone, Reba. He got to get the feel first. I asked you did you play any. That why they call you Guitar?"

"Not cause I do play. Because I wanted to. When I was real little. So they tell me."

"Where'd you ever see a guitar?"

"It was a contest, in a store down home in Florida. I saw it when my mother took me downtown with her. I was just a baby. It was one of those things where you guess how many beans in the big glass jar and you win a guitar. I cried for it, they said. And always asked about it."

"You should of called Reba. She'd get it for you."

"No, you couldn't buy it. You had to give the number of jellybeans."

"I heard you. Reba would of known how many. Reba wins things. She ain't never lost nothing."

"Really?" Guitar smiled, but he was doubtful. "She lucky?"

"Sure I'm lucky." Reba grinned. "People come from everywhere to get me to stand in for 'em at drawings and give them numbers to play. It works pretty well for them, and it always works for me. I win everything I try to win and lots of things I don't even try to win."

"Got to where won't nobody sell her a raffle ticket. They just want her to hold theirs."

"See this?" Reba put her hand down in the top of her dress and pulled out a diamond ring attached to a string. "I won this last year. I was the . . . what was it, Mama?"

"Five hundred thousandth."

"Five hundred . . . no it wasn't. That ain't what they said."

"Half a million is what they said."

"That's right. The half a millionth person to walk into Sears and Roebuck." Her laughter was gay and proud.

"They didn't want to give it to her," said Hagar, "cause she looked so bad."

Guitar was astonished. "I remember that contest, but I don't remember hearing nothing 'bout no colored person winning it." Guitar, a habitual street roamer, believed he knew every public thing going on in the city.

"Nobody did. They had picture-taking people and everything waiting for the next person to walk in the door. But they never did put my picture in the paper. Me and Mama looked, too, didn't we?" She glanced at Pilate for confirmation and went on. "But they put the picture of the man who won second prize in. He won a war bond. He was white."

"Second prize?" Guitar asked. "What kind of 'second prize'? Either you the half-millionth person or you ain't. Can't be no next-to-the-half-millionth."

"Can if the winner is Reba," Hagar said. "The only reason they got a second was cause she was the first. And the only reason they gave it to her was because of them cameras."

"Tell 'em why you was in Sears, Reba."

"Looking for a toilet." Reba threw her head back to let the laughter escape. Her hands were stained with blackberry juice, and when she wiped the tears from her eyes she streaked the purple from her nose to her cheekbone. Much lighter than Pilate or Hagar, Reba had the simple eyes of an infant. All of them had a guileless look about them, but complication and something more lurked behind Pilate's and Hagar's faces. Only Reba, with her light pimply skin and deferential manner, looked as though her simplicity might also be vacuousness.

"Ain't but two toilets downtown they let colored in: Mayflower Restaurant and Sears. Sears was closer. Good thing nature wasn't in a hurry. They kept me there fifteen minutes gettin my name and address to send the diamond over to me. But I wouldn't let 'em send it to me. I kept asking them, Is this a real contest? I don't believe you."

"It was worth a diamond ring to get you out of there. Drawing a crowd and getting ready to draw flies," said Hagar.

"What're you going to do with the ring?" Milkman asked her.

"Wear it. Seldom I win something I like."

"Everything she win, she give away," Hagar said.

"To a man," said Pilate.

"She don't never keep none of it. . . ."

"That's what she want to win—a man. . . ."

"Worse'n Santa Claus. . . ."

"Funny kind of luck ain't no luck at all. . . ."

"*He* comes just once a year. . . ."

Hagar and Pilate pulled the conversation apart, each yanking out some thread of comment more to herself than to Milkman or Guitar—or even Reba, who had dropped her ring back inside her dress and was smiling sweetly, and deftly separating the royal-purple berries from their twigs.

Milkman was five feet seven then but it was the first time in his life that he remembered being completely happy. He was with his friend, an older boy—wise and kind and fearless. He was sitting comfortably in the notorious wine house; he was surrounded by women who seemed to enjoy him and who laughed out loud. And he was in love. No wonder his father was afraid of them.

"When will this wine be ready?" he asked.

"This batch? Few weeks," Pilate said.

"You gonna let us have some?" Guitar smiled.

"Sure. You want some now? Plenty wine in the cellar."

"I don't want that. I want some of this. Some of the wine I made."

"You think you made this?" Pilate laughed at him. "You think this all there is to it? Picking a few berries?"

"Oh." Guitar scratched his head. "I forgot. We got to mash them in our bare feet."

"Feet? Feet?" Pilate was outraged. "Who makes wine with they feet?"

"Might taste good, Mama," said Hagar.

"Couldn't taste no worse," Reba said.

"Your wine any good, Pilate?" asked Guitar.

"Couldn't tell you."

"Why not?"

"Never tasted it."

Milkman laughed. "You sell wine you don't even taste?"

"Folks don't buy it for the taste. Buy it to get drunk."

Reba nodded. "Used to anyway. Ain't buying nothing now."

"Don't nobody want no cheap home brew. The Depression's over," Hagar said. "Everybody got work now. They can afford to buy Four Roses."

"Plenty still buy," Pilate told her.

"Where you get the sugar for it?" Guitar asked.

"Black market," said Reba.

"What 'plenty'? Tell the truth, Mama. If Reba hadn't won that hundred pounds of groceries, we'd have starved last winter."

"Would not." Pilate put a fresh piece of twig in her mouth.

"We *would* have."

"Hagar, don't contradict your mama," Reba whispered.

"Who was gonna feed us?" Hagar was insistent. "Mama can go for months without food. Like a lizard."

"Lizard live that long without food?" asked Reba.

"Girl, ain't nobody gonna let you starve. You ever had a hungry day?" Pilate asked her granddaughter.

"Course she ain't," said her mother.

Hagar tossed a branch to the heap on the floor and rubbed her fingers. The tips were colored a deep red. "Some of my days were hungry ones."

With the quickness of birds, the heads of Pilate and Reba shot up. They peered at Hagar, then exchanged looks.

"Baby?" Reba's voice was soft. "You been hungry, baby? Why didn't you say so?" Reba looked hurt. "We get you anything you want, baby. Anything. You *been* knowing that."

Pilate spit her twig into the palm of her hand. Her face went still. Without those moving lips her face was like a mask. It seemed to Milkman that somebody had just clicked off a light.

He looked at the faces of the women. Reba's had crumpled. Tears were streaming down her cheeks. Pilate's face was still as death, but alert as though waiting for some signal. Hagar's profile was hidden by her hair. She leaned forward, her elbows on her thighs, rubbing fingers that looked bloodstained in the lessening light. Her nails were very very long.

The quiet held. Even Guitar didn't dare break it.

Then Pilate spoke. "Reba. She don't mean food."

Realization swept slowly across Reba's face, but she didn't answer. Pilate began to hum as she returned to plucking the berries. After a moment, Reba joined her, and they hummed together in perfect harmony until Pilate took the lead:

> *O Sugarman don't leave me here*
> *Cotton balls to choke me*
> *O Sugarman don't leave me here*
> *Buckra's arms to yoke me. . . .*

When the two women got to the chorus, Hagar raised her head and sang too.

> *Sugarman done fly away*
> *Sugarman done gone*
> *Sugarman cut across the sky*
> *Sugarman gone home.*

Milkman could hardly breathe. Hagar's voice scooped up what little pieces of heart he had left to call his own. When he thought he was going to faint from the weight of what he was feeling, he risked a glance at his friend and saw the setting sun gilding Guitar's eyes, putting into shadow a slow smile of recognition.

Delicious as the day turned out to be for Milkman, it was even more so because it included secrecy and defiance, both of which dissipated within an hour of his father's return. Freddie had let Macon Dead know that his son had spent the afternoon "drinking in the wine house."

"He's lying! We didn't drink nothing. Nothing. Guitar didn't even get the glass of water he asked for."

"Freddie never lies. He misrepresents, but he never lies."

"He lied to you."

"About the wine-drinking? Maybe. But not about you being there, huh?"

"No, sir. Not about that." Milkman softened his tone a bit, but succeeded in keeping the edge of defiance in his voice.

"Now, what were your instructions from me?"

"You told me to stay away from there. To stay away from Pilate."

"Right."

"But you never told me why. They're our cousins. She's your own sister."

"And you're my own son. And you will do what I tell you to do. With or without explanations. As long as your feet are under my table, you'll do in this house what you are told."

At fifty-two, Macon Dead was as imposing a man as he had been at forty-two, when Milkman thought he was the biggest thing in the world. Bigger even than the house they lived in. But today he had seen a woman who was just as tall and who had made him feel tall too.

"I know I'm the youngest one in this family, but I ain't no baby. You treat me like I was a baby. You keep saying you don't have to explain nothing to me. How do you think that makes me feel? Like a baby, that's what. Like a twelve-year-old baby!"

"Don't you raise your voice to me."

"Is that the way your father treated you when you were twelve?"

"Watch your mouth!" Macon roared. He took his hands out of his pockets but didn't know what to do with them. He was momentarily confused. His son's question had shifted the scenery. He was seeing himself at twelve, standing in Milkman's shoes and feeling what he himself had felt for his own father. The numbness that had settled on him when he saw the man he loved and admired fall off the fence; something wild ran through him when he watched the body twitching in the dirt. His father had sat for five nights on a split-rail fence cradling a shotgun and in the end died protecting his property. Was that what this boy felt for him? Maybe it was time to tell him things.

"Well, did he?"

"I worked right alongside my father. Right alongside him. From the time I was four or five we worked together. Just the two of us. Our mother was dead. Died when Pilate was born. Pilate was just a baby. She stayed over at another farm in the daytime. I carried her over there myself in my arms every morning. Then I'd go back across the fields and meet my father. We'd hitch President Lincoln to the plow and . . . That's what we called her: President Lincoln. Papa said Lincoln was a good plow hand before he was President and you shouldn't take a good plow hand away from his work. He called our farm Lincoln's Heaven. It was a little bit a place. But it looked big to me then. I know now it must a been a little bit a place, maybe a hundred and fifty acres. We tilled fifty. About eighty of it was woods. Must of been a fortune in oak and pine; maybe that's what they wanted—the lumber, the oak and the pine. We had a pond that was four acres. And a stream, full of fish. Right down in the heart of a valley. Prettiest mountain you ever saw, Montour Ridge. We lived in Montour County. Just north of the Susquehanna. We had a four-stall hog pen. The big barn was forty feet by a hundred and forty—hip-roofed too. And all around in the mountains was deer and wild turkey. You ain't tasted nothing till you taste wild turkey the way Papa cooked it. He'd burn it real fast in the fire. Burn it black all over. That sealed it. Sealed the juices in. Then he'd let it roast on a spit for twenty-four hours. When you cut the black burnt part off, the meat underneath was tender, sweet, juicy. And we had fruit trees. Apple, cherry. Pilate tried to make me a cherry pie once."

Macon paused and let the smile come on. He had not said any of this for years. Had not even reminisced much about it recently. When he was first married he used to talk about Lincoln's Heaven to Ruth. Sitting on the porch swing in the dark, he would re-create the land that was to have been his. Or when he was just starting out in the business of buying houses, he would lounge around the barbershop and swap stories with the men there. But for years he hadn't had that kind of time, or interest. But now he was doing it again, with his son, and every detail of that land was clear in his mind: the well, the apple orchard, President Lincoln; her foal, Mary Todd; Ulysses S. Grant, their cow; General Lee, their hog. That was the way he knew what history he remembered. His father couldn't read, couldn't write; knew only what he saw and heard tell of. But he had etched in Macon's mind certain historical figures, and as a boy in school, Macon thought of the personalities of his horse, his hog, when he read about these people. His father may have called their plow horse President Lincoln as a joke, but Macon always thought of Lincoln with fondness since he had loved him first as a strong, steady, gentle, and obedient horse. He even liked General Lee, for one spring they slaughtered him and ate the best pork outside Virginia, "from the butt to the smoked ham to the ribs to the sausage to the jowl to the feet to the tail to the head cheese"—for eight months. And there was cracklin in November.

"General Lee was all right by me," he told Milkman, smiling. "Finest general I ever knew. Even his balls was tasty. Circe made up the best pot of maws she ever cooked. Huh! I'd forgotten that woman's name. That was it, Circe. Worked at a big farm some white people owned in Danville, Pennsylvania. Funny how things get away from you. For years you can't remember nothing. Then just like that, it all comes back to you. Had a dog run, they did. That was the big sport back then. Dog races. White people did love their dogs. Kill a nigger and comb their hair at the same time. But I've seen grown white men cry about their dogs."

His voice sounded different to Milkman. Less hard, and his speech was different. More southern and comfortable and soft. Milkman spoke softly too. "Pilate said somebody shot your father. Five feet into the air."

"Took him sixteen years to get that farm to where it was paying. It's all dairy country up there now. Then it wasn't. Then it was . . . nice."

"Who shot him, Daddy?"

Macon focused his eyes on his son. "Papa couldn't read, couldn't even sign his name. Had a mark he used. They tricked him. He signed something, I don't know what, and they told him they owned his property. He never read nothing. I tried to teach him, but he said he couldn't remember those little marks from one day to the next. Wrote one word in his life—Pilate's name; copied it out of the Bible. That's what she got folded up in that earring. He should have let me teach him. Everything bad that ever happened to him happened because he couldn't read. Got his name messed up cause he couldn't read."

"His name? How?"

"When freedom came. All the colored people in the state had to register with the Freedmen's Bureau."

"Your father was a slave?"

"What kind of foolish question is that? Course he was. Who hadn't been in 1869? They all had to register. Free and not free. Free and used-to-be-slaves. Papa was in his teens and went to sign up, but the man behind the desk was drunk. He asked Papa where he was born. Papa said Macon. Then he asked him who his father was. Papa said, 'He's dead.' Asked him who owned him, Papa said, 'I'm free.' Well, the Yankee wrote it all down, but in the wrong spaces. Had him born in Dunfrie, wherever the hell that is, and in the space for his name the fool wrote, 'Dead' comma 'Macon.' But Papa couldn't read so he never found out what he was registered as till Mama told him. They met on a wagon going North. Started talking about one thing and another, told her about being a freedman and showed off his papers to her. When she looked at his paper she read him out what it said."

"He didn't have to keep the name, did he? He could have used his real name, couldn't he?"

"Mama liked it. Liked the name. Said it was new and would wipe out the past. Wipe it all out."

"What was his real name?"

"I don't remember my mother too well. She died when I was four. Light-skinned, pretty. Looked like a white woman to me. Me and Pilate don't take nothing after her. If you ever have a doubt we from Africa, look at Pilate. She look just like Papa and he looked like all them pictures you ever see of Africans. A Pennsylvania African. Acted like one too. Close his face up like a door."

"I saw Pilate's face like that." Milkman felt close and confidential now that his father had talked to him in a relaxed and intimate way.

"I haven't changed my mind, Macon. I don't want you over there."

"Why? You still haven't said why."

"Just listen to what I say. That woman's no good. She's a snake, and can charm you like a snake, but still a snake."

"You talking about your own sister, the one you carried in your arms to the fields every morning."

"That was a long time ago. You seen her. What she look like to you? Somebody nice? Somebody normal?"

"Well, she . . ."

"Or somebody cut your throat?"

"She didn't look like that, Daddy."

"Well she *is* like that."

"What'd she do?"

"It ain't what she did; it's what she is."

"What is she?"

"A snake, I told you. Ever hear the story about the snake? The man who saw a little baby snake on the ground? Well, the man saw this baby snake bleeding and hurt. Lying there in the dirt. And the man felt sorry for it and picked it up and put it in his basket and took it home. And he fed it and took care of it till it was big and strong. Fed it the same thing he ate. Then one day, the snake turned on him and bit him. Stuck his poison tongue right in the man's heart. And while he was laying there dying, he turned to the snake and asked him, 'What'd you do that for?' He said, 'Didn't I take good care of you? Didn't I save your life?' The snake said, 'Yes.' 'Then what'd you do it for? What'd you kill me for?' Know what the snake said? Said, 'But you knew I was a snake, didn't you?' Now, I mean for you to stay out of that wine house and as far away from Pilate as you can."

Milkman lowered his head. His father had explained nothing to him.

"Boy, you got better things to do with your time. Besides, it's time you started learning how to work. You start Monday. After school come to my office; work a couple of hours there and learn what's real. Pilate can't teach you a thing you can use in this world. Maybe the next, but not this one. Let me tell you right now the one important thing you'll ever need to know: Own things. And let the things you own own other things. Then you'll own yourself and other people too. Starting Monday, I'm going to teach you how."

# Chapter 3

Life improved for Milkman enormously after he began working for Macon. Contrary to what his father hoped, there was more time to visit the wine house. Running errands for Macon's rent houses gave him leave to be in Southside and get to know the people Guitar knew so well. Milkman was young and he was friendly—just the opposite of his father—and the tenants felt at ease enough with him to tease him, feed him, confide in him. But it was hard to see much of Guitar. Saturdays were the only days he was certain to find him. If Milkman got up early enough on Saturday morning, he could catch his friend before Guitar went roaming the streets and before he himself had to help Macon collect rents. But there were days in the week when they agreed to skip school and hang out, and on one of those days Guitar took him to Feather's pool hall on Tenth Street, right in the middle of the Blood Bank area.

It was eleven o'clock in the morning when Guitar pushed open the door and shouted, "Hey, Feather! Give us a couple of Red Caps."

Feather, a short squat man with sparse but curly hair, looked up at Guitar, then at Milkman, and frowned.

"Get him out of here."

Guitar stopped short and followed the little man's gaze to Milkman's face and back again. The half-dozen men there playing pool turned around at the sound of Feather's voice. Three of them were air force pilots, part of the 332nd Fighter Group. Their beautiful hats and gorgeous leather jackets were carefully arranged on chairs. Their hair was cut close to the skull; their shirt cuffs were turned neatly back on their forearms; their white scarves hung in snowy rectangles from their hip pockets. Silver chains glistened at their necks and they looked faintly amused as they worked chalk into the tips of their cues.

Guitar's face shone with embarrassment. "He's with me," he said.

"I said get him outta here."

"Come on, Feather, he's my friend."

"He's Macon Dead's boy, ain't he?"

"So what?"

"So get him outta here."

"He can't help who his daddy is." Guitar had his voice under control.

"Neither can I. Out."

"What his daddy do to you?"

"Nothing yet. That's why I want him outta here."

"He ain't like his daddy."

"He ain't got to be like him—*from* him is enough."

"I'll be responsible for—"

"Stop messing with me, Guitar. Get him out. He ain't old enough to have wet dreams."

The pilots laughed and a man in a gray straw hat with a white band said, "Aw, let the boy stay, Feather."

"You shut your mouth. I'm running this."

"What harm can he do? A twelve-year-old kid." He smiled at Milkman, who stopped himself from saying, No, thirteen.

"But it ain't your problem, is it?" asked Feather. "His daddy ain't your landlord, is he, and you ain't got no operating license to hang on to either. You ain't got nothing. . . ."

Feather turned on the man with the white hatband the same acid manner he'd used with the boys. Guitar took the opportunity offered by Feather's new target to shoot his hand out like a double-edged hatchet slamming into a tree, and shout, "Later for you, man. Come on. Let's shake this place." His voice now was loud and deep—loud enough and deep enough for two. Milkman slid his hands into his back pockets and followed his friend to the door. He stretched his neck a little to match the chilly height he hoped the soldiers had seen in his eyes.

Silently they ambled down Tenth Street until they reached a stone bench that jutted from the sidewalk near the curb. They stopped there and sat down, their backs to the eyes of two men in white smocks who were watching them. One of the men leaned in the doorway of a barbershop. The other sat in a chair tilted back to the plate-glass window of the shop. They were the owners of the barbershop, Railroad Tommy and Hospital Tommy. Neither boy spoke, not to the men nor to each other. They sat and watched the traffic go by.

"Have all the halls of academe crumbled, Guitar?" Hospital Tommy spoke from his chair. His eyes were milky, like those of very old people, but the rest of him was firm, lithe, and young-looking. His tone was casual but suggested authority nonetheless.

"No, sir." Guitar answered him over his shoulder.

"Then what, pray, are you doing out here in the streets at this time of day?"

Guitar shrugged. "We just took a day off, Mr. Tommy."

"And your companion? Is he on sabbatical too?"

Guitar nodded. Hospital Tommy talked like an encyclopedia and Guitar had to guess at most of his words. Milkman kept looking at the cars going by.

"Neither one of you appears to be having much fun on your holiday. You could have stayed in the halls of academe and looked evil."

Guitar fished for a cigarette and offered one to Milkman. "Feather made me mad is all."

"Feather?"

"Yeah. He wouldn't let us in. I go in there all the time. All the time and he don't say nothing. But today he throws us out. Said my friend here is too young. Can you beat that? Feather? Worrying about somebody's age?"

"I didn't know Feather had so much as a brain cell to worry with."

"He don't. Just showing off is all. He wouldn't even let me have a bottle of beer."

Railroad Tommy laughed softly from the doorway. "Is that all? He wouldn't let you have a beer?" He rubbed the back of his neck and then crooked a finger at Guitar. "Come over here, boy, and let me tell you about some other stuff you are not going to have. Come on over here."

Reluctantly they stood up and sidled closer to the laughing man.

"You think that's something? Not having a beer? Well, let me ask you something. You ever stood stock still in the galley of the Baltimore and Ohio dining car in the middle of the night when the kitchen closed down and everything's neat and ready for the next day? And the engine's highballing down the track and three of your buddies is waiting for you with a brand-new deck of cards?"

Guitar shook his head. "No, I never . . ."

"That's right, you never. And you never going to. That's one more thrill you not going to have, let alone a bottle of beer."

Guitar smiled. "Mr. Tommy," he began, but Tommy cut him off.

"You ever pull fourteen days straight and come home to a sweet woman, clean sheets, and a fifth of Wild Turkey? Eh?" He looked at Milkman. "Did you?"

Milkman smiled and said, "No, sir."

"No? Well, don't look forward to it, cause you not going to have that either."

Hospital Tommy drew a pinfeather toothpick from under his smock. "Don't tease the boy, Tommy."

"Who's teasing? I'm telling him the truth. He ain't going to have it. Neither one of 'em going to have it. And I'll tell you something else you not going to have. You not going to have no private coach with four red velvet chairs that swivel around in one place whenever you want 'em to. No. And you not going to have your own special toilet and your own special-made eight-foot bed either. And a valet and a cook and a secretary to travel with you and do everything you say. Everything: get the right temperature in your hot-water bottle and make sure the smoking tobacco in the silver humidor is fresh each and *every* day. That's something else you not going to have. You ever have five thousand dollars of cold cash money in your pocket and walk into a bank and tell the bank man you want such and such a house on such and such a street and he sell it to you right then? Well, you won't ever have it. And you not going to have a governor's mansion, or eight thousand acres of timber to sell. And you not going to have no ship under your command to sail on, no train to run, and you can join the 332nd if you want to and shoot down a thousand German planes all by yourself and land in Hitler's backyard and whip him with your own hands, but you never going to have four stars on your shirt front, or even three. And you not going to have no breakfast tray brought in to you early in the morning with a red rose on it and two warm croissants and a cup of hot chocolate. Nope. Never. And no pheasant buried in coconut leaves for twenty days and stuffed with wild rice and cooked over a wood fire so tender and delicate it make you cry. And no Rothschild '29 or even Beaujolais to go with it."

A few men passing by stopped to listen to Tommy's lecture. "What's going on?" they asked Hospital Tommy.

"Feather refused them a beer," he said. The men laughed.

"And *no* baked Alaska!" Railroad Tommy went on. "None! You never going to have that."

"No baked Alaska?" Guitar opened his eyes wide with horror and grabbed his throat. "You breaking my heart!"

"Well, now. That's something you will have—a broken heart." Railroad Tommy's eyes softened, but the merriment in them died suddenly. "And folly. A whole lot of folly. You can count on it."

"Mr. Tommy, suh," Guitar sang in mock humility, "we just wanted a bottle of beer is all."

"Yeah," said Tommy. "Yeah, well, welcome aboard."

"What's a baked Alaska?" They left the Tommys just as they had found them and continued down Tenth Street.

"Something sweet," answered Guitar. "A dessert."

"Taste good?"

"I don't know. I can't eat sweets."

"You can't?" Milkman was amazed. "Why not?"

"Makes me sick."

"You don't like nothing sweet?"

"Fruit, but nothing with sugar. Candy, cake, stuff like that. I don't even like to smell it. Makes me want to throw up."

Milkman searched for a physical cause. He wasn't sure he trusted anybody who didn't like sweets. "You must have sugar diabetes."

"You don't get sugar diabetes from not eating sugar. You get it from eating too much sugar."

"Then what is it, then?"

"I don't know. It makes me think of dead people. And white people. And I start to puke."

"Dead people?"

"Yeah. And white people."

"I don't get it."

Guitar said nothing, so Milkman continued, "How long you been like that?"

"Since I was little. Since my father got sliced up in a sawmill and his boss came by and gave us kids some candy. Divinity. A big sack of divinity. His wife made it special for us. It's sweet, divinity is. Sweeter than syrup. Real sweet. Sweeter than . . ." He stopped walking and wiped from his forehead the beads of sweat that were collecting there. His eyes paled and wavered. He spit on the sidewalk. "Ho—hold it," he whispered, and stepped into a space between a fried-fish restaurant and Lilly's Beauty Parlor.

Milkman waited on the sidewalk, staring at the curtained window of the beauty shop. Beauty shops always had curtains or shades up. Barbershops didn't. The women didn't want anybody on the street to be able to see them getting their hair done. They were ashamed.

When Guitar emerged, his eyes were teary from the effort of dry heaving. "Come on," he said. "Let's get us some weed. That's one thing I can have."

By the time Milkman was fourteen he had noticed that one of his legs was shorter than the other. When he stood barefoot and straight as a pole, his left foot was about half an inch off the floor. So he never stood straight; he slouched or leaned or stood with a hip thrown out, and he never told anybody about it—ever. When Lena said, "Mama, what is he walking like *that* for?" he said, "I'll walk any way I want to, including over your ugly face." Ruth said, "Be quiet, you two. It's just growing pains, Lena." Milkman knew better. It wasn't a limp—not at all—just the suggestion of one, but it looked like an affected walk, the strut of a very young man trying to appear more sophisticated than he was. It bothered him and he acquired movements and habits to disguise what to him was a burning defect. He sat with his left ankle on his right knee, never the other way around. And he danced each new dance with a curious stiff-legged step that the girls loved and other boys eventually copied. The deformity was mostly in his mind. Mostly, but not completely, for he did have shooting pains in that leg after several hours on a basketball court. He favored it, believed it was polio, and felt secretly connected to the late President Roosevelt for that reason. Even when everybody was raving about Truman because he had set up a Committee on Civil Rights,

Milkman secretly preferred FDR and felt very very close to him. Closer, in fact, to him than to his own father, for Macon had no imperfection and age seemed to strengthen him. Milkman feared his father, respected him, but knew, because of the leg, that he could never emulate him. So he differed from him as much as he dared. Macon was clean-shaven; Milkman was desperate for a mustache. Macon wore bow ties; Milkman wore four-in-hands. Macon didn't part his hair; Milkman had a part shaved into his. Macon hated tobacco; Milkman tried to put a cigarette in his mouth every fifteen minutes. Macon hoarded his money; Milkman gave his away. But he couldn't help sharing with Macon his love of good shoes and fine thin socks. And he did try, as his father's employee, to do the work the way Macon wanted it done.

Macon was delighted. His son belonged to him now and not to Ruth, and he was relieved at not having to walk all over town like a peddler collecting rents. It made his business more dignified, and he had time to think, to plan, to visit the bank men, to read the public notices, auctions, to find out what plots were going for taxes, unclaimed heirs' property, where roads were being built, what supermarkets, schools; and who was trying to sell what to the government for the housing projects that were going to be built. The quickie townlets that were springing up around war plants. He knew as a Negro he wasn't going to get a big slice of the pie. But there were properties nobody wanted yet, or little edges of property somebody didn't want Jews to have, or Catholics to have, or properties nobody knew were of any value yet. There was quite a bit of pie filling oozing around the edge of the crust in 1945. Filling that could be his. Everything had improved for Macon Dead during the war. Except Ruth. And years later when the war was over and that pie filling had spilled over into his very lap, had stickied his hands and weighed his stomach down into a sagging paunch, he still wished he had strangled her back in 1921. She hadn't stopped spending occasional nights out of the house, but she was fifty years old now and what lover could she have kept so long? What lover could there be that even Freddie didn't know about? Macon decided it was of no importance, and less and less often did he get angry enough to slap her. Particularly after the final time, which became final because his son jumped up and knocked him back into the radiator.

Milkman was twenty-two then and since he had been fucking for six years, some of them with the same woman, he'd begun to see his mother in a new light. She was no longer the person who worried him about galoshes and colds and food, who stood in the way of most of the little pleasures he could take at home because they all involved some form of dirt, noise, or disarray. Now he saw her as a frail woman content to do tiny things; to grow and cultivate small life that would not hurt her if it died: rhododendron, goldfish, dahlias, geraniums, imperial tulips. Because these little lives did die. The goldfish floated to the top of the water and when she tapped the side of the bowl with her fingernail they did not flash away in a lightning arc of terror. The rhododendron leaves grew wide and green and when their color was at its deepest and waxiest, they suddenly surrendered it and lapsed into limp yellow hearts. In a way she was jealous of death. Inside all that grief she felt when the doctor died, there had been a bit of pique too, as though he had chosen a more interesting subject than life—a more provocative companion than she was—and had deliberately followed death when it beckoned. She was fierce in the presence of death, heroic even, as she was at no other time. Its threat gave her direction, clarity, audacity. Regardless of what Macon had done, she'd always suspected that the doctor didn't have to die if he hadn't wanted to. And it may have been that suspicion of personal failure and rejection (plus a smidgen of revenge against Macon) that made her lead her husband down paths from which there was no exit save violence. Lena thought Macon's rages unaccountable. But Corinthians began to see a plan. To see how her mother had learned to bring her husband to a point, not of power (a nine-year-old girl could slap Ruth and get away with it), but of helplessness. She would begin by describing some incident in which she was a sort of honest buffoon. It began as a piece of pleasant dinner conversation, harmless on the surface because no one at the table was required to share her embarrassment; but all were able to admire her honesty and to laugh at her ignorance.

She had gone to the wedding of Mrs. Djvorak's granddaughter. Anna Djvorak was an old Hungarian woman who had been one of her father's patients. He'd had many working-class white patients and some middle-class white women who thought he was handsome. Anna Djvorak was convinced that the doctor had miraculously saved her son's life by not sending him to the tuberculosis sanatorium back in 1903. Almost everybody who did go to the "san," as they called it, died in it. Anna didn't know that the doctor had no practicing privileges there, just as he had none at Mercy. Nor did she know that the cure for tuberculosis in 1903 was precisely the one most detrimental to the patients. All she knew was that the doctor had prescribed a certain diet, hours of rest to be rigidly adhered to, and cod-liver oil twice a day. The boy survived. It was natural that she would want the miracle doctor's daughter at the wedding of this son's youngest daughter. Ruth went and when the congregation went to the altar to receive the host, she went also. Kneeling there with her head bowed, she was not aware that the priest was left with the choice of placing the wafer on her hat or skipping her. He knew immediately that she was not Catholic since she did not raise her head at his words and push out her tongue for the wafer to be carefully placed there.

"Corpus Domini Nostri Jesu Christi," said the priest, and then, to her, a sharp whisper: "Ssss. Raise your head!" She looked up, saw the wafer and the acolyte holding a little silver tray under it. "Corpus Domini Nostri Jesu Christi custodiat animam tuam . . ." The priest held the host toward her and she opened her mouth.

Later, at the reception, the priest asked her point-blank whether she was Catholic.

"No. I'm Methodist," she said.

"I see," he said. "Well, the sacraments of the Church are reserved for—" Just then old Mrs. Djvorak interrupted him.

"Father," she said, "I want you to meet one of my dearest

friends. Dr. Foster's daughter. Her father saved Ricky's life. Ricky wouldn't be here today if . . ."

Father Padrew smiled and shook Ruth's hand. "Very pleased to meet you, Miss Foster."

It was a simple occurrence, elaborately told. Lena listened and experienced each phrase of her mother's emotion from religious ecstasy to innocent confidence to embarrassment. Corinthians listened analytically, expectantly—wondering how her mother would develop this anecdote into a situation in which Macon would either lash out at her verbally or hit her. Milkman was only half listening.

" 'Are you Catholic?' he asked me. Well, I was embarrassed for a minute, but then I said, 'No. I'm Methodist.' And he started to tell me that only Catholics could take communion in a Catholic church. Well, I never heard of that. Anybody can take communion, I thought. At our church anybody can come up on the first Sunday. Well, before he could get it out, Anna came up and said, 'Father, I want you to meet one of my dearest friends. Dr. Foster's daughter.' Well, the priest was all smiles then. And shook my hand and said he was *very* pleased and honored to make my acquaintance. So it all turned out all right. But honestly, I didn't know. I went up there as innocent as a lamb."

"You didn't know that only Catholics take communion in a Catholic church?" Macon Dead asked her, his tone making it clear that he didn't believe her.

"No, Macon. How would I know?"

"You see them put up their own school, keep their kids out of public schools, and you still think their religious stuff is open to anybody who wants to drop in?"

"Communion is communion."

"You're a silly woman."

"Father Padrew didn't think so."

"You made a fool of yourself."

"Mrs. Djvorak didn't think so."

"She was just trying to keep the wedding going, keep you from fucking it up."

"Macon, please don't use that language in front of the children."

"What goddam children? Everybody in here is old enough to vote."

"There is no call for an argument."

"You make a fool of yourself in a Catholic church, embarrass everybody at the reception, and come to the table to gloat about how wonderful you were?"

"Macon . . ."

"And sit there lying, saying you didn't know any better?"

"Anna Djvorak wasn't the least bit—"

"Anna Djvorak don't even know your name! She called you *Dr. Foster's daughter!* I bet you one hundred dollars she still don't know your name! You by yourself ain't nobody. You your daddy's daughter!"

"That's so," said Ruth in a thin but steady voice. "I certainly am my daddy's daughter." She smiled.

Macon didn't wait to put his fork down. He dropped it on the table while his hand was on its way across the bread plate becoming the fist he smashed into her jaw.

Milkman hadn't planned any of it, but he had to know that one day, after Macon hit her, he'd see his mother's hand cover her lips as she searched with her tongue for any broken teeth, and discovering none, tried to adjust the partial plate in her mouth without anyone noticing—and that on that day he would not be able to stand it. Before his father could draw his hand back, Milkman had yanked him by the back of his coat collar, up out of his chair, and knocked him into the radiator. The window shade flapped and rolled itself up.

"You touch her again, one more time, and I'll kill you."

Macon was so shocked at being assaulted he could not speak. He had come to believe, after years of creating respect and fear wherever he put his foot down, after years of being the tallest man in every gathering, that he was impregnable. Now he crept along the wall looking at a man who was as tall as he was—and forty years younger.

Just as the father brimmed with contradictory feelings as he crept along the wall—humiliation, anger, and a grudging feeling of pride in his son—so the son felt his own contradictions. There was the pain and shame of seeing his father crumple before any man—even himself. Sorrow in discovering that the pyramid was not a five-thousand-year wonder of the civilized world, mysteriously and permanently constructed by generation after generation of hardy men who had died in order to perfect it, but that it had been made in the back room at Sears, by a clever window dresser, of papier-mâché, guaranteed to last for a mere lifetime.

He also felt glee. A snorting, horse-galloping glee as old as desire. He had won something and lost something in the same instant. Infinite possibilities and enormous responsibilities stretched out before him, but he was not prepared to take advantage of the former, or accept the burden of the latter. So he cock-walked around the table and asked his mother, "Are you all right?"

She was looking at her fingernails. "Yes, I'm fine."

Milkman looked at his sisters. He had never been able to really distinguish them (or their roles) from his mother. They were in their early teens when he was born; they were thirty-five and thirty-six now. But since Ruth was only sixteen years older than Lena, all three had always looked the same age to him. Now when he met his sisters' eyes over the table, they returned him a look of hatred so fresh, so new, it startled him. Their pale eyes no longer appeared to blur into their even paler skin. It seemed to him as though charcoal lines had been drawn around their eyes; that two drag lines had been smudged down their cheeks, and their rosy lips were swollen in hatred so full it was about to burst through. Milkman had to blink twice before their faces returned to the vaguely alarmed blandness he was accustomed to. Quickly he left the room, realizing there was no one to thank him—or abuse him. His action was his alone. It would change nothing between his parents. It would change nothing inside them. He had knocked his father down and perhaps there were some new positions on the chessboard, but the game would go on.

Sleeping with Hagar had made him generous. Or so he thought. Wide-spirited. Or so he imagined. Wide-spirited and generous enough to defend his mother, whom he almost never thought about, and to deck his father, whom he both feared and loved.

Back in his bedroom, Milkman fiddled with things on his dresser. There was a pair of silver-backed brushes his mother had given him when he was sixteen, engraved with his initials, the abbreviated degree designation of a doctor. He and his mother had joked about it and she hinted strongly that he ought to consider going to medical school. He'd foisted her off with "How would that look? M.D., M.D. If you were sick, would you go see a man called Dr. Dead?"

She laughed but reminded him that his middle name was Foster. Couldn't he use Foster as a last name? Dr. Macon Foster. Didn't that sound fine? He had to admit that it did. The silver-backed brushes were a constant reminder of what her wishes for him were—that he not stop his education at high school, but go on to college and medical school. She had as little respect for her husband's work as Macon had for college graduates. To Milkman's father, college was time spent in idleness, far away from the business of life, which was learning to own things. He was eager for his daughters to go to college—where they could have found suitable husbands—and one, Corinthians, did go. But it was pointless for Milkman, particularly since his son's presence was a real help to him in the office. So much so that he had been able to get his bank friends to speak to some of their friends and get his son moved out of 1-A draft classification and into a "necessary to support family" status.

Milkman stood before his mirror and glanced, in the low light of the wall lamp, at his reflection. He was, as usual, unimpressed with what he saw. He had a fine enough face. Eyes women complimented him on, a firm jaw line, splendid teeth. Taken apart, it looked all right. Even better than all right. But it lacked coherence, a coming together of the features into a total self. It was all very tentative, the way he looked, like a man peeping around a corner of someplace he is not supposed to be, trying to make up his mind whether to go forward or to turn back. The decision he made would be extremely important, but the way in which he made the decision would be careless, haphazard, and uninformed.

Standing there in the lamplight, trying not to think of how his father had looked creeping along the wall, he heard a knock at his door. He didn't want to see the face of Lena or Corinthians, nor to have any secret talk with his mother. But he was not any happier to see his father looming there in the hall. A line of blood was still visible in the thin cut at the corner of Macon's mouth. But he stood straight, and his eyes were steady.

"Look, Daddy," Milkman began, "I—"

"Don't say anything," Macon said, pushing past him. "Sit down."

Milkman moved toward the bed. "Look here, let's try to forget this. If you promise—"

"I told you to sit down. And down is what I mean." Macon's voice was low, but his face looked like Pilate's. He closed the door. "You a big man now, but big ain't nearly enough. You have to be a whole man. And if you want to be a whole man, you have to deal with the whole truth."

"You don't have to do any of this, you know. I don't need to know everything between you and Mama."

"I do have to do it and you do need to know it. If you're in the business of raising your fist at your father, you better have some intelligence behind that fist the next time you throw it. Nothing I'm about to say is by way of apology or excuse. It's just information.

"I married your mother in 1917. She was sixteen, living alone with her father. I can't tell you I was in love with her. People didn't require that as much as they do now. Folks were expected to be civilized to one another, honest, and—and clear. You relied on people being what they said they were, because there was no other way to survive. The important thing, when you took a wife, was that the two of you agreed on what was important.

"Your mother's father never liked me and I have to say I was very disappointed in him. He was just about the biggest Negro in this city. Not the richest, but the most respected. But a bigger hypocrite never lived. Kept all his money in four different banks. Always calm and dignified. I thought he was naturally that way until I found out he sniffed ether. Negroes in this town worshipped him. He didn't give a damn about them, though. Called them cannibals. He delivered both your sisters himself and each time all he was interested in was the color of their skin. He would have disowned you. I didn't like the notion of his being his own daughter's doctor, especially since she was also my wife. Mercy wouldn't take colored then. Anyway, Ruth wouldn't go to any other doctor. I tried to get a midwife for her, but the doctor said midwives were dirty. I told him a midwife delivered me, and if a midwife was good enough for my mother, a midwife was good enough for his daughter. Well, we had some words between us about it, and I ended up telling him that nothing could be nastier than a father delivering his own daughter's baby. That stamped it. We had very little to say after that, but they did it anyway. Both Lena and Corinthians. They let me do the naming by picking a word blind, but that was all. Your sisters are just a little over a year apart, you know. And both times he was there. She had her legs wide open and he was there. I know he was a doctor and doctors not supposed to be bothered by things like that, but he was a man before he was a doctor. I knew then they'd ganged up on me forever—the both of them—and no matter what I did, they managed to have things their way. They made sure I remembered whose house I was in, where the china came from, how he sent to England for the Waterford bowl, and again for the table they put it on. That table was so big they had to take it apart to get it in the door. He was always bragging about how he was the second man in the city to have a two-horse carriage.

"Where I'd come from, the farm we had, that was nothing to them. And what I was trying to do—they didn't have any interest in that. Buying shacks in shacktown, they called it.

'How's shacktown?' That's the way he'd greet me in the evenings.

"But it wasn't that. I could put up with that, because I knew what I wanted, and pretty much how to get it. So I could put up with that. Did put up with it. It was something else, something I couldn't put my finger on. I tried to get him to spend some of that money out of those four banks once. Some track land was going for a lot of money—railroad money. Erie Lackawanna was buying. I had a good hunch where the track would be laid. I walked all around over there, the Shore Road, the docks, the fork in routes 6 and 2. I figured out just where the tracks would have to go. And found land I could have got cheap and sold back to the railroad agents. He wouldn't lend me a dime. If he had, he would have died a rich man, instead of a fair-to-middling one. And I would have been way ahead. I asked your mother to talk him into it. I told her exactly where the Erie was headed. She said it had to be *his* decision; she couldn't influence him. She told me, her husband, that. Then I began to wonder who she was married to—me or him.

"Well, he took sick." Macon stopped, as though the mention of illness reminded him of his own frailty, and pulled a large white handkerchief out of his pocket. Gingerly he pressed it against the thin cut on his lip. He looked at the faint stain it made on his handkerchief. "All that ether," he said, "must have got in his blood. They had another name for it, but I know it was that ether. He just lay down and started swelling up. His body did; his legs and arms just wasted away. He couldn't see patients anymore, and for the first time in his life the pompous donkey found out what it was like to have to be sick and pay another donkey to make you well. One of them doctors, the one that was taking care of him—one of the same ones wouldn't let him set foot in their hospital, and who, if he had delivered *their* daughter's or wife's baby, had even thought of it, would have run him out of here on a rail—one of them, the ones he thought worth his attention, well, he came in here with some magic potion, Radiathor, and told him it would cure him. Ruth was all excited. And for a few days he was better. Then he got sicker. Couldn't move, holes were forming in his scalp. And he just lay there in that bed where your mother still sleeps and then he died there. Helpless, fat stomach, skinny arms and legs, looking like a white rat. He couldn't digest his food, you know. Had to drink all his meals and swallow something after every meal. I believe to this day that was ether too.

"The night he died, I'd been over on the other side of town, fixing a porch that fell down. Mr. Bradlee's house. Porch had been leaning for twenty years, and then just fell down, split clean away from the foundation. I got some men to help me and went over there to get it back up so the people wouldn't have to jump to get out the house and climb up three feet to get in it. Somebody tiptoed up to me and said, 'Doctor died.' Ruth, they said, was upstairs with him. I figured she was upset and went up right away to comfort her. I didn't have time to change clothes from working on the porch, but I went up anyway. She was sitting in a chair next to his bed, and the minute she saw me she jumped up and screamed at me, 'You dare come in here like that? Clean yourself! Clean up before you come in here!' It vexed me some, but I do respect the dead. I went and washed up. Took a bath, put on a clean shirt and collar, and went back in." Macon paused again and touched his cut lip as though that were where the pain that showed in his eyes was coming from.

"In the bed," he said, and stopped for so long Milkman was not sure he was going to continue. "In the bed. That's where she was when I opened the door. Laying next to him. Naked as a yard dog, kissing him. Him dead and white and puffy and skinny, and she had his fingers in her mouth.

"Now, I want you to know I had a terrible time after that. I started thinking all sorts of things. If Lena and Corinthians were my children. I come to know pretty quick they were, cause it was clear that bastard couldn't fuck nothing. Ether took care of whatever he had in that area long before I got there. And he wouldn't have been so worried about what color skin they had unless they were coming from me. Then I thought about his delivering Ruth's babies. I'm not saying that they had contact. But there's lots of things a man can do to please a woman, even if he can't fuck. Whether or not, the fact is she was in that bed sucking his fingers, and if she do that when he was dead, what'd she do when he was alive? Nothing to do but kill a woman like that. I swear, many's the day I regret she talked me out of killing her. But I wasn't looking forward to spending the rest of my days on some rock pile. But you see, Macon, sometimes I can't catch hold of myself quick enough. It just gets out. Tonight, when she said, 'Yes, I am my daddy's daughter,' and gave that little smirk . . ." Macon looked up at his son. The door of his face had opened; his skin looked iridescent. With only a minor break in his voice, he told him, "I am not a bad man. I want you to know that. Or believe it. No man ever took his responsibilities more seriously than I have. I'm not making claims to sainthood, but you have to know it all. I'm forty years older than you and I don't have another forty in me. Next time you take it into your head to jump me, I want you to think about the man you think you whipping. And think about the fact that next time I might not let you. Old as I am, I might not let you."

He stood up and pushed his handkerchief into his back pocket.

"Don't say anything now. But think about everything I've said."

Macon turned the doorknob, and without a backward glance, left the room.

Milkman sat on the edge of his bed; everything was still except for the light buzzing in his head. He felt curiously disassociated from all that he had heard. As though a stranger that he'd sat down next to on a park bench had turned to him and begun to relate some intimacy. He was entirely sympathetic to the stranger's problems—understood perfectly his view of what had happened to him—but part of his sympathy came from the fact that he himself was not involved or in any way threatened by the stranger's story. It was quite the opposite from the feeling he'd had an hour or less ago. The alien who had just

walked out of his room was also the man he felt passionately
enough about to strike with all the fervor he could summon up.
Even now he could feel the tingle in his shoulder that had
signaled the uncontrollable urge to smash his father's face. On
the way upstairs to his room he had felt isolated, but righteous.
He was a man who saw another man hit a helpless person. And
he had interfered. Wasn't that the history of the world? Isn't
that what men did? Protected the frail and confronted the King
of the Mountain? And the fact that the frail was his mother and
the King of the Mountain his father made it more poignant, but
did not change the essential facts. No. He would not pretend
that it was love for his mother. She was too insubstantial, too
shadowy for love. But it was her vaporishness that made her
more needful of defense. She was not a maternal drudge, her
mind pressed flat, her shoulders hunched under the burden of
housework and care of others, brutalized by a bear of a man.
Nor was she the acid-tongued shrew who defended herself with
a vicious vocabulary and a fast lip. Ruth was a pale but complicated woman given to deviousness and ultra-fine manners. She
seemed to know a lot and understand very little. It was an
interesting train of thought, and new for him. Never had he
thought of his mother as a person, a separate individual, with a
life apart from allowing or interfering with his own.

Milkman put on his jacket and left the house. It was seven-
thirty in the evening and not yet dark. He wanted to walk and
breathe some other air. He wouldn't know what to feel until he
knew what to think. And it was difficult thinking in that room
where the silver-backed brushes with the M.D. initials shone in
the light and where the chair his father had just sat in still held
the imprint of his buttocks in the cushion. As the stars made
themselves visible, Milkman tried to figure what was true and
what part of what was true had anything to do with him. What
was he supposed to do with this new information his father had
dumped on him? Was it an effort to cop a plea? How was he
supposed to feel about the two of them now? Was it *true*, first
of all? Did his mother . . . had his mother made it with her

own father? Macon had said no. That the doctor was impotent. How did he know? Well, he must have known what he was talking about, because he was much too eager for it to be true to let it go if there were any possibility it could have taken place. Still, he had admitted there were "other things" a man could do to please a woman. "Goddam," Milkman said aloud. "What the fuck did he tell me all that shit for?" He didn't want to know any of it. There was nothing he could do about it. The doctor was dead. You can't do the past over.

Milkman's confusion was rapidly turning to anger. "Strange motherfuckers," he whispered. "Strange." If he wanted me to lay off, he thought, why didn't he just say that? Just come to me like a man and say, Cool it. You cool it and I'll cool it. We'll both cool it. And I'd say, Okay, you got it. But no. He comes to me with some way-out tale about how come and why.

Milkman was heading toward Southside. Maybe he could find Guitar. A drink with Guitar would be just the thing. Or if he couldn't find Guitar, he'd go see Hagar. No. He didn't want to talk to Hagar, to any woman, just yet. Talk about strange. Now, that was a really strange bunch. His whole family was a bunch of crazies. Pilate singing all day and talking off the wall. Reba turning on for everything in pants. And Hagar . . . well, she was just fine, but still, she wasn't regular. She had some queer ways. But at least they were fun and not full of secrets.

Where would Guitar be? Never anywhere when you really needed him. A real pop-up. Popped up anywhere, anytime, but never on time. Milkman realized he was whispering every now and then and that people on the street were looking at him. Suddenly it seemed to him that there were a lot of people out for that time of day. Where the hell was everybody going? He made an effort not to vocalize his thoughts.

"You want to be a whole man, you have to deal with the whole truth," his father had said. Couldn't I be a whole man without knowing all that? "You better have some intelligence behind that fist." Okay. What intelligence? That my mama screwed her daddy. That my grandfather was a high-yellow nigger who loved ether and hated black skin. So what did he let you marry his daughter for? So he could screw her without the neighbors knowing it? Did you ever catch them doing it? No. You just felt something you couldn't put your finger on. His money, probably. He wouldn't let you put your finger on that, would he? And his daughter wouldn't help you, would she? So you figured they must be gettin it on the operating table. If he'd given you those four bankbooks to do what you liked, to buy up the Erie Lackawanna Railroad, he could have had her all he liked, right? He could have come right in your bed, and the three of you could have had a ball. He'd get one tit and you'd get . . . the . . . other. . . .

Milkman stopped dead in his tracks. Cold sweat broke out on his neck. People jostled him trying to get past the solitary man standing in their way. He had remembered something. Or believed he remembered something. Maybe he'd dreamed it and it was the dream he remembered. The picture was developing, of the two men in the bed with his mother, each nibbling on a breast, but the picture cracked and in the crack another picture emerged. There was this green room, a very small green room, and his mother was sitting in the green room and her breasts were uncovered and somebody was sucking them and the somebody was himself. So? So what? My mother nursed me. Mothers nurse babies. Why the sweat? He walked on, hardly noticing the people pushing past him, their annoyed, tight faces. He tried to see more of the picture, but couldn't. Then he heard something that he knew was related to the picture. Laughter. Somebody he couldn't see, in the room laughing . . . at him and at his mother, and his mother is ashamed. She lowers her eyes and won't look at him. "Look at me, Mama. Look at me." But she doesn't and the laughter is loud now. Everybody is laughing. Did he wet his pants? Is his mother ashamed because while he was nursing he wet his pants? What pants? He didn't wear pants then. He wore diapers. Babies always wet their diapers. Why does he think he has pants on? Blue pants with elastic around the calf. Little blue corduroy knickers. Why is he dressed that way?

Is that what the man is laughing at? Because he is a tiny baby dressed in blue knickers? He sees himself standing there. "Look at me, Mama," is all he can think of to say. "Please look at me." Standing? He is a tiny baby. Nursing in his mother's arms. He can't stand up.

"I couldn't stand up," he said aloud, and turned toward a shop window. There was his face leaning out of the upturned collar of his jacket, and he knew. "My mother nursed me when I was old enough to talk, stand up, and wear knickers, and somebody saw it and laughed and—and that is why they call me Milkman and that is why my father never does and that is why my mother never does, but everybody else does. And how did I forget that? And why? And if she did that to me when there was no reason for it, when I also drank milk and Ovaltine and everything else from a glass, then maybe she did other things with her father?"

Milkman closed his eyes and then opened them. The street was even more crowded with people, all going in the direction he was coming from. All walking hurriedly and bumping against him. After a while he realized that nobody was walking on the other side of the street. There were no cars and the street lights were on, now that darkness had come, but the sidewalk on the other side of the street was completely empty. He turned around to see where everybody was going, but there was nothing to see except their backs and hats pressing forward into the night. He looked again at the other side of Not Doctor Street. Not a soul.

He touched the arm of a man in a cap who was trying to get past him. "Why is everybody on this side of the street?" he asked him.

"Watch it, buddy," the man snapped, and moved on with the crowd.

Milkman walked on, still headed toward Southside, never once wondering why he himself did not cross over to the other side of the street, where no one was walking at all.

He believed he was thinking coldly, clearly. He had never

loved his mother, but had always known that she had loved him. And that had always seemed right to him, the way it should be. Her confirmed, eternal love of him, love that he didn't even have to earn or deserve, seemed to him natural. And now it was decomposing. He wondered if there was anyone in the world who liked him. Liked him for himself alone. His visits to the wine house seemed (before his talk with his father) an extension of the love he had come to expect from his mother. Not that Pilate or Reba felt the possessive love for him that his mother did, but they had accepted him without question and with all the ease in the world. They took him seriously too. Asked him questions and thought all his responses to things were important enough to laugh at or quarrel with him about. Everything he did at home was met with quiet understanding from his mother and his sisters (or indifference and criticism from his father). The women in the wine house were indifferent to nothing and understood nothing. Every sentence, every word, was new to them and they listened to what he said like bright-eyed ravens, trembling in their eagerness to catch and interpret every sound in the universe. Now he questioned them. Questioned everybody. His father had crept along the wall and then come upstairs with a terrible piece of news. His mother had been portrayed not as a mother who simply adored her only son, but as an obscene child playing dirty games with whatever male was near—be it her father or her son. Even his sisters, the most tolerant and accommodating of all the women he knew, had changed their faces and rimmed their eyes with red and charcoal dust.

Where was Guitar? He needed to find the one person left whose clarity never failed him, and unless he was out of the state, Milkman was determined to find him.

His first stop, Tommy's Barbershop, was fruitful. Guitar was there with several other men, leaning in various attitudes, but all listening to something.

As Milkman entered and spotted Guitar's back, he was so relieved he shouted, "Hey, Guitar!"

"Sh!" said Railroad Tommy. Guitar turned around and motioned him to come in but to be quiet. They were listening to the radio and muttering and shaking their heads. It was some time before Milkman discovered what they were so tense about. A young Negro boy had been found stomped to death in Sunflower County, Mississippi. There were no questions about who stomped him—his murderers had boasted freely—and there were no questions about the motive. The boy had whistled at some white woman, refused to deny he had slept with others, and was a Northerner visiting the South. His name was Till.

Railroad Tommy was trying to keep the noise down so he could hear the last syllable of the newscaster's words. In a few seconds it was over, since the announcer had only a few speculations and even fewer facts. The minute he went on to another topic of news, the barbershop broke into loud conversation. Railroad Tommy, the one who had tried to maintain silence, was himself completely silent now. He moved to his razor strop while Hospital Tommy tried to keep his customer in the chair. Porter, Guitar, Freddie the janitor, and three or four other men were exploding, shouting angry epithets all over the room. Apart from Milkman, only Railroad Tommy and Empire State were quiet—Railroad Tommy because he was preoccupied with his razor and Empire State because he was simple, and probably mute, although nobody seemed sure about that. There was no question whatever about his being simple.

Milkman tried to focus on the crisscrossed conversations.

"It'll be in the morning paper."

"Maybe it will, and maybe it won't," said Porter.

"It was on the radio! Got to be in the paper!" said Freddie.

"They don't put that kind of news in no white paper. Not unless he raped somebody."

"What you bet? What you bet it'll be in there?" said Freddie.

"Bet anything you can lose," Porter answered.

"You on for five."

"Wait a minute," Porter shouted. "Say where."

"What you mean, 'where'? I got five says it'll be in the morning paper."

"On the sports page?" asked Hospital Tommy.

"Or the funny papers?" said Nero Brown.

"No, man. Front page. I bet five dollars on front page."

"What the fuck is the difference?" shouted Guitar. "A kid is stomped and you standin round fussin about whether some cracker put it in the paper. He stomped, ain't he? Dead, ain't he? Cause he whistled at some Scarlett O'Hara cunt."

"What'd he do it for?" asked Freddie. "He knew he was in Mississippi. What he think that was? Tom Sawyer Land?"

"So he whistled! So what!" Guitar was steaming. "He supposed to die for that?"

"He from the North," said Freddie. "Acting big down in Bilbo country. Who the hell he think he is?"

"Thought he was a man, that's what," said Railroad Tommy.

"Well, he thought wrong," Freddie said. "Ain't no black men in Bilbo country."

"The hell they ain't," said Guitar.

"Who?" asked Freddie.

"Till. That's who."

"He dead. A dead man ain't no man. A dead man is a corpse. That's all. A corpse."

"A living coward ain't a man either," said Porter.

"Who you talking to?" Freddie was quick to get the personal insult.

"Calm down, you two," said Hospital Tommy.

"You!" shouted Porter.

"You calling me a coward?" Freddie wanted to get the facts first.

"If the shoe fits, put your rusty foot in it."

"You all gonna keep that up, you have to get out of my shop."

"Tell that nigger somethin," said Porter.

"I'm serious now," Hospital Tommy went on. "There is no cause for all this. The boy's dead. His mama's screaming. Won't let them bury him. That ought to be enough colored blood on the streets. You want to spill blood, spill the crackers' blood that bashed his face in."

"Oh, they'll catch them," said Walters.

"Catch 'em? Catch 'em?" Porter was astounded. "You out of your fuckin mind? They'll catch 'em, all right, and give 'em a big party and a medal."

"Yeah. The whole town planning a parade," said Nero.

"They got to catch 'em."

"So they catch 'em. You think they'll get any time? Not on your life!"

"How can they *not* give 'em time?" Walters' voice was high and tight.

"How? Just *don't*, that's how." Porter fidgeted with his watch chain.

"But everybody knows about it now. It's all over. Everywhere. The law is the law."

"You wanna bet? This is sure money!"

"You stupid, man. Real stupid. Ain't no law for no colored man except the one sends him to the chair," said Guitar.

"They say Till had a knife," Freddie said.

"They always say that. He could of had a wad of bubble gum, they'd swear it was a hand grenade."

"I still say he shoulda kept his mouth shut," said Freddie.

"You should keep yours shut," Guitar told him.

"Hey, man!" Again Freddie felt the threat.

"South's bad," Porter said. "Bad. Don't nothing change in the good old U.S. of A. Bet his daddy got his balls busted off in the Pacific somewhere."

"If they ain't busted already, them crackers will see to it. Remember them soldiers in 1918?"

"Ooooo. Don't bring all that up. . . ."

The men began to trade tales of atrocities, first stories they had heard, then those they'd witnessed, and finally the things that had happened to themselves. A litany of personal humiliation, outrage, and anger turned sicklelike back to themselves as humor. They laughed then, uproariously, about the speed with which they had run, the pose they had assumed, the ruse they had invented to escape or decrease some threat to their manliness, their humanness. All but Empire State, who stood, broom in hand and drop-lipped, with the expression of a very intelligent ten-year-old.

And Guitar. His animation had died down, leaving its traces in his eyes.

Milkman waited until he could get his attention. Then they both left, walking silently down the street.

"What is it? You looked pissed when you came in."

"Nothing," said Milkman. "Where can we get a drink?"

"Mary's?"

"Naw. Too many broads hasslin you."

"It's just eight-thirty. Cedar Lounge don't open till nine."

"Shit. *You* think. I'm tired."

"I got a taste at the pad," Guitar offered.

"Solid. Your box working?"

"Uh uh. Still broke."

"I need some music. Music and a taste."

"Then it'll have to be Miss Mary. I'll keep the ladies working elsewhere."

"Yeah? I want to see you tell those ladies what to do."

"Come on, Milk. This ain't New York, choices are limited."

"Okay. Mary's."

They walked a few blocks to the corner of Rye and Tenth streets. When they passed a tiny bakery, Guitar swallowed hard and quickened his steps. Mary's was the bar/lounge that did the best business in the Blood Bank—although each of the three other corners had a similar place—because of Mary herself, a pretty but overpainted barmaid/part-owner, who was sassy, funny, and good company for the customers. Whores worked her bar in safety; lonely drunks could drink there in peace; cruisers found chickens or hawks—whichever they preferred, even jailbait; restless housewives were flattered there and danced their heels off; teen-agers learned "life rules" there; and everybody found excitement there. For in Mary's the lights made everybody beautiful, or if not beautiful, then fascinating. The music gave tone and texture to conversations that would put you to sleep anywhere else. And the food and drink provoked people into behavior that resembled nothing less than high drama.

But all that began around eleven o'clock. It was practically empty at eight-thirty in the evening, when Guitar and Milkman arrived. They slid into a booth and ordered Scotch and water. Milkman drank his up quickly and ordered another before asking Guitar, "How come they call me Milkman?"

"How the fuck would I know? That's your name, ain't it?"

"My name is Macon Dead."

"You drag me all the way over here to tell me your name?"

"I need to know it."

"Aw, drink up, man."

"You know your name, don't you?"

"Cut the shit. What's on your mind?"

"I decked my old man."

"Decked?"

"Yeah. Hit him. Knocked him into the fuckin radiator."

"What'd he do to you?"

"Nothin."

"Nothin? You just up and popped him?"

"Yeah."

"For no reason?"

"He hit my mother."

"Oh."

"He hit her. I hit him."

"That's tough."

"Yeah."

"I mean it."

"I know." Milkman sighed heavily. "I know."

"Listen. I can understand how you feel."

"Uh uh. You can't understand. Unless it happens to you, you can't understand."

"Yes I can. You know I used to hunt a lot. When I was a kid down home—"

"Oh, shit, do we have to hear about Alabama again?"

"Not Alabama. Florida."

"Whatever."

"Just listen, Milkman. Listen to me. I used to hunt a lot. From the time I could walk almost and I was good at it. Everybody said I was a natural. I could hear anything, smell anything, and see like a cat. You know what I mean? A natural. And I was never scared—not of the dark or shadows or funny sounds, and I was never afraid to kill. Anything. Rabbit, bird, snakes, squirrels, deer. And I was little. It never bothered me. I'd take a shot at anything. The grown men used to laugh about it. Said I was a natural-born hunter. After we moved up here with my grandmother, that was the only thing about the South I missed. So when my grandmother used to send us kids back home in the summer, all I thought about was hunting again. They'd pile us on the bus and we'd spend the summer with my grandmother's sister, Aunt Florence. Soon's I got there I looked for my uncles, to go out in the woods. And one summer—I was about ten or eleven, I guess—we all went out and I went off on my own. I thought I saw deer tracks. It wasn't the season for deer, but that didn't bother me any. If I saw one I killed one. I was right about the tracks; it was a deer, but spaced funny—not wide apart like I thought they should be, but still a deer. You know they step in their own prints. If you never saw them before you'd think a two-legged creature was jumping. Anyway, I stayed on the trail until I saw some bushes. The light was good and all of a sudden I saw a rump between the branches. I dropped it with the first shot and finished it with the next. Now, I want to tell you I was feeling good. I saw myself showing my uncles what I'd caught. But when I got up to it—and I was going real slow because I thought I might have to shoot it again—I saw it was a doe. Not a young one; she was old, but she was still a doe. I felt . . . bad. You know what I mean? I killed a doe. A doe, man."

Milkman was gazing at Guitar with the wide steady eyes of a man trying to look sober.

"So I know how you felt when you saw your father hit your mother. It's like that doe. A man shouldn't do that. You couldn't help what you felt."

Milkman nodded his head, but it was clear to Guitar that nothing he had said had made any difference. Chances were Milkman didn't even know what a doe was, and whatever it was, it wasn't his mother. Guitar ran his finger around the rim of his glass.

"What'd she do, Milk?"

"Nothin. Smiled. He didn't like her smile."

"You're not making sense. Talk sense. And slow down. You know you can't hold liquor."

"What you mean, I can't hold liquor?"

" 'Scuse me. Help yourself."

"I'm trying to have a serious conversation and you talking shit, Guitar."

"I'm listening."

"And I'm talking."

"Yes, you talking, but what are you saying? Your papa clips your mama cause she smiles at him. You clip him cause he clipped her. Now, is that the way you all spend the evening in your house or is there something else you're trying to say?"

"Came up to talk to me afterwards."

"Who?"

"My old man."

"What'd he say?"

"Said I had to be a whole man and know the whole thing."

"Go on."

"He was gonna buy the Erie Lackawanna, but my mother wouldn't let him."

"Oh, yeah? Maybe she needs beatin."

"That's very funny, man."

"Why ain't you laughing, then?"

"I am laughing. Inside."

"Milk?"

"Yeah?"

"Your daddy slapped your mama, right?"

"Right. Right."

"You hit him, right?"

"Right."

"Nobody appreciates what you did. Right?"

"Hey, Guitar. You right again."

"Not your mother, not your sisters, and your daddy appreciates it least of all."

"Least of all. Right."

"So he bawls you out."

"Yep. No. No. He . . ."

"He talks quiet to you?"

"Right!"

"Explains things to you."

"Yeah."

"About why he hit her."

"Uh huh."

"And it's all about something that happened a long time ago? Before you were born?"

"You got it! You are a very smart little colored boy. And I am going to tell Oxford University about you."

"And you wish he'd kept it to himself because it don't concern you and you can't do nothin about it anyway."

"You have just passed the course. Guitar Bains, Ph.D."

"But it bothers you just the same?"

"Let me think." Milkman closed his eyes and tried to prop his chin on his hand, but it was too difficult. He was trying to get as drunk as possible as rapidly as possible. "Yes. Well, it did bother me. Before I came in here it did. I don't know, Guitar." He became serious and his face had the still and steady look of a grown man trying not to vomit . . . or cry.

"Forget it, Milk. Whatever it is, forget it. It ain't nothin. Whatever he told you, forget it."

"I hope I can. I sure hope I can."

"Listen, baby, people do funny things. Specially us. The cards are stacked against us and just trying to stay in the game, stay alive and in the game, makes us do funny things. Things we can't help. Things that make us hurt one another. We don't even know why. But look here, don't carry it inside and don't give it to nobody else. Try to understand it, but if you can't, just forget it and keep yourself strong, man."

"I don't know, Guitar. Things seem to be getting to me, you know?"

"Don't let 'em. Unless you got a plan. Look at Till. They got to him too. Now he's just an item on WJR's evening news."

"He was crazy."

"No. Not crazy. Young, but not crazy."

"Who cares if he fucks a white girl? Anybody can do that. What's he bragging for? Who cares?"

"Crackers care."

"Then they're crazier'n he is."

"Of course. But they're alive and crazy."

"Yeah, well, fuck Till. I'm the one in trouble."

"Did I hear you right, brother?"

"All right. I didn't mean that. I . . ."

"What's your trouble? You don't like your name?"

"No." Milkman let his head fall to the back of the booth. "No, I don't like my name."

"Let me tell you somethin, baby. Niggers get their names the way they get everything else—the best way they can. The best way they can."

Milkman's eyes were blurred now and so were his words. "Why can't we get our stuff the right way?"

"The best way is the right way. Come on. I'll take you home."

"No, I can't go back there."

"No? Where then?"

"Let me stay in your pad."

"Oh, man, you know my situation. One of us'll have to sleep on the floor. Besides . . ."

"I'll sleep on the floor."

"Besides, I may have company."

"No shit?"

"No shit. Come on, let's go."

"I ain't going home, Guitar. Hear me?"

"Want me to take you over to Hagar's?" Guitar motioned to the waitress for the check.

"Hagar's. Yeah. Sweet Hagar. Wonder what her name is."

"You just said it."

"I mean her last name. Her daddy's name."

"Ask Reba." Guitar paid their bar bill and helped Milkman negotiate to the door. The wind had risen and cooled. Guitar flapped his elbows against the cold.

"Ask anybody *but* Reba," said Milkman. "Reba don't know her own last name."

"Ask Pilate."

"Yeah. I'll ask Pilate. Pilate knows. It's in that dumb-ass box hanging from her ear. Her own name and everybody else's. Bet mine's in there too. I'm gonna ask her what my name is. Say, you know how my old man's daddy got his name?"

"Uh uh. How?"

"Cracker gave it to him."

"Sho 'nough?"

"Yep. And he took it. Like a fuckin sheep. Somebody should have shot him."

"What for? He was already Dead."

# Chapter 4

Once again he did his Christmas shopping in a Rexall drugstore. It was late, the day before Christmas Eve, and he hadn't had the spirit or energy or presence of mind to do it earlier or thoughtfully. Boredom, which had begun as a mild infection, now took him over completely. No activity seemed worth the doing, no conversation worth having. The fluttery preparations at home seemed fake and dingy. His mother was going on as she did every year about the incredible price of trees and butter. As though their tree would be anything other than it had always been: the huge shadowy thing in a corner burdened with decorations she had had since she was a girl. As if her fruitcakes were edible, or her turkey done all the way to the bone. His father gave them all envelopes of varying amounts of money, never thinking that just once they might like something he actually went into a department store and selected.

The gifts Milkman had to buy were few and easily chosen in a drugstore. Cologne and dusting powder for Magdalene called Lena; a compact for Corinthians; a five-pound box of chocolates for his mother. And some shaving equipment for his father. In fifteen minutes he was done. The only problem gift was Hagar's. It was hard to select something hurriedly for her since she liked everything but preferred nothing. More important, he wasn't sure he wanted to keep it up. Keep up the whole business of "going with" Hagar. He seldom took her anywhere except to the movies and he never took her to parties where people of his own set danced and laughed and developed intrigues among themselves. Everybody who knew him knew about Hagar, but she was considered his private honey pot, not a real or legitimate girl friend—not someone he might marry. And only one or two of the various women he dated "seriously" ever put up a fight about her since they believed she was less than a rival.

Now, after more than a dozen years, he was getting tired of her. Her eccentricities were no longer provocative and the stupefying ease with which he had gotten and stayed between her legs had changed from the great good fortune he'd considered it, to annoyance at her refusal to make him hustle for it, work for it, do something difficult for it. He didn't even have to pay for it. It was so free, so abundant, it had lost its fervor. There was no excitement, no galloping of blood in his neck or his heart at the thought of her.

She was the third beer. Not the first one, which the throat receives with almost tearful gratitude; nor the second, that confirms and extends the pleasure of the first. But the third, the one you drink because it's there, because it can't hurt, and because what difference does it make?

Perhaps the end of the year was a good time to call it off. It wasn't going anywhere and it was keeping him lazy, like a pampered honey bear who had only to stick out his paw for another scoop, and so had lost the agility of the tree-climbers, the bee-fighters, but not the recollection of how thrilling the search had been.

He would buy her something for Christmas, of course, something nice to remember him by, but nothing that would give her any ideas about marriage. There was some costume jewelry on display. She might like that, but it would pale before the diamond ring Reba had stuck down in her dress. A Timex? She would never look at it. Staring at the glass tube that housed the watches, he found himself getting angry. All this indecision about what to get for Hagar was new. At Christmases past he simply chose (or had his sisters choose) from a long list of things that Hagar had mentioned specifically. Things quite out of place in her household: a navy-blue satin bathrobe (this for a woman who lived in a house that had no bathroom); a chubby; a snood with a velvet bow; a rhinestone bracelet with earrings to match; patent leather pumps; White Shoulders cologne. Milkman used to wonder at her specificity and her acquisitiveness until he reminded himself that Pilate and Reba celebrated no holidays. Yet their generosity was so wholehearted it looked like carelessness, and they did their best to satisfy every whim Hagar had. When he first took her in his arms, Hagar was a vain and somewhat distant creature. He liked to remember it that way—that he took her in his arms—but in truth it was she who called him back into the bedroom and stood there smiling while she unbuttoned her blouse.

From the time he first saw her, when he was twelve and she was seventeen, he was deeply in love with her, alternately awkward and witty in her presence. She babied him, ignored him, teased him—did anything she felt like, and he was grateful just to see her do anything or be any way. A good part of the enthusiasm with which he collected his father's rents was because of the time it gave him to visit the wine house and, hopefully, find Hagar there. He was free to drop in anytime and after school he tried to make sure he saw her.

Years passed and his puppy breath came as fast as ever in Hagar's presence. It slowed finally, after Guitar took him to his first Southside party, and after he found himself effortlessly popular with girls of his own age and in his own neighborhood. But while his breath was no longer that of a puppy, Hagar could still whip it into a pant when he was seventeen and she was twenty-two. Which she did on the dullest flattest day he could remember, a throw-away day in March when he drove his father's two-tone Ford over to her house for two bottles of wine. Milkman was much sought after and depended upon to secure the liquor he and his under-twenty-one friends believed vital to a party. When he got to Pilate's he walked in on a domestic crisis.

Reba's new man friend had asked her for a small loan and she had told him that she didn't have any money at all. The man, who had received two or three nice presents from her unasked, thought she was lying and was trying to tell him to shove off. They were quarreling in the backyard—that is, the man was quarreling. Reba was crying and trying to convince him that what she'd said was true. Just after Milkman opened the door, Hagar came running from the bedroom, where she'd been looking out the back window. She screamed to Pilate, "Mama! He's hitting her! I saw him! With his fist, Mama!"

Pilate looked up from a fourth-grade geography book she was reading and closed it. Slowly, it seemed to Milkman, she walked over to a shelf that hung over the dry sink, put the geography book on it, and removed a knife. Slowly still, she walked out the front door—there was no back door—and as soon as she did, Milkman could hear Reba's screams and the man's curses.

It didn't occur to him to stop Pilate—her mouth was not moving and her earring flashed fire—but he did follow her, as did Hagar, around to the back of the house, where, approaching the man from the back, she whipped her right arm around his neck and positioned the knife at the edge of his heart. She waited until the man felt the knife point before she jabbed it skillfully, about a quarter of an inch through his shirt into the skin. Still holding his neck, so he couldn't see but could feel the blood making his shirt sticky, she talked to him.

"Now, I'm not going to kill you, honey. Don't you worry none. Just be still a minute, the heart's right here, but I'm not going to stick it in any deeper. Cause if I stick it in any deeper, it'll go straight through your heart. So you have to be real still, you hear? You can't move a inch cause I might lose control. It's just a little hole now, honey, no more'n a pin scratch. You might lose about two tablespoons of blood, but no more. And if you're real still, honey, I can get it back out without no mistake. But before I do that, I thought we'd have a little talk."

The man closed his eyes. Sweat ran from his temples down the sides of his face. A few neighbors who had heard Reba's screams had gathered in Pilate's backyard. They knew right away that the man was a newcomer to the city. Otherwise he would have known a few things about Reba, one of which was that she gave away everything she had and if there was a case quarter in that house she'd have given it to him; and more important, he would have known not to fool with anything that belonged to Pilate, who never bothered anybody, was helpful to everybody, but who also was believed to have the power to step out of her skin, set a bush afire from fifty yards, and turn a man into a ripe rutabaga—all on account of the fact that she had no navel. So they didn't have much sympathy for him. They just craned their necks to hear better what Pilate was telling him.

"You see, darlin, that there is the only child I got. The first baby I ever had, and if you could turn around and see my face, which of course you can't cause my hand might slip, you'd know she's also the last. Women are foolish, you know, and mamas are the most foolish of all. And you know how mamas are, don't you? You got a mama, ain't you? Sure you have, so you know what I'm talking about. Mamas get hurt and nervous when somebody don't like they children. First real misery I ever had in my life was when I found out somebody—a little teeny tiny boy it was—didn't like my little girl. Made me so mad, I didn't know what to do. We do the best we can, but we ain't got the strength you men got. That's why it makes us so sad if a grown man start beating up on one of us. You know what I mean? I'd hate to pull this knife out and have you try some other time to act mean to my little girl. Cause one thing I know for sure: whatever she done, she's been good to *you*. Still, I'd hate to push it in more and have your mama feel like I do now. I confess, I don't know what to do. Maybe you can help me. Tell me, what should I do?"

The man struggled for breath and Pilate eased up on his throat but not his heart.

"Lemme go," he whispered.

"Hmmmmm?"

"Lemme go. I . . . won't never . . . put a hand on her. I promise."

"A real promise, sugar?"

"Yeah. I promise. You won't never see me no more."

Reba sat on the ground, her arms around her knees, staring through her unswollen eye at the scene as though she were at a picture show. Her lip was split and her cheek was badly bruised, and though her skirt and hands were stained with her effort to stop the blood pouring from her nose, a little still trickled down.

Pilate plucked the knife out of the man's shirt and took her arm away. He lurched a little, looked down at the blood on his clothes and up at Pilate, and licking his lips, backed all the way to the side of the house under Pilate's gaze. Her lips didn't start moving again until he was out of sight and running down the road.

All attention turned to Reba, who was having difficulty trying to stand up. She said she thought something was broken inside in the place where he'd kicked her. Pilate felt her ribs and said nothing was broken. But Reba said she wanted to go to the hospital. (It was her dream to be a patient in a hospital; she was forever trying to get admitted, since in her picture-show imagination, it was a nice hotel. She gave blood there as often as they would let her, and stopped only when the blood bank was moved to an office-type clinic some distance away from Mercy.) She was insistent now, and Pilate surrendered her judgment to Reba's. A neighbor offered to drive them and off they went, leaving Milkman to buy his wine from Hagar.

He was delighted with the performance and followed Hagar into the house to laugh and talk excitedly about it. She was as tranquil as he was agitated, as monosyllabic as he was garrulous.

"Was that something? Wow! She's two inches taller than he is, and she's talking about weak."

"We are weak."

"Compared to what? A B-52?"

"Every woman's not as strong as she is."

"I hope not. Half as strong is too much."

"Well, muscle strength is one thing. I meant women are weak in other ways."

"Name some. I want you to name some for me. Where are you weak?"

"I don't mean me. I mean other women."

"You don't have any weakness?"

"I haven't found any."

"I suppose you think you can whip me." It was the seventeen-year-old's constant preoccupation—who could whip him.

"Probably," said Hagar.

"Ha! Well, I guess I better not try to prove you wrong. Pilate might be back with her knife."

"Pilate scare you?"

"Yeah. Don't she scare you?"

"No. Nobody scares me."

"Yeah. You tough. I know you tough."

"Not tough. I just don't let people tell me what to do. I do what I want."

"Pilate tells you what to do."

"But I don't have to do it, if I don't want to."

"Wish I could say the same for my mother."

"Your mother boss you?"

"Well . . . not boss exactly." Milkman floundered for a word to describe the nagging he thought he was a victim of.

"How old are you now?" asked Hagar. She lifted her eyebrows like a woman mildly interested in the age of a small child.

"Seventeen."

"You old enough to be married." Hagar said it with the strong implication that he should not allow his mother to have any say about what he did.

"I'm waiting for you," he said, trying to regain (or acquire) some masculine flippancy.

"Be a long wait."

"Why?"

Hagar sighed as if her patience was being tried. "I'd like to be in love with the man I marry."

"Try me. You could learn if you'd try."

"You're too young for me."

"State of mind," he said.

"Uh huh. My mind."

"You're like all women. Waiting for Prince Charming to come trotting down the street and pull up in front of your door. Then you'll sweep down the steps and powie! Your eyes meet and he'll yank you up on his horse and the two of you ride off into the wind. Violins playing and 'courtesy of MGM' stamped on the horse's butt. Right?"

"Right," she said.

"What you going to do in the meantime?"

"Watch the lump grow in a little boy's pants."

Milkman smiled, but he was not amused. Hagar laughed. He jumped up to grab her, but she ran into the bedroom and shut the door. He rubbed his chin with the back of his hand and looked at the door. Then he shrugged and picked up the two bottles of wine.

"Milkman?" Hagar stuck her head out the door. "Come in here."

He turned around and put the bottles down on the table. The door was open, but he couldn't see her, could only hear her laughing, a low private laugh as though she had won a bet. He moved so quickly he forgot to duck the green sack hanging from the ceiling. A hickey was forming on his forehead by the time he got to her. "What you all got in there?" he asked her.

"That's Pilate's stuff. She calls it her inheritance." Hagar was unbuttoning her blouse.

"What'd she inherit? Bricks?" Then he saw her breasts.

"This is what I do in the meantime," she said.

Their tossing and giggling had been free and open then and they began to spend as much time in Guitar's room when he was at work as Guitar himself did when he was home. She became a quasi-secret but permanent fixture in his life. Very much a tease, sometimes accommodating his appetites, sometimes refusing. He never knew when or why she would do either. He assumed Reba and Pilate knew, but they never made any reference to the change in his relationship to Hagar. While he had lost some of his twelve-year-old's adoration of her, he was delighted to be sleeping with her and she was odd, funny, quirky company, spoiled, but artlessly so and therefore more refreshing than most of the girls his own age. There were months when Hagar would not see him, and then he'd appear one day and she was all smiles and welcome.

After about three years or so of Hagar's on-again-off-again passion, her refusals dwindled until finally, by the time he'd hit his father, they were nonexistent. Furthermore, she began to wait for him, and the more involved he got with the other part of his social life, the more reliable she became. She began to pout, sulk, and accuse him of not loving her or wanting to see her anymore. And though he seldom thought about his age, she was very aware of hers. Milkman had stretched his carefree boyhood out for thirty-one years. Hagar was thirty-six—and nervous. She placed duty squarely in the middle of their relationship; he tried to think of a way out.

He paid the clerk for the presents he had chosen and left the drugstore, having made up his mind to call it off.

I'll remind her that we are cousins, he thought. He would not buy her a present at all; instead he would give her a nice piece of money. Explain that he wanted her to get something really nice for herself, but that his gift-giving was compromising her. That he was not what she needed. She needed a steady man who could marry her. He was standing in her way. And since they were related and all, she should start looking for someone else. It hurt him, he would say, deeply hurt him, after all these years, but if you loved somebody as he did her, you had to think of them first. You couldn't be selfish with somebody you loved.

Having thought so carefully of what he would say to her, he felt as though he had already had the conversation and had settled everything. He went back to his father's office, got some cash out of the safe, and wrote Hagar a nice letter which ended: "Also, I want to thank you. Thank you for all you have meant to me. For making me happy all these years. I am signing this letter with love, of course, but more than that, with gratitude."

And he did sign it with love, but it was the word "gratitude" and the flat-out coldness of "thank you" that sent Hagar spinning into a bright blue place where the air was thin and it was silent all the time, and where people spoke in whispers or did not make sounds at all, and where everything was frozen except for an occasional burst of fire inside her chest that crackled away until she ran out into the streets to find Milkman Dead.

Long after he'd folded the money and the letter into an envelope, Milkman sat on at his father's desk. He added and re-added columns of figures, always eighty cents too little or eighty cents too much. He was still distracted and edgy, and all of it was not because of the problem of Hagar. He'd had a conversation with Guitar some time ago about the dragnet. A young boy, about sixteen years old, on his way home from school, had been strangled with what was believed to be a rope, and his head was bashed in. The state troopers cooperating with the local police said the way in which the boy had been killed was similar to the way another boy had been killed on New Year's Eve in 1953, and the way four grown men had been killed in 1955—the strangulation, the smashing of the face. In the poolrooms and in Tommy's Barbershop, the word was that Winnie Ruth Judd had struck again. The men laughed about it and repeated for the benefit of newcomers the story of how, in 1932, Winnie Ruth, a convicted murderer, who axed and dismembered her victims and stuffed them in trunks, was committed to a state asylum for the criminally insane, and escaped two or three times each year.

Once she had walked two hundred miles through two states before they caught her. Because there was a brutal killing in the city in December of that year, during the time Winnie Ruth was at large, Southside people were convinced that she had done it. From then on when some particularly nasty murder was reported, the Negroes said it was Winnie Ruth. They said that because Winnie Ruth was white and so were the victims. It was their way of explaining what they believed was white madness—crimes planned and executed in a truly lunatic manner against total strangers. Such murders could only be committed by a fellow lunatic of the race and Winnie Ruth Judd fit the description. They believed firmly that members of their own race killed one another for good reasons: violation of another's turf (a man is found with somebody else's wife); refusal to observe the laws of hospitality (a man reaches into his friend's pot of mustards and snatches out the meat); or verbal insults impugning their virility, honesty, humanity, and mental health. More important, they believed the crimes they committed were legitimate because they were committed in the heat of passion: anger, jealousy, loss of face, and so on. Bizarre killings amused them, unless of course the victim was one of their own.

They speculated about Winnie Ruth's motives for this recent murder. Somebody said she was raunchy from being cooped up and went looking for a lay. But she knew better than to expect a grown man to want her, so she went for a schoolboy. Another said she probably didn't like saddle shoes and when she got out of the loony bin and walked four hundred miles to safety, the first thing she saw was a kid wearing saddle shoes and she couldn't take it—ran amok.

Amid the jokes, however, was a streak of unspoken terror. The police said there had been a witness who thought he saw a "bushy-haired Negro" running from the schoolyard where the body was found.

"The same bushy-haired Negro they saw when Sam Sheppard axed his wife," said Porter.

"Hammered, man," said Guitar. "Twenty-seven hammer blows."

"Great Jesus. Why he do twenty-seven? That's a hard killin."

"Every killing is a hard killing," said Hospital Tommy. "Killing anybody is hard. You see those movies where the hero puts his hands around somebody's neck and the victim coughs a little bit and expires? Don't believe it, my friends. The human body is robust. It can gather strength when it's in mortal danger."

"You kill anybody in the war, Tommy?"

"I put my hand to a few."

"With your hands?"

"Bayonet, friend. The men of the Ninety-second used bayonets. Belleau Wood glittered with them. Fairly glittered."

"How'd it feel?"

"Unpleasant. Extremely unpleasant. Even when you know he'll do the same to you, it's still a very indelicate thing to do."

They laughed as usual at Tommy's proper way of speaking.

"That's because you didn't want to be in the army no way," said a fat man. "What about if you was roaming the streets and met up with Orval Faubus?"

"Boy, I'd love to kill that sucker," a heavy-set man said.

"Keep saying that. They'll soon have your ass downtown."

"My hair ain't bushy."

"They'll make it bushy."

"They'll take some brass knuckles and make your *head* bushy and call it hair."

Aside from Empire State's giggle, which was wholehearted, it had seemed to Milkman then that the laughter was wan and nervous. Each man in that room knew he was subject to being picked up as he walked the street and whatever his proof of who he was and where he was at the time of the murder, he'd have a very uncomfortable time being questioned.

And there was one more thing. For some time Milkman had been picking up hints that one or more of these murders had in fact been either witnessed or committed by a Negro. Some slip, someone knowing some detail about the victim. Like whether or not Winnie Ruth couldn't stand saddle shoes. Did the boy have on saddle shoes? Did the newspaper say so? Or was that just one of the fanciful details a good jokester would think of.

The two Tommys were cleaning up. "Closed," they said to a

man who poked his face in the door. "Shop's closing." The conversation died down and the men who were just hanging around seemed reluctant to go. Guitar too, but finally he slipped on his jacket, shadow-boxed with Empire State, and joined Milkman at the door. Southside shops were featuring feeble wreaths and lights, made more feeble by the tacky Yuletide streamers and bells the city had strung up on the lampposts. Only downtown were the lights large, bright, festive, and full of hope.

The two men walked down Tenth Street, headed for Guitar's room.

"Freaky," said Milkman. "Some freaky shit."

"Freaky world," said Guitar. "A freaky, fucked-up world."

Milkman nodded. "Railroad Tommy said the boy had on saddle shoes."

"Did he?" Guitar asked.

"Did he? You know he did. You were laughing right along with the rest of us."

Guitar glanced at him. "What you opening your nose for?"

"I know when I'm being put off."

"Then that's what it is, man. Nothing else. Maybe I don't feel like discussing it."

"You mean you don't feel like discussing it with me. You were full of discussion in Tommy's."

"Look, Milk, we've been tight a long time, right? But that don't mean we're not different people. We can't always think the same way about things. Can't we leave it like that? There are all kinds of people in this world. Some are curious, some ain't; some talk, some scream; some are kickers and other people are kicked. Take your daddy, now. He's a kicker. First time I laid eyes on him, he was kicking us out of our house. That was a difference right there between you and me, but we got to be friends anyway. . . ."

Milkman stopped and forced Guitar to stop too and turn around. "I know you're not going to give me a bullshit lecture."

"No lecture, man. I'm trying to tell you something."

"Well, tell me. Don't give me no fuckin bullshit lecture."

"What do you call a lecture?" asked Guitar. "When *you* don't talk for two seconds? When you have to listen to somebody else instead of talk? Is that a lecture?"

"A lecture is when somebody talks to a thirty-one-year-old man like he's a ten-year-old kid."

"You want me to talk or not?"

"Go ahead. Talk. Just don't talk to me in that funny tone. Like you a teacher and I'm some snot-nosed kid."

"That's the problem, Milkman. You're more interested in my tone than in what I'm saying. I'm trying to say that we don't have to agree on everything; that you and me are different; that—"

"You mean you got some secret shit you don't want me to know about."

"I mean there are things that interest me that don't interest you."

"How you know they don't interest me?"

"I know you. Been knowing you. You got your high-tone friends and your picnics on Honoré Island and you can afford to spend fifty percent of your brainpower thinking about a piece of ass. You got that red-headed bitch and you got a Southside bitch and no telling what in between."

"I don't believe it. After all these years you putting me down because of where I live?"

"Not where you live—where you hang out. You don't live nowhere. Not Not Doctor Street *or* Southside."

"You begrudge me—"

"I don't begrudge you a thing."

"You're welcome everywhere I go. I've tried to get you to come to Honoré—"

"Fuck Honoré! You hear me? The only way I'll go to that nigger heaven is with a case of dynamite and a book of matches."

"You used to like it."

"I never liked it! I went with you, but I never liked it. Never."

"What's wrong with Negroes owning beach houses? What

do you want, Guitar? You mad at every Negro who ain't scrubbing floors and picking cotton. This ain't Montgomery, Alabama."

Guitar looked at him, first in rage, and then he began to laugh. "You're right, Milkman. You have never in your life said a truer word. This definitely is not Montgomery, Alabama. Tell me. What would you do if it was? If this turned out to be another Montgomery?"

"Buy a plane ticket."

"Exactly. Now you know something about yourself you didn't know before: who you are and what you are."

"Yeah. A man that refuses to live in Montgomery, Alabama."

"No. A man that can't live there. If things ever got tough, you'd melt. You're not a serious person, Milkman."

"Serious is just another word for miserable. I know all about serious. My old man is serious. My sisters are serious. And nobody is more serious than my mother. She's so serious, she wasting away. I was looking at her in the backyard the other day. It was as cold as a witch's tit out there, but she had to get some bulbs in the ground before the fifteenth of December, she said. So there she was on her knees, digging holes in the ground."

"So? I miss the point."

"The point is that she wanted to put those bulbs in. She didn't have to. She likes to plant flowers. She really likes it. But you should have seen her face. She looked like the unhappiest woman in the world. The most miserable. So where's the fun? I've never in my whole life heard my mother laugh. She smiles sometimes, even makes a little sound. But I don't believe she has ever laughed out loud."

Without the least transition and without knowing he was going to, he began to describe to Guitar a dream he had had about his mother. He called it a dream because he didn't want to tell him it had really happened, that he had really seen it.

He was standing at the kitchen sink pouring the rest of his coffee down the drain when he looked through the window and saw Ruth digging in the garden. She made little holes and tucked something that looked like a small onion in them. As he stood there, mindlessly watching her, tulips began to grow out of the holes she had dug. First a solitary thin tube of green, then two leaves opened up from the stem—one on each side. He rubbed his eyes and looked again. Now several stalks were coming out of the ground behind her. Either they were bulbs she had already planted or they had been in the sack so long they had germinated. The tubes were getting taller and taller and soon there were so many of them they were pressing up against each other and up against his mother's dress. And still she didn't notice them or turn around. She just kept digging. Some of the stems began to sprout heads, bloody red heads that bobbed over and touched her back. Finally she noticed them, growing and nodding and touching her. Milkman thought she would jump up in fear—at least surprise. But she didn't. She leaned back from them, even hit out at them, but playfully, mischievously. The flowers grew and grew, until he could see only her shoulders above them and her flailing arms high above those bobbing, snapping heads. They were smothering her, taking away her breath with their soft jagged lips. And she merely smiled and fought them off as though they were harmless butterflies.

He knew they were dangerous, that they would soon suck up all the air around her and leave her limp on the ground. But she didn't seem to guess this at all. Eventually they covered her and all he could see was a mound of tangled tulips bent low over her body, which was kicking to the last.

He described all of that to Guitar as though the dream emphasized his point about the dangers of seriousness. He tried to be as light-hearted as possible in the telling, but at the end, Guitar looked him in the eyes and said, "Why didn't you go help her?"

"What?"

"Help her. Pull her out from underneath."

"But she liked it. She was having fun. She liked it."

"Are you sure?" Guitar was smiling.

"Sure I'm sure. It was my dream."

"It was *your* mother too."

"Aw, man, why you making something out of it that ain't there? You're making the whole thing into something superserious, just to prove your point. First I'm wrong for not living in Alabama. Then I'm wrong for not behaving right in my own dream. Now I'm wrong for dreaming it. You see what I mean? The least little thing is a matter of life and death to you. You're getting to be just like my old man. He thinks if a paper clip is in the wrong drawer, I should apologize. What's happening to everybody?"

"Looks like everybody's going in the wrong direction but you, don't it?"

Milkman swallowed. He remembered that long-ago evening after he hit his father how everybody was crammed on one side of the street, going in the direction he was coming from. Nobody was going his way. It was as though Guitar had been in that dream too.

"Maybe," he said. "But I know where I'm going."

"Where?"

"Wherever the party is."

Guitar smiled. His teeth were as white as the snowflakes that were settling on his jacket. "Merry Christmas," he said, "and Happy New Year." He waved his hand and cut around the corner to his street. He was lost in the snowy shadows of Southside before Milkman could ask him where he was going or tell him to wait.

Now he closed the accounts book in Sonny's Shop and gave up on the column of numbers. Something was happening to Guitar, had already happened to him. He was constantly chafing Milkman about how he lived, and that conversation was just one more example of how he'd changed. No more could Milkman run up the stairs to his room to drag him off to a party or a bar. And he didn't want to talk about girls or getting high. Sports were about the only things he was still enthusiastic about, and music. Other than that, he was all gloom and golden eyes. And politics.

It was that atmosphere of earnestness he provoked that led Milkman to talking about his family more than he would normally do and that also led him to defend with flippant remarks the kind of life he led. Pussy and Honoré parties. Guitar knew that wasn't all he was interested in, didn't he? He knew Milkman had other interests. Such as? he asked himself. Well, he was very good in his father's business, for one thing. Excellent, in fact. But he had to admit right away that real estate was of no real interest to him. If he had to spend the rest of his life thinking about rents and property, he'd lose his mind. But he was going to spend the rest of his life doing just that, wasn't he? That's what his father assumed and he supposed that was what he had assumed as well.

Maybe Guitar was right—partly. His life was pointless, aimless, and it was true that he didn't concern himself an awful lot about other people. There was nothing he wanted bad enough to risk anything for, inconvenience himself for. Still, what right had Guitar to talk? He didn't live in Montgomery either; all he did was work at that automobile factory and sneak off places—nobody knew where—and hang around Tommy's Barbershop. He never kept a woman more than a few months—the time span that he said was average before she began to make "permanent-arrangement-type noises."

He ought to get married, Milkman thought. Maybe I should too. Who? There were lots of women around and he was very much the eligible bachelor to the Honoré crowd. Maybe he'd pick one—the redhead. Get a nice house. His father would help him find one. Go into a real partnership with his father and . . . And what? There had to be something better to look forward to. He couldn't get interested in money. No one had ever denied him any, so it had no exotic attraction. Politics—at least barbershop politics and Guitar's brand—put him to sleep. He was bored. Everybody bored him. The city was boring. The racial problems that consumed Guitar were the most boring of all. He wondered what they would do if they didn't have black and white problems to talk about. Who would they be if they couldn't describe the insults, violence, and oppression that their lives (and the television news) were made up of? If they didn't have Kennedy or Elijah to quarrel about? They excused themselves for everything. Every job of work undone, every bill unpaid, every illness, every death was The Man's fault. And Guitar was becoming just like them—except he made no excuses for himself—just agreed, it seemed to Milkman, with every grievance he heard.

Milkman went into the bathroom, which served also as a pantry, and plugged in the hot plate to make himself some instant coffee. While he was there, he heard a rapid tapping on the windowpane. He stepped back into the office and saw Freddie's eyes through the lettering. Milkman unlocked the door.

"Hey, Freddie. What's up?"

"Looking for a warm spot. They got me runnin tonight. Christmas comin and all, all I do is run up and down the street." Freddie's janitor duties at the department store were supplemented by his function as a messenger and package deliverer.

"They give you a new truck yet?" Milkman asked him.

"You crazy? The engine have to fall out on the ground before they give me a decent one."

"I put some coffee water on. Have a cup?"

"Just what I'm lookin for. Saw your lights and thought there's got to be a hot cup a coffee in there. You wouldn't happen to have a little taste to go in it, would ya?"

"Just so happens I do."

"Atta boy."

Milkman went into the bathroom, lifted the lid from the toilet tank, and took out the half-pint bottle he kept hidden from Macon, who wouldn't have alcohol on the premises. He brought the bottle into the office, put it on the desk, and went back to make up two cups of coffee. When he reentered, Freddie was trying to look as though he hadn't already turned the pint up to his mouth. They laced their coffee and Milkman looked around for his cigarettes.

"Hard times, boy," Freddie said absently, after his first sip. "Hard times." Then, as though he noticed something missing, he asked, "Where's your buddy?"

"You mean Guitar?"

"Yeah. Guitar. Where's he?"

"Haven't seen him in a few days. You know Guitar. He'll disappear on you in a minute." Milkman noticed how white Freddie's hair was.

"How old are you, Freddie?"

"Who knows? They made dirt in the morning and me that afternoon." He giggled. "But I been around a long long time."

"You born here?"

"Naw. Down south. Jacksonville, Florida. Bad country, boy. Bad, bad country. You know they ain't even got an orphanage in Jacksonville where colored babies can go? They have to put 'em in jail. I tell people that talk about them sit-ins I was *raised* in jail, and it don't scare me none."

"I didn't know you were an orphan."

"Well, not a regular orphan. I had people and all, but my mama died and nobody would take me in. It was on account of the way she died that nobody would take me."

"How'd she die?"

"Ghosts."

"Ghosts?"

"You don't believe in ghosts?"

"Well"—Milkman smiled—"I'm willing to, I guess."

"You better believe, boy. They're here."

"Here?" Milkman didn't glance around the office, but he wanted to. The wind howled outside in the blackness and Freddie, looking like a gnome, flashed his gold teeth. "I don't mean in this room necessarily. Although they could be." He cocked his head and listened. "No. I mean they in the world."

"You've seen some?"

"Plenty. Plenty. Ghosts killed my mother. I didn't see that, of course, but I seen 'em since."

"Tell me about them."

"No I ain't. I don't do no talkin 'bout the ghosts I seen. They don't like that."

"Well, tell me about the one you didn't see. The one killed your mother."

"Oh. Well. That one. She was walking cross the yard with this neighbor friend of hers and they both looked up and saw a woman comin down the road. They stopped and waited to see who she was. When the woman got near, the neighbor called out howdy and soon's she said the word, the woman turned into a white bull. Right before their eyes. My mama fell down on the ground in labor pain right then and there. When I was born and they showed me to her, she screamed and passed out. Never *did* come to. My father died two months before I was born, and they couldn't get none of my people and nobody else to take a baby brought here by a white bull."

Milkman started laughing. He didn't mean to hurt Freddie's feelings, but he couldn't stop the laughter, and the more he tried, the more it came.

Freddie looked more surprised than hurt. "You don't believe me, do you?"

Milkman couldn't answer, he was laughing so hard.

"Okay," Freddie said, and threw up his hands. "Okay, laugh on. But they's a lot of strange things you don't know nothin about, boy. You'll learn. Lot of strange things. Strange stuff goin on right in this here town."

Milkman's laughter was under control now. "What? What strange stuff is happening in this town? I haven't seen any white bulls lately."

"Open your eyes. Ask your buddy. He knows."

"What buddy?"

"Your buddy Guitar. Ask him what strange stuff been happenin. Ask him how come he runnin round with Empire State all of a sudden."

"Empire State?"

"That's right. Empire State."

"Nobody runs around with Empire State. He's a nut. He just stands around with a broom, dribbling spit. He can't even talk."

"He *don't* talk. That don't mean he can't. Only reason he don't is cause he found his wife in bed with another man long time ago, and ain't found nothing to say since then."

"Well, what's Guitar doing with him?"

"Good question. Police would like to know the answer to that too."

"How'd you get from Empire State to the police?"

"You ain't heard? People say the police is lookin for a colored man what killed that white boy in the schoolyard."

"I know that. Everybody knows that."

"Well, the description fits State. And Guitar been takin him places. Hidin him, I believe."

"What's so strange about that? You know Guitar is like that. He'll hide anybody the law is looking for. He hates white people, especially cops, and anybody they're after can count on him for help."

"You don't understand. Him and State ain't actin like they just hidin him. They actin like he did it."

"You a little drunk, Freddie?"

"Yeah, I'm a little drunk, but that don't change nothin. Look here. Remember when Emmet Till was killed? Back in fifty-three? Well, right after that, a white boy was killed in the schoolyard, wasn't he?"

"I don't know. I can't remember the dates of murders I haven't committed."

"You don't know?" Freddie was incredulous.

"No. Are you saying State did it?"

"I'm sayin he acts like it and I'm sayin Guitar knows, and I'm sayin somethin strange is goin on. That's what I'm sayin."

He's mad at me, thought Milkman, because I laughed at his mother and that white bull story. So he's trying to get back at me.

"Keep your eyes open," Freddie went on. "Just keep them open." He looked in the pint bottle, saw it was empty, and got up to leave. "Yep. Some strange goings on round here. But don't put my name in it if you hear anything. Was just like this when that insurance man jumped off the roof. Ever hear tell of him?"

"Seems like I did."

"That must a been when you was a little bitty baby, 1931.

Well, it was some strange stuff then too." Freddie buttoned his coat and pulled his flap-eared cap down as far as it would go. "Well, thanks for the coffee, boy. Did me a lot of good. A lot of good." He took his gloves out of his pocket and moved to the door.

"You're welcome, Freddie. Merry Christmas if I don't see you before that."

"Same to you. And your folks. Tell Mr. Dead and your mother I said Merry Christmas." He was smiling again. When he reached the door he put on his gloves. Then he turned his head slowly and faced Milkman. "Tell you somebody else might know about what's goin on. Corinthians. Ask Corinthians."

He flashed his gold merrily and was gone.

# Chapter 5

Nothing happened to the fear. He lay in Guitar's bed face-up in the sunlight, trying to imagine how it would feel when the ice pick entered his neck. But picturing a spurt of wine-red blood and wondering if the ice pick would make him cough didn't help. Fear lay like a pair of crossed paws on his chest.

He closed his eyes and threw his arm over his face to keep the light from overexposing his thoughts. In the darkness that his arm made he could see ice picks coming down faster than raindrops had when he tried as a little boy to catch them with his tongue.

Five hours ago, before he knocked on Guitar's door, he had stood on the top step, dripping in the summer rain that still patted the window, imagining that the drops were tiny steely picks. Then he knocked on the door.

"Yeah?" The voice was lightly aggressive; Guitar never opened his door to a knock anymore before finding out who it was.

"Me—Milkman," he answered, and waited for the clicking sounds of three locks being released.

Milkman walked in, hunching his shoulders under his wet suit jacket. "Anything to drink?"

"Now, you know better'n that." Guitar was smiling, his golden eyes dimmed for the moment. They had not seen much of each other since that argument about Honoré versus Alabama, but the quarrel had been cleansing for both of them. They were easy with each other now that they didn't have to pretend. When in conversation they came to the battleground of difference, their verbal sparring was full of good humor. Furthermore, their friendship had been tested in more immediate ways. The last six months had been dangerous for Milkman, and Guitar had come to his aid over and over again.

"Coffee, then," said Milkman. He sat on the bed with the heaviness of a very old man. "How long you gonna keep that up?"

"Forever. It's over, man. No booze. How about some tea?"

"Jesus."

"Loose too. Bet you thought tea grew in little bags."

"Oh, Christ."

"Like Louisiana cotton. Except the black men picking it wear diapers and turbans. All over India that's all you see. Bushes with little bitsy white tea bags blossoming. Right?"

"Gimme the tea, Guitar. Just the tea. No geography."

"No geography? Okay, no geography. What about some history in your tea? Or some sociopolitico— No. That's still geography. Goddam, Milk, I do believe my whole life's geography."

"Don't you wash pots out for people before you cook water in them?"

"For example, I live in the North now. So the first question come to mind is North of what? Why, north of the South. So North exists because South does. But does that mean North is different from South? No way! South is just south of North. . . ."

"You don't put the fuckin leaves in the boiling water. You pour the water *over* the leaves. In a pot, man. In a teapot!"

"But there is some slight difference worth noticing. Northerners, for example—born and bi ?d ones, that is—are picky about their food. Well, not about the food. They actually don't give a shit about the food. What they're picky about is the trappings. You know what I mean? The pots and shit. Now, they're real funny about pots. But tea? They don't know Earl Grey from old man Lipton's instant."

"I want tea, man. Not won-ton shredded wheat."

"Old man Lipton dye him up some shredded *New York Times* and put it in a cute little white bag and northern Negroes run amok. Can't contain themselves. Ever notice that? How they love them little white bags?"

"Oh, Jesus."

"He's a Northerner too. Lived in Israel, but a Northerner in His heart. His bleeding heart. His cute little old bleeding red heart. Southerners think they own Him, but that's just because the first time they laid eyes on Him, He was strung up on a tree. They can relate to that, see. Both the stringer and the strung. But Northerners know better. . . ."

"Who you talking about? Black people or white people?"

"Black? White? Don't tell me you're one of those racial Negroes? Who said anything about black people? This is just a geography lesson." Guitar handed Milkman a steaming cup of tea.

"Yeah, well, if this is tea, I'm a soft-fried egg."

"See what I mean? Picky. Why you got to be a *soft*-fried egg? Why can't you be just a fried egg? Or just a plain old egg? And why a egg anyway? Negro's been a lotta things, but he ain't never been no egg."

Milkman began to laugh. Guitar had done it again. He'd come to the door sopping wet, ready to roll over and die, and now he was laughing, spilling tea, and choking out his reply: "How come? How come a nigger can't be a egg? He can be a egg if he wants to."

"Nope. Can't be no egg. It ain't in him. Something about his genes. His genes won't let him be no egg no matter how hard he tries. Nature says no. 'No, you can't be no egg, nigger. Now, you can be a crow if you wanna. Or a big baboon. But not no egg. Eggs is difficult, complicated. Fragile too. And white.' "

"They got brown eggs."

"Miscegenation. Besides, don't nobody want 'em."

"French people do."

"In France, yeah. But not in the Congo. Frenchman in the Congo won't touch a brown egg."

"Why won't he?"

"Scared of 'em. Might do something to his skin. Like the sun."

"French people love the sun. They're always trying to get in the sun. On the Riviera—"

"They try to get in the French sun, but not the Congo sun. In the Congo they hate the sun."

"Well, I got a right to be what I want to be, and I want to be a egg."

"Fried?"

"Fried."

"Then somebody got to bust your shell."

Quicker than a pulse beat, Guitar had changed the air. Milkman wiped his mouth, avoiding Guitar's eyes because he knew the phosphorus was back in them. The little room stood at attention in the quiet. It was a second-story porch walled in to make a room-for-rent so the landlady could get an income from it and have a watchman too. Its outside stairway made it perfect for a bachelor. Especially a secretive one like Guitar Bains.

"Can I have the pad tonight?" Milkman asked him. He examined his fingernails.

"To cop?"

Milkman shook his head.

Guitar didn't believe him. Didn't believe his friend really wanted to be alone the night before the day of his own murder. "That's scary, man. Very scary."

Milkman didn't answer.

"You're not obliged to go through no number, you know. Not for me. Everybody knows you're brave when you want to be."

Milkman looked up but still did not answer.

"Still and all," Guitar went on carefully, "you might get your heart cut out. Then you'll be just another brave nigger what got wasted."

Milkman reached for the Pall Mall package. It was empty, so he pulled a longish butt from the Planter's peanut butter jar top that was Guitar's ashtray for the day. He stretched out on the bed, letting his long fingers rub the pocket places in his clothes where matches might be. "Everything's cool," he said.

"Shit," said Guitar. "Ain't nothing cool. Nothing, nowhere. Even the North Pole ain't cool. You think so, go on up there and watch them fuckin glaciers ice your ass. And what the glaciers don't get the polar bears will." Guitar stood up, his head almost touching the ceiling. Annoyed by Milkman's indifference, he relieved his agitation by straightening up the room. He pulled an empty crate from underneath the straight-backed chair leaning in the corner, and started dumping trash into the box: dead matches from the window sill, pork bones from the barbecue he had eaten the day before. He crumpled the pleated paper cups that had been overflowing with cole slaw and fired them into the crate. "Every nigger I know wants to be cool. There's nothing wrong with controlling yourself, but can't nobody control other people." He looked sideways at Milkman's face, alert for any sign, any opening. This kind of silence was new. Something must have happened. Guitar was genuinely worried about his friend, but he also didn't want anything to happen in his room that would bring the police there. He picked up the peanut-butter-top ashtray.

"Wait. There's still some good butts in there." Milkman spoke softly.

Guitar dumped the whole ashtray into the box.

"What'd you do that for? You know we don't have no cigarettes."

"Then move your ass and go get some."

"Come on, Guitar. Cut the shit." Milkman rose from the bed and reached for the crate. He would have gotten it except Guitar stepped back and flung it all the way across the room, letting the mess settle right back where it came from. Graceful and economical as a cat, he arced his arm out of the swing and slammed his fist up against the wall, forming a barrier to any move Milkman might make.

"Pay attention." Guitar's voice was low. "Pay attention when I'm trying to tell you something."

Head to head, toe to toe they stood. Milkman's left foot hovered above the floor, and Guitar's eyes with their phosphorous lights singed his heart a little, but he took the stare. "And if I don't? What then, man? You gonna do me in? My name is Macon, remember? I'm already Dead."

Guitar didn't smile at the familiar joke, but there was enough recognition of it in his face to soften the glare in his eyes.

"Somebody ought to tell your murderer that," said Guitar.

Milkman gave a short laugh and moved back toward the bed. "You worry too much, Guitar."

"I worry just enough. But right now I need to know how come you ain't worried at all. You come up here knowing it's the thirtieth day. Knowing if anybody wants to find you they come here if not first then last. And you ask me to leave you by yourself. Just tell me what you doing."

"Look," Milkman said. "Out of all those times, I was scared just twice: the first time and the third. I've been handling it ever since, right?"

"Yeah, but something's funny this time."

"Ain't nothing funny."

"Yeah, it is. You. You funny."

"No I'm not. Just tired. Tired of dodging crazy people, tired of this jive town, of running up and down these streets getting nowhere. . . ."

"Well, you're home free if tired is all you are. Soon you'll have all the rest you ever need. Can't promise you the bed's comfortable, but morticians don't make mattresses."

"Maybe she won't come this time."

"She ain't missed in six months. You countin on her taking a holiday or something?"

"I can't hide from that bitch no more. I got to stop it. I don't want to go through this again a month from now."

"Why don't you get her people to do something?"

"I am her people."

"Listen, Milk, I'll split if you say so. But just listen to me a minute. That broad had a Carlson skinning knife last time. You know how sharp a Carlson skinning knife is? Cut you like a laser, man."

"I know."

"No, you don't know. You was up under the bar when me and Moon grabbed her."

"I know what she had."

"Won't be no Moon in this room tomorrow. And no Guitar either, if I listen to you. This time she might have a pistol."

"What fool is gonna give a colored woman a pistol?"

"Same fool that gave Porter a shotgun."

"That was years ago."

"It ain't even that that bothers me. It's the way you acting. Like you want it. Like you looking forward to it."

"Where'd you think that up?"

"Look at you. You all dressed up."

"I had to work in Sonny's Shop. You know my old man makes me dress up like this when I'm behind the desk."

"You had time to change. It's past midnight."

"Okay. So I'm clean. So I'm looking forward to it. I just got through telling you I don't want to hide no more. . . ."

"It's a secret, ain't it? You got yourself a secret."

"That makes two of us."

"Two? You and her?"

"No. You and me. You've been making some funny smoke screens lately." Milkman looked up at Guitar and smiled. "Just so you don't think I ain't noticed."

Guitar grinned back. Now that he knew there was a secret, he settled down into the groove of their relationship.

"Okay, Mr. Dead, sir. You on your own. Would you ask your visitor to kind of neaten things up a little before she goes? I don't want to come back and have to look through a pile of cigarette butts for your head. Be nice if it was laying somewhere I could spot it right off. And if it's her head that's left behind, well, there's some towels in the closet on the shelf in the back."

"Rest your mind, boy. Ain't nobody giving up no head."

They laughed then at the suitableness of the unintended pun, and it was in the sound of this laughter that Guitar picked up his brown leather jacket and started out the door.

"Cigarettes!" Milkman called after him. "Bring me some cigarettes before you disappear."

"Gotcha!" Guitar was halfway down the stairs. Already his thoughts had left Milkman and had flown ahead to the house where six old men waited for him.

He didn't come back that night.

Milkman lay quietly in the sunlight, his mind a blank, his lungs craving smoke. Gradually his fear of and eagerness for death returned. Above all he wanted to escape what he knew, escape the implications of what he had been told. And all he knew in the world about the world was what other people had told him. He felt like a garbage pail for the actions and hatreds of other people. He himself did nothing. Except for the one time he had hit his father, he had never acted independently, and that act, his only one, had brought unwanted knowledge too, as well as some responsibility for that knowledge. When his father told him about Ruth, he joined him in despising her, but he felt put upon; felt as though some burden had been given to him and that he didn't deserve it. None of that was his fault, and he didn't want to have to think or be or do something about any of it.

In that mood of lazy righteousness he wallowed in Guitar's bed, the same righteousness that had made him tail his mother like a secret agent when she left the house a week or so ago.

Returning home from a party, he had hardly pulled Macon's Buick up to the curb and turned off the car lights when he saw his mother walking a little ahead of him down Not Doctor Street. It was one-thirty in the morning, but in spite of the hour and her turned-up coat collar, there was no air of furtiveness about her at all. She was walking in what seemed to him a determined manner. Neither hurried nor aimless. Just the even-paced walk of a woman on her way to some modest but respectable work.

When Ruth turned the corner, Milkman waited a minute and started up the car. Creeping, not letting the engine slide into high gear, he drove around the corner. She was standing at the bus stop, so Milkman waited in the shadows until the bus came and she boarded it.

Surely this was no meeting of lovers. The man would have picked her up nearby somewhere. No man would allow a woman he had any affection for to come to him on public transportation in the middle of the night, especially a woman as old as Ruth. And what man wanted a woman over sixty anyway?

Following the bus was a nightmare; it stopped too often, too long, and it was difficult to tail it, hide, and watch to see if she got off. Milkman turned on the car radio, but the music, which he hoped would coat his nerve ends, only splayed them. He was very nervous and thought seriously about turning back.

Finally the bus pulled up at the intracounty train station. Its last stop. There, among the few remaining passengers, he saw her go into the lobby of the station. He believed he'd lost her. He'd never find out what train she was taking. He thought again of going back home. It was late, he was exhausted, and he wasn't sure he wanted to know any more about his mother. But having come this far, he realized it was foolish to turn back now and leave things forever up in the air. He parked in the lot and walked slowly toward the station. Maybe she's not taking a train, he thought. Maybe he meets her in the station.

He looked around carefully before pushing open the doors. There was no sign of her inside. It was a small, plain building. Old but well lit. Looming over the modest waiting room was the Great Seal of Michigan, in vivid Technicolor, painted, probably, by some high school art class. Two pink deer reared up on their hind legs, facing each other, and an eagle perched at eye level between them. The eagle's wings were open and looked like raised shoulders. Its head was turned to the left; one fierce eye bored into that of a deer. Purple Latin words stretched in a long ribbon beneath the seal: *Si Quaeris Peninsulam Amoenam Circumspice.* Milkman didn't understand the Latin and he didn't understand why the wolverine state had a buck painted on the seal. Or were they does? He remembered Guitar's story about killing one. "A man shouldn't do that." Milkman felt a quick beat of something like remorse, but he shook it off and resumed his search for his mother. He walked to the back of the station. Still no sight of her. Then he noticed that there was an upper platform, stairs leading to it, and an arrow with the words FAIR-FIELD AND NORTHEASTERN SUBURBS painted on it. Perhaps she was up there. He moved cautiously toward the stairs, glancing up and all around lest he see her or miss her. A loudspeaker broke the silence, announcing the arrival of the two-fifteen train to Fairfield Heights, leaving from the upper platform. He dashed up the stairs then just in time to see Ruth step into a car, and to jump into another car himself.

The train made ten stops at about ten-minute intervals. He leaned out between the cars at each stop to see if she was getting off. After the sixth stop, he asked the conductor when the next train returned to the city. "Five forty-five a.m.," he said.

Milkman looked at his watch. It was already three o'clock. When the conductor called out, "Fairfield Heights. Last stop," a half hour later, Milkman looked out again and this time he saw her disembark. He darted behind the three-sided wooden structure that sheltered waiting passengers from the wind until he heard her wide rubber heels padding down the steps.

Beyond the shelter along the street below were stores—all closed now: newsstands, coffee shops, stationery shops, but no houses. The wealthy people of Fairfield did not live near a train station and very few of their houses could even be seen from the road. Nevertheless, Ruth walked in her even-paced way down the street and in just a few minutes was at the wide winding lane that led into Fairfield Cemetery.

As Milkman stared at the ironwork arched over the entrance, he remembered snatches of his mother's chatter about having looked so very carefully for a cemetery for the doctor's body— someplace other than the one where Negroes were all laid together in one area. And forty years ago Fairfield was farm country with a county cemetery too tiny for anybody to care whether its dead were white or black.

Milkman leaned against a tree and waited at the entrance. Now he knew, if he'd had any doubts, that all his father had told him was true. She was a silly, selfish, queer, faintly obscene woman. Again he felt abused. Why couldn't anybody in his whole family just be normal?

He waited for an hour before she came out.

"Hello, Mama," he said. He tried to make his voice sound as coolly cruel as he felt; just as he tried to frighten her by stepping out suddenly from behind the tree.

He succeeded. She stumbled in alarm and took a great gulp of air into her mouth.

"Macon! Is that you? You're here? Oh, my goodness. I . . ." She tried desperately to normalize the situation, smiling wanly and blinking her eyes, searching for words and manners and civilization.

Milkman stopped her. "You come to lay down on your father's grave? Is that what you've been doing all these years? Spending a night every now and then with your father?"

Ruth's shoulders seemed to slump, but she said in a surprisingly steady voice, "Let's walk toward the train stop."

Neither said a word during the forty-five minutes they waited in the little shelter for the train back to the city. The sun came up and pointed out the names of young lovers painted on the wall. A few men were walking up the stairs to the platform.

When the train backed in from its siding they still had not spoken. Only when the wheels were actually turning and the engine had cleared its throat did Ruth begin, and she began in the middle of a sentence as though she had been thinking it all through since she and her son left the entrance to Fairfield Cemetery.

". . . because the fact is that I am a small woman. I don't mean little; I mean small, and I'm small because I was pressed small. I lived in a great big house that pressed me into a small package. I had no friends, only schoolmates who wanted to touch my dresses and my white silk stockings. But I didn't think I'd ever need a friend because I had him. I was small, but he was big. The only person who ever really cared whether I lived or died. Lots of people were *interested* in whether I lived or died, but he cared. He was not a good man, Macon. Certainly he was an arrogant man, and often a foolish and destructive one. But he cared whether and he cared how I lived, and there was, and is, no one else in the world who ever did. And for that I would do anything. It was important for me to be in his presence, among his things, the things he used, had touched. Later it was just important for me to know that he was in the world. When he left it, I kept on reigniting that cared-for feeling that I got from him.

"I am not a strange woman. I am a small one.

"I don't know what all your father has told you about me down in that shop you all stay in. But I know, as well as I know my own name, that he told you only what was flattering to him. I know he never told you that he killed my father and that he tried to kill you. Because both of you took my attention away from him. I know he never told you that. And I know he never told you that he threw my father's medicine away, but it's true. And I couldn't save my father. Macon took away his medicine and I just didn't know it, and I wouldn't have been able to save you except for Pilate. Pilate was the one brought you here in the first place."

"Pilate?" Milkman was coming awake. He had begun listening to his mother with the dulled ear of someone who was about to be conned and knew it.

"Pilate. Old, crazy, sweet Pilate. Your father and I hadn't had physical relations since my father died, when Lena and Corinthians were just toddlers. We had a terrible quarrel. He threatened to kill me. I threatened to go to the police about what he had done to my father. We did neither. I guess my father's money was more important to him than the satisfaction of killing me. And I would have happily died except for my babies. But he did move into another room and that's the way things stayed until I couldn't stand it anymore. Until I thought I'd really die if I had to live that way. With nobody touching me, or even looking as though they'd like to touch me. That's when I started coming to Fairfield. To talk. To talk to somebody who wanted to listen and not laugh at me. Somebody I could trust. Somebody who trusted me. Somebody who was . . . interested in me. For my own self. I didn't care if that somebody was under the ground. You know, I was twenty years old when your father stopped sleeping in the bed with me. That's hard, Macon. Very hard. By the time I was thirty . . . I think I was just afraid I'd die that way.

"Then Pilate came to town. She came into this city like she owned it. Pilate, Reba, and Reba's little baby. Hagar. Pilate came to see Macon right away and soon as she saw me she knew what my trouble was. And she asked me one day, 'Do you want him?' 'I want somebody,' I told her. 'He's as good as anybody,' she said. 'Besides, you'll get pregnant and your baby ought to be his. He ought to have a son. Otherwise this be the end of us.'

"She gave me funny things to do. And some greenish-gray grassy-looking stuff to put in his food." Ruth laughed. "I felt like a doctor, like a chemist doing some big important scientific experiment. It worked too. Macon came to me for four days. He even came home from his office in the middle of the day to be with me. He looked puzzled, but he came. Then it was over. And two months later I was pregnant. When he found out about it, he immediately suspected Pilate and he told me to get rid of the baby. But I wouldn't and Pilate helped me stand him off. I wouldn't have been strong enough without her. She saved my life. And yours, Macon. She saved yours too. She watched you like you were her own. Until your father threw her out."

Milkman leaned his head against the cold handbar that was attached to the seat in front of him. He held it there, letting its chill circle his head. Then he turned to his mother. "Were you in the bed with your father when he was dead? Naked?"

"No. But I did kneel there in my slip at his bedside and kiss his beautiful fingers. They were the only part of him that wasn't . . ."

"You nursed me."

"Yes."

"Until I was . . . old. Too old."

Ruth turned toward her son. She lifted her head and looked deep into his eyes. "And I also prayed for you. Every single night and every single day. On my knees. Now you tell me. What harm did I do you on my knees?"


That was the beginning. Now it was all going to end. In a little while she would walk in the door and this time he would let her do it. Afterward there would be no remembrance of who he was or where. Of Magdalene called Lena and First Corinthians, of his father trying to stop him dead before he was born. Of the brilliant bitterness between his father and his mother, a bitterness as smooth and fixed as steel. And he wouldn't have those waking dreams or hear those awful words his mother had spoken to him: What harm? What harm did I do you on my knees?

He could hear her footsteps, and then the sound of the doorknob turning, sticking, and turning again. He knew, without uncovering his eyes, that she was right there, looking at him through the window.

Hagar. Killing, ice-pick-wielding Hagar, who, shortly after a Christmas thank-you note, found herself each month searching the barrels and cupboards and basement shelves for some comfortably portable weapon with which to murder her true love.

The "thank you" cut her to the quick, but it was not the

reason she ran scurrying into cupboards looking for weapons. That had been accomplished by the sight of Milkman's arms around the shoulders of a girl whose silky copper-colored hair cascaded over the sleeve of his coat. They were sitting in Mary's, smiling into glasses of Jack Daniel's on the rocks. The girl looked a little like Corinthians or Lena from the back, and when she turned, laughing, toward Milkman, and Hagar saw her gray eyes, the fist that had been just sitting in her chest since Christmas released its forefinger like the blade of a skinning knife. As regularly as the new moon searched for the tide, Hagar looked for a weapon and then slipped out of her house and went to find the man for whom she believed she had been born into the world. Being five years older than he was and his cousin as well did nothing to dim her passion. In fact her maturity and blood kinship converted her passion to fever, so it was more affliction than affection. It literally knocked her down at night, and raised her up in the morning, for when she dragged herself off to bed, having spent another day without his presence, her heart beat like a gloved fist against her ribs. And in the morning, long before she was fully awake, she felt a longing so bitter and tight it yanked her out of a sleep swept clean of dreams.

She moved around the house, onto the porch, down the streets, to the fruit stalls and the butchershop, like a restless ghost, finding peace nowhere and in nothing. Not in the first tomato off the vine, split open and salted lightly, which her grandmother put before her. Not the six-piece set of pink glass dishes Reba won at the Tivoli Theater. And not the carved wax candle that the two of them made for her, Pilate dipping the wick and Reba scratching out tiny flowers with a nail file, and put in a genuine store-bought candleholder next to her bed. Not even the high fierce sun at noon, nor the ocean-dark evenings. Nothing could pull her mind away from the mouth Milkman was not kissing, the feet that were not running toward him, the eye that no longer beheld him, the hands that were not touching him.

She toyed, sometimes, with her unsucked breasts, but at some point her lethargy dissipated of its own accord and in its place was wilderness, the focused meanness of a flood or an avalanche of snow which only observers, flying in a rescue helicopter, believed to be an indifferent natural phenomenon, but which the victims, in their last gulp of breath, knew was both directed and personal. The calculated violence of a shark grew in her, and like every witch that ever rode a broom straight through the night to a ceremonial infanticide as thrilled by the black wind as by the rod between her legs; like every fed-up-to-the-teeth bride who worried about the consistency of the grits she threw at her husband as well as the potency of the lye she had stirred into them; and like every queen and every courtesan who was struck by the beauty of her emerald ring as she tipped its poison into the old red wine, Hagar was energized by the details of her mission. She stalked him. Whenever the fist that beat in her chest became that pointing finger, when any contact with him at all was better than none, she stalked him. She could not get his love (and the possibility that he did not think of her at all was intolerable), so she settled for his fear.

On those days, her hair standing out from her head like a thundercloud, she haunted Southside and Not Doctor Street until she found him. Sometimes it took two days, or three, and the people who saw her passed the word along that Hagar "done took off after Milkman again." Women watched her out of their windows. Men looked up from their checker games and wondered if she'd make it this time. The lengths to which lost love drove men and women never surprised them. They had seen women pull their dresses over their heads and howl like dogs for lost love. And men who sat in doorways with pennies in their mouths for lost love. "Thank God," they whispered to themselves, "thank God I ain't never had one of them graveyard loves." Empire State himself was a good example of one. He'd married a white girl in France and brought her home. Happy as a fly and just as industrious, he lived with her for six years until he came home to find her with another man. Another black man. And when he discovered that his white wife loved not only him, not only this other black man, but the whole race, he sat down, closed his mouth, and never said another word. Railroad Tommy had given him a janitor's job to save him from the poorhouse, workhouse, or nuthouse, one.

So Hagar's forays were part and parcel of the mystery of having been "lifed" by love, and while the manifestation it took was a source of great interest to them, the consequences were not. After all, it served him right, messing with his own cousin.

Luckily for Milkman, she had proved, so far, to be the world's most inept killer. Awed (even in the midst of her anger) by the very presence of her victim, she trembled violently and her knife thrusts and hammer swings and ice-pick jabs were clumsy. As soon as the attempt had been thwarted by a wrist grab from behind or a body tackle from the front or a neat clip on the jaw, she folded up into herself and wept cleansing tears right there and later under Pilate's strap—to which she submitted with relief. Pilate beat her, Reba cried, and Hagar crouched. Until the next time. Like this time when she turned the doorknob of Guitar's little bachelor room.

It was locked. So she swung one leg over the porch railing and fiddled with the window. Milkman heard the noises, heard the window shake, but refused to move or take his arm away from his eyes. Even when he heard the tinkle and clatter of glass he did not move.

Hagar put her shoe back on before reaching into the window hole she had made and turning the catch. It took her the longest time to raise the window. She was hanging lopsided over the railing, one leg supporting her weight. The window slid in a crooked path up its jamb.

Milkman refused to look. Perspiration collected in the small of his back and ran out of his armpit down his side. But the fear was gone. He lay there as still as the morning light, and sucked the world's energy up into his own will. And willed her dead. Either she will kill me or she will drop dead. Either I am to live in this world on my terms or I will die out of it. If I am to live in it, then I want her dead. One or the other. Me or her. Choose.

Die, Hagar. Die. Die. Die.

But she didn't. She crawled into the room and walked over to the little iron bed. In her hand was a butcher knife, which she raised high over her head and brought down heavily toward the smooth neck flesh that showed above his shirt collar. The knife struck his collarbone and angled off to his shoulder. A small break in the skin began to bleed. Milkman jerked, but did not move his arm nor open his eyes. Hagar raised the knife again, this time with both hands, but found she could not get her arms down. Try as she might, the ball joint in her shoulders would not move. Ten seconds passed. Fifteen. The paralyzed woman and the frozen man.

At the thirtieth second Milkman knew he had won. He moved his arm and opened his eyes. His gaze traveled to her strung-up, held-up arms.

Oh, she thought, when she saw his face, I had forgotten how beautiful he is.

Milkman sat up, swung his legs over the side of the bed, and stood.

"If you keep your hands just that way," he said, "and then bring them down straight, straight and fast, you can drive that knife right smack in your cunt. Why don't you do that? Then all your problems will be over." He patted her cheek and turned away from her wide, dark, pleading, hollow eyes.


She stood that way for a long time, and it was an even longer time before anybody found her. They could have guessed where she was, though. If anybody missed her for a while they could guess. Even Ruth knew now. A week earlier she had learned from Freddie that Hagar had tried to kill Milkman six times in as many months. She stared at his golden teeth and said, "Hagar?" She hadn't laid eyes on her in years; had been to Pilate's house only once in her life—a very long time ago.

"Hagar?"

"Hagar. Shore Hagar."

"Does Pilate know?"

"Course she do. Whip her every time, but it don't do no good."

Ruth was relieved. For a moment she imagined that Pilate, who had brought her son to life in the first place, was now bound to see him dead. But right after that moment of relief, she felt hurt because Milkman had not told her himself. Then she realized that he really didn't tell her anything, and hadn't for years. Her son had never been a person to her, a separate real person. He had always been a passion. Because she had been so desperate to lie with her husband and have another baby by him, the son she bore was first off a wished-for bond between herself and Macon, something to hold them together and reinstate their sex lives. Even before his birth he was a strong feeling—a feeling about the nasty greenish-gray powder Pilate had given her to be stirred into rain water and put into food. But Macon came out of his few days of sexual hypnosis in a rage and later when he discovered her pregnancy, tried to get her to abort. Then the baby became the nausea caused by the half ounce of castor oil Macon made her drink, then a hot pot recently emptied of scalding water on which she sat, then a soapy enema, a knitting needle (she inserted only the tip, squatting in the bathroom, crying, afraid of the man who paced outside the door), and finally, when he punched her stomach (she had been about to pick up his breakfast plate, when he looked at her stomach and punched it), she ran to Southside looking for Pilate. She had never walked through that part of town, but she knew the street Pilate lived on, though not the house. Pilate had no telephone and no number on her house. Ruth had asked some passer-by where Pilate lived and was directed to a lean brown house set back from the unpaved road. Pilate was sitting on a chair; Reba was cutting Pilate's hair with a barber's clippers. That was the first time she saw Hagar, who was four or five years old then. Chubby, with four long braids, two like horns over each ear, two like tails at the back of her neck. Pilate comforted Ruth, gave her a peach, which Ruth could not eat because the fuzz made her sick. She listened to what Ruth said and sent Reba to the store for a box of Argo cornstarch. She sprinkled a little of it into her hand and offered it to Ruth, who obediently took a lump and put it in her mouth. As soon as she tasted it, felt its crunchiness, she asked for more, and ate half a box before she left. (From then on she ate cornstarch, cracked ice, nuts, and once in a fit she put a few tiny pebbles of gravel in her mouth. "When you expectin, you have to eat what the baby craves," Pilate said, " 'less it come in the world hongry for what you denied it." Ruth could not bite enough. Her teeth were on edge with the yearning. Like the impulse of a cat to claw, she searched for crunchy things, and when there was nothing, she would grind her teeth.)

Gnashing the cornstarch, Ruth let Pilate lead her into the bedroom, where the woman wrapped her in a homemade-on-the-spot girdle—tight in the crotch—and told her to keep it on until the fourth month and "don't take no more mess off Macon and don't ram another thing up in your womb." She also told her not to worry. Macon wouldn't bother her no more; she, Pilate, would see to it. (Years later Ruth learned that Pilate put a small doll on Macon's chair in his office. A male doll with a small painted chicken bone stuck between its legs and a round red circle painted on its belly. Macon knocked it out of the chair and with a yardstick pushed it into the bathroom, where he doused it with alcohol and burned it. It took nine separate burnings before the fire got down to the straw and cotton ticking of its insides. But he must have remembered the round fire-red stomach, for he left Ruth alone after that.)

When the baby was born the day after she stood in the snow, with cloth roses at her feet and a man with blue wings above her head, she regarded him as a beautiful toy, a respite, a distraction, a physical pleasure as she nursed him—until Freddie (again Freddie) caught her at it; then he was no longer her velveteened toy. He became a plain on which, like the cowboys and Indians in the movies, she and her husband fought. Each one befuddled by the values of the other. Each one convinced of his own purity and outraged by the idiocy he saw in the other. She was the Indian, of course, and lost her land, her customs, her integrity to the cowboy and became a spread-eagled footstool resigned to her fate and holding fast to tiny irrelevant defiances.

But who was this son of hers? This tall man who had flesh on the outside and feelings on the inside that she knew nothing of, but somebody did, knew enough about him to want to kill him. Suddenly, the world opened up for her like one of her imperial tulips and revealed its evil yellow pistil. She had been husbanding her own misery, shaping it, making of it an art and a Way. Now she saw a larger, more malevolent world outside her own. Outside the fourposter bed where Doctor had bubbled and rotted (all but his beautiful hands, which were the only things his grandson had inherited). Outside her garden and the fishbowl where her goldfish died. She had thought it was all done. That she had won out over the castor oil, and the pot of steam that had puckered and burned her skin so she could not bear to urinate or sit with her daughters at the table where they cut and sewed. She had had the baby anyway, and although it did nothing to close the break between herself and Macon, there he was, her single triumph.

Now Freddie was telling her that it wasn't done and over yet. Somebody was still trying to kill him. To deprive her of the one aggressive act brought to royal completion. And the person who was threatening his life was someone who shared Macon's blood.

"That hurts," she said aloud to Freddie as she folded into her pocket the rent money he handed her. "That hurts, you know."

She climbed the porch steps and went into the kitchen. Without knowing what her foot was planning to do, she kicked the cabinet door with the worn lock under the sink. It answered her kick with a tiny whine before it sneaked open again. Ruth looked at it and kicked it closed once more. Again it whined and opened right back up.

"I want you closed," she whispered. "Closed."

The door stayed open.

"Closed. You hear me? Closed. Closed. Closed." She was screaming by now.

Magdalene called Lena, hearing her shouts, ran down the stairs and into the kitchen. She found her mother staring at the sink and commanding it.

"Mother?" Lena was frightened.

Ruth looked up at her. "What is it?"

"I don't know. . . . I thought I heard you saying something."

"Get somebody to fix that door. I want it shut. Tight."

Lena stared as Ruth hurried past and when she heard her mother running up the stairs, she put her fingers to her lips in disbelief. Ruth was sixty-two years old. Lena had no idea she could move that fast.

Her passions were narrow but deep. Long deprived of sex, long dependent on self-manipulation, she saw her son's imminent death as the annihilation of the last occasion she had been made love to.

With the same determined tread that took her to the graveyard six or seven times a year, Ruth left the house and caught the number 26 bus and sat down right in back of the driver. She took her glasses off and wiped them on the hem of her skirt. She was serene and purposeful as always when death turned his attention to someone who belonged to her, as she was when death breathed in her father's wispy hair and blew the strands about. She had the same calmness and efficiency with which she cared for the doctor, putting her hand on death's chest and holding him back, denying him, keeping her father alive even past the point where he wanted to be alive, past pain on into disgust and horror at having to smell himself in his next breath. Past that until he was too sick to fight her efforts to keep him alive, lingering in absolute hatred of this woman who would not grant him peace, but kept her shining lightish eyes fixed on him like magnets holding him from the narrow earth he longed for.

Ruth wiped her glasses clean so she could see the street signs as they passed ("Eat cherries," Pilate had told her, "and you won't have to wear them little windows over your eyes"), her mind empty except for getting there—to Darling Street, where Pilate lived and where, she supposed, Hagar lived too. How had that chubby little girl weighed down with hair become a knife-the marvelous biting and crunching it allowed her. Now she merely ground her teeth as she stepped out to the porch and made her way around the side of the house through the nicotiana growing all wild and out of control.

A woman sat on a bench, her hands clasped between her knees. It was not Pilate. Ruth stood still and looked at the woman's back. It didn't look like death's back at all. It looked vulnerable, soft, like an easily wounded shin, full of bone but susceptible to the slightest pain.

"Reba?" she said.

The woman turned around and fastened on her the most sorrowful eyes Ruth had ever seen.

"Reba's gone," she said, the second word sounding as if the going were permanent. "Can I do something for you?"

"I'm Ruth Foster."

Hagar stiffened. A lightning shot of excitement ran through her. Milkman's mother: the silhouette she had seen through the curtains in an upstairs window on evenings when she stood across the street hoping at first to catch him, then hoping just to see him, finally just to be near the things he was familiar with. Private vigils held at night, made more private because they were expressions of public lunacy. The outline she'd seen once or twice when the side door opened and a woman shook crumbs from a tablecloth or dust from a small rug onto the ground. Whatever Milkman had told her about his mother, whatever she had heard from Pilate and Reba, she could not remember, so overwhelmed was she in the presence of *his* mother. Hagar let her morbid pleasure spread across her face in a smile.

Ruth was not impressed. Death always smiled. And breathed. And looked helpless like a shinbone, or a tiny speck of black on the Queen Elizabeth roses, or film on the eye of a dead goldfish.

"You are trying to kill him." Ruth's voice was matter-of-fact. "If you so much as bend a hair on his head, so help me Jesus, I will tear your throat out."

Hagar looked surprised. She loved nothing in the world except this woman's son, wanted him alive more than anybody, but hadn't the least bit of control over the predator that lived wielding would-be killer out to get her son? Maybe Freddie lied. Maybe. She'd see.

When the banks disappeared and small shops in between rickety houses came into view, Ruth pulled the cord. She stepped down and walked toward the underpass that cut across Darling Street. It was a long walk and she was sweating by the time she got to Pilate's house. The door was open, but nobody was inside. The house smelled fruity and she remembered how the peach had nauseated her the last time she was there. Here was the chair she had collapsed in. There the candlemaker's rack, the pan where Pilate's homemade soap hardened into a yellowish-brown slab. This house had been a haven then, and in spite of the cold anger she felt now, it still looked like an inn, a safe harbor. A flypaper roll entirely free of flies curled down from the ceiling not far from a sack that hung there too. Ruth looked into the bedroom and saw three little beds, and like Goldilocks, she walked over to the nearest one and sat down. There was no back door to this two-room house, just a big room where they lived and this bedroom. It had a cellar that one could enter only from the outside under a metal door that slanted away from the house and opened onto stone stairs.

Ruth sat still, letting the anger and determination jell. She wondered whose bed it was and lifted up the blanket and saw only mattress ticking. The same was true of the next bed, but not of the third. It had sheets, a pillow, and a pillow slip. That would be Hagar's, she thought. The anger unjelled and flooded through her. She left the room, pressing her fury back so she would be able to wait and wait until somebody returned. Pacing the floor of the outer room, her elbows in the palms of her hands, she suddenly heard humming that seemed to be coming from the back of the house. Pilate, she thought. Pilate hummed and chewed things all the time. Ruth would ask her first if what Freddie said was true. She needed Pilate's calm view, her honesty and equilibrium. Then she would know what to do. Whether to unfold her arms and let the rage out to do whatever it might, or . . . She tasted again the Argo cornstarch and felt inside her. Totally taken over by her anaconda love, she had no self left, no fears, no wants, no intelligence that was her own. So it was with a great deal of earnestness that she replied to Ruth. "I'll try not to. But I can't make you a for-certain promise."

Ruth heard the supplication in her words and it seemed to her that she was not looking at a person but at an impulse, a cell, a red corpuscle that neither knows nor understands why it is driven to spend its whole life in one pursuit: swimming up a dark tunnel toward the muscle of a heart or an eye's nerve end that it both nourished and fed from.

Hagar lowered her eyelids and gazed hungrily down the figure of the woman who had been only a silhouette to her. The woman who slept in the same house with him, and who could call him home and he would come, who knew the mystery of his flesh, had memory of him as long as his life. The woman who knew him, had watched his teeth appear, stuck her finger in his mouth to soothe his gums. Cleaned his behind, Vaselined his penis, and caught his vomit in a fresh white diaper. Had fed him from her own nipples, carried him close and warm and safe under her heart, and who had opened her legs far far wider than she herself ever had for him. Who even now could walk freely into his room if she wanted to and smell his clothes, stroke his shoes, and lay her head on the very spot where he had lain his. But what was more, so much more, this thin lemon-yellow woman knew with absolute certainty what Hagar would willingly have her throat torn out to know: that she would see him this very day. Jealousy loomed so large in her it made her tremble. Maybe you, she thought. Maybe it's you I should be killing. Maybe then he will come to me and let me come to him. He is my home in this world. And then, aloud, "He is my home in this world."

"And I am his," said Ruth.

"And he wouldn't give a pile of swan shit for either one of you."

They turned then and saw Pilate leaning on the window sill. Neither knew how long she'd been there.

"Can't say as I blame him neither. Two growed-up women

talkin 'bout a man like he was a house or needed one. He ain't a house, he's a man, and whatever he need, don't none of you got it."

"Leave me alone, Mama. Just leave me alone."

"You already alone. If you want more alone, I can knock you into the middle of next week, and leave you there."

"You're botherin me!" Hagar was shouting and digging her fingers in her hair. It was an ordinary gesture of frustration, but its awkwardness made Ruth know that there was something truly askew in this girl. That here was the wilderness of Southside. Not the poverty or dirt or noise, not just extreme unregulated passion where even love found its way with an ice pick, but the absence of control. Here one lived knowing that at any time, anybody might do anything. Not wilderness where there was system, or the logic of lions, trees, toads, and birds, but wild wilderness where there was none.

She had not recognized it in Pilate, whose equilibrium overshadowed all her eccentricities and who was, in any case, the only person she knew of strong enough to counter Macon. Although Ruth had been frightened of her the first time she saw her—when she knocked on the kitchen door way back then, looking, as she said, for her brother Macon. (Ruth was still frightened of her a little. Not just her short hair cut regularly like a man's, or her large sleepy eyes and busy lips, or the smooth smooth skin, hairless, scarless, and wrinkleless. For Ruth had actually seen it. The place on her stomach where a navel should have been and was not. Even if you weren't frightened of a woman who had no navel, you certainly had to take her very seriously.)

Now she held up her hand, imperiously, and silenced Hagar's whines.

"Sit down there. Sit down and don't leave this yard."

Hagar slumped and moved slowly back to her bench.

Pilate turned her eyes to Ruth. "Come on in. Rest yourself before you hop on that bus again."

They sat down at the table facing each other.

"Peaches kind of dried up on me in this heat," said Pilate, and she reached for a peck basket which held about a half dozen. "But there should be some good ones left in here. Can I slice you up some?"

"No, thank you," said Ruth. She was trembling a little now. After the tension, the anger, the bravado of her earlier state of mind, followed by the violence of Pilate's words to her grand-daughter, this quiet social-tea tone disarmed her, threw her too soon and too suddenly back into the mannered dignity that was habitual for her. Ruth pressed her hands together in her lap to stop the shaking.

They were so different, these two women. One black, the other lemony. One corseted, the other buck naked under her dress. One well read but ill traveled. The other had read only a geography book, but had been from one end of the country to another. One wholly dependent on money for life, the other indifferent to it. But those were the meaningless things. Their similarities were profound. Both were vitally interested in Macon Dead's son, and both had close and supportive post-humous communication with their fathers.

"The last time I was here you offered me a peach. My visit was about my son then too."

Pilate nodded her head and with her right thumbnail slit the peach open.

"You won't never be able to forgive her. For just tryin to do it you won't never be able to forgive her. But it looks to me like you ought to be able to understand her. Think on it a minute. You ready now to kill her—well, maim her anyway—because she's tryin to take him away from you. She's the enemy to you because she wants to take him out of your life. Well, in her eyes there's somebody who wants to take him out of her life too—him. So he's her enemy. He's the one who's tryin to take himself out of her life. And she'll kill him before she lets him do that. What I'm sayin is that you both got the same idea.

"I do my best to keep her from it. She's my baby too, you know, but I tear her up every time she try. Just for the tryin, mind you, because I know one thing sure: she'll never pull it off. He come in the world tryin to keep from gettin killed. Layin in your stomach, his own papa was tryin to do it. And you helped some too. He had to fight off castor oil and knittin needles and being blasted with hot steam and I don't know what all you and Macon did. But he made it. When he was at his most helpless, he made it. Ain't nothin goin to kill him but his own ignorance, and won't no woman ever kill him. What's likelier is that it'll be a woman save his life."

"Nobody lives forever, Pilate."

"Don't?"

"Of course not."

"Nobody?"

"Of course, nobody."

"I don't see why not."

"Death is as natural as life."

"Ain't nothin natural about death. It's the most unnatural thing they is."

"You think people should live forever?"

"Some people. Yeah."

"Who's to decide? Which ones should live and which ones shouldn't?"

"The people themselves. Some folks want to live forever. Some don't. I believe they decide on it anyway. People die when they want to and if they want to. Don't nobody have to die if they don't want to."

Ruth felt a chill. She'd always believed that her father wanted to die. "I wish I could count on your faith as far as my son was concerned. But I think I'd be a really foolish woman if I did that. You saw your own father die, just like I did; you saw him killed. Do you think he wanted to die?"

"I saw Papa shot. Blown off a fence five feet into the air. I saw him wigglin on the ground, but not only did I not see him die, I seen him since he was shot."

"Pilate. You all buried him yourselves." Ruth spoke as if she were talking to a child.

"Macon did."

"It's the same thing."

"Macon seen him too. After he buried him, after he was blown off that fence. We both seen him. I see him still. He's helpful to me, real helpful. Tells me things I need to know."

"What things?"

"All kinds of things. It's a good feelin to know he's around. I tell you he's a person I can always rely on. I tell you somethin else. He's the *only* one. I was cut off from people early. You can't know what that was like. After my papa was blown off that fence, me and Macon wandered around for a few days until we had a fallin out and I went off on my own. I was about twelve, I think. When I cut out by myself, I headed for Virginia. I thought I remembered that was where my papa had people. Or my mother did. Seemed to me like I remembered somebody sayin that. I don't remember my mother because she died before I was born."

"*Before* you were born? How could she . . . ?"

"She died and the next minute I was born. But she was dead by the time I drew air. I never saw her face. I don't even know what her name was. But I do remember thinkin she come from Virginia. Anyways, that's where I struck out for. I looked around for somebody to take me in, give me a little work for a while so I could earn some money to get on down there. I walked for seven days before I found a place with a preacher's family. A nice place except they made me wear shoes. They sent me to school, though. A one-room place, where everybody sat. I was twelve, but since this was my first school I had to sit over there with the little bitty children. I didn't mind it too much; matter of fact, I liked a lot of it. I loved the geography part. Learning about that made me want to read. And the teacher was tickled at how much I liked geography. She let me have the book and I took it home with me to look at. But then the preacher started pattin on me. I was so dumb I didn't know enough to stop him. But his wife caught him at it, thumbin my breasts, and put me out. I took my geography book off with me.

I could of stayed in that town cause they was plenty of colored people to take me in. In them days, anybody too old to work kept the children. Grown folks worked and left their kids in other people's houses. But him being the preacher and all like that, I figured I ought to make tracks. I was broke as a haint cause the place didn't carry no wages. Just room and board. So I just took my geography book and a rock I picked up for a souvenir and lit out.

"It was a Sunday when I met up with some pickers. Folks call 'em migrants nowadays; then they was just called pickers. They took me in and treated me fine. I worked up in New York State pickin beans, then we'd move to another place and pick a different crop. Everyplace I went I got me a rock. They was about four or five families all together in the crew. All of them related one way or another. But they was good people and treated me fine. I stayed with them for three years, I believe, and the main reason I stayed on was a woman there I took to. A root worker. She taught me a lot and kept me from missin my own family, Macon and Papa. I didn't have a thought in my head of ever leavin them, but I did. I had to. After a while they didn't want me around no more." Pilate sucked a peach stone and her face was dark and still with the memory of how she was "cut off" so early from other people.

The boy. The nephew, or was it the cousin, of the woman who worked roots. When she was fifteen, and the rain was so heavy they had to stay in the shacks (those who had them—the others had tents) because nothing could be harvested in that pouring rain, the boy and Pilate lay down together. He was no older than she was and while everything about her delighted him, nothing about her surprised him. So it was with no malice whatsoever that one evening after supper he mentioned to some of the men (but within listening distance of the women) that he didn't know that some folks had navels and some didn't. The men and the women raised their eyes at his remark, and asked him to explain what he meant. He got it out, finally, after many false starts—he thought they were alarmed because he had taken the pretty girl with the single earring to bed—but he soon discovered that the navel thing was what bothered them.

The root woman was assigned the job of finding out if what he said was true or not. She called Pilate into her shack one day later. "Lay down," she said. "I want to check on something." Pilate lay down on the straw pallet. "Now lift up your dress," the woman said. "More. All the way up. Higher." And then her eyes flew open wide and she put her hand over her mouth. Pilate leaped up. "What? What is it?" She looked down at herself, thinking a snake or a poisonous spider had crawled over her legs.

"Nothin," the woman said. Then, "Child, where's your navel?"

Pilate had never heard the word "navel" and didn't know what the woman was talking about. She looked down at her legs, parted on the rough ticking. "Navel?" she asked.

"You know. This." And the woman pulled up her own dress and slipped the elastic of her bloomers down over her fat stomach. Pilate saw the little corkscrew thing right in the middle, the little piece of skin that looked like it was made for water to drain down into, like the little whirlpools along the edges of a creek. It was just like the thing her brother had on his stomach. He had one. She did not. He peed standing up. She squatting down. He had a penis like a horse did. She had a vagina like the mare. He had a flat chest with two nipples. She had teats like the cow. He had a corkscrew in his stomach. She did not. She thought it was one more way in which males and females were different. The boy she went to bed with had one too. But until now she had never seen another woman's stomach. And from the horror on the older woman's face she knew there was something wrong with not having it.

"What's it for?" she asked.

The woman swallowed. "It's for . . . it's for people who were born natural."

Pilate didn't understand that, but she did understand the conversation she had later with the root worker and some other women in the camp. She was to leave. They were very sorry, they liked her and all, and she was such a good worker and a big help to everybody. But she had to leave just the same.

"On account of my stomach?" But the women would not answer her. They looked at the ground.

Pilate left with more than her share of earnings, because the women did not want her to go away angry. They thought she might hurt them in some way if she got angry, and they also felt pity along with their terror of having been in the company of something God never made.

Pilate went away. Again she headed for Virginia. But now she knew how to harvest in a team and looked for another migrant crew, or a group of women who had followed their men to some seasonal work as brickmakers, iron workers, shipyard workers. In her three years picking, she had seen a number of these women, their belongings stuffed into wagons heading for the towns and cities that sought out and transported black men to various crafts that could be practiced only when the weather permitted. The companies did not encourage the women to come—they did not want an influx of poor colored settlers in those towns—but the women came anyway and took jobs as domestics and farm helpers in the towns, and lived wherever housing was free or dirt cheap. But Pilate did not want a steady job in a town where a lot of colored people lived. All her encounters with Negroes who had established themselves in businesses or trades in those small midwestern towns had been unpleasant. Their wives did not like the trembling unhampered breasts under her dress, and told her so. And though the men saw many raggedy black children, Pilate was old enough to disgrace them. Besides, she wanted to keep moving.

Finally she was taken on by some pickers heading home, stopping for a week's work here and there, wherever they could find it. Again she took a man to bed, and again she was expelled. Only this time there was no polite but firm pronouncement, nor any generous share of profits. They simply left her one day, moved out while she was in the town buying thread. She got back to campground to find nothing but a dying fire, a bag of rocks, and her geography book propped up on a tree. They even took her tin cup.

She had six copper pennies, five rocks, the geography book, and two spools of black thread—heavyweight No. 30. Right there she knew she must decide on whether to get to Virginia or settle in a town where she would probably have to wear shoes. So she did both—the latter to make the former possible. With the six pennies, the book, the rocks, and the thread, she walked back to town. Black women worked in numbers at two places in that town: the laundry and, across the street from it, the hotel/ whorehouse. Pilate chose the laundry and walked in, saying to the three young girls elbow deep in water there, "Can I stay here tonight?"

"Nobody in here at night."

"I know. Can I stay?"

They shrugged. The next day Pilate was hired as a washer-woman at ten cents a day. She worked there, ate there, slept there, and saved her dimes. Her hands, well calloused from years of harvesting, were stripped of their toughness and became soft in the wash water. Before her hands could get the different but equally tough skin of a laundress, her knuckles split with the rubbing and wringing, and ran blood into the rinse tubs. She almost ruined an entire batch of sheets, but the other girls covered for her, giving the sheets a second rinse.

One day she noticed a train steaming away from the town. "Where does it go to?" she asked.

"South," they said.

"How much does it cost?"

They laughed. "They freight trains," they told her. Only two passenger cars, and no colored allowed.

"Well, how do colored people get where they want to go?"

"Ain't supposed to go nowhere," they said, "but if they do, have to go by wagon. Ask at the livery stable when the next wagon is going down. The livery people always know when somebody is getting ready to take off."

She did, and by the end of October, just before cold weather set in, she was on her way to West Virginia, which was close anyway, according to her geography book. When she got to Virginia itself, she realized that she didn't know in what part of the state to look for her people. There were more Negroes there than she'd ever seen, and the comfort she felt in their midst she kept all her life.

Pilate had learned, whenever she was asked her name, to give only her first name. The last name had a bad effect on people. Now she was forced to ask if anybody knew of a family called Dead. People frowned and said, "No, never heard of any such."

She was in Culpeper, Virginia, washing clothes in a hotel, when she learned that there was a colony of Negro farmers on an island off the coast of Virginia. They grew vegetables, had cattle, made whiskey, and sold a little tobacco. They did not mix much with other Negroes, but were respected by them and self-sustaining. And you could get to them only by boat. On a Sunday, she convinced the ferryman to take her there, when his work was done, in his skiff.

"What you want over there?" he asked.

"Work."

"You don't want to work over there," he said.

"Why not?"

"Them folks keep to theyselves too much."

"Take me. I'll pay."

"How much?"

"A nickel."

"Great Jesus! You on. Be here at nine-thirty."

There were twenty-five or thirty families on that island and when Pilate made it clear that she wasn't afraid of work, but didn't like the mainland and the confinement of town, she was taken in. She worked there for three months, hoeing, fishing, plowing, planting, and helping out at the stills. All she had to do, she thought, was keep her belly covered. And it was true. At sixteen now, she took a lover from one of the island families and managed to keep direct light from ever hitting her stomach. She also managed to get pregnant, and to the great consternation of the island women, who were convinced their menfolk were the most desirable on earth—which accounted for so much intermarrying among them—Pilate refused to marry the man, who was eager to take her for his wife. Pilate was afraid that she wouldn't be able to hide her stomach from a husband forever. And once he saw that uninterrupted flesh, he would respond the same way everybody else had. Yet, incredible as they found her decision, nobody asked her to leave. They watched over her and gave her fewer and lighter chores as her time drew near. When her baby was born, a girl, the two midwives in attendance were so preoccupied with what was going on between her legs they never even noticed her smooth balloon of a stomach.

The first thing the new mother looked for in her baby girl was the navel, which she was relieved to see. Remembering how she got the name that was folded in her ear, when the nine days' waiting was done she asked one of the women for a Bible. There was a hymnal, they said, but not a Bible on the island. Everybody who wanted to go to services had to go to the mainland.

"Can you tell me a nice name for a girl that's in the Bible?" Pilate asked.

"Oh, plenty," they said, and reeled off a score, from which she chose Rebecca and shortened it to Reba.

It was right after Reba was born that her father came to her again. Pilate had become extremely depressed and lonely after the birth. The baby's father was forbidden to see her, since she had not "healed" yet, and she spent some dark lonely hours along with the joyous ones with the baby. Clear as day, her father said, "Sing. Sing," and later he leaned in at the window and said, "You just can't fly on off and leave a body."

Pilate understood all of what he told her. To sing, which she did beautifully, relieved her gloom immediately. And she knew he was telling her to go back to Pennsylvania and collect what was left of the man she and Macon had murdered. (The fact that she had struck no blow was irrelevant. She was part of her brother's act, because, then, she and he were one.) When the child was six months old, she asked the mother of the baby's father to keep it, and left the island for Pennsylvania. They tried to discourage her because it was getting to be winter, but she paid them no attention.

A month later she returned with a sack, the contents of which she never discussed, which she added to her geography book and the rocks and the two spools of thread.

When Reba was two years old, Pilate was seized with restlessness. It was as if her geography book had marked her to roam the country, planting her feet in each pink, yellow, blue or green state. She left the island and began the wandering life that she kept up for the next twenty-some-odd years, and stopped only after Reba had a baby. No place was like the island ever again. Having had one long relationship with a man, she sought another, but no man was like that island man ever again either.

After a while, she stopped worrying about her stomach, and stopped trying to hide it. It occurred to her that although men fucked armless women, one-legged women, hunchbacks and blind women, drunken women, razor-toting women, midgets, small children, convicts, boys, sheep, dogs, goats, liver, each other, and even certain species of plants, they were terrified of fucking her—a woman with no navel. They froze at the sight of that belly that looked like a back; became limp even, or cold, if she happened to undress completely and walked straight toward them, showing them, deliberately, a stomach as blind as a knee.

"What are you? Some kinda *mer*maid?" one man had shouted, and reached hurriedly for his socks.

It isolated her. Already without family, she was further isolated from her people, for, except for the relative bliss on the island, every other resource was denied her: partnership in marriage, confessional friendship, and communal religion. Men frowned, women whispered and shoved their children behind them. Even a traveling side show would have rejected her, since her freak quality lacked that important ingredient—the grotesque. There was really nothing to see. Her defect, frightening and exotic as it was, was also a theatrical failure. It needed intimacy, gossip, and the time it took for curiosity to become drama.

Finally Pilate began to take offense. Although she was hampered by huge ignorances, but not in any way unintelligent, when she realized what her situation in the world was and would probably always be she threw away every assumption she had learned and began at zero. First off, she cut her hair. That was one thing she didn't want to have to think about anymore. Then she tackled the problem of trying to decide how she wanted to live and what was valuable to her. When am I happy and when am I sad and what is the difference? What do I need to know to stay alive? What is true in the world? Her mind traveled crooked streets and aimless goat paths, arriving sometimes at profundity, other times at the revelations of a three-year-old. Throughout this fresh, if common, pursuit of knowledge, one conviction crowned her efforts: since death held no terrors for her (she spoke often to the dead), she knew there was nothing to fear. That plus her alien's compassion for troubled people ripened her and—the consequence of the knowledge she had made up or acquired—kept her just barely within the boundaries of the elaborately socialized world of black people. Her dress might be outrageous to them, but her respect for other people's privacy—which they were all very intense about—was balancing. She stared at people, and in those days looking straight into another person's eyes was considered among black people the height of rudeness, an act acceptable only with and among children and certain kinds of outlaws—but she never made an impolite observation. And true to the palm oil that flowed in her veins, she never had a visitor to whom she did not offer food before one word of conversation—business or social—began. She laughed but never smiled and in 1963, when she was sixty-eight years old, she had not shed a tear since Circe had brought her cherry jam for breakfast.

She gave up, apparently, all interest in table manners or hygiene, but acquired a deep concern for and about human relationships. Those twelve years in Montour County, where she had been treated gently by a father and a brother, and where she herself was in a position to help farm animals under her care, had taught her a preferable kind of behavior. Preferable to that of the men who called her mermaid and the women who swept up her footprints or put mirrors on her door.

She was a natural healer, and among quarreling drunks and fighting women she could hold her own, and sometimes mediated a peace that lasted a good bit longer than it should have because it was administered by someone not like them. But most important, she paid close attention to her mentor—the father who appeared before her sometimes and told her things. After Reba was born, he no longer came to Pilate dressed as he had been on the woods' edge and in the cave, when she and Macon had left Circe's house. Then he had worn the coveralls and heavy shoes he was shot in. Now he came in a white shirt, a blue collar, and a brown peaked cap. He wore no shoes (they were tied together and slung over his shoulder), probably because his feet hurt, since he rubbed his toes a lot as he sat near her bed or on the porch, or rested against the side of the still. Along with winemaking, cooking whiskey became the way Pilate began to make her steady living. That skill allowed her more freedom hour by hour and day by day than any other work a woman of no means whatsoever and no inclination to make love for money could choose. Once settled in as a small-time bootlegger in the colored section of a town, she had only occasional police or sheriff problems, for she allowed none of the activities that often accompanied wine houses—women, gambling—and she more often than not refused to let her customers drink what they bought from her on the premises. She made and sold liquor. Period.

After Reba grew up and began to live from one orgasm to another, taking time out to produce one child, Hagar, Pilate thought it might be time for a change. Not because of Reba, who was quite content with the life her mother and she lived, but because of her granddaughter. Hagar was prissy. She hated, even as a two-year-old, dirt and disorganization. At three she was already vain and beginning to be proud. She liked pretty clothes. Astonished as Pilate and Reba were by her wishes, they enjoyed trying to fulfill them. They spoiled her, and she, as a favor to their indulgence, hid as best she could the fact that they embarrassed her.

Pilate decided to find her brother, if he was still alive, for the child, Hagar, needed family, people, a life very different from what she and Reba could offer, and if she remembered anything about Macon, he would be different. Prosperous, conventional, more like the things and people Hagar seemed to admire. In addition, Pilate wanted to make peace between them. She asked her father where he was, but he just rubbed his feet and shook his head. So for the first time, Pilate went voluntarily to the police, who sent her to the Red Cross, who sent her to the Salvation Army, who sent her to the Society of Friends, who sent her back to the Salvation Army, who wrote to their command posts in large cities from New York to St. Louis and from Detroit to Louisiana and asked them to look in the telephone directory, where in fact one captain's secretary found him listed. Pilate was surprised that they were successful, but the captain was not, because there could hardly be many people with such a name.

They made the trip in style (one train and two buses), for Pilate had a lot of money; the crash of 1929 had produced so many buyers of cheap home brew she didn't even need the collection the Salvation Army took up for her. She arrived with suitcases, a green sack, a full-grown daughter, and a granddaughter, and found her brother truculent, inhospitable, embarrassed, and unforgiving. Pilate would have moved on immediately except for her brother's wife, who was dying of lovelessness then, and seemed to be dying of it now as she sat at the table across from her sister-in-law listening to her life story, which Pilate was making deliberately long to keep Ruth's mind off Hagar.

# Chapter 6

"I took her home. She was standing in the middle of the room when I got there. So I just took her home. Pitiful. Really pitiful."

Milkman shrugged. He didn't want to talk about Hagar, but it was a way to sit Guitar down and get around to asking him something else.

"What'd you do to her?" asked Guitar.

"What'd I do to *her*? You saw her with a butcher knife and you ask me that?"

"I mean before. That's a messed-up lady."

"I did what you do to some woman every six months—called the whole thing off."

"I don't believe you."

"It's the truth."

"No. It had to be something more."

"You calling me a liar?"

"Take it any way you want. But that girl's hurt—and the hurt came from you."

"What's the matter with you? You've been watching her try

to kill me for months and I never laid a hand on her. Now you sit there worried about her. All of a sudden you're police. You've been wearing a halo a lot lately. You got a white robe too?"

"What's that supposed to mean?"

"It means I'm tired of being criticized by you. I know we don't see eye to eye on a lot of things. I know you think I'm lazy—not serious, you say—but if we're friends . . . I don't meddle you, do I?"

"No. Not at all."

Several minutes passed while Milkman played with his beer and Guitar sipped tea. They were sitting in Mary's Place on a Sunday afternoon a few days after Hagar's latest attempt on his life.

"You're not smoking?" asked Milkman.

"No. I quit. Feel a hell of a lot better too." There was another pause before Guitar continued. "You ought to stop yourself."

Milkman nodded. "Yeah. If I stay around you I will. I'll stop smoking, fucking, drinking—everything. I'll take up a secret life and hanging out with Empire State."

Guitar frowned. "Now who's meddling?"

Milkman sighed and looked straight at his friend. "I am. I want to know why you were running around with Empire State last Christmas."

"He was in trouble. I helped him."

"That's all?"

"What else?"

"I don't know what else. But I know there is something else. Now, if it's something I can't know, okay, say so. But something's going on with you. And I'd like to know what it is."

Guitar didn't answer.

"We've been friends a long time, Guitar. There's nothing you don't know about me. I can tell you anything—whatever our differences, I know I can trust you. But for some time now it's been a one-way street. You know what I mean? I talk to you, but you don't talk to me. You don't think I can be trusted?"

"I don't know if you can or not."

"Try me."

"I can't. Other people are involved."

"Then don't tell me about other people; tell me about you."

Guitar looked at him for a long time. Maybe, he thought. Maybe I can trust you. Maybe not, but I'll risk it anyway because one day . . .

"Okay," he said aloud, "but you have to know that what I tell you can't go any further. And if it does, you'll be dropping a rope around my neck. Now do you still want to know it?"

"Yeah."

"You sure?"

"I'm sure."

Guitar poured some more hot water over his tea. He looked into his cup for a minute while the leaves settled slowly to the bottom. "I suppose you know that white people kill black people from time to time, and most folks shake their heads and say, 'Eh, eh, eh, ain't that a shame?'"

Milkman raised his eyebrows. He thought Guitar was going to let him in on some deal he had going. But he was slipping into his race bag. He was speaking slowly, as though each word had to count, and as though he were listening carefully to his own words. "I can't suck my teeth or say 'Eh, eh, eh.' I had to do something. And the only thing left to do is balance it; keep things on an even keel. Any man, any woman, or any child is good for five to seven generations of heirs before they're bred out. So every death is the death of five to seven generations. You can't stop them from killing us, from trying to get rid of us. And each time they succeed, they get rid of five to seven generations. I help keep the numbers the same.

"There is a society. It's made up of a few men who are willing to take some risks. They don't initiate anything; they don't even choose. They are as indifferent as rain. But when a Negro child, Negro woman, or Negro man is killed by whites and nothing is done about it by *their* law and *their* courts, this society selects a similar victim at random, and they execute him or her in a similar manner if they can. If the Negro was hanged, they hang; if a Negro was burnt, they burn; raped and murdered, they rape and murder. If they can. If they can't do it precisely in the same manner, they do it any way they can, but they do it. They call themselves the Seven Days. They are made up of seven men. Always seven and only seven. If one of them dies or leaves or is no longer effective, another is chosen. Not right away, because that kind of choosing takes time. But they don't seem to be in a hurry. Their secret is time. To take the time, to last. Not to grow; that's dangerous because you might become known. They don't write their names in toilet stalls or brag to women. Time and silence. Those are their weapons, and they go on forever.

"It got started in 1920, when that private from Georgia was killed after his balls were cut off and after that veteran was blinded when he came home from France in World War I. And it's been operating ever since. I am one of them now."

Milkman had held himself very still all the time Guitar spoke. Now he felt tight, shriveled, and cold.

"You? You're going to kill people?"

"Not people. White people."

"But why?"

"I just told you. It's necessary; it's got to be done. To keep the ratio the same."

"And if it isn't done? If it just goes on the way it has?"

"Then the world is a zoo, and I can't live in it."

"Why don't you just hunt down the ones who did the killing? Why kill innocent people? Why not just those who did it?"

"It doesn't matter who did it. Each and every one of them could do it. So you just get any one of them. There are no innocent white people, because every one of them is a potential nigger-killer, if not an actual one. You think Hitler surprised them? You think just because they went to war they thought he was a freak? Hitler's the most natural white man in the world. He killed Jews and Gypsies because he didn't have us. Can you see those Klansmen shocked by him? No, you can't."

"But people who lynch and slice off people's balls—they're crazy, Guitar, crazy."

"Every time somebody does a thing like that to one of us,

they say the people who did it were crazy or ignorant. That's like saying they were drunk. Or constipated. Why isn't cutting a man's eyes out, cutting his nuts off, the kind of thing you never get too drunk or ignorant to do? Too crazy to do? Too constipated to do? And more to the point, how come Negroes, the craziest, most ignorant people in America, don't get that crazy and that ignorant? No. White people are unnatural. As a race they are unnatural. And it takes a strong effort of the will to overcome an unnatural enemy."

"What about the nice ones? Some whites made sacrifices for Negroes. Real sacrifices."

"That just means there are one or two natural ones. But they haven't been able to stop the killing either. They are outraged, but that doesn't stop it. They might even speak out, but that doesn't stop it either. They might even inconvenience themselves, but the killing goes on and on. So will we."

"You're missing the point. There're not just one or two. There're a lot."

"Are there? Milkman, if Kennedy got drunk and bored and was sitting around a potbellied stove in Mississippi, he might join a lynching party just for the hell of it. Under those circumstances his unnaturalness would surface. But I know I wouldn't join one no matter how drunk I was or how bored, and I know you wouldn't either, nor any black man I know or ever heard tell of. Ever. In any world, at any time, just get up and go find somebody white to slice up. But they *can* do it. And they don't even do it for profit, which is why they do most things. They do it for fun. Unnatural."

"What about . . ." Milkman searched his memory for some white person who had shown himself unequivocally supportive of Negroes. "Schweitzer. Albert Schweitzer. Would he do it?"

"In a minute. He didn't care anything about those Africans. They could have been rats. He was in a laboratory testing *himself*—proving he could work on human dogs."

"What about Eleanor Roosevelt?"

"I don't know about the women. I can't say what their women would do, but I do remember that picture of those white mothers holding up their babies so they could get a good look at some black men burning on a tree. So I have my suspicions about Eleanor Roosevelt. But *none* about Mr. Roosevelt. You could've taken him and his wheelchair and put him in a small dusty town in Alabama and given him some tobacco, a checkerboard, some whiskey, and a rope and he'd have done it too. What I'm saying is, under certain conditions they would *all* do it. And under the same circumstances we would not. So it doesn't matter that some of them *haven't* done it. I listen. I read. And now I know that they know it too. They know they are unnatural. Their writers and artists have been saying it for years. Telling them they are unnatural, telling them they are depraved. They call it tragedy. In the movies they call it adventure. It's just depravity that they try to make glorious, natural. But it ain't. The disease they have is in their blood, in the structure of their chromosomes."

"You can prove this, I guess. Scientifically?"

"No."

"Shouldn't you be able to prove it before you act on something like that?"

"Did they prove anything scientifically about us before they killed us? No. They killed us first and then tried to get some scientific proof about why we should die."

"Wait a minute, Guitar. If they are as bad, as unnatural, as you say, why do you want to be like them? Don't you want to be better than they are?"

"I am better."

"But now you're doing what the worst of them do."

"Yes, but I am reasonable."

"Reasonable? How?"

"I am not, one, having fun; two, trying to gain power or public attention or money or land; three, angry at anybody."

"You're not angry? You must be!"

"Not at all. I hate doing it. I'm afraid to do it. It's hard to do it when you aren't angry or drunk or doped up or don't have a personal grudge against the person."

"I can't see how it helps. I can't see how it helps anybody."

"I told you. Numbers. Balance. Ratio. And the earth, the land."

"I'm not understanding you."

"The earth is soggy with black people's blood. And before us Indian blood. Nothing can cure them, and if it keeps on there won't be any of us left and there won't be any land for those who are left. So the numbers have to remain static."

"But there are more of them than us."

"Only in the West. But still the ratio can't widen in their favor."

"But you should want everybody to know that the society exists. Then maybe that would help stop it. What's the secrecy for?"

"To keep from getting caught."

"Can't you even let other Negroes know about it? I mean to give us hope?"

"No."

"Why not?"

"Betrayal. The possibility of betrayal."

"Well, let *them* know. Let white people know. Like the Mafia or the Klan; frighten them into behaving."

"You're talking foolishness. How can you let one group know and not the other? Besides, we are not like them. The Mafia is unnatural. So is the Klan. One kills for money, the other kills for fun. And they have huge profits and protection at their disposal. We don't. But it's not about other people knowing. We don't even tell the victims. We just whisper to him, 'Your Day has come.' The beauty of what we do is its secrecy, its smallness. The fact that nobody needs the unnatural satisfaction of talking about it. Telling about it. We don't discuss it among ourselves, the details. We just get an assignment. If the Negro was killed on a Wednesday, the Wednesday man takes it; if he was killed on Monday, the Monday man takes that one. And we just notify one another when it's completed, not how or who. And if it ever gets to be too much, like it was for Robert Smith, we do *that* rather than crack and tell somebody. Like Porter. It was getting him down. They thought somebody would have to take over his day. He just needed a rest and he's okay now."

Milkman stared at his friend and then let the spasm he had been holding back run through him. "I can't buy it, Guitar."

"I know that."

"There's too much wrong with it."

"Tell me."

"Well, for one thing, you'll get caught eventually."

"Maybe. But if I'm caught I'll just die earlier than I'm supposed to—not better than I'm supposed to. And how I die or when doesn't interest me. What I die *for* does. It's the same as what I live for. Besides, if I'm caught they'll accuse me and kill me for one crime, maybe two, never for all. And there are still six other days in the week. We've been around for a long long time. And believe me, we'll be around for a long long time to come."

"You can't marry."

"No."

"Have children."

"No."

"What kind of life is that?"

"Very satisfying."

"There's no love in it."

"No love? No love? Didn't you hear me? What I'm doing ain't about hating white people. It's about loving us. About loving you. My whole life is love."

"Man, you're confused."

"Am I? When those concentration camp Jews hunt down Nazis, are they hating Nazis or loving dead Jews?"

"It's not the same thing."

"Only because they have money and publicity."

"No; because they turn them over to the courts. You kill and you don't kill the killers. You kill innocent people."

"I told you there are no—"

"And you don't correct a thing by—"

"We poor people, Milkman. I work at an auto plant. The rest

of us barely eke out a living. Where's the money, the state, the country to finance our justice? You say Jews try their catches in a court. Do we have a court? Is there one courthouse in one city in the country where a jury would convict them? There are places right now where a Negro still can't testify against a white man. Where the judge, the jury, the court, are legally bound to ignore anything a Negro has to say. What that means is that a black man is a victim of a crime only when a white man says he is. Only then. If there was anything like or near justice or courts when a cracker kills a Negro, there wouldn't have to be no Seven Days. But there ain't; so we are. And we do it without money, without support, without costumes, without newspapers, without senators, without lobbyists, and without illusions!"

"You sound like that red-headed Negro named X. Why don't you join him and call yourself Guitar X?"

"X, Bains—what difference does it make? I don't give a damn about names."

"You miss his point. His point is to let white people know you don't accept your slave name."

"I don't give a shit what white people know or even think. Besides, I do accept it. It's part of who I am. Guitar is *my* name. Bains is the slave master's name. And I'm all of that. Slave names don't bother me; but slave status does."

"And knocking off white folks changes your slave status?"

"Believe it."

"Does it do anything for my slave status?"

Guitar smiled. "Well, doesn't it?"

"Hell, no." Milkman frowned. "Am I going to live any longer because you all read the newspaper and then ambush some poor old white man?"

"It's not about you living longer. It's about how you live and why. It's about whether your children can make other children. It's about trying to make a world where one day white people will think before they lynch."

"Guitar, none of that shit is going to change how I live or how any other Negro lives. What you're doing is crazy. And something else: it's a habit. If you do it enough, you can do it to anybody. You know what I mean? A torpedo is a torpedo, I don't care what his reasons. You can off anybody you don't like. You can off me."

"We don't off Negroes."

"You hear what you said? *Negroes*. Not Milkman. Not 'No, I can't touch *you*, Milkman,' but 'We don't off Negroes.' Shit, man, suppose you all change your parliamentary rules?"

"The Days are the Days. It's been that way a long time."

Milkman thought about that. "Any other young dudes in it? Are all the others older? You the only young one?"

"Why?"

"Cause young dudes are subject to change the rules."

"You worried about yourself, Milkman?" Guitar looked amused.

"No. Not really." Milkman put his cigarette out and reached for another one. "Tell me, what's your day?"

"Sunday. I'm the Sunday man."

Milkman rubbed the ankle of his short leg. "I'm scared for you, man."

"That's funny. I'm scared for you too."

# Chapter 7

Truly landlocked people know they are. Know the occasional Bitter Creek or Powder River that runs through Wyoming; that the large tidy Salt Lake of Utah is all they have of the sea and that they must content themselves with *bank*, *shore*, and *beach* because they cannot claim a coast. And having none, seldom dream of flight. But the people living in the Great Lakes region are confused by their place on the country's edge—an edge that is border but not coast. They seem to be able to live a long time believing, as coastal people do, that they are at the frontier where final exit and total escape are the only journeys left. But those five Great Lakes which the St. Lawrence feeds with memories of the sea are themselves landlocked, in spite of the wandering river that connects them to the Atlantic. Once the people of the lake region discover this, the longing to leave becomes acute, and a break from the area, therefore, is necessarily dream-bitten, but necessary nonetheless. It might be an appetite for other streets, other slants of light. Or a yearning to be surrounded by strangers. It may even be a wish to hear the solid click of a door closing behind their backs.

For Milkman it was the door click. He wanted to feel the heavy white door on Not Doctor Street close behind him and know that he might be hearing the catch settle into its groove for the last time.

"You'll own it all. All of it. You'll be free. Money is freedom, Macon. The only real freedom there is."

"I know, Daddy, I know. But I have to get away just the same. I'm not leaving the country; I just want to be on my own. Get a job on my own, live on my own. You did it at sixteen. Guitar at seventeen. Everybody. I'm still living at home, working for you—not because I sweated for the job, but because I'm your son. I'm over thirty years old."

"I need you here, Macon. If you were going to go, you should have gone five years ago. Now I've come to depend on you." It was difficult for him to beg, but he came as close to it as he could.

"Just a year. One year. Stake me for a year and let me go. When I come back, I'll work a year for nothing and pay you back."

"It's not the money. It's you being here, taking care of this. Taking care of all I'm going to leave you. Getting to know it, know how to handle it."

"Let me use some of it now, when I need it. Don't do like Pilate, put it in a green sack and hang it from the wall so nobody can get it. Don't make me wait until—"

"What did you say?" As suddenly as an old dog drops a shoe when he smells raw meat, Macon Dead dropped his pleading look and flared his nostrils with some new interest.

"I said give me a little bit—"

"No. Not that. About Pilate and a sack."

"Yeah. Her sack. You've seen it, haven't you? That green sack she got hanging from the ceiling? She calls it her inheritance. You can't get from one side of the room to the other without cracking your head on it. Don't you remember it?"

Macon was blinking rapidly, but he managed to calm himself and say, "I've never set foot in Pilate's house in my life. I looked in there once, but it was dark and I didn't see anything hanging down from the ceiling. When's the last time you saw it?"

"Maybe nine or ten months ago. What about it?"

"You think it's still there?"

"Why wouldn't it be?"

"You say it's green. You know for sure it's green?"

"Yeah, green. Grass green. What is it? What's bothering you?"

"She told you it was her inheritance, huh?" Macon was smiling, but so craftily that Milkman could hardly recognize it as a smile.

"No. She didn't; Hagar did. I was walking across the room toward the . . . uh . . . toward the other side and I'm tall enough for it to be in my way. I bumped my head on it. Made a hickey too. When I asked Hagar what it was she said, 'Pilate's inheritance.' "

"And it made a hickey on your head?"

"Yeah. Felt like bricks. What're you going to do, sue her?"

"You had any lunch?"

"It's ten-thirty, Daddy."

"Go to Mary's. Get us a couple of orders of barbecue. Meet me in the park across from Mercy. We'll eat lunch there."

"Daddy . . ."

"Go on now. Do what I say. Go on, Macon."


They met in the little public park across the street from Mercy Hospital. It was full of pigeons, students, drunks, dogs, squirrels, children, trees, and secretaries. The two colored men sat down on an iron bench a little away from the most crowded part, but not the edge. They were very well dressed, too well dressed to be eating pork out of a box, but on that warm September day it seemed natural, a perfect addition to the mellowness that pervaded the park.

Milkman was curious about his father's agitation, but not alarmed. So much had been going on, so many changes. Besides, he knew whatever was making his father fidget and look around to see if anyone was too near had to do with something his father wanted, not something he wanted himself. He could look at his father coolly now that he had sat on that train and listened to his mother's sad sad song. Her words still danced around in his head. "What harm did I do you on my knees?"

Deep down in that pocket where his heart hid, he felt used. Somehow everybody was using him for something or as something. Working out some scheme of their own on him, making him the subject of their dreams of wealth, or love, or martyrdom. Everything they did seemed to be about him, yet nothing he wanted was part of it. Once before he had had a long talk with his father, and it ended up with his being driven further from his mother. Now he had had a confidential talk with his mother, only to discover that before he was born, before the first nerve end had formed in his mother's womb, he was the subject of great controversy and strife. And now the one woman who claimed to love him more than life, more than her life, actually loved him more than *his* life, for she had spent half a year trying to relieve him of it. And Guitar. The one sane and constant person he knew had flipped, had ripped open and was spilling blood and foolishness instead of conversation. He was a fit companion for Empire State. So now he waited with curiosity, but without excitement or hope, for this latest claim.

"Listen to me. Just eat your meat and listen to me. Don't interrupt, because I might lose my train of thought.

"A long time ago, I told you about when I was a boy on the farm. About Pilate and me. About my father getting killed. I never finished the story; I never told you all of it. The part I left out was about me and Pilate. I tried to keep you away from her and said she was a snake. Now I'm going to tell you why."

A red ball rolled to his feet, and Macon picked it up and threw it back to a little girl. He made sure she was safely back in her mother's view before he began his story.

Six days after the first Macon Dead died, his children, a twelve-year-old Pilate and a sixteen-year-old Macon Dead, found themselves homeless. Bewildered and grieving, they went to the house of the closest colored person they knew: Circe, the midwife who had delivered them both and who was there when their mother died and when Pilate was named. She worked in a large house—a mansion—outside Danville, for a family of what was then called gentlemen farmers. The orphans called to Circe from the vegetable garden early in the morning as soon as they saw the smoke from the cook stove rising. Circe let them in, pressing her hands together with relief, and saying how glad she was to see them alive. She hadn't known what had happened to them after the killing. Macon explained that he had buried his father himself, down by that part of the stream on Lincoln's Heaven where they used to fish together, the place where he had caught that nine-pound trout. The grave was shallower than it ought to be, but he'd piled rocks there.

Circe told them to stay with her until they could all figure out what to do, someplace for them to go. She hid them in that house easily. There were rooms the family seldom went into, but if they weren't safe, she was prepared to share her own room (which was off limits to everybody in the house). It was small, though, so they agreed to stay in a pair of rooms on the third floor that were used only for storage. Circe would bring them food, water to wash in, and she would empty their slop jar.

Macon asked if they couldn't work there; would her mistress take them on as kitchen help, yard help, anything?

Circe bit her tongue trying to get the words out. "You crazy? You say you saw the men what killed him. You think they don't know you saw them? If they kill a growed man, what you think they do to you? Be sensible. We got to plan and figure this thing out."

Macon and Pilate stayed there two weeks, not a day longer. He had been working hard on a farm since he was five or six years old and she was born wild. They couldn't bear the stillness, the walls, the boredom of having nothing to do but wait for the day's excitement of eating and going to the toilet. Anything was better than walking all day on carpeting, than eating the soft bland food white people ate, than having to sneak a look at the sky from behind ivory curtains.

Pilate began to cry the day Circe brought her white toast and cherry jam for breakfast. She wanted her own cherries, from her own cherry tree, with stems and seeds; not some too-sweet mashed mush. She thought she would die if she couldn't hold her mouth under Ulysses S. Grant's teat and squirt the warm milk into her mouth, or pull a tomato off its vine and eat it where she stood. Craving certain specific foods had almost devastated her. That, plus the fact that her earlobe was sore from the operation she had performed on herself, had her near hysteria. Before they left the farm, she'd taken the scrap of brown paper with her name on it from the Bible, and after a long time trying to make up her mind between a snuffbox and a sunbonnet with blue ribbons on it, she took the little brass box that had belonged to her mother. Her miserable days in the mansion were spent planning how to make an earring out of the box which would house her name. She found a piece of wire, but couldn't get it through. Finally, after much begging and whining, Circe got a Negro blacksmith to solder a bit of gold wire to the box. Pilate rubbed her ear until it was numb, burned the end of the wire, and punched it through her earlobe. Macon fastened the wire ends into a knot, but the lobe was swollen and running pus. At Circe's instruction she put cobwebs on it to draw the pus out and stop the bleeding.

On the night of the day she cried so about the cherries, the two of them decided that when her ear got better, they would leave. It was too much of a hardship on Circe anyway for them to stay there, and if her white folks found out about them, they might let her go.

One morning Circe climbed all the way to the third floor with a covered plate of scrapple and found two empty rooms. They didn't even take a blanket. Just a knife and a tin cup.

The first day out was joyous for them. They ate raspberries and apples; they took off their shoes and let the dewy grass and sun-warmed dirt soothe their feet. At night they slept in a hay-stack, so grateful for open air even the field mice and the ticks were welcome bedmates.

The next day was pleasant but less exciting. They bathed in a curve of the Susquehanna and then wandered in a southerly direction, keeping to fields, woods, stream beds, and little-used paths, headed, they thought, for Virginia, where Macon believed they had people.

On the third day they woke to find a man that looked just like their father sitting on a stump not fifty yards away. He was not looking at them; he was just sitting there. They would have called out to him or run toward him except he was staring right past them with such distance in his eyes, he frightened them. So they ran away. All day long at various intervals they saw him: staring down into duck ponds; framed by the Y of a sycamore tree; shading his eyes from the sun as he peered over a rock at the wide valley floor beneath them. Each time they saw him they backed off and went in the opposite direction. Now the land itself, the only one they knew and knew intimately, began to terrify them. The sun was blazing down, the air was sweet, but every leaf that the wind lifted, every rustle of a pheasant hen in a clump of ryegrass, sent needles of fear through their veins. The cardinals, the gray squirrels, the garden snakes, the butter-flies, the ground hogs and rabbits—all the affectionate things that had peopled their lives ever since they were born became ominous signs of a presence that was searching for them, follow-ing them. Even the river's babbling sounded like the call of a liquid throat waiting, just waiting for them. That was in the daylight. How much more terrible was the night.

Just before dark, when the sun had left them alone, when they were coming out of some woods looking around for the crest of the hill where they could see, perhaps, a farm, an aban-doned shed—anyplace where they could spend the night—they saw a cave, and at its mouth stood their father. This time he motioned for them to follow him. Faced with the choice of the limitless nighttime woods and a man who looked like their father, they chose the latter. After all, if it was their father, he wouldn't hurt them, would he?

Slowly they approached the mouth of the cave, following their father's beckoning hand and his occasional backward glance.

They looked into the cave and saw nothing but a great maw of darkness. Their father had disappeared. If they stayed near the lip, they thought, it was as good a place as any to spend the night; perhaps he was simply looking out for them, showing them what to do and where to go. They made themselves as comfortable as they could on a rock formation that jutted out like a shelf from a hip-high mass of stone. There was nothing behind them that they could see and only the certainty of bats to disturb them. Yet it was nothing to that other darkness—outside.

Toward morning, Macon woke from a light and fitful sleep, with a terrific urge to relieve his bowels, the consequence of three days' diet of wild fruit. Without waking his sister, he climbed off the shelf, and shy of squatting on the crown of a hill in a new sun, he walked a little farther back into the cave. When he was finished, the darkness had disintegrated somewhat, and he saw, some fifteen feet in front of him, a man stirring in his sleep. Macon tried to button his pants and get away without waking him, but the leaves and twigs crunching under his feet pulled the man all the way out of his sleep. He raised his head, turned over, and smiled. Macon saw that he was very old, very white, and his smile was awful.

Macon stepped back, one hand outstretched behind him, thinking all the while of how his father's body had twitched and danced for whole minutes in the dirt. He touched the cave's wall and a piece of it gave way in his hand. Closing his fingers around it, he threw it at the grinning man's head, hitting him just above the eye. Blood spurted out and knocked the smile off the pale face, but did not stop the man from coming and coming, all the time wiping blood from his face and smearing it on his shirt.

Macon got hold of another rock, but missed that time. The man kept coming.

The scream that boomed down the cave tunnel and woke the bats came just when Macon thought he had taken his last living breath. The bleeding man turned toward the direction of the scream and looked at the colored girl long enough for Macon to pull out his knife and bring it down on the old man's back. He crashed forward, then turned his head to look up at them. His mouth moved and he mumbled something that sounded like "What for?" Macon stabbed him again and again until he stopped moving his mouth, stopped trying to talk, and stopped jumping and twitching on the ground.

Panting with the exertion of slashing through an old man's rib cage, Macon ran back to get the blanket the man had been sleeping on. He wanted the dead man to disappear, to be covered, hidden, to be gone. When he snatched the blanket, a large tarpaulin came with it and he saw three boards positioned across what looked like a shallow pit. He paused and then kicked the boards aside. Underneath were little gray bags, their necks tied with wire, arranged like nest eggs. Macon picked one of them up and was amazed at its weight.

"Pilate," he called. "Pilate."

But she was growing roots where she stood, and staring open-mouthed at the dead man. Macon had to pull her by the arm over to the hole where the bags lay. After some difficulty with the wire (he ended up having to use his teeth), he got one open and shook the gold nuggets it held out into the leaves and twigs that lay on the floor of the cave.

"Gold," he whispered, and immediately, like a burglar out on his first job, stood up to pee.

Life, safety, and luxury fanned out before him like the tail-spread of a peacock, and as he stood there trying to distinguish each delicious color, he saw the dusty boots of his father standing just on the other side of the shallow pit.

"It *is* Papa!" said Pilate. And as if in answer to her recognition, he took a deep breath, rolled his eyes back, and whispered, "Sing. Sing," in a hollow voice before he melted away again.

Pilate darted around the cave calling him, looking for him, while Macon piled the sacks of gold into the tarpaulin.

"Let's go, Pilate. Let's get out of here."

"We can't take that." She pointed a finger at his bundle.

"What? Not take it? You lost your mind?"

"That's stealing. We killed a man. They'll be after us, all over. If we take his money, then they'll think that's why we did it. We got to leave it, Macon. We can't get caught with no bags of money."

"This ain't money; it's gold. It'll keep us for life, Pilate. We can get us another farm. We can—"

"Leave it, Macon! Leave it! Let them find it just where it was!" Then she began to shout, "Papa! Papa!"

Macon slapped her and the little brass box dangled on her ear. She cupped it in her hands for a moment and then leaped on her brother like an antelope. They fought right there in front of the dead man's staring eyes. Pilate was almost as strong as Macon, but no real match for him, and he probably would have beaten her unconscious had she not got his knife, not yet dry from the old man's blood, and held it ready for his heart.

Macon stood very still and watched her eyes. He began calling her ugly names, but she didn't answer. He backed out of the cave and walked a little distance away.

All day he waited for her to come out. All day she stayed there. When night came he just sat, at the foot of a tree, unafraid of all the night things that had terrified him before, eyes wide open, waiting for her to stick her woolly head out of the cave. There was no sound from her direction and he waited the whole night. At dawn he crept forward a foot at a time, hoping he would catch her asleep. Just then he heard some dogs and knew hunters were walking nearby. He ran as fast as he could through the woods until he couldn't hear the dogs anymore.

Another day and a night he spent trying to work his way back to the cave and avoid the hunters if they were still about. Finally he got there, three days and two nights later. Inside the cave the dead man was still looking placidly up at him, but the tarpaulin and the gold were gone.

The secretaries went away. So did the children and the dogs. Only the pigeons, the drunks, and the trees were left in the little park.

Milkman had eaten almost none of his barbecue. He was watching his father's face, shining with perspiration and the emotions of memory.

"She took it, Macon. After all that, she took the gold."

"How do you know? You didn't see her take it," said Milkman.

"The tarpaulin was green." Macon Dead rubbed his hands together. "Pilate came to this city in 1930. Two years later they call back all the gold. I figured she spent it all in the twenty or so years since I'd seen her, since she was living like poor trash when she got here. It was natural for me to believe she'd got rid of it all. Now you tell me she got a green sack full of something hard enough to give you a hickey on your head when you bumped into it. That's the gold, boy. That's it!"

He turned to his son full face and licked his lips. "Macon, get it and you can have half of it; go wherever you want. Get it. For both of us. Please get it, son. Get the gold."

# Chapter 8

Every night now Guitar was seeing little scraps of Sunday dresses—white and purple, powder blue, pink and white, lace and voile, velvet and silk, cotton and satin, eyelet and grosgrain. The scraps stayed with him all night and he remembered Magdalene called Lena and Corinthians bending in the wind to catch the heart-red pieces of velvet that had floated under the gaze of Mr. Robert Smith. Only Guitar's scraps were different. The bits of Sunday dresses that he saw did not fly; they hung in the air quietly, like the whole notes in the last measure of an Easter hymn.

Four little colored girls had been blown out of a church, and his mission was to approximate as best he could a similar death of four little white girls some Sunday, since he was the Sunday man. He couldn't do it with a piece of wire, or a switchblade. For this he needed explosives, or guns, or hand grenades. And that would take money. He knew that the assignments of the Days would more and more be the killing of white people in groups, since more and more Negroes were being killed in groups. The single, solitary death was going rapidly out of fashion, and the Days might as well prepare themselves for it.

So when Milkman came to him with a proposal to steal and share a cache of gold, Guitar smiled. "Gold?" He could hardly believe it.

"Gold."

"Nobody got gold, Milkman."

"Pilate does."

"It's against the law to have gold."

"That's why she got it. She can't use it, and she can't report its being stolen since she wasn't supposed to have it in the first place."

"How do we get rid of it—get greenbacks for it?"

"Leave that to my father. He knows bank people who know other bank people. They'll give him legal tender for it."

"Legal tender." Guitar laughed softly. "How much legal tender will it bring?"

"That's what we have to find out."

"What's the split?"

"Three ways."

"Your papa know that?"

"Not yet. He thinks it's two ways."

"When you gonna tell him?"

"Afterwards."

"Will he go for it?"

"How can he *not* go for it?"

"When do we get it?"

"Whenever we want to."

Guitar spread his palm. "My man." Milkman slapped his hand. "Legal tender. Legal tender. I love it. Sounds like a virgin bride." Guitar rubbed the back of his neck and lifted his face to the sun in a gesture of expansiveness and luxury.

"Now we have to come up with something. A way to get it," said Milkman.

"Be a breeze. A cool cool breeze," Guitar continued, smiling at the sun, his eyes closed as though to ready himself for the gold by trying out a little bit of the sun's.

"A breeze?" Now that Guitar was completely enthusiastic, Milkman's own excitement was blunted. Something perverse made him not want to hand the whole score to his friend on a platter. There should be some difficulty, some complication in this adventure. "We just walk over there and snatch it off the wall, right? And if Pilate or Reba say anything, we just knock them out the way. That what you have in mind?" He summoned as much irony as he could into his voice.

"Defeatism. That's what you got. Defeatism."

"Common sense is what I got."

"Come on, old dude. Your pappy give you a good thing and you want to fight it."

"I'm not fighting. I just want to get out alive and breathing so what I snatch does me some good. I don't want to have to give it to a brain surgeon to pull an ice pick out the back of my head."

"Can't no ice pick get through the back of your head, nigger."

"Can get through my heart."

"What you doin with a heart anyway?"

"Pumping blood. And I'd like to keep on pumping it."

"Okay. We got us a problem. A little bitty problem: how can two big men get a fifty-pound sack out of a house with three women in it—women who all together don't weigh three hundred pounds."

"What you have to weigh to pull a trigger?"

"What trigger? Nobody in that house got a gun."

"You don't know what Hagar's got."

"Look, Milk. She's been trying to kill you for almost a year. Used everything she could get her hands on and never once did she use a gun."

"So? Maybe she's thinking. Wait till next month."

"Next month she'll be too late, won't she?" Guitar leaned his head over to the side and smiled at Milkman, an engaging boyish smile. Milkman hadn't seen him this relaxed and cordial in a long

long time. He wondered if that's why he had let him in on it. Obviously he could pull it off alone, but maybe he wanted to see Guitar warm and joking again, his face open and smiling instead of with that grim reaper look.

They met again on Sunday on route 6 away from the colored part of town. A road consisting of used-car lots, Dairy Queens, and White Castle hamburger places. It was empty of shoppers that morning—nothing but the occasional sound of automobiles breaking the graveyard silence of the cars in the lots, lined up like tombstones.

Since that last conversation—the important one in which Guitar explained his work, not the brief chancy talks they'd had afterward—Milkman wished he had the nerve to ask Guitar the question that was bothering him. "Has he?" He could hardly phrase the question in his own mind, and certainly could never say it aloud. Guitar had impressed him with the seriousness and the dread of the work of the Days, and the danger. He had said that the Days never even talked about the details among themselves, so Milkman was sure any inquiry from him would only make Guitar sullen again. And cold. But the question was there. "Has he done it? Has he really killed somebody?" Like the old men on Tenth Street, now he bought the morning and evening papers, and once every two weeks the black newspaper, and read nervously, looking for reports of murders that appeared suspicious, pointless. When he found one, he followed the news stories until a suspect was found. Then he had to see if there were any black people murdered by someone other than their own.

"Did you do it yet?" He was like a teen-age girl wondering about the virginity of her friend, the friend who has a look, a manner newly minted—different, separate, focused somehow. "Did you do it yet? Do you know something both exotic and ordinary that I have not felt? Do you now know what it's like to risk your one and only self? How did it feel? Were you afraid? Did it change you? And if I do it, will it change me too?"

Maybe he could ask him one day, but not this day when it was so much like old times. Taking risks together the way they did when Milkman was twelve and Guitar was a teen-ager and they swaggered, haunched, leaned, straddled, ran all over town trying to pick fights or at least scare somebody: other boys, girls, dogs, pigeons, old women, school principals, drunks, ice cream vendors, and the horses of junkyard men. When they succeeded they rode the wind and covered their mouths to aggravate their laughter. And when they didn't, when somebody out-insulted them, or ignored them, or sent them running, they wisecracked and name-called until the sweat of embarrassment evaporated from the palms of their hands. Now they were men, and the terror they needed to provoke in others, if for no other reason than to feel it themselves, was rarer but not lighter. Dominion won by fear and secured by fear was still sweeter than any that could be got another way. (Except for women, whom they liked to win with charm but keep with indifference.)

It was like that again now, and Milkman didn't want to lose it.

There was something else too. Guitar had placed himself willingly and eagerly in a life cause that would always provide him with a proximity to knife-cold terror. Milkman knew his own needs were milder, for he could thrive in the presence of someone who inspired fear. His father, Pilate, Guitar. He gravitated toward each one, envious of their fearlessness now, even Hagar's, in spite of the fact that she was no longer a threat, but a fool who wanted not his death so much as his attention. Guitar could still create the sense of danger and life lived on the cutting edge. So Milkman had brought him into this scheme only partially for his help. Mostly because this escapade cried out for a cutting edge to go with its larklike quality. With Guitar as his co-conspirator, Milkman could look forward to both fun and fear.

They sauntered on down route 6, stopping frequently to examine the cars, gesticulating, bantering each other about the best way to burglarize a shack that, as Guitar said, "didn't have a door or window with a lock."

"But it's got people," Milkman insisted. "Three. All crazy."

"Women."

"Crazy women."

"Women."

"You're forgetting, Guitar, how Pilate got the gold in the first place. She waited in a cave with a dead man for three days to haul it out, and that was when she was twelve. If she did that at twelve to get it, what you think she'll do now when she's almost seventy to keep it?"

"We don't have to be rough. Cunning is all we need to be."

"Okay. Tell me how you gonna cunning them out of the house."

"Well, let's see now." Guitar stopped to scratch his back on a telephone pole. He closed his eyes, in either the ecstasy of relief or the rigors of concentration. Milkman stared off into the sky for inspiration, and while glancing toward the rooftops of the used-car places, he saw a white peacock poised on the roof of a long low building that served as headquarters for Nelson Buick. He was about to accept the presence of the bird as one of those waking dreams he was subject to whenever indecisiveness was confronted with reality, when Guitar opened his eyes and said, "Goddam! Where'd that come from?"

Milkman was relieved. "Must of come from the zoo."

"That raggedy-ass zoo? Ain't nothing in there but two tired monkeys and some snakes."

"Well, where then?"

"Beats me."

"Look—she's flying down." Milkman felt again his unrestrained joy at anything that could fly. "Some jive flying, but look at her strut."

"He."

"Huh?"

"He. That's a he. The male is the only one got that tail full of jewelry. Son of a bitch. Look at that." The peacock opened its tail wide. "Let's catch it. Come on, Milk," and Guitar started to run toward the fence.

"What for?" asked Milkman, running behind him. "What we gonna do if we catch him?"

"Eat him!" Guitar shouted. He swung easily over the double pipes that bordered the lot and began to circle the bird at a distance, holding his head a little to the side to fool the peacock, which was strutting around a powder-blue Buick. It closed its tail and let the tips trail in the gravel. The two men stood still, watching.

"How come it can't fly no better than a chicken?" Milkman asked.

"Too much tail. All that jewelry weighs it down. Like vanity. Can't nobody fly with all that shit. Wanna fly, you got to give up the shit that weighs you down."

The peacock jumped onto the hood of the Buick and once more spread its tail, sending the flashy Buick into oblivion.

"Faggot." Guitar laughed softly. "White faggot."

Milkman laughed too, and they watched a while more before leaving the used cars and the pure white peacock.

But the bird had set them up. Instead of continuing the argument about how they would cop, they began to fantasize about what the gold could buy when it became legal tender. Guitar, eschewing his recent asceticism, allowed himself the pleasure of waking up old dreams: what he would buy for his grandmother and her brother, Uncle Billy, the one who had come up from Florida to help raise them all after his father died; the marker he would buy for his father's grave, "pink with lilies carved on it"; then stuff for his brother and sisters, and his sisters' children. Milkman fantasized too, but not for the stationary things Guitar described. Milkman wanted boats, cars, airplanes, and the command of a large crew. He would be whimsical, generous, mysterious with his money. But all the time he was laughing and going on about what he would do and how he planned to live, he was aware of a falseness in his voice. He wanted the money—desperately, he believed—but other than making tracks out of the city, far away from Not Doctor Street, and Sonny's Shop, and Mary's Place, and Hagar, he could not visualize a life that much different from the one he had. New people. New places. Command. That was what he wanted in his life. And he couldn't get deep into Guitar's talk of elegant clothes for himself and his brother, sumptuous meals for Uncle Billy, and week-long card games in which the stakes would be a yard and a half and then a deuce and a quarter. He screamed and shouted "Wooeeeee!" at Guitar's list, but because his life was not unpleasant and even had a certain amount of luxury in addition to its comfort, he felt off center. He just wanted to beat a path away from his parents' past, which was also their present and which was threatening to become his present as well. He hated the acridness in his mother's and father's relationship, the conviction of righteousness they each held on to with both hands. And his efforts to ignore it, transcend it, seemed to work only when he spent his days looking for whatever was light-hearted and without grave consequences. He avoided commitment and strong feelings, and shied away from decisions. He wanted to know as little as possible, to feel only enough to get through the day amiably and to be interesting enough to warrant the curiosity of other people— but not their all-consuming devotion. Hagar had given him this last and more drama than he could ever want again. He'd always believed his childhood was sterile, but the knowledge Macon and Ruth had given him wrapped his memory of it in septic sheets, heavy with the odor of illness, misery, and unforgiving hearts. His rebellions, minor as they were, had all been in the company of, or shared with, Guitar. And this latest Jack and the Beanstalk bid for freedom, even though it had been handed to him by his father—assigned almost—stood some chance of success.

He had half expected his friend to laugh at him, to refuse with some biting comment that would remind Milkman that Guitar was a mystery man now, a man with blood-deep responsibilities. But when he watched Guitar's face as he described what could be had almost for the asking, he knew right away he hadn't guessed wrong. Maybe the professional assassin had had enough, or had changed his mind. Had he . . . ? "Did you . . . ?" As he listened to him go over each detail of meals, clothes, tombstones, he wondered if Guitar simply could not resist the lure of something he had never had—money.

Guitar smiled at the sun, and talked lovingly of televisions, and brass beds, and week-long card games, but his mind was on the wonders of TNT.

By the time they'd exhausted their imaginative spending, it was almost noon and they were back on the edge of Southside. They picked up where they'd left off in the discussion of the scheme. Guitar was ready now; Milkman was still cautious. Too cautious for Guitar.

"I don't understand you. You come running after me with a dynamite proposition, and for three days we talk about it, the best news I've had since pussy, but when we get down to business, you come up with some shit about how it can't be done. You shucking me or what?"

"What would I be shucking for? I didn't have to tell you about it."

"I don't know. I don't even know why you doing it. You know about me—you can guess why I'm in it. But money ain't never been what you needed or couldn't get."

Milkman ignored the reference to why Guitar was "in it," and said as calmly as he could, "I need it to get away. I told you, man. I got to get out of here. Be on my own."

"On *your* own? With a million-dollar wallet, you call that on your own?"

"Fuck you. What difference does it make why I want it?"

"Cause I'm not sure you do want it. At least not bad enough to go ahead and cop."

"I just want it right. No hassles. No . . . You know, burglary is a serious crime. I don't want to end up in—"

"What burglary? This ain't no burglary. This is Pilate."

"So?"

"So! They're your people."

"They're still people, and people scream."

"What's the worst? What's the worst thing can happen? We

bust in, right? Suppose all three of them are there. They're women. What can they do? Whip us?"

"Maybe."

"Come on! Who? Hagar? Right up in your face she blows it. Pilate? She loves you, boy. She wouldn't touch you."

"You believe that?"

"Yeah, I believe it! Look. You got qualms, tell me about them. Because you related? Your daddy's more related than you are, and it's his idea."

"It's not that."

"Then what?"

"They're crazy, Guitar. Nobody knows what they'll do; *they* don't even know."

"I know they're crazy. Anybody live like they do, selling fifty-cent wine and peeing in a bucket, with one million dollars hanging over their nappy heads, has to be. You scared of craziness? If you are, *you're* crazy."

"I don't want to be caught, that's all. I don't want to do time. I want to plan it so neither one happens. How come that's too much to ask? To plan."

"It don't look like planning. Looks like stalling."

"It is planning. Planning how to get them out the house. How to get us in the house. How to cut that sack off the ceiling and then get back out the house and on down the street. And it's hard to plan with them. They're not regular. They don't have regular habits. And then there's the wineheads. One of them liable to drop in any old time. They're not clock people, Guitar. I don't believe Pilate knows how to tell time except by the sun."

"They sleep at night."

"Anybody sleep can wake up."

"Anybody woke up can be knocked down."

"I don't want to knock nobody down. I want them gone when we hit."

"And what's gonna make them leave?"

Milkman shook his head. "An earthquake, maybe."

"Then let's make an earthquake."

"How?"

"Set the house on fire. Put a skunk in there. A bear. Something. Anything."

"Be serious, man."

"I'm trying, baby. I'm trying. Don't they go nowhere?"

"All together?"

"All together."

Milkman shrugged. "Funerals. They go to funerals. And circuses."

"Oh, man! We have to wait for somebody to die? Or for Ringling Brothers to come to town?"

"I'm trying to figure it out is all. At the moment we don't have a chance."

"Well, if a man don't *have* a chance, then he has to *take* a chance!"

"Be reasonable."

"Reasonable? You can't get no pot of gold being reasonable. Can't nobody get no gold being reasonable. You have to be unreasonable. How come you don't know that?"

"Listen to me. . . ."

"I just quit listening. You listen! You got a life? Live it! Live the motherfuckin life! Live it!"

Milkman's eyes opened wide. He tried hard not to swallow, but the clarion call in Guitar's voice filled his mouth with salt. The same salt that lay in the bottom of the sea and in the sweat of a horse's neck. A taste so powerful and necessary that stallions galloped miles and days for it. It was new, it was delicious, and it was his own. All the tentativeness, doubt, and inauthenticity that plagued him slithered away without a trace, a sound.

Now he knew what his hesitation had been all about. It was not to give an unnatural complexity to a simple job; nor was it to keep Guitar on hold. He had simply not believed in it before. When his father told him that long story, it really seemed like Jack and the Beanstalk . . . some fairy tale mess. He hadn't believed it was really there, or really gold, or that he could really have it just for the taking. It was too simple. But Guitar believed it, gave it a crisp concreteness, and what's more, made it into an act, an important, real, and daring thing to do. He felt a self inside himself emerge, a clean-lined definite self. A self that could join the chorus at Railroad Tommy's with more than laughter. He could tell this. The only other real confrontation he'd had was hitting his father, but that wasn't the kind of story that stirred the glitter up in the eyes of the old men in Tommy's.

Milkman didn't think through any of this clearly. He only tasted the salt and heard the hunter's horn in Guitar's voice.

"Tomorrow," he said. "Tomorrow night."

"What time?"

"One-thirty. I'll pick you up."

"Beautiful."

Far down the road, a long way from Milkman and Guitar, the peacock spread its tail.

On autumn nights, in some parts of the city, the wind from the lake brings a sweetish smell to shore. An odor like crystallized ginger, or sweet iced tea with a dark clove floating in it. There is no explanation for the smell either, since the lake, on September 19, 1963, was so full of mill refuse and the chemical wastes of a plastics manufacturer that the hair of the willows that stood near the shore was thin and pale. Carp floated belly up onto the beach, and the doctors at Mercy knew, but did not announce, that ear infections were a certainty for those who swam in those waters.

Yet there was this heavy spice-sweet smell that made you think of the East and striped tents and the *sha-sha-sha* of leg bracelets. The people who lived near the lake hadn't noticed the smell for a long time now because when air conditioners came, they shut their windows and slept a light surface sleep under the motor's drone.

So the ginger sugar blew unnoticed through the streets, around the trees, over roofs, until, thinned out and weakened a little, it reached Southside. There, where some houses didn't even have screens, let alone air conditioners, the windows were thrown wide open to whatever the night had to offer. And there the ginger smell was sharp, sharp enough to distort dreams and make the sleeper believe the things he hungered for were right at hand. To the Southside residents who were awake on such nights, it gave all their thoughts and activity a quality of being both intimate and far away. The two men standing near the pines on Darling Street—right near the brown house where wine drinkers went—could smell the air, but they didn't think of ginger. Each thought it was the way freedom smelled, or justice, or luxury, or vengeance.

Breathing the air that could have come straight from a marketplace in Accra, they stood for what seemed to them a very long time. One leaned against a tree, his foot hovering off the ground. Finally one touched the elbow of the other and they both moved toward an open window. With no trouble at all, they entered. Although they had stood deliberately in the dark of the pine trees, they were unprepared for the deeper darkness that met them there in that room. Neither had seen that kind of blackness, not even behind their own eyelids. More unsettling than the darkness, however, was the fact that in contrast to the heat outside (the slumbering ginger-laden heat that had people wiping sweat from their neck folds), it was as cold as ice in Pilate's house.

Suddenly the moon came out and shone like a flashlight right into the room. They both saw it at the same time. It hung heavy, hung green like the green of Easter eggs left too long in the dye. And like Easter, it promised everything: the Risen Son and the heart's lone desire. Complete power, total freedom, and perfect justice. Guitar knelt down before it and wove his fingers together into a footstep. Milkman hoisted himself up, one hand on Guitar's head, and shifted himself until he sat on Guitar's shoulders. Slowly Guitar stood up. Milkman felt upward along the sack until he found its neck. He thought the rope would have to be cut, and was annoyed to find the sack hung by wire instead.

He hoped the knife would be enough, because they hadn't figured on wire and had brought neither pincers nor a wire cutter. The sound of the grating knife filled the room. No one, he thought, could sleep through that. At last some few strands broke and it was only a moment before the entire blackness was severed. They'd figured on the weight of the sack being enough to tumble them the minute it was cut free, and planned that at a whispered signal, Guitar would bend his knees and sink down so Milkman's feet would hit the floor almost immediately. But there was no need for this graceful footwork; the bag was much lighter than they had anticipated, and Milkman made it down quite easily. As soon as they both regained balance, there was a huge airy sigh that each one believed was made by the other. Milkman handed his knife to Guitar, who closed it and tucked it in his back pocket. There was the deep sigh again and an even more piercing chill. Holding the sack by its neck and its bottom, Milkman followed Guitar to the window. Once Guitar had cleared the sill, he reached back to help Milkman over. The moonlight was playing tricks on him, for he thought he saw the figure of a man standing right behind his friend. Enveloped by the heat they'd left a few minutes earlier, they walked swiftly away from the house and out onto the road.

At another open window on the same side of the house, the one next to the sink where Hagar washed her hair and where Reba put pintos to soak, a woman's face appeared. "What the devil they want that for?" she wondered. Then she picked at the window sill until she had a splinter of wood and put it in her mouth.

# Chapter 9

Amanuensis. That was the word she chose, and since it was straight out of the nineteenth century, her mother approved, relishing the blank stares she received when she told her lady guests what position her daughter had acquired with the State Poet Laureate. "She's Michael-Mary Graham's amanuensis." The rickety Latin word made the work her daughter did (she, after all, wasn't required to work) sound intricate, demanding, and totally in keeping with her education. And the women didn't dare ask for further details (they tried to remember its sound, but still couldn't find it in the dictionary), for they were suitably impressed by the name of Michael-Mary Graham. It was a lie, of course, even as the simpler word "secretary" was a lie, but Ruth repeated it with confidence because she believed it was true. She did not know then, and never found out, that Corinthians was Miss Graham's maid.

Unfit for any work other than the making of red velvet roses, she had a hard time finding employment befitting her degree. The three years she had spent in college, a junior year in France, and being the granddaughter of the eminent Dr. Foster should have culminated in something more elegant than the two uniforms that hung on Miss Graham's basement door. That all these advantages didn't was still incredible to her. It had been assumed that she and Magdalene called Lena would marry well—but hopes for Corinthians were especially high since she'd gone to college. Her education had taught her how to be an enlightened mother and wife, able to contribute to the civilization—or in her case, the civilizing—of her community. And if marriage was not achieved, there were alternative roles: teacher, librarian, or . . . well, something intelligent and public-spirited. When neither of these fates tapped her on the forehead right away, she simply waited. High toned and high yellow, she believed what her mother was also convinced of: that she was a prize for a professional man of color. So there were vacations and weekends in other cities as well as visits and teas in her own, where and when such men appeared. The first of the black doctors to move there, in the forties when she graduated, had a son five years her junior. The second, a dentist, had two infant girls; the third was a very old physician (rumored to be an alcoholic), whose two sons were already raising families. Then there were teachers, two lawyers, a mortician—but on the few occasions when eligible bachelors were among them, Corinthians was not their choice. She was pretty enough, pleasant enough, and her father had the money they could rely on if needed, but she lacked drive. These men wanted wives who could manage, who were not so well accustomed to middle-class life that they had no ambition, no hunger, no hustle in them. They wanted their wives to like the climbing, the acquiring, and the work it took to maintain status once it was achieved. They wanted wives who would sacrifice themselves and appreciate the hard work and sacrifice of their husbands. Corinthians was a little too elegant. Bryn Mawr in 1940. France in 1939. That was a bit much. Fisk, Howard, Talledega, Tougaloo—that was their hunting territory. A woman who spoke French and who had traveled on the *Queen Mary* might not have the proper attitude toward future patients or clients, and if the man was a teacher, he steered clear of a woman who had a better education than he did. At one point post office workers were even being considered suitable for Lena and Corinthians, but that was long after they had reached thirty-five, and after Ruth came to terms with the savage fact that her daughters were not going to marry doctors. It was a shock to them all, which they managed to withstand by not accepting a more complete truth: that they probably were not going to marry anybody.

Magdalene called Lena seemed resigned to her life, but when Corinthians woke up one day to find herself a forty-two-year-old maker of rose petals, she suffered a severe depression which lasted until she made up her mind to get out of the house. So her search for work—which was shock number two—was intense. The twenty-one years that she had been out of college worked against her for a teaching job. She had none of the "new" courses now required by the board of education. She considered going to the state teachers' school to take the required courses, even went to the administration building to register. But the sight of those torpedo breasts under fuzzy blue sweaters, the absolute nakedness of those young faces, drove her out of the building and off the campus like a leaf before a hailstorm. Which was too bad, because she had no real skills. Bryn Mawr had done what a four-year dose of liberal education was designed to do: unfit her for eighty percent of the useful work of the world. First, by training her for leisure time, enrichments, and domestic mindlessness. Second, by a clear implication that she was too good for such work. After graduation she returned to a work world in which colored girls, regardless of their background, were in demand for one and only one kind of work. And by 1963, Corinthians' main concern was simply that her family not know that she had been doing it for two years.

She avoided the other maids on the street, and those whom she saw regularly on the bus assumed that she had some higher household position than theirs since she came to work in high-heeled shoes and only a woman who didn't have to be on her feet all day could stand the pressure of heels on the long ride home. Corinthians was careful; she carried no shopping bag of shoes, aprons, or uniforms. Instead she had a book. A small gray book on which *Contes de Daudet* was printed in gold lettering on its cover. Once she was inside Miss Graham's house she changed into her uniform (which was a discreet blue anyway, not white) and put on a pair of loafers before she dropped to her knees with the pail of soapy water.

Miss Graham was delighted with Corinthians' dress and slightly uppity manners. It gave her house the foreign air she liked to affect, for she was the core, the very heartbeat, of the city's literary world. Michael-Mary Graham was very considerate of Corinthians. When she had large dinner parties, a Swedish cook was hired and the heavy work was done by the old white rummy she shared with the Goodwill Industries. Nor was she impatient with Corinthians' undistinguished everyday cooking, for Michael-Mary ate several small plain meals. It was also a pleasure and a relief to have a maid who read and who seemed to be acquainted with some of the great masters of literature. So nice to give a maid a copy of *Walden* for Christmas rather than that dreary envelope, and to be able to say so to her friends. In the world Michael-Mary Graham inhabited, her mild liberalism, a residue of her Bohemian youth, and her posture of sensitive lady poet passed for anarchy.

Corinthians was naïve, but she was not a complete fool. She never let her mistress know she had ever been to college or Europe or could recognize one word of French that Miss Graham had not taught her (*entrez*, for example). Actually, the work Corinthians did was good for her. In that house she had what she never had in her own: responsibility. She flourished in a way, and exchanged arrogance occasionally for confidence. The humiliation of wearing a uniform, even if it was blue, and deceiving people was tempered by the genuine lift which came of having her own money rather than receiving an allowance like a child. And she was surprised to discover that the amount of neatly folded bills Michael-Mary handed her each Saturday at noon was within two dollars of the amount real secretaries took home each week.

Other than scrubbing the kitchen tile and keeping a hard shine on the wooden floors, the work was not hard. The poetess lived alone and shaped her time and activities carefully in order to meet the heavy demands of artistic responsibility. Being a poet she could, of course, do little else. Marriage, children—all had been sacrificed to the Great Agony and her home was a tribute to the fastidiousness of her dedication (and the generosity of her father's will). Colors, furnishings, and appointments had been selected for their inspirational value. And she was fond of saying, in deprecating some item, "I couldn't write a line with *that* in the house." *That* might be a vase, the new toilet bowl the plumbers hauled in, a plant, or even the Christmas wreath St. John's third-grade class presented to her in gratitude for the moving reading she'd given at their holiday assembly. Every morning between ten and noon she wrote, and every afternoon between three and four-fifteen. Evenings were often given over to discussions and meetings with local poets, painters, musicians, and writers of fiction, at which they praised or condemned other artists, scorned the marketplace and courted it. Of this group Michael-Mary Graham was the queen, for her poetry had been published—first in 1938, in a volume called *Seasons of My Soul;* there was a second collection in 1941, called *Farther Shores.* What was more, her poems had appeared in at least twenty small literary magazines, two "slicks," six college journals, and the Sunday supplements of countless newspapers. She was also the winner, between 1938 and 1958, of nine Poet of the Year awards, culminating finally in the much-coveted State Poet Laureateship. At the ceremony, her most famous poem, "Watchword," was performed by the Choral Speech Society of St. John's High School. None of that, however, had mitigated the reluctance of her publishers to bring out her complete collected works (tentatively called *The Farthest Shore*). But there was no question in her mind that they would come around.

When Miss Graham first saw Corinthians, she was not at all

impressed with her. First, because the prospective employee came ten minutes early for the interview and Michael-Mary, who adhered to her schedule to the minute, was forced to answer the door in a print peignoir. Already irritated by this lapse, she was further disenchanted by the woman's delicate frame. Obviously she could not put up the screens, take down the storm windows, or endure any sustained heavy cleaning. But when she learned the woman's name, Michael-Mary was so charmed by the sound of "Corinthians Dead," she hired her on the spot. As she told friends later, her poetic sensibility overwhelmed her good judgment.

They got on well together, mistress and maid, and by the sixth month of her stay, Michael-Mary suggested that she learn how to type. So Corinthians was almost on her way to becoming an amanuensis after all.

Shortly after Miss Graham encouraged her to take typing so she might be helpful with some of her mistress's work, a black man sat down next to Corinthians on the bus. She took little notice of him—only that he was ill-dressed and appeared elderly. But soon she became aware that he was staring at her. A quick corner-of-the-eye peek to verify this was met by his radiant smile. Corinthians turned her head and kept it so until he got off.

The next day he was there again. Once more she made her disdain clear. The rest of the week passed without his watchful eyes. But on the following Monday he was back, looking at her with an expression that stopped just short of a leer. These occasional meetings went on for a month or so. Corinthians thought she should be afraid of him, for something in his manner suggested waiting—a confident, assured waiting. Then one morning he dropped a white envelope on the seat beside her just before he got off the bus. She let it lie there all the way to her stop, but couldn't resist scooping it up as surreptitiously as possible when she stood to pull the cord.

Standing at the stove, waiting for Michael-Mary's milk to skim, she opened the envelope and withdrew a greeting card.

Raised letters of the word "Friendship" hung above a blue and yellow bouquet of flowers and were repeated inside above a verse.

> *Friendship is an outstretched hand,*
> *A smile of warm devotion.*
> *I offer both to you this day,*
> *With all the heart's emotion.*

A white hand of no particular sex held another, smaller, blue and yellow bouquet. There was no signature.

Corinthians threw it in the brown paper bag opened for the day's garbage. It stayed there all day, but it also stayed on her mind. When evening came, she reached down through the grapefruit rind, the tea leaves, and the salami casing to find it, brush it clean, and transfer it to her purse. She couldn't explain to herself why. The man was a complete nuisance and his flirtation an insult. But no one, not anyone at all, had made any attempt (any serious attempt) to flirt with her in a long time. At the very least the card was good for conversation. She wished he had signed it, not because she wanted to know his name, but so it would look more authentic—otherwise somebody might think she bought it herself.

For two weeks afterward the man was not on the bus. When he did appear, it was hard for Corinthians not to speak or acknowledge his presence. As they neared the place where he usually got off, he leaned over to her and said, "I truly hope you didn't mind." She looked up, gave him a small smile, and shook her head. He said nothing more.

But on subsequent days they did exchange greetings and finally they began to talk. In a while they were chatting (carefully, guardedly) and she, at least, was looking forward to his being there. By the time she knew that his name was Henry Porter and that he had occasional yard work in that part of town, she was glad she had never shown or mentioned either the card or the man to anyone.

Pleasant as their conversations were, they were also curious.

Each took care not to ask the other certain questions—for fear he or she would have to volunteer the same information. What part of town do you live in? Do you know Mr. So-and-so?

Eventually Mr. Porter offered to pick Corinthians up after work. He didn't own a car, he said, but borrowed a friend's sometimes. Corinthians agreed, and the result was a pair of middle-aged lovers who behaved like teen-agers—afraid to be caught by their parents in a love relationship they were too young for. He took her for rides in an old gray Oldsmobile—to the country, to drive-in movies—and they sat over bad coffee in certain dime stores where they were not likely to be recognized.

Corinthians knew she was ashamed of him, that she would have to add him to the other secret, the nature of her work, that he could never set foot in her house. And she hated him a lot for the shame she felt. Hated him sometimes right in the middle of his obvious adoration of her, his frequent compliments about her looks, her manners, her voice. But those swift feelings of contempt never lasted long enough for her to refuse those drive-in movie sessions where she was the sole object of someone's hunger and satisfaction.

At some point Corinthians began to suspect that Porter's discretion was not only in deference to who she was (her position and all), but also because he too didn't want to be discovered. Her first thought was that he was married. His denials, accompanied by a wistful smile which she interpreted as a sly one, only aggravated her suspicions. Finally, to prove his bachelorhood as well as to indulge himself in a real bed, he invited her to his room. She declined immediately and repeatedly for several days until he accused her of the very thing that was absolutely true: that she was ashamed of him.

"Ashamed of you?" Her eyes and mouth went wide with surprise (genuine surprise, because she never thought he would guess it). "If I were ashamed I wouldn't see you at all, let alone *this* way." Her hand pointed toward the world outside the car they sat in: the row upon row of automobiles in the hot drive-in movie lot.

Porter traced her cheek line with his knuckle. "Well, then? The things you tell me can't be true and not true at the same time."

"I've never told you anything except what was true. I thought we both knew . . . understood . . . the problem."

"Maybe," he said. "Let's hear it, Corrie." His knuckles stroked her jaw line. "Let's hear the problem."

"My father. It's only my father . . . the way he is."

"How is he?"

Corinthians shrugged. "You know as well as I do. He never wanted us to mix with . . . people. He's very strict."

"And that's the reason you won't come home with me?"

"I'm sorry. I have to live there. I can't let him know about us. Not yet." But when? she thought. If not at forty-four, then when? If not now, when even my pubic hair is turning gray and when my breasts have dropped of their own accord—then when?

Porter spoke her own question aloud. "When, then?" And she could not answer him right away. She put her fingers to her forehead and said, "I don't know. I honestly don't know."

It was such a fake gesture to go along with her fake feelings of moral and filial commitment that she knew right away how foolish she seemed. The things they did in that old car, the things she'd let her tongue say, as recently as five minutes ago . . . and now to caress her temples and say in Michael-Mary's reading voice, "I don't know," embarrassed her and must have disgusted Porter, for he took his hand from her face and put it on the steering wheel. Right at the beginning of the second feature, he started the car and moved it slowly down the gravel aisle.

Neither spoke until the car entered downtown traffic. It was ten-thirty. She'd told her mother she would be typing manuscript for Miss Graham until very late. "In this heat?" was all her mother said. Corinthians sat quietly, feeling shame but not thinking the word, until she realized that he was driving her to the bus stop where he always let her out to walk home the way she normally would. In a sudden flash she knew he was never going to see her again, and the days rolled out before her like a dingy gray carpet in an unfurnished, unpeopled hall-for-rent.

"Are you taking me home?" She succeeded in keeping the anxiety out of her voice—succeeded too well, for her words sounded arrogant and careless.

He nodded and said, "I don't want a doll baby. I want a woman. A grown-up woman that's not scared of her daddy. I guess you don't want to be a grown-up woman, Corrie."

· She stared through the windshield. A grown-up woman? She tried to think of some. Her mother? Lena? The dean of women at Bryn Mawr? Michael-Mary? The ladies who visited her mother and ate cake? Somehow none of them fit. She didn't know any grown-up women. Every woman she knew was a doll baby. Did he mean like the women who rode on the bus? The other maids, who were not hiding what they were? Or the black women who walked the streets at night?

"You mean like those women on the bus? You can have one of *them*, you know. Why don't you drop a greeting card in one of *their* laps?" His words had hit home; she had been compared —unfavorably, she believed—with the only people she knew for certain she was superior to. "They'd love to have a greeting card dropped in their lap. Just love it. But oh, I forgot. You couldn't do that, could you, because they wouldn't be able to read it. They'd have to take it home and wait till Sunday and give it to the preacher to read it to them. Of course when they heard it they might not know what it meant. But it wouldn't matter— they'd see the flowers and the curlicues all over the words and they'd be happy. It wouldn't matter a bit that it was the most ridiculous, most clichéd, most commercial piece of tripe the drugstore world has to offer. They wouldn't know mediocrity if it punched them right in their fat faces. They'd laugh and slap their fat thighs and take you right on into their kitchens. Right up on the breakfast table. But you wouldn't give them a fifteen-cent greeting card, would you?—no matter how silly and stupid it was—because they're grown-up women and you don't have to court *them*. You can just come right out and say, 'Hello there, come on to my room tonight.' Right? Isn't that so? Isn't that so?" She was close to screaming. "But no. You wanted a lady. Somebody who knows how to sit down, how to dress, how to eat the food on her plate. Well, there is a difference between a woman and a lady, and I know you know which one I am."

Porter pulled the car over to the curb, and without shutting off the motor, leaned across her and opened the door. Corinthians got out and did her best to slam it, but the rusty hinges of the borrowed Oldsmobile did not accommodate her. She had to settle for the gesture.

By the time she reached number 12 Not Doctor Street, her trembling had become uncontrollable. Suddenly the shaking stopped and she froze at the steps. Two seconds later she turned on her heel and ran back down the street to where Porter had stopped the car. The moment she had put her foot on the step leading up to the porch, she saw her ripeness mellowing and rotting before a heap of red velvet scraps on a round oak table. The car was still there, its motor purring. Corinthians ran toward it faster than she had ever run in her life, faster than she'd cut across the grass on Honoré Island when she was five and the whole family went there for a holiday. Faster even than the time she flew down the stairs having seen for the first time what the disease had done to her grandfather. She put her hand on the door handle and found it locked. Porter was sitting pretty much the way he was when she'd tried to slam the door. Bending down, she rapped on the window. Porter's profile did not move. She rapped again, louder, mindless of who might see her under the gray beech tree just around the corner from home. So close and yet so far, she felt as though she were in a dream; there, but not there, within a hair's breadth but not reaching it.

She was First Corinthians Dead, daughter of a wealthy property owner and the elegant Ruth Foster, granddaughter of the magnificent and worshipped Dr. Foster, who had been the second man in the city to have a two-horse carriage, and a woman who had turned heads on every deck of the *Queen Mary* and had Frenchmen salivating all over Paris. Corinthians Dead, who had held herself pure all these years (well, almost all, and almost pure), was now banging on the car-door window of a yardman. But she would bang forever to escape the velvet. The red velvet that had flown all over the snow that day when she and Lena and her mother had walked past the hospital on their way to the department store. Her mother was pregnant—a fact that had embarrassed Corinthians when first she learned of it. All she could think of was how her friends would laugh when they found out she had a pregnant mother. Her relief was sweet when she discovered that it was too soon to show. But by February her mother was heavy and needed to get out of the house, to exercise a little. They'd walked slowly through the snow, watching carefully for icy places. Then as they passed Mercy, there was a crowd watching a man on the roof. Corinthians had seen him before her mother did, but when Ruth looked up she was so startled she dropped the basket, scattering the roses everywhere. Corinthians and Lena busied themselves picking them up, wiping the snow from the cloth on their coats, all the while peeping at the man in blue wings on the hospital roof. They were laughing, Lena and she; collecting the roses, looking up at the man, and laughing from fear, embarrassment, and giddiness. It was all mixed together—the red velvet, the screams, and the man crashing down on the pavement. She had seen his body quite clearly, and to her astonishment, there was no blood. The only red in view was in their own hands and in the basket. Her mother's moans were getting louder and she seemed to be sinking into the ground. A stretcher came at last for the doll-broken body (all the more doll-like because there was no blood), and finally a wheelchair for her mother, who was moving straight into labor.

Corinthians continued to make roses, but she hated that stupid hobby and gave Lena any excuse to avoid it. They spoke to her of death. First the death of the man in the blue wings. Now her own. For if Porter did not turn his head and lean toward the door to open it for her, Corinthians believed she would surely die. She banged her knuckles until they ached to get the attention of the living flesh behind the glass, and would have smashed her fist through the window just to touch him, feel his heat, the only thing that could protect her from a smothering death of dry roses.

He did not move. In a panic, lest he shift gears and drive away, leaving her alone in the street, Corinthians climbed up on the fender and lay full out across the hood of the car. She didn't look through the windshield at him. She just lay there, stretched across the car, her fingers struggling for a grip on steel. She thought of nothing. Nothing except what her body needed to do to hang on, to never let go. Even if he drove off at one hundred miles an hour, she would hang on. Her eyes were shut tight with the effort of clinging to the hood, and she didn't hear the door open and shut, nor Porter's footsteps as he moved around to the front of the car. She screamed at first when he put his hand on her shoulders and began pulling her gently into his arms. He carried her to the passenger's side of the car, stood her on her feet while he opened the door and helped her ease into the seat. In the car, he pressed her head onto his shoulder and waited for her soft crying to wane before he left the driver's seat to pick up the purse she had let fall on the sidewalk. He drove away then to number 3 Fifteenth Street, a house owned by Macon Dead, where sixteen tenants lived, and where there was an attic window, from which this same Henry Porter had screamed, wept, waved a shotgun, and urinated over the heads of the women in the yard.

It was not yet midnight and hot—hot enough to make people angry, had it not been for a pleasant smell in the air, like sweet ginger. Corinthians and Porter entered the hall that opened off the front door. Except for a hem of light under the kitchen door, where a card game was in progress, there was no sign of any other tenant.

Corinthians saw only the bed, an iron bed painted hospital white. She sank down on it as soon as she got into the room and stretched out, feeling bathed, scoured, vacuumed, and for the first time simple. Porter undressed after she did and lay down beside her. They were quiet for a minute, then he turned over and parted her legs with his.

Corinthians looked down at him. "Is this for me?" she asked.

"Yes," he said. "Yes, this is for you."

"Porter."

"This is . . . for you. Instead of roses. And silk underwear and bottles of perfume."

"Porter."

"Instead of chocolate creams in a heart-shaped box. Instead of a big house and a great big car. Instead of long trips . . ."

"Porter."

". . . in a clean white boat."

"No."

"Instead of picnics . . ."

"No."

". . . and fishing . . ."

"No."

". . . and being old together on a porch."

"No."

"This is for you, girl. Oh, yes. This is for you."

They woke at four o'clock in the morning, or rather she did. When she opened her eyes she saw him staring at her and those were either tears in his eyes or sweat. It was very hot in that room in spite of the open window.

"The bathroom," she murmured. "Where is the bathroom?"

"Down the hall," he said. Then, apologetically, "Can I get you something?"

"Oh." She pushed a few strands of matted damp hair from her forehead. "Something to drink, please. Something cold."

He dressed quickly, leaving off his shirt and his socks, and left the room. Corinthians got up too and began to put her clothes on. Since there seemed to be no mirror in the room, she stood in front of the open window and used the upper part of the pane, dark enough to show her reflection, to smooth her hair. Then she noticed the walls. What she had assumed to be wallpaper as she entered and fell on the bed was in fact calendars. Row after row of calendars: S. &. J. Automobile Parts, featuring a 1939 Hudson; the Cuyahoga River Construction Company ("We build to please—We're pleased to build"); Lucky Hart Beauty Products (a wavy-haired lady smiling out of a heavily powdered face); the *Call and Post* newspaper. But most of them were from the North Carolina Mutual Life Insurance Company. They literally covered the walls, each one turned to December. It was as though he'd kept every calendar since 1939. Some of them were large cards displaying all twelve months and on those she noticed circles drawn around dates.

Porter came in while she was gazing at them. He held a glass of iced water, the cubes jammed to the rim.

"Why do you keep calendars?" she asked.

He smiled. "Passes the time. Here. Drink your drink. It'll cool you."

She took the glass and sipped a little from it, trying to keep the ice from touching her teeth as she looked at him over the rim. Standing there, barefoot, her hair damp with sweat and sticking to her cheeks like paint, she felt easy. In place of vanity she now felt a self-esteem that was quite new. She was grateful to him, this man who rented a tiny room from her father, who ate with a knife and did not even own a pair of dress shoes. A perfect example of the men her parents had kept her from (and whom she had also kept herself from) all her life because such a man was known to beat his woman, betray her, shame her, and leave her. Corinthians moved close to him, tilted his chin up with her fingers, and planted a feathery kiss on his throat. He held her head in his hands until she closed her eyes and tried to set the glass down on a tiny table.

"Uh uh. It'll be light soon. Gotta get you home."

She obeyed and finished dressing herself. They walked as softly as possible down the stairs and past the wide triangle of light that lay on the floor in front of the kitchen door. The men were still at their card game, but the door was partially open now. Porter and Corinthians moved quickly past, just out of the light.

Still a voice called, "Who that? Mary?"

"No. Just me. Porter."

"Porter?" The voice was incredulous. "What shift you on?"

"Catch you later," said Porter and opened the front door before the speaker's curiosity could propel him into the hall.

Corinthians slid as close to Porter as the floor gear of the car allowed, her head resting on the seat back. She closed her eyes once more and took deep breaths of the sweet air her brother had been inhaling three hours ago.

"Hadn't you better fix your hair?" Porter asked. He thought she was beautiful like that, girlish, but he didn't want her excuse to her parents, if they were still awake, to sound ridiculous.

She shook her head. She wouldn't have collected her hair into a ball at her nape now for anything in the world.

Porter parked under the same tree where Corinthians had thrown herself across the hood of the car. Now, after a whispered confession, she walked the four blocks, no longer afraid to mount the porch steps.

As soon as she closed the door she heard voices and instinctively touched her loose hair. The voices came from beyond the dining room, from behind the closed kitchen door. Men's voices. Corinthians blinked. She had just come from a house in which men sat in a lit kitchen talking in loud excited voices, only to meet an identical scene at home. She wondered if this part of the night, a part she was unfamiliar with, belonged, had always belonged, to men. If perhaps it was a secret hour in which men rose like giants from dragon's teeth and, while the women slept, clustered in their kitchens. On tiptoe she approached the door. Her father was speaking.

"You still haven't explained to me why you brought him along."

"What difference does it make now?" That was her brother's voice.

"He knows about it," said her father. "That's what difference."

"About what? There's nothing to know. It was a bust." Milkman's voice swelled like a blister.

"It was a mistake, not a bust. It just means it's somewhere else. That's all."

"Yeah. The mint. You want me to go to the mint?"

"No!" Macon struck the table. "It's got to be there. It's got to."

Corinthians couldn't make sense out of what they were talking about with so much passion, and she didn't want to stay there and learn, lest it distract her from the contentment she was feeling. She left them and climbed the stairs to her own bed.

Downstairs in the kitchen, Milkman folded his arms on the table and put his head down. "I don't care. I don't care where it is."

"It was just a mistake," said his father. "One little mess-up. That don't mean we have to pull out."

"You call being thrown in jail a little mess-up?"

"You out, ain't you? You was only there twenty minutes."

"Two hours."

"Wouldn't have been two minutes if you had called me soon's you got there. Sooner. Should have called me soon's they picked you up."

"Police cars don't have telephones in them." Milkman was weary. He lifted his head and let it rest in his hand, directing his words into his shirt sleeve.

"They would have let you, if it had just been you. Soon as you told them your name they would have let you go. But you was with that Southside nigger. That's what did it."

"That is *not* what did it. It was riding around with a sack of rocks and human bones that did it. Human bones. Which is, if you're a halfway intelligent cop, a hint that there must have been a human being connected to them bones at one time."

"Of course at one time. But not tonight. There couldn't have been a human attached to the bones yesterday. It takes time for a body to be a skeleton. They know that. And don't tell me it wasn't Guitar they was suspicious of. That yellow-eyed nigger looks like he might do anything."

"They didn't see his eyes when they told us to pull over. They didn't see nothing. They just sideswiped us, and told us to get out. Now, what was that for? What'd they stop us for? We wasn't speeding. Just driving along." Milkman searched for cigarettes. He got angry again when he thought about bending over the car, his legs spread, his hands on the hood, while the policeman fingered his legs, his back, his ass, his arms. "What business they got stopping cars that ain't speeding?"

"They stop anybody they want to. They saw you was colored, that's all. And they're looking for the Negro that killed that boy."

"Who said it was a Negro?"

"Paper said it."

"They always say that. Every time . . ."

"What difference does it make? If you'd been alone and told them your name they never would have hauled you in, never would have searched the car, and never would have opened that sack. They know me. You saw how they acted when I got there."

"They didn't act any different when you got there. . . ."

"What?"

"They acted different when you took that sucker off in the corner and opened your wallet."

"You better be thankful I got a wallet."

"I am. God knows I am."

"And that would have been the end of it, except for that Southside nigger. Hadn't been for him, they wouldn't of had to get Pilate down there." Macon rubbed his knees. The idea of having to depend on Pilate to get his son out of jail humiliated him. "Raggedy bootlegging bitch."

"She's still a bitch?" Milkman began to chuckle. Exhaustion and the slow release of tension made him giddy. "You thought she stole it. All these years . . . all these years you've been holding that against her." He was laughing out right now. "How she sneaked out of some cave with a big bag of gold that must have weighed a hundred pounds over her shoulder, all over the country for fifty years and didn't spend none of it, just hung it from the ceiling like a fuckin sack of onions." Milkman put his head back and let the laughter fill the kitchen. Macon was silent. "Fifty years . . . You been thinking about that gold for fifty years! Oh, shit. This is some crazy shit. . . ." Tears of laughter were running from his eyes. "Crazy. All of you. Just straight-out, laid-back crazy. I should of known. The whole thing was crazy; everything about it was crazy—the whole idea."

"What's crazier? Her hauling a sack of gold around all this time, or hauling a dead man's bones around? Huh? Which one?" Macon asked.

"I don't know. I really don't know."

"If she do one, she could do the other. She's the one they should have kept. When you all told them the bones belonged to her, they should have locked her up soon's she walked in the door."

Milkman wiped the tears on his sleeve. "Lock her up for what? After that story she told?" He started laughing again. "She came in there like Louise Beaver and Butterfly McQueen all rolled up in one. 'Yassuh, boss. Yassuh, boss. . . .'"

"She didn't say that."

"Almost. She even changed her voice."

"I told you she was a snake. Drop her skin in a split second."

"She didn't even look the same. She looked short. Short and pitiful."

"That's cause she wanted it back. She wanted them to let her have the bones back."

"Her poor husband's bones, that she didn't have no money to bury. Pilate got a husband somewhere?"

"Does the Pope?"

"Well, she got 'em back. They gave 'em to her."

"She knew what she was doing, all right."

"Yeah, she knew. But how did she know so fast? I mean she came in there . . . you know . . . prepared. She had it all to-gether when she got there. Cop must have told her everything when he picked her up and brought her to the station."

"Uh uh. They don't do that."

"Then how did she know?"

"Who knows what Pilate knows?"

Milkman shook his head. "Only The Shadow knows." He was still amused, but earlier, when he and Guitar had sat hand-cuffed on a wooden bench, his neck skin had crawled with fear.

"White man's bones," Macon said. He stood up and yawned. The dark of the sky was softened now. "Nigger bitch roaming around with a white man's bones." He yawned again. "I'll never understand that woman. I'm seventy-two years old and I'm going to die not understanding one thing about her." Macon walked toward the kitchen door and opened it. Then he turned around and said to Milkman, "But you know what that means, don't you? If she took the white man's bones and left the gold, then the gold must still be there." He shut the door before his son could protest.

Well, it would rot there, thought Milkman. If anybody even mentions the word "gold," I'm going to have to take his teeth out. He sat on there in the kitchen, wishing for more coffee, but too tired to get up and fix it. In a minute his mother would be downstairs; she had got up when he and Macon had come in, but Macon sent her back upstairs. Milkman fished for another ciga-rette and watched dawn eclipse the electric light over the sink. It was a cheery sun, which suggested another hot day. But the stronger it got, the more desolate he became. Alone, without Macon, he let the events of the night come back to him—he remembered little things, details, and yet he wasn't sure these details had really happened. Perhaps he made them up. Pilate *had* been shorter. As she stood there in the receiving room of the jail, she didn't even come up to the sergeant's shoulder—and the sergeant's head barely reached Milkman's own chin. But Pilate was as tall as he was. When she whined to the policeman, verify-ing Milkman's and Guitar's lie that they had ripped off the sack as a joke on an old lady, she had to look up at him. And her hands were shaking as she described how she didn't know the sack was gone until the officer woke her up; that she couldn't imagine why anybody would want to run off with her husband's bones; that her husband had been lynched in Mississippi fifteen years ago, and that they wouldn't let her cut him down, and that she left town then and that when she went back the body had dropped off the rope of its own accord, so she collected it and tried to bury it, but the "funeral peoples" wanted fifty dollars for a coffin, and the carpenter wanted twelve-fifty for a pine box and she just didn't have no twelve dollars and fifty cents so she just carried what was left of Mr. Solomon (she always called him Mr. Solomon cause he was such a dignified colored man) and put it in a sack and kept it with her. "Bible say what so e'er the Lord hath brought together, let no man put asunder—Matthew Twenty-one: Two. We was bony fide and legal wed, suh," she pleaded. Even her eyes, those big sleepy old eyes, were small as she went on: "So I thought I just as well keep him near me and when I die they can put him in the same hole as me. We'll raise up to Judgment Day together. Hand in hand."

Milkman was astonished. He thought Pilate's only acquaintance with the Bible was the getting of names out of it, but she quoted it, apparently, verse and chapter. Furthermore, she had looked at Milkman and Guitar and Macon like she didn't know who exactly they were. In fact, when asked if she knew them, she pointedly said, "Not this man, here," looking at her brother, "but I do believe I've noticed this fella around the neighborhood." Here she motioned toward Guitar, who sat there like marble with the eyes of a dead man. Later, as Macon drove them all home—Pilate sitting in front, Guitar and himself in the back—Guitar never said a word. His anger was like heat shimmering out of his skin, making the hot air blowing in through the open window seem refreshing by comparison.

And again there was a change. Pilate was tall again. The top of her head, wrapped in a silk rag, almost touched the roof of the car, as did theirs. And her own voice was back. She spoke, but to Macon only, and nobody else spoke at all. In a conversational tone, like somebody picking up a story that had been interrupted in the telling, she told her brother something quite different from what she told the policemen.

"I spent that whole day and night in there, and when I looked out the next morning you was gone. I was scared I would run into you, but I didn't see hide nor hair of you. It was three years or more 'fore I went back. The winter it was. Snow was everywhere and I couldn't hardly find my way. I looked up Circe first, then went looking for the cave. It was a hard trek, I can tell you, and I was in frail condition. Snow piled up every which way. But you should of known better than to think I'd go back there for them little old bags. I wasn't stuttin 'em when I first laid eyes on 'em, I sure wasn't thinking about them three years later. I went cause Papa told me to. He kept coming to see me, off and on. Tell me things to do. First he just told me to sing, to keep on singing. 'Sing,' he'd whisper. 'Sing, sing.' Then right after Reba was born he came and told me outright: 'You just can't fly on off and leave a body,' he tole me. A human life is precious. You shouldn't fly off and leave it. So I knew right away what he meant cause he was right there when we did it. He meant that if you take a life, then you own it. You responsible for it. You can't get rid of nobody by killing them. They still there, and they yours now. So I had to go back for it. And I did find the cave. And there he was. Some wolves or something must have drug it cause it was right in the mouth of the cave, laying up, sitting up almost, on that very rock we slept on. I put him in my sack, piece by piece. Some cloth was still on him, but his bones was clean and dry. I've had it every since. Papa told me to, and he was right, you know. You can't take a life and walk off and leave it. Life is life. Precious. And the dead you kill is yours. They stay with you anyway, in your mind. So it's a better thing, a more better thing to have the bones right there with you wherever you go. That way, it frees up your mind."

Fucks up your mind, thought Milkman, fucks it up for good. He pulled himself up from the table. He had to get some sleep before he went looking for Guitar.

Staggering up the stairs, he remembered Pilate's back as she got out of the Buick—not bent at all under the weight of the sack. And he remembered how Guitar glared at her as she walked away from the car. When Macon dropped him off, he neither answered nor turned his head at Milkman's "See y' later."

Milkman woke at noon. Somebody had come into his room and placed a small fan on the floor near the foot of his bed. He listened to the whirring for a long time before he got up and went into the bathroom to fill the tub. He lay there in lukewarm water, still sweating, too hot and tired to soap himself. Every now and then he flicked water on his face, letting it wet his two-day-old beard. He wondered if he could shave without slicing his chin open. The tub was uncomfortable, too short for him to stretch out, though he remembered when he could almost swim in it. Now he looked down at his legs. The left one looked just as long as the other. His eyes traveled up his body. The touch of the policeman's hand was still there—a touch that made his flesh jump like the tremor of a horse's flank when flies light on it. And something more. Something like shame stuck to his skin. Shame at being spread-eagled, fingered, and handcuffed. Shame at having stolen a skeleton, like a kid on a Halloween trick-or-treat prank rather than a grown man making a hit. Shame at needing both his father and his aunt to get him off. Then more shame at seeing his father with an accommodating "we all understand how it is" smile—buckle before the policemen. But nothing was like the shame he felt as he watched and listened to Pilate. Not just her Aunt Jemima act, but the fact that she was both adept at it and willing to do it—for him. For the one who had just left her house carrying what he believed was her inheritance. It didn't matter that he also believed she had "stolen" it. . . . From whom? From a dead man? From his father, who was also stealing it? Then and now? He had stolen it too, and what's more, he had been prepared—at least he told himself he had been prepared—to knock her down if she had come into the room while he was in the act of stealing it. To knock down an old black lady who had cooked him his first perfect egg, who had shown him the sky, the blue of it, which was like her mother's ribbons, so that from then on when he looked at it, it had no distance, no remoteness, but was intimate, familiar, like a room that he lived in, a place where he belonged. She had told him stories, sung him songs, fed him bananas and corn bread and, on the first cold day of the year, hot nut soup. And if his mother was right, this old black lady—in her late sixties, but with the skin and agility of a teen-aged girl—had brought him into the world when only a miracle could have. It was this woman, whom he would have knocked senseless, who shuffled into the police station and did a little number for the cops—opening herself up wide for their amusement, their pity, their scorn, their mockery, their disbelief, their meanness, their whimsy, their annoyance, their power, their anger, their boredom—whatever would be useful to her and to himself.

Milkman sloshed his legs in the water. He thought again of how Guitar had looked at Pilate—the jeweled hatred in his eyes. He had no right to that look. Suddenly, Milkman knew the answer to the question he had never been able to ask Guitar. Guitar could kill, would kill, and probably had killed. The Seven Days was the consequence of this ability, but not its origin. No. He had no cause to look at her like that, Milkman thought, and heaving himself upright in the tub, he soaped himself hurriedly.

The September heat blasted him as soon as he got outside, and wiped out the pleasant effects of his bath. Macon had taken the Buick—age forced him to walk less—so Milkman went on foot to Guitar's house. As he rounded the corner, he noticed a familiar-looking gray Oldsmobile, a jagged crack in the rear window, parked in front of the house. Several men were inside and two were standing outside: Guitar and Railroad Tommy. Milkman slowed his steps. Tommy was talking, while Guitar nodded his head. Then the two men shook hands—a handshake Milkman had never seen before: first Tommy held Guitar's hand in both his own, then Guitar held Tommy's hand in his two. Tommy got in the car and Guitar dashed around the house to the side stairs that led to his room. The Oldsmobile—Milkman figured it was a 1953 or 1954 model—made a tight U-turn and headed toward him. When it passed by, all the occupants looked straight ahead. Porter was driving, with Empire State in the middle and Railroad Tommy on the far side, and in the back seat was Hospital Tommy and a man named Nero. Milkman didn't know the other man.

That must be *them*, he thought. His heart beat wildly. Six men, one of them Porter, and Guitar. Those are the Days. And that car. That was the car that let Corinthians off near the house sometimes. Milkman had first assumed his sister had an occasional lift home from her job. Later, since she never mentioned it, and also because she seemed quieter and rounder lately, he decided she was seeing some man on the sly. He thought it funny, sweet and a little sad. But now he knew that whoever she was seeing belonged to that car and belonged to the Seven Days. Foolish woman, he thought. Of all the people to pick. She was so silly. So silly. Jesus!

He wasn't up to Guitar now. He would see him later.


People behaved much better, were more polite, more understanding when Milkman was drunk. The alcohol didn't change him at all, but it had a tremendous impact on whomever he saw while he was under its influence. They looked better, never spoke above a whisper, and when they touched him, even to throw him out of the house party because he had peed in the kitchen sink, or when they picked his pockets as he dozed on a bench at the bus station, they were gentle, loving.

He stayed that way, swaying from light buzz to stoned, for two days and a night, and would have extended it to at least another day but for a sobering conversation with Magdalene called Lena, to whom he had not said more than four consecutive sentences since he was in the ninth grade.

She was waiting for him at the top of the stairs when he came home early one morning. Wrapped in a rayon robe and without her glasses, she looked unreal yet kind, like the man who had picked his pocket a short while ago.

"Come here. I want to show you something. Can you come in here for a minute?" She was whispering.

"Can't it wait?" He was kind too; and he was proud of the civility in his voice, considering how tired he was.

"No," she said. "No. You have to see it now. Today. Just look at it."

"Lena, I'm really beat out . . ." he began in sweet reasonableness.

"It won't take more'n a minute. It's important."

He sighed and followed her down the hall into her bedroom. She walked to the window and pointed. "Look down there."

In what seemed to him like elegant if slow motion, Milkman went to the window, parted the curtain, and followed her pointing finger with his eyes. All he saw was the lawn at the side of the house. Not a thing was moving there, but in the light of early day he thought he might have missed it.

"What?"

"That little maple. Right there." She pointed to a tiny maple tree about four feet high. "The leaves should be turning red now. September is almost over. But they're not; they're just shriveling and falling down green."

He turned to her and smiled. "You said it was important." He was not angry, not even irritated, and he enjoyed his equanimity.

"It is important. Very important." Her voice was soft; she kept on staring at the tree.

"Then tell me. I've got to go to work in a few minutes."

"I know. But you can spare me a minute, can't you?"

"Not to stare at a dead bush, I can't."

"It's not dead yet. But it will be soon. The leaves aren't turning this year."

"Lena, you been in the sherry?"

"Don't make fun of me," she said, and there was a hint of steel in her voice.

"But you have, haven't you?"

"You're not paying any attention to me."

"I am. I'm standing here listening to you tell me the news of the day—that a bush is dying."

"You don't remember it, do you?"

"Remember it?"

"You peed on it."

"I what?"

"You peed on it."

"Lena, maybe we can discuss this later. . . ."

"And on me."

"Uh . . . Lena, I have done some things in my life. Some things I don't feel too good about. But I swear to God I never peed on you."

"It was summer. The year Daddy had that Packard. We went for a ride and you had to go to the bathroom. Remember?"

Milkman shook his head. "No. I don't remember that."

"I took you. We were in the country and there was no place else to go. So they made me take you. Mama wanted to, but Daddy wouldn't let her. And he wouldn't go himself. Corinthians turned up her nose and refused outright, so they made me go. I had on heels too. I was a girl too, but they made me go. You and I had to slide down a little slope off the shoulder of the road. It was pretty back in there. I unbuttoned your pants and turned away so you could be private. Some purple violets were growing all over the grass, and wild jonquil. I picked them and took some twigs from a tree. When I got home I stuck them in the ground right down there." She nodded toward the window. "Just made a hole and stuck them in. I always liked flowers, you know. I was the one who started making artificial roses. Not Mama. Not Corinthians. Me. I loved to do it. It kept me . . . quiet. That's why they make those people in the asylum weave baskets and make rag rugs. It keeps them quiet. If they didn't have the baskets they might find out what's really wrong and . . . do something. Something terrible. After you peed on me, I wanted to kill you. I even tried to once or twice. In little ways:

leaving soap in your tub, things like that. But you never slipped and broke your neck, or fell down the stairs or anything." She laughed a little. "But then I saw something. The flowers I'd stuck in the ground, the ones you peed on—well, they died, of course, but not the twig. It lived. It's that maple. So I wasn't mad about it anymore—the pee, I mean—because the tree was growing. But it's dying now, Macon."

Milkman rubbed the corner of his eye with his ring finger. He was so sleepy. "Yeah, well, that was a helluva piss, wouldn't you say? You want me to give it another shot?"

Magdalene called Lena drew one hand out of the pocket of her robe and smashed it across his mouth. Milkman stiffened and made an incomplete gesture toward her. She ignored it and said, "As surely as my name is Magdalene, you are the line I will step across. I thought because that tree was alive that it was all right. But I forgot that there are all kinds of ways to pee on people."

"You listen here." Milkman was sober now and he spoke as steadily as he could. "I'm going to make some allowance for your sherry—up to a point. But you keep your hands off me. What is all this about peeing on people?"

"You've been doing it to us all your life."

"You're crazy. When have I ever messed over anybody in this house? When did you ever see me telling anybody what to do or giving orders? I don't carry no stick; I live and let live, you know that."

"I know you told Daddy about Corinthians, that she was seeing a man. Secretly. And—"

"I *had* to. I'd love for her to find somebody, but I *know* that man. I—I've been around him. And I don't think he . . ." Milkman stopped, unable to explain. About the Days, about what he suspected.

"Oh?" Her voice was thick with sarcasm. "You have somebody else in mind for her?"

"No."

"No? But he's Southside, and not good enough for her? It's good enough for you, but not for her, right?"

"Lena . . ."

"What do you know about somebody not being good enough for somebody else? And since when did you care whether Corinthians stood up or fell down? You've been laughing at us all your life. Corinthians. Mama. Me. Using us, ordering us, and judging us: how we cook your food; how we keep your house. But now, all of a sudden, you have Corinthians' welfare at heart and break her up from a man you don't approve of. Who are you to approve or disapprove anybody or anything? I was breathing air in the world thirteen years before your lungs were even formed. Corinthians, twelve. You don't know a single thing about either one of us—we made roses; that's all you knew —but now you know what's best for the very woman who wiped the dribble from your chin because you were too young to know how to spit. Our girlhood was spent like a found nickel on you. When you slept, we were quiet; when you were hungry, we cooked; when you wanted to play, we entertained you; and when you got grown enough to know the difference between a woman and a two-toned Ford, everything in this house stopped for you. You have yet to wash your own underwear, spread a bed, wipe the ring from your tub, or move a fleck of your dirt from one place to another. And to this day, you have never asked one of us if we were tired, or sad, or wanted a cup of coffee. You've never picked up anything heavier than your own feet, or solved a problem harder than fourth-grade arithmetic. Where do you get the *right* to decide our lives?"

"Lena, cool it. I don't want to hear it."

"I'll tell you where. From that hog's gut that hangs down between your legs. Well, let me tell you something, baby brother: you will need more than that. I don't know where you will get it or who will give it to you, but mark my words, you will need more than that. He has forbidden her to leave the house, made her quit her job, evicted the man, garnisheed his wages, and it is all because of you. You are exactly like him. Exactly. I didn't go to college because of him. Because I was afraid of what he might do to Mama. You think because you hit him once that we all believe you were protecting her. Taking her side. It's a lie. You were taking over, letting us know you had the right to tell her and all of us what to do."

She stopped suddenly and Milkman could hear her breathing. When she started up again, her voice had changed; the steel was gone and in its place was a drifting, breezy music. "When we were little girls, before you were born, he took us to the icehouse once. Drove us there in his Hudson. We were all dressed up, and we stood there in front of those sweating black men, sucking ice out of our handkerchiefs, leaning forward a little so as not to drip water on our dresses. There were other children there. Barefoot, naked to the waist, dirty. But we stood apart, near the car, in white stockings, ribbons, and gloves. And when he talked to the men, he kept glancing at us, us and the car. The car and us. You see, he took us there so they could see us, envy us, envy him. Then one of the little boys came over to us and put his hand on Corinthians' hair. She offered him her piece of ice and before we knew it, *he* was running toward us. He knocked the ice out of her hand into the dirt and shoved us both into the car. First he displayed us, then he splayed us. All our lives were like that: he would parade us like virgins through Babylon, then humiliate us like whores in Babylon. Now he has knocked the ice out of Corinthians' hand again. And you are to blame." Magdalene called Lena was crying. "You are to blame. You are a sad, pitiful, stupid, selfish, hateful man. I hope your little hog's gut stands you in good stead, and that you take good care of it, because you don't have anything else. But I want to give you notice." She pulled her glasses out of her pocket and put them on. Her eyes doubled in size behind the lenses and were very pale and cold. "I don't make roses anymore, and you have pissed your last in this house."

Milkman said nothing.

"Now," she whispered, "get out of my room."

Milkman turned and walked across the room. It was good advice, he thought. Why not take it? He closed the door.

# Part II

# Chapter 10

When Hansel and Gretel stood in the forest and saw the house in the clearing before them, the little hairs at the nape of their necks must have shivered. Their knees must have felt so weak that blinding hunger alone could have propelled them forward. No one was there to warn or hold them; their parents, chastened and grieving, were far away. So they ran as fast as they could to the house where a woman older than death lived, and they ignored the shivering nape hair and the softness in their knees. A grown man can also be energized by hunger, and any weakness in his knees or irregularity in his heartbeat will disappear if he thinks his hunger is about to be assuaged. Especially if the object of his craving is not gingerbread or chewy gumdrops, but gold.

Milkman ducked under the boughs of black walnut trees and walked straight toward the big crumbling house. He knew that an old woman had lived in it once, but he saw no signs of life there now. He was oblivious to the universe of wood life that did live there in layers of ivy grown so thick he could have sunk his arm in it up to the elbow. Life that crawled, life that slunk and crept and never closed its eyes. Life that burrowed and scurried, and life so still it was indistinguishable from the ivy stems on which it lay. Birth, life, and death—each took place on the hidden side of a leaf. From where he stood, the house looked as if it had been eaten by a galloping disease, the sores of which were dark and fluid.

One mile behind him were macadam and the reassuring sounds of an automobile or two—one of which was Reverend Cooper's car, driven by his thirteen-year-old nephew.

Noon, Milkman had told him. Come back at noon. He could just as easily have said twenty minutes, and now that he was alone, assaulted by what city people regard as raucous silence, he wished he had said five minutes. But even if the boy hadn't had chores to do, it would be foolish to be driven fifteen miles out-side Danville on "business" and stay a hot minute.

He should never have made up that elaborate story to disguise his search for the cave; somebody might ask him about it. Be-sides, lies should be very simple, like the truth. Excessive detail was simply excess. But he was so tired after the long bus ride from Pittsburgh, coming right after the luxury of the flight, he was afraid he wouldn't be convincing.

The airplane ride exhilarated him, encouraged illusion and a feeling of invulnerability. High above the clouds, heavy yet light, caught in the stillness of speed ("Cruise," the pilot said), sitting in intricate metal become glistening bird, it was not pos-sible to believe he had ever made a mistake, or could. Only one small thought troubled him—that Guitar was not there too. He would have loved it—the view, the food, the stewardesses. But Milkman wanted to do this by himself, with no input from any-body. This one time he wanted to go solo. In the air, away from real life, he felt free, but on the ground, when he talked to Guitar just before he left, the wings of all those other people's nightmares flapped in his face and constrained him. Lena's anger, Corinthians' loose and uncombed hair, matching her slack lips, Ruth's stepped-up surveillance, his father's bottomless greed, Hagar's hollow eyes—he did not know whether he deserved any of that, but he knew he was fed up and he knew he had to leave quickly. He told Guitar of his decision before he told his father.

"Daddy thinks the stuff is still in the cave."

"Could be." Guitar sipped his tea.

"Anyway, it's worth checking out. At least we'll know once and for all."

"I couldn't agree more."

"So I'm going after it."

"By yourself?"

Milkman sighed. "Yeah. Yeah. By myself. I need to get out of here. I mean I really have to go away somewhere."

Guitar put his cup down and folded his hands in front of his mouth. "Wouldn't it be easier with the two of us? Suppose you have trouble?"

"It might be easier, but it might look more suspicious with two men instead of one roaming around the woods. If I find it, I'll haul it back and we'll split it up just like we agreed. If I don't, well, I'll be back anyway."

"When you leaving?"

"Tomorrow morning."

"What's your father say about you going alone?"

"I haven't told him yet. You're the only one knows so far." Milkman stood up and went to the window that looked out on Guitar's little porch. "Shit."

Guitar was watching him carefully. "What's the matter?" he asked. "Why you so low? You don't act like a man on his way to the end of the rainbow."

Milkman turned around and sat on the sill. "I hope it *is* a rainbow, and nobody has run off with the pot, cause I need it."

"Everybody needs it."

"Not as bad as me."

Guitar smiled. "Look like you really got the itch now. More than before."

"Yeah, well, everything's worse than before, or maybe it's the same as before. I don't know. I just know that I want to live my own life. I don't want to be my old man's office boy no more. And as long as I'm in this place I will be. Unless I have my own money. I have to get out of that house and I don't want to owe anybody when I go. My family's driving me crazy. Daddy wants me to be like him and hate my mother. My mother wants me to think like her and hate my father. Corinthians won't speak to me; Lena wants me out. And Hagar wants me chained to her bed or dead. Everybody wants something from me, you know what I mean? Something they think they can't get anywhere else. Something they think I got. I don't know what it is—I mean what it is they really want."

Guitar stretched his legs. "They want your life, man."

"My life?"

"What else?"

"No. Hagar wants my life. My family . . . they want—"

"I don't mean that way. I don't mean they want your dead life; they want your living life."

"You're losing me," said Milkman.

"Look. It's the condition our condition is in. Everybody wants the life of a black man. Everybody. White men want us dead or quiet—which is the same thing as dead. White women, same thing. They want us, you know, 'universal,' human, no 'race consciousness.' Tame, except in bed. They like a little racial loincloth in the bed. But outside the bed they want us to be individuals. You tell them, 'But they lynched my papa,' and they say, 'Yeah, but you're better than the lynchers are, so forget it.' And black women, they want your whole self. Love, they call it, and understanding. 'Why don't you *understand* me?' What they mean is, Don't love anything on earth except me. They say, 'Be responsible,' but what they mean is, Don't go anywhere where I ain't. You try to climb Mount Everest, they'll tie up your ropes. Tell them you want to go to the bottom of the sea—just for a look—they'll hide your oxygen tank. Or you don't even have to go that far. Buy a horn and say you want to play. Oh, they love the music, but only after you pull eight at the post office. Even if you make it, even if you stubborn and

mean and you get to the top of Mount Everest, or you do play
and you good, real good—that still ain't enough. You blow your
lungs out on the horn and they want what breath you got left to
hear about how you love them. They want your full attention.
Take a risk and they say you not for real. That you don't love
them. They won't even let you risk your own life, man, your
*own* life—unless it's over them. You can't even die unless it's
about them. What good is a man's life if he can't even choose
what to die for?"

"Nobody can choose what to die for."

"Yes you can, and if you can't, you can damn well try to."

"You sound bitter. If that's what you feel, why are you playing your numbers game? Keeping the racial ratio the same and
all? Every time I ask you what you doing it for, you talk about
love. Loving Negroes. Now you say—"

"It *is* about love. What else but love? Can't I love what I
criticize?"

"Yeah, but except for skin color, I can't tell the difference
between what the white women want from us and what the
colored women want. You say they all want our life, our living
life. So if a colored woman is raped and killed, why do the Days
rape and kill a white woman? Why worry about the colored
woman at all?"

Guitar cocked his head and looked sideways at Milkman. His
nostrils flared a little. "Because she's *mine*."

"Yeah. Sure." Milkman didn't try to keep disbelief out of his
voice. "So everybody wants to kill us, except black men, right?"

"Right."

"Then why did my father—who is a very black man—try to
kill me before I was even born?"

"Maybe he thought you were a little girl; I don't know. But I
don't have to tell you that your father is a very strange Negro.
He'll reap the benefits of what we sow, and there's nothing we
can do about that. He behaves like a white man, thinks like a
white man. As a matter of fact, I'm glad you brought him up.
Maybe you can tell me how, after losing everything his own

father worked for to some crackers, after *seeing* his father shot down by them, how can he keep his knees bent? Why does he love them so? And Pilate. She's worse. She saw it too and, first, goes back to get a cracker's bones for some kind of crazy self-punishment, and second, leaves the cracker's gold right where it was! Now, is that voluntary slavery or not? She slipped into those Jemima shoes cause they fit."

"Look, Guitar. First of all, my father doesn't care whether a white man lives or swallows lye. He just wants what they have. And Pilate is a little nuts, but she wanted us out of there. If she hadn't been smart, both our asses would be cooling in the joint right now."

"My ass. Not yours. She wanted you out, not me."

"Come on. That ain't even fair."

"No. Fair is one more thing I've given up."

"But to Pilate? What for? She knew what we did and still she bailed us out. Went down for us, clowned and crawled for us. You saw her face. You ever see anything like it in your life?"

"Once. Just once," said Guitar. And he remembered anew how his mother smiled when the white man handed her the four ten-dollar bills. More than gratitude was showing in her eyes. More than that. Not love, but a willingness to love. Her husband was sliced in half and boxed backward. He'd heard the mill men tell how the two halves, not even fitted together, were placed cut side down, skin side up, in the coffin. Facing each other. Each eye looking deep into its mate. Each nostril inhaling the breath the other nostril had expelled. The right cheek facing the left. The right elbow crossed over the left elbow. And he had worried then, as a child, that when his father was wakened on Judgment Day his first sight would not be glory or the magnificent head of God—or even the rainbow. It would be his own other eye.

Even so, his mother had smiled and shown that willingness to love the man who was responsible for dividing his father up throughout eternity. It wasn't the divinity from the foreman's wife that made him sick. That came later. It was the fact that instead of life insurance, the sawmill owner gave his mother forty dollars "to tide you and them kids over," and she took it happily and bought each of them a big peppermint stick on the very day of the funeral. Guitar's two sisters and baby brother sucked away at the bone-white and blood-red stick, but Guitar couldn't. He held it in his hand until it stuck there. All day he held it. At the graveside, at the funeral supper, all the sleepless night. The others made fun of what they believed was his miserliness, but he could not eat it or throw it away, until finally, in the outhouse, he let it fall into the earth's stinking hole.

"Once," he said. "Just once." And felt the nausea all over again. "The crunch is here," he said. "The big crunch. Don't let them Kennedys fool you. And I'll tell you the truth: I hope your daddy's right about what's in that cave. And I sure hope you don't have no second thoughts about getting it back here."

"What's that supposed to mean?"

"It means I'm nervous. Real nervous. I need the bread."

"If you're in a hurt, I can let you have—"

"Not *me*. *Us*. We have work to do, man. And just recently"—Guitar squinted his eyes at Milkman—"just recently one of us was put out in the streets, by somebody I don't have to name. And his wages were garnisheed cause this somebody said two months rent was owing. This somebody needs two months rent on a twelve-by-twelve hole in the wall like a fish needs side pockets. Now we have to take care of this man, get him a place to stay, pay the so-called back rent, and—"

"That was my fault. Let me tell you what happened. . . ."

"No. Don't tell me nothing. You ain't the landlord and you didn't put him out. You may have handed him the gun, but you didn't pull the trigger. I'm not blaming you."

"Why not? You talk about my father, my father's sister, and you'll talk about my sister too if I let you. Why you trust me?"

"Baby, I hope I never have to ask myself that question."

It ended all right, that gloomy conversation. There was no real anger and nothing irrevocable was said. When Milkman left, Guitar opened his palm as usual and Milkman slapped it. Maybe it was fatigue, but the touching of palms seemed a little weak.

At the Pittsburgh airport he discovered that Danville was 240 miles northeast, and not accessible by any public transportation other than a Greyhound bus. Reluctantly, unwilling to give up the elegance he had felt on the flight, he taxied from the airport to the bus station and settled himself for two idle hours before the Greyhound left. By the time he boarded, the inactivity, the picture magazines he'd read, the strolls in the streets near the station, had exhausted him. He fell asleep fifteen minutes outside Pittsburgh. When he woke it was late in the afternoon, with an hour more to go before he reached Danville. His father had raved about the beauty of this part of the country, but Milkman saw it as merely green, deep into its Indian summer but cooler than his own city, although it was farther south. The mountains, he thought, must make for the difference in temperature. For a few minutes he tried to enjoy the scenery running past his window, then the city man's boredom with nature's repetition overtook him. Some places had lots of trees, some did not; some fields were green, some were not, and the hills in the distance were like the hills in every distance. Then he watched signs—the names of towns that lay twenty-two miles ahead, seventeen miles to the east, five miles to the northeast. And the names of junctions, counties, crossings, bridges, stations, tunnels, mountains, rivers, creeks, landings, parks, and lookout points. Everybody had to do his act, he thought, for surely anybody who was interested in Dudberry Point already knew where it was.

He had two bottles of Cutty Sark in his suitcase, along with two shirts and some underwear. The large suitcase, he thought, would have its real load on the return trip. Now he wished he had not checked it under the bus, for he wanted a drink right then. According to his watch, the gold Longines his mother had given him, it would be another twenty minutes before a stop. He lay back on the headrest and tried to fall asleep. His eyes were creasing from the sustained viewing of uneventful countryside.

In Danville he was astonished to learn that the bus depot was a diner on route 11 where the counterman sold bus tickets, hamburgers, coffee, cheese and peanut butter crackers, cigarettes, candy and a cold-cut plate. No lockers, no baggage room, no taxi, and now he realized no men's room either.

Suddenly he felt ridiculous. What was he supposed to do? Put his suitcase down and ask the man: Where is the cave near the farm where my father lived fifty-eight years ago? He knew nobody, had no names except the first name of an old lady who was now dead. And rather than call any more attention to himself in this tiny farming town than his beige three-piece suit, his button-down light-blue shirt and black string tie, and his beautiful Florsheim shoes had already brought, he asked the counterman if he could check his bag there. The man gazed at the suitcase and seemed to be turning the request over in his mind.

"I'll pay," said Milkman.

"Leave 'er here. Back a the pop crates," the man said. "When you wanna pick 'er up?"

"This evening," he said.

"Fine. She'll be right here."

Milkman left the diner/bus station with a small satchel of shaving things and walked out into the streets of Danville, Pennsylvania. He'd seen places like this in Michigan, of course, but he never had to do anything in them other than buy gas. The three stores on the street were closing up for the night. It was five-fifteen and about a dozen people, all told, were walking on the sidewalks. One of them a Negro. A tall man, elderly, with a brown peaked cap and an old-fashioned collar. Milkman followed him for a while, then caught up to him and said, "Say, I wonder if you could help me." He smiled as he spoke.

The man turned around but did not answer. Milkman wondered if he had offended him in some way. Finally the man nodded and said, "Do what I can." He had a slight country lilt, like that of the white man at the counter.

"I'm looking for . . . Circe, a lady named Circe. Well, not

her, but her house. Do you know where she used to live? I'm from out of town. I just got off the bus. I have some business to take care of here, an insurance policy, and I need to check on some property out there."

The man was listening and apparently not going to interrupt him, so Milkman ended his sentence lamely with: "Can you help me?"

"Reverend Cooper would know," said the man.

"Where can I find him?" Milkman felt something missing from the conversation.

"Stone Lane. Follow this here street till you come to the post office. Go on around the post office and that'll be Windsor. The next street is Stone Lane. He lives in there."

"Will there be a church there?" Milkman assumed a preacher lived next door to his church.

"No. No. Church ain't got no parsonage. Reverend Cooper lives in Stone Lane. Yella house, I believe."

"Thanks," said Milkman. "Thanks a lot."

"Mighty welcome," said the man. "Good evenin'." And he walked away.

Milkman considered whether to go back for his suitcase, abandoned the idea, and followed the directions given him. An American flag identified the post office, a frame structure next to a drugstore that served also as the Western Union office. He turned left at the corner, but noticed there were no street signs anywhere. How could he find Windsor or Stone Lane if there were no signs? He walked through a residential street, another and another, and he was just about to go back to the drugstore and look under "A.M.E." or "A.M.E. Zion" in the telephone directory when he saw a yellow-and-white house. Maybe this is it, he thought. He climbed the steps, determined to mind his manners. A thief should be polite and win goodwill.

"Good evening. Is Reverend Cooper here?"

A woman was standing in the doorway. "Yes, he's here. Would you like to come in? I'll call him."

"Thank you." Milkman entered a tiny hall and waited.

A short chubby man appeared, fingering his glasses. "Yes, sir? You wanted to see me?" His eyes ran rapidly over Milkman's clothes, but his voice betrayed no excessive curiosity.

"Yes. Uh . . . how are you?"

"Fine. Fine. And you?"

"Pretty good." Milkman felt as awkward as he sounded. He had never had to try to make a pleasant impression on a stranger before, never needed anything from a stranger before, and did not remember ever asking anybody in the world how they were. I might as well say it all, he thought. "I could use your help, sir. My name is Macon Dead. My father is from around—"

"Dead? Macon Dead, you say?"

"Yes." Milkman smiled apologetically for the name. "My father—"

"Well, I'll be." Reverend Cooper took off his glasses. "Well, I'll be! Esther!" He threw his voice over his shoulder without taking his eyes off his guest. "Esther, come here!" Then to Milkman: "I know your people!"

Milkman smiled and let his shoulders slump a little. It was a good feeling to come into a strange town and find a stranger who knew your people. All his life he'd heard the tremor in the word: "I live here, but my *people* . . ." or: "She acts like she ain't got no *people*," or: "Do any of your *people* live there?" But he hadn't known what it meant: links. He remembered Freddie sitting in Sonny's Shop just before Christmas, saying, "None of my people would take me in." Milkman beamed at Reverend Cooper and his wife. "You do?"

"Sit on down here, boy. You the son of the Macon Dead I knew. Oh, well, now, I don't mean to say I knew him all that well. Your daddy was four or five years older than me, and they didn't get to town much, but everybody round here remembers the old man. Old Macon Dead, your granddad. My daddy and him was good friends. A blacksmith, my daddy was. I'm the only one got the call. Well well well." Reverend Cooper grinned and massaged his knees. "Oh, Lord, I'm forgetting myself. You must be hungry. Esther, get him something to fill himself up on."

"Oh, no. No, thank you, sir. Maybe a little something to drink. I mean if you do drink, that is."

"Sure. Sure. Nothing citified, I'm sorry to say, but— Esther!" She was on her way to the kitchen. "Bring some glasses and get that whiskey out the cupboard. This here's Macon Dead's boy and he's tired and needs a drink. Tell me, how'd you find me? Don't tell me your daddy remembered me?"

"He probably does, but I met a man in the street and he told me how to find you."

"You asked him for me?" Reverend Cooper wanted to get all the facts straight. Already he was framing the story for his friends: how the man came to his house first, how he asked for him. . . .

Esther returned with a Coca-Cola tray, two glasses, and a large mayonnaise jar of what looked like water. Reverend Cooper poured it warm and neat into the two glasses. No ice, no water—just pure rye whiskey that almost tore Milkman's throat when he swallowed it.

"No. I didn't ask for you by name. I asked him if he knew where a woman named Circe used to live."

"Circe? Yes. Lord, old Circe!"

"He told me to talk to you."

Reverend Cooper smiled and poured more whiskey. "Everybody round here knows me and I know everybody."

"Well, I know my father stayed with her awhile, after they . . . when they . . . after his father died."

"They had a fine place. Mighty fine. Some white folks own it now. Course that's what they wanted. That's why they shot him. Upset a lot of people here, a whole lot of people. Scared 'em too. But didn't your daddy have a sister name of Pilate?"

"Yes, sir. Pilate."

"Still living, is she?"

"Oh, yes. Very much living."

"Issat so? Pretty girl, real pretty. My daddy was the one made the earring for her. That's how we knew they was alive. After Old Macon Dead was killed, nobody knew whether the children was dead too or what. Then a few weeks passed and Circe came to my daddy's shop. Right across from where the post office is now—that's where my daddy's blacksmith shop was. She came in there with this little metal box with a piece of paper bag folded up in it. Pilate's name was written on it. Circe didn't tell Daddy anything, but that he was to make a earring out of it. She stole a brooch from the folks she worked for. My daddy took the gold pin off it and soldered it to the box. So we knew they was alive and Circe was taking care of 'em. They'd be all right with Circe. She worked for the Butlers—rich white folks, you know—but she was a good midwife in those days. Delivered everybody. Me included."

Maybe it was the whiskey, which always made other people gracious when he drank it, but Milkman felt a glow listening to a story come from this man that he'd heard many times before but only half listened to. Or maybe it was being there in the place where it happened that made it seem so real. Hearing Pilate talk about caves and woods and earrings on Darling Street, or his father talk about cooking wild turkey over the automobile noise of Not Doctor Street, seemed exotic, something from another world and age, and maybe not even true. Here in the parsonage, sitting in a cane-bottomed chair near an upright piano and drinking homemade whiskey poured from a mayonnaise jar, it was real. Without knowing it, he had walked right by the place where Pilate's earring had been fashioned, the earring that had fascinated him when he was little, the fixing of which informed the colored people here that the children of the murdered man were alive. And this was the living room of the son of the man who made the earring.

"Did anybody ever catch the men who did it—who killed him?"

Reverend Cooper raised his eyebrows. "Catch?" he asked, his face full of wonder. Then he smiled again. "Didn't have to catch 'em. They never went nowhere."

"I mean did they have a trial; were they arrested?"

"Arrested for what? Killing a nigger? Where did you say you was from?"

"You mean nobody did anything? Didn't even try to find out who did it?"

"Everybody knew who did it. Same people Circe worked for—the Butlers."

"And nobody did anything?" Milkman wondered at his own anger. He hadn't felt angry when he first heard about it. Why now?

"Wasn't nothing to do. White folks didn't care, colored folks didn't dare. Wasn't no police like now. Now we got a county sheriff handles things. Not then. Then the circuit judge came through just once or twice a year. Besides, the people what did it owned half the county. Macon's land was in their way. Folks just was thankful the children escaped."

"You said Circe worked for the people who killed him. Did she know that?"

"Course she did."

"And she let them stay there?"

"Not out in the open. She hid them."

"Still, they were in the same house, right?"

"Yep. Best place, I'd say. If they came to town somebody'd see 'em. Nobody would think of looking there."

"Did Daddy—did my father know that?"

"I don't know what he knew, if Circe ever told him. I never saw him after the murder. None of us did."

"Where are they? The Butlers. They still live here?"

"Dead now. Every one of 'em. The last one, the girl Elizabeth, died a couple years back. Barren as a rock and just as old. Things work out, son. The ways of God are mysterious, but if you live it out, just live it out, you see that it always works out. Nothing they stole or killed for did 'em a bit a good. Not one bit."

"I don't care whether it did them good. The fact is they did somebody else harm."

Reverend Cooper shrugged. "White folks different up your way?"

"No, I guess not. . . . Sometimes, though, you can do something."

"What?" The preacher looked genuinely interested.

Milkman couldn't answer except in Guitar's words, so he said nothing.

"See this here?" The reverend turned around and showed Milkman a knot the size of a walnut that grew behind his ear. "Some of us went to Philly to try and march in an Armistice Day parade. This was after the First World War. We were invited and had a permit, but the people, the white people, didn't like us being there. They started a fracas. You know, throwing rocks and calling us names. They didn't care nothing 'bout the uniform. Anyway, some police on horseback came—to quiet them down, we thought. They ran *us* down. Right under their horses. This here's what a hoof can do. Ain't that something?"

"Jesus God."

"You wouldn't be here to even things up, would you?" The preacher leaned over his stomach.

"No. I'm passing through, that's all. Just thought I'd look around. I wanted to see the farm. . . ."

"Cause any evening up left to do, Circe took care of."

"What'd she do?"

"Hah! What didn't she do?"

"Sorry I didn't come out here long time ago. I would have liked to meet her. She must have been a hundred years old when she died."

"Older. Was a hundred when I was a boy."

"Is the farm nearby?" Milkman appeared mildly interested.

"Not too far."

"I sort of wanted to see where it was since I'm out this way. Daddy talked so much about it."

"It's right back of the Butler place, about fifteen miles out. I can take you there. My old piece of car's in the shop, but it was supposed to be ready yesterday. I'll check on it."

Milkman waited four days for the car to be ready. Four days at Reverend Cooper's house as his guest, and the purpose of long visits from every old man in the town who remembered his father or his grandfather, and some who'd only heard. They all repeated various aspects of the story, all talked about how beautiful Lincoln's Heaven was. Sitting in the kitchen, they looked at Milkman with such rheumy eyes, and spoke about his grandfather with such awe and affection, Milkman began to miss him too. His own father's words came back to him: "I worked right alongside my father. Right alongside him." Milkman thought then that his father was boasting of his manliness as a child. Now he knew he had been saying something else. That he loved his father; had an intimate relationship with him; that his father loved him, trusted him, and found him worthy of working "right alongside" him. "Something went wild in me," he'd said, "when I saw him on the ground."

His was the genuine feeling that Milkman had faked when Reverend Cooper described the hopelessness of "doing anything." These men remembered both Macon Deads as extraordinary men. Pilate they remembered as a pretty woods-wild girl "that couldn't nobody put shoes on." Only one of them remembered his grandmother. "Good-lookin, but looked like a white woman. Indian, maybe. Black hair and slanted-up eyes. Died in childbirth, you know." The more the old men talked—the more he heard about the only farm in the county that grew peaches, real peaches like they had in Georgia, the feasts they had when hunting was over, the pork kills in the winter and the work, the backbreaking work of a going farm—the more he missed something in his life. They talked about digging a well, fashioning traps, felling trees, warming orchards with fire when spring weather was bad, breaking young horses, training dogs. And in it all was his own father, the second Macon Dead, their contemporary, who was strong as an ox, could ride bareback and barefoot, who, they agreed, outran, outplowed, outshot, outpicked, outrode them all. He could not recognize that stern, greedy, unloving man in the boy they talked about, but he loved the boy they described and loved that boy's father, with his hip-roofed barn, his peach trees, and Sunday break-of-dawn fishing parties in a fish pond that was two acres wide.

They talked on and on, using Milkman as the ignition that gunned their memories. The good times, the hard times, things that changed, things that stayed the same—and head and shoulders above all of it was the tall, magnificent Macon Dead, whose death, it seemed to him, was the beginning of their own dying even though they were young boys at the time. Macon Dead was the farmer they wanted to be, the clever irrigator, the peach-tree grower, the hog slaughterer, the wild-turkey roaster, the man who could plow forty in no time flat and sang like an angel while he did it. He had come out of nowhere, as ignorant as a hammer and broke as a convict, with nothing but free papers, a Bible, and a pretty black-haired wife, and in one year he'd leased ten acres, the next ten more. Sixteen years later he had one of the best farms in Montour County. A farm that colored their lives like a paintbrush and spoke to them like a sermon. "You see?" the farm said to them. "See? See what you can do? Never mind you can't tell one letter from another, never mind you born a slave, never mind you lose your name, never mind your daddy dead, never mind nothing. Here, this here, is what a man can do if he puts his mind to it and his back in it. Stop sniveling," it said. "Stop picking around the edges of the world. Take advantage, and if you can't take advantage, take disadvantage. We live here. On this planet, in this nation, in this county right here. Nowhere else! We got a home in this rock, don't you see! Nobody starving in my home; nobody crying in my home, and if I got a home you got one too! Grab it. Grab this land! Take it, hold it, my brothers, make it, my brothers, shake it, squeeze it, turn it, twist it, beat it, kick it, kiss it, whip it, stomp it, dig it, plow it, seed it, reap it, rent it, buy it, sell it, own it, build it, multiply it, and pass it on—can you hear me? Pass it on!"

But they shot the top of his head off and ate his fine Georgia peaches. And even as boys these men began to die and were dying still. Looking at Milkman in those nighttime talks, they

yearned for something. Some word from him that would re-
kindle the dream and stop the death they were dying. That's
why Milkman began to talk about his father, the boy they
knew, the son of the fabulous Macon Dead. He bragged a little
and they came alive. How many houses his father owned (they
grinned); the new car every two years (they laughed); and
when he told them how his father tried to buy the Erie Lackawanna (it sounded better that way), they hooted with joy.
That's him! That's Old Macon Dead's boy, all right! They
wanted to know everything and Milkman found himself rattling
off assets like an accountant, describing deals, total rents income,
bank loans, and this new thing his father was looking into—the
stock market.

Suddenly, in the midst of his telling, Milkman wanted the
gold. He wanted to get up right then and there and go get it.
Run to where it was and snatch every grain of it from under the
noses of the Butlers, who were dumb enough to believe that if
they killed one man his whole line died. He glittered in the light
of their adoration and grew fierce with pride.

"Who'd your daddy marry?"

"The daughter of the richest Negro doctor in town."

"That's him! That's Macon Dead!"

"Send you all to college?"

"Sent my sisters. I work right alongside him in our office."

"Hah! Keep you home to get that money! Macon Dead
gonna always make him some money!"

"What kinda car he drive?"

"Buick. Two-twenty-five."

"Great God, a deuce and a quarter! What year?"

"This year!"

"That's him! That's Macon Dead! He gonna buy the Erie
Lackawanna! If he want it, he'll get it! Bless my soul. Bet he
worry them white folks to death. Can't nobody keep him down!
Not no Macon Dead! Not in this world! And not in the next!
Haw! Goddam! The Erie Lacka*wan*na!"

After all the waiting, Reverend Cooper couldn't go. His preaching income was supplemented by freightyard work and he was called for an early shift. His nephew, called Nephew since he was their only one, was assigned to drive Milkman out to the farm—as close as they could get. Nephew was thirteen and barely able to see over the steering wheel.

"Does he have a license?" Milkman asked Mrs. Cooper.

"Not yet," she said, and when she saw his consternation she explained that farm kids drove early—they had to.

Milkman and Nephew started out right after breakfast. It took them the better part of an hour because the roads were curving two-lanes and they spent twenty minutes behind a light truck they couldn't pull around. Nephew spoke very little. He seemed interested only in Milkman's clothes, which he took every opportunity to examine. Milkman decided to give him one of his shirts, and asked him to stop by the bus station to pick up the suitcase he'd left there.

Finally Nephew slowed down on a stretch of road that showed no houses at all. He stopped.

"What's the matter? You want me to drive?"

"No, sir. This is it."

"What's it? Where?"

"Back in there." He pointed to some bushes. "The road to the Butler place is in there and the farm's back behind it. You got to walk it. Car won't make it."

Nothing was truer; as it turned out, Milkman's feet could hardly make it over the stony road covered with second growth. He had asked Nephew to wait, thinking he would survey the area quickly and come back later on his own. But the boy had chores, he said, and would be back whenever Milkman wanted him to be there.

"An hour," said Milkman.

"Take me an hour just to get back to town," said Nephew.

"Reverend Cooper said you were to take me. Not leave me stranded."

"My mama whip me, I don't do my chores."

Milkman was annoyed, but because he didn't want the boy to think he was nervous about being left out there alone, he agreed to having him come back at—he glanced at his heavy, overdesigned watch—at noon. It was nine o'clock then.

His hat had been knocked off by the first branches of the old walnut trees, so he held it in his hand. His cuffless pants were darkened by the mile-long walk over moist leaves. The quiet fairly roared in his ears. He was uncomfortable and a little anxious, but the gold loomed large in his mind, as did the faces of the men he'd drunk with last night, and he stepped firmly onto the gravel and leaves of the driveway which circled the biggest house he'd ever seen.

This is where they stayed, he thought, where Pilate cried when given cherry jam. He stood still a moment. It must have been beautiful, must have seemed like a palace to them, but neither had ever spoken of it in any terms but how imprisoned they felt, how difficult it was to see the sky from their room, how repelled they were by the carpets, the draperies. Without knowing who killed their father, they instinctively hated the murderers' house. And it did look like a murderer's house. Dark, ruined, evil. Never, not since he knelt by his window sill wishing he could fly, had he felt so lonely. He saw the eyes of a child peer at him over the sill of the one second-story window the ivy had not covered. He smiled. Must be myself I'm seeing—thinking about how I used to watch the sky out the window. Or maybe it's the light trying to get through the trees. Four graceful columns supported the portico, and the huge double door featured a heavy, brass knocker. He lifted it and let it fall; the sound was soaked up like a single raindrop in cotton. Nothing stirred. He looked back down the path and saw the green maw out of which he had come, a greenish-black tunnel, the end of which was nowhere in sight.

The farm, they said, was right in back of the Butler place, but knowing how different their concept of distance was, he thought he'd better get moving. If he found what he was looking for he would have to come back at night—with equipment, of course, but also with some familiarity with the area. On impulse he reached out his hand and tried to turn the doorknob. It didn't budge. Half turning to leave—literally as an afterthought —he pushed the door and it swung open with a sigh. He leaned in. The smell prevented him from seeing anything more than the absence of light did. A hairy animal smell, ripe, rife, suffocating. He coughed and looked for somewhere to spit, for the odor was in his mouth, coating his teeth and tongue. He pulled a handkerchief from his back pocket, held it over his nose, backed away from the open door, and had just begun to spill the little breakfast he'd eaten when the odor disappeared and, quite suddenly, in its place was a sweet spicy perfume. Like ginger root—pleasant, clean, seductive. Surprised and charmed by it, he retraced his steps and went inside. After a second or two he was able to see the hand-laid and hand-finished wooden floor in a huge hall, and at its farther end a wide staircase spiraling up into the dark. His eyes traveled up the stairs.

He had had dreams as a child, dreams every child had, of the witch who chased him down dark alleys, between lawn trees, and finally into rooms from which he could not escape. Witches in black dresses and red underskirts; witches with pink eyes and green lips, tiny witches, long rangy witches, frowning witches, smiling witches, screaming witches and laughing witches, witches that flew, witches that ran, and some that merely glided on the ground. So when he saw the woman at the top of the stairs there was no way for him to resist climbing up toward her outstretched hands, her fingers spread wide for him, her mouth gaping open for him, her eyes devouring him. In a dream you climb the stairs. She grabbed him, grabbed his shoulders and pulled him right up against her and tightened her arms around him. Her head came to his chest and the feel of that hair under his chin, the dry bony hands like steel springs rubbing his back, her floppy mouth babbling into his vest, made him dizzy, but he knew that always, always at the very instant of the pounce or the gummy embrace he would wake with a scream and an erection. Now he had only the erection.

Milkman closed his eyes, helpless to pull away before the completion of the dream. What made him surface from it was a humming sound around his knees. He looked down and there, surrounding him, was a pack of golden-eyed dogs, each of which had the intelligent child's eyes he had seen from the window. Abruptly the woman let him go and he looked down at her too. Beside the calm, sane, appraising eyes of the dogs, her eyes looked crazy. Beside their combed, brushed gun-metal hair, hers was wild and filthy.

She spoke to the dogs. "Go on away. Helmut, go on. Horst, move." She waved her hands and the dogs obeyed.

"Come, come," she said to Milkman. "In here." She took his hand in both of hers, and he followed her—his arm outstretched, his hand in hers—like a small boy being dragged reluctantly to bed. Together they weaved among the bodies of the dogs that floated around his legs. She led him into a room, made him sit on a gray velvet sofa, and dismissed all the dogs but two that lay at her feet.

"Remember the Weimaraners?" she asked, settling herself, pulling her chair close to him.

She was old. So old she was colorless. So old only her mouth and eyes were distinguishable features in her face. Nose, chin, cheekbones, forehead, neck all had surrendered their identity to the pleats and crochetwork of skin committed to constant change.

Milkman struggled for a clear thought, so hard to come by in a dream: Perhaps this woman is Circe. But Circe is dead. This woman is alive. That was as far as he got, because although the woman was talking to him, she might in any case still be dead—as a matter of fact, she *had* to be dead. Not because of the wrinkles, and the face so old it could not be alive, but because out of the toothless mouth came the strong, mellifluent voice of a twenty-year-old girl.

"I knew one day you would come back. Well, that's not entirely true. Some days I doubted it and some days I didn't think about it at all. But you see, I was right. You did come."

It was awful listening to that voice come from that face. Maybe something was happening to his ears. He wanted to hear the sound of his own voice, so he decided to take a chance on logic.

"Excuse me. I'm his son. I'm Macon Dead's son. Not the one you knew."

She stopped smiling.

"My name is Macon Dead too, but I'm thirty-two years old. You knew my father and his father too." So far, so good. His voice was the same. Now he needed only to know if he had assessed the situation correctly. She did not answer him. "You're Circe, aren't you?"

"Yes; Circe," she said, but she seemed to have lost all interest in him. "My name is Circe."

"I'm just visiting," he said. "I spent a couple of days with Reverend Cooper and his wife. They're the ones brought me out here."

"I thought you were him. I thought you came back to see me. Where is he? *My* Macon?"

"Back home. He's alive. He told me about you. . . ."

"And Pilate. Where is she?"

"There too. She's fine."

"Well, you look like him. You really do." But she didn't sound convinced.

"He's seventy-two years old now," said Milkman. He thought that would clear things up, make her know he couldn't be the Macon she knew, who was sixteen when she last saw him. But all she said was "Uhn," as though seventy-two, thirty-two, any age at all, meant nothing whatsoever to her. Milkman wondered how old she really was.

"Are you hungry?" she asked.

"No. Thank you. I ate breakfast."

"So you've been staying with that little Cooper boy?"

"Yes, ma'am."

"A runt. I told him not to smoke, but children don't listen."

"Do you mind if I do?" Milkman was relaxing a little and he hoped the cigarette would relax him more.

She shrugged. "Do what you like. Everybody does what he likes nowadays anyway."

Milkman lit the cigarette and the dogs hummed at the sound of the match, their eyes glittering toward the flame.

"Ssh!" whispered Circe.

"Beautiful," said Milkman.

"What's beautiful?"

"The dogs."

"They're not beautiful, they're strange, but they keep things away. I'm completely worn out taking care of 'em. They belonged to Miss Butler. She bred them, crossbred them. Tried for years to get them in the AKC. They wouldn't permit it."

"What did you call them?"

"Weimaraners. German."

"What do you do with them?"

"Oh, I keep some. Sell some. Till we all die in here together." She smiled.

She had dainty habits which matched her torn and filthy clothes in precisely the way her strong young cultivated voice matched her wizened face. Her white hair—braided, perhaps; perhaps not—she touched as though replacing a wayward strand from an elegant coiffure. And her smile—an opening of flesh like celluloid dissolving under a drop of acid—was accompanied by a press of fingers on her chin. It was this combination of daintiness and cultivated speech that misled Macon and invited him to regard her as merely foolish.

"You should get out once in a while."

She looked at him.

"Is this your house now? Did they will you this? Is that why you have to stay here?"

She pressed her lips over her gums. "The only reason I'm here alone is because she died. She killed herself. All the money was gone, so she killed herself. Stood right there on the landing where you were a minute ago and threw herself off the banister. She didn't die right away, though; she lay in the bed a week or two and there was nobody here but us. The dogs were in the kennel then. I brought her in the world, just like I did her mother and her grandmother before that. Birthed just about everybody in the county, I did. Never lost one either. Never lost nobody but your mother. Well, grandmother, I guess she was. Now I birth dogs."

"Some friend of Reverend Cooper said she looked white. My grandmother. Was she?"

"No. Mixed. Indian mostly. A good-looking woman, but fierce, for the young woman I knew her as. Crazy about her husband too, overcrazy. You know what I mean? Some women love too hard. She watched over him like a pheasant hen. Nervous. Nervous love."

Milkman thought about this mixed woman's great-granddaughter, Hagar, and said, "Yes. I know what you mean."

"But a good woman. I cried like a baby when I lost her. Like a baby. Poor Sing."

"What?" He wondered if she lisped.

"I cried like a baby when I—"

"No. I mean what did you call her?"

"Sing. Her name was Sing."

"Sing? Sing Dead. Where'd she get a name like that?"

"Where'd you get a name like yours? White people name Negroes like race horses."

"I suppose so. Daddy told me how they got their name."

"What'd he tell you?"

Milkman told her the story about the drunken Yankee.

"Well, he didn't have to keep the name. She made him. She made him keep that name," Circe said when he was through.

"She?"

"Sing. His wife. They met on a wagon going North. Ate pecans all the way, she told me. It was a wagonful of ex-slaves going to the promised land."

"Was she a slave too?"

"No. No indeed. She always bragged how she was never a slave. Her people neither."

"Then what was she doing on that wagon?"

"I can't answer you because I don't know. Never crossed my mind to ask her."

"Where were they coming from? Georgia?"

"No. Virginia. Both of them lived in Virginia, her people and his. Down around Culpeper somewhere. Charlemagne or something like that."

"I think that's where Pilate was for a while. She lived all over the country before she came to us."

"Did she ever marry that boy?"

"What boy?"

"The boy she had the baby by."

"No. She didn't marry him."

"Didn't think she would. She was too ashamed."

"Ashamed of what?"

"Her stomach."

"Oh, that."

"Borned herself. I had very little to do with it. I thought they were both dead, the mother and the child. When she popped out you could have knocked me over. I hadn't heard a heartbeat anywhere. She just came on out. Your daddy loved her. Hurt me to hear they broke away from one another. So it does me good to hear they're back together again." She had warmed up talking about the past and Milkman decided not to tell her that Macon and Pilate just lived in the same city. He wondered how she knew about their split, and if she knew what they broke apart about.

"You knew about their quarrel?" he asked quietly, nonchalantly.

"Not the substance. Just the fact. Pilate came back here just after her baby was born. One winter. She told me they split up when they left here and she hadn't seen him since."

"Pilate told me they lived in a cave for a few days after they left this house."

"Is that right? Must have been Hunters Cave. Hunters used it to rest up in there sometimes. Eat. Smoke. Sleep. That's where they dumped Old Macon's body."

"They who? I thought . . . My father said he buried him. Down by a creek or a river someplace where they used to fish."

"He did. But it was too shallow and too close to the water. The body floated up at the first heavy rain. Those children hadn't been gone a month when it floated up. Some men were fishing down there and saw this body, a Negro. So they knew who it was. Dumped it in the cave, and it was summer too. You'd think they would have buried a body in the summer. I told Mrs. Butler I thought it was a disgrace."

"Daddy doesn't know that."

"Well, don't tell him. Let him have his peace. It's hard enough with a murdered father; he don't need to know what happened to the body."

"Did Pilate tell you why she came back here?"

"Yes. She said her father told her to. She had visits from him, she said."

"I'd like to see that cave. Where he's . . . where they put him."

"Won't be anything left to see now. That's been a long time ago."

"I know, but maybe there's something I can bury properly."

"Now, that's a thought worth having. The dead don't like it if they're not buried. They don't like it at all. You won't have trouble finding it. You go back out the road you came in on. Go north until you come to a stile. It's falling down, but you'll see it's a stile. Right in there the woods are open. Walk a little way in and you'll come to a creek. Cross it. There'll be some more woods, but ahead you'll see a short range of hills. The cave is right on the face of those hills. You can't miss it. It's the only one there. Tell your daddy you buried him properly, in a grave-yard. Maybe with a headstone. A nice headstone. I hope they find me soon enough and somebody'll take pity on me." She looked at the dogs. "Hope they find me soon and don't let me lay in here too long."

Milkman swallowed as her thought touched his mind. "People come to see you, don't they?"

"Dog buyers. They come every now and then. They'll find me, I guess."

"Reverend Cooper . . . They think you're dead."

"Splendid. I don't like those Negroes in town. Dog people come and the man that delivers the dog food once a week. They come. They'll find me. I just hope it's soon."

He loosened his collar and lit another cigarette. Here in this dim room he sat with the woman who had helped deliver his father and Pilate; who had risked her job, her life, maybe, to hide them both after their father was killed, emptied their slop jars, brought them food at night and pans of water to wash. Had even sneaked off to the village to have the girl Pilate's name and snuffbox made into an earring. Then healed the ear when it got infected. And after all these years was thrilled to see what she believed was one of them. Healer, deliverer, in another world she would have been the head nurse at Mercy. Instead she tended Weimaraners and had just one selfish wish: that when she died somebody would find her before the dogs ate her.

"You should leave this place. Sell the damn dogs. I'll help you. You need money? How much?" Milkman felt a flood of pity and thought gratitude made her smile at him. But her voice was cold.

"You think I don't know how to walk when I want to walk? Put your money back in your pocket."

Rebuffed from his fine feelings, Milkman matched her cold tone: "You loved those white folks that much?"

"Love?" she asked. "Love?"

"Well, what are you taking care of their dogs for?"

"Do you know why she killed herself? She couldn't stand to see the place go to ruin. She couldn't live without servants and money and what it could buy. Every cent was gone and the taxes took whatever came in. She had to let the upstairs maids go, then the cook, then the dog trainer, then the yardman, then the chauffeur, then the car, then the woman who washed once a week. Then she started selling bits and pieces—land, jewels, furniture. The last few years we ate out of the garden. Finally she couldn't take it anymore. The thought of having no help, no money—well, she couldn't take that. She had to let everything go."

"But she didn't let you go." Milkman had no trouble letting his words snarl.

"No, she didn't let me go. She killed herself."

"And you still loyal."

"You don't listen to people. Your ear is on your head, but it's not connected to your brain. I said she killed herself rather than do the work I'd been doing all my life!" Circe stood up, and the dogs too. "Do you hear me? She saw the work I did all her days and *died*, you hear me, *died* rather than live like me. Now, what do you suppose she thought I was! If the way I lived and the work I did was so hateful to her she killed herself to keep from having to do it, and you think I stay on here because I loved her, then you have about as much sense as a fart!"

The dogs were humming and she touched their heads. One stood on either side of her. "They loved this place. Loved it. Brought pink veined marble from across the sea for it and hired men in Italy to do the chandelier that I had to climb a ladder and clean with white muslin once every two months. They loved it. Stole for it, lied for it, killed for it. But I'm the one left. Me and the dogs. And I will never clean it again. Never. Nothing. Not a speck of dust, not a grain of dirt, will I move. Everything in this world they lived for will crumble and rot. The chandelier already fell down and smashed itself to pieces. It's down there in the ballroom now. All in pieces. Something gnawed through the cords. Ha! And I want to see it all go, make sure it does go, and that nobody fixes it up. I brought the dogs in to make sure. They keep strangers out too. Folks tried to get in here to steal things after she died. I set the dogs on them. Then I just brought them all right in here with me. You ought to see what they did to her bedroom. Her walls didn't have wallpaper. No. Silk brocade that took some Belgian women six years to make. She loved it—oh, how much she loved it. Took thirty Weimaraners one day to rip it off the walls. If I thought the stink wouldn't strangle you, I'd show it to you." She looked at the walls around her. "This is the last room."

"I wish you'd let me help you," he said after a while.

"You have. You came in here and pretended it didn't stink and told me about Macon and my sweet little Pilate."

"Are you sure?"

"Never surer."

They both stood and walked down the hall. "Mind how you step. There's no light." Dogs came from everywhere, humming. "Time for their feeding," she said. Milkman started down the stairs. Halfway down, he turned and looked up at her.

"You said his wife made him keep the name. Did you ever know his real name?"

"Jake, I believe."

"Jake what?"

She shrugged, a Shirley Temple, little-girl-helpless shrug. "Jake was all she told me."

"Thanks," he called back, louder than he needed to, but he wanted his gratitude to cut through the stink that was flooding back over the humming of the dogs.

But the humming and the smell followed him all the way back down the tunnel to the macadam road. When he got there it was ten-thirty. Another hour and a half before Nephew would be back. Milkman paced the shoulder of the road, making plans. When should he return? Should he try to rent a car or borrow the preacher's? Had Nephew got his suitcase? What equipment would he need? Flashlight and what else? What story should be in his mind in case he was discovered? Of course: looking for his grandfather's remains—to collect them and take them for a proper burial. He paced further, and then began to stroll in the direction Nephew would be coming from. After a few minutes, he wondered if he was going the right way. He started back, but just then saw the ends of two or three wooden planks sticking out of the brush. Maybe this was the stile Circe had described to him. Not exactly a stile, but the remains of one. Circe had not left that house in years, he thought. Any stile she knew of would have to be in disrepair now. And if her directions were accurate, he might make it there and back before twelve. At least he would be able to check it out in the daylight.

Gingerly, he parted the brush and walked a little way into the woods. He didn't see even a trace of a track. But as he kept on a bit, he heard water and followed the sound, which seemed to be just ahead of the next line of trees. He was deceived. He walked for fifteen minutes before he came to it. "Cross it," she'd said, and he thought there would be a bridge of some sort. There was none. He looked across and saw hills. It must be there. Right there. He calculated that he could just make it in the hour or so left before he should be back on the road. He sat down, took off his shoes and socks, stuffed the socks in his pocket, and rolled up his pants. Holding his shoes in his hand, he waded in. Unprepared for the coldness of the water and the slimy stones at the bottom, he slipped to one knee and soaked his shoes trying to break his fall. He righted himself with difficulty and poured the water out of his shoes. Since he was already wet, there was no point in turning back; he waded on out. After half a minute, the creek bed dropped six inches and he fell again, only now he went completely under and got a glimpse of small silvery translucent fish as his head went down. Snorting water, he cursed the creek, which was too shallow to swim and too rocky to walk. He should have pulled a stick to check depth before he put his foot down, but his excitement had been too great. He went on, feeling with his toes for firm footing before he put his weight down. It was slow moving—the water was about two or three feet deep and some twelve yards wide. If he hadn't been so eager, maybe he could have found a narrower part to cross. Thoughts of what he should have done instead of just plunging in, fruitless as they were, irritated him so that they kept him moving until he made it to the other side. He threw his shoes on the dry ground and hoisted himself up and out on the bank. Breathless, he reached for his cigarettes and found them soaked. He lay back on the grass and let the high sunshine warm him. He opened his mouth so the clear air could bathe his tongue.

After a while he sat up and put on the wet socks and shoes. He looked at his watch to check the time. It ticked, but the face was splintered and the minute hand was bent. Better move, he thought, and struck out for the hills, which, deceptive as the sound of the creek, were much farther away than they seemed. He had no idea that simply walking through trees, bushes, on untrammeled ground could be so hard. Woods always brought to his mind City Park, the tended woods on Honoré Island where he went for outings as a child and where tiny convenient paths led you through. "He leased ten acres of virgin woods and cleared it all," said the men describing the beginning of Old Macon Dead's farm. Cleared this? Chopped down this? This stuff he could barely walk through?

He was sweating into his wet shirt and just beginning to feel the result of sharp stones on his feet. Occasionally he came to a clear space and he'd alter his direction as soon as the low hills came back into view.

Finally flat ground gave way to a gentle upward slope of bushes, saplings, and rock. He walked along its edge, looking for an opening. As he moved southward, the skirts of the hills were rockier and the saplings fewer. Then he saw, some fifteen to twenty feet above him, a black hole in the rock which he could get to by a difficult, but not dangerous, climb, made more difficult by the thin smooth soles of his shoes. He wiped sweat from his forehead on his coat sleeve, slipped off the narrow black tie that hung open around his collar and put it in his pocket.

The salt taste was back in his mouth and he was so agitated by what he believed, hoped, he would find there, he had to put his hands on warm stone to dry them. He thought of the pitiful hungry eyes of the old men, their eagerness for some word of defiant success accomplished by the son of Macon Dead; and of the white men who strutted through the orchards and ate the Georgia peaches after they shot his grandfather's head off. Milkman took a deep breath and began to negotiate the rocks.

As soon as he put his foot on the first stone, he smelled money, although it was not a smell at all. It was like candy and sex and soft twinkling lights. Like piano music with a few strings in the background. He'd noticed it before when he waited under the pines near Pilate's house; more when the moon lit up the green sack that hung like a kept promise from her ceiling; and most when he tumbled lightly to the floor, sack in hand. Las Vegas and buried treasure; numbers dealers and Wells Fargo wagons; race track pay windows and spewing oil wells; craps, flushes, and sweepstakes tickets. Auctions, bank vaults, and heroin deals. It caused paralysis, trembling, dry throats, and sweaty palms. Urgency, and the feeling that "they" had been mastered or were on your side. Quiet men stood up and threw a queen down on the table hard enough to break her neck. Women sucked their bottom lips and put little red disks down in numbered squares. Lifeguards, A-students, eyed cash registers and speculated on how far away the door was. To win. There was nothing like it in the world.

Milkman became agile, pulling himself up the rock face, digging his knees into crevices, searching with his fingers for solid earth patches or ledges of stone. He left off thinking and let his body do the work. He stood up, finally, on level ground twenty feet to the right of the mouth of the cave. There he saw a crude footpath he might have found earlier if he had not been so hasty. That was the path the hunters used and that Pilate and his father had also used. None of them tore their clothes as he had, climbing twenty feet of steep rock.

He entered the cave and was blinded by the absence of light. He stepped back out and reentered, cupping his eyes. After a while, he could distinguish the ground from the wall of the cave. There was the ledge of rock where they'd slept, much larger than he had pictured. And worn places on the floor where fires had once burned, and several boulders standing around the entrance—one with a kind of V-shaped crown. But where were the bones? Circe said they dumped him in here. Farther back, probably, back where the shallow pit was. Milkman had no flashlight and his matches were certainly wet, but he tried to find a dry one anyway. Only one or two even sputtered. The rest were dead. Still, his eyes were getting used to the dark. He pulled a branch from a bush that grew near the entrance and bending forward, let it graze the ground before him as he walked. He had gone thirty or forty feet when he noticed the cave's walls were closer together. He could not see the roof at all. He stopped and began to move slowly sideways, the branch tip scratching a yard or so ahead. The side of his hand grazed rock and he flung the dry bat shit off it and moved to the left. The branch struck air. He stopped again, and lowered the tip until it touched ground again. Raising it up and down, and pressing it back and around, he could tell that he had found the pit. It was about two feet deep and maybe eight feet wide. Frantically he scraped the branch around the bottom. It hit something hard, again something else hard. Milkman swallowed and dropped to his knees. He squinted his eyes as hard as he could, but he couldn't see a thing. Suddenly he remembered a lighter in his vest pocket. He dropped the branch and fumbled for it, almost faint from the money smell—the twinkling lights, the piano music. He pulled it out, praying it would light. On the second try, it burst into flame and he peered down. The lighter went out. He snapped it back and held his hand over its fragile flame. At the bottom of the hole he saw rocks, boards, leaves, even a tin cup, but no gold. Stretched out on his stomach, holding the lighter in one hand, he swept the bottom with the other, clawing, pulling, fingering, poking. There were no fat little pigeon-breasted bags of gold. There was nothing. Nothing at all. And before he knew it, he was hollering a long, *awwww* sound into the pit. It triggered the bats, which swooped suddenly and dived in the darkness over his head. They startled him and he leaped to his feet, whereupon the sole of his right shoe split away from the soft cordovan leather. The bats drove him out in a lopsided run, lifting his foot high to accommodate the flopping sole.

In the sunlight once more, he stopped for breath. Dust, tears, and too bright light were in his eyes, but he was too angry and disgusted to rub them. He merely threw the lighter in a wide

high arc into the trees at the foot of the hills and limped down
the footpath, paying no attention to the direction he was going.
He put his feet down wherever was most convenient. Quite
suddenly, it seemed to him, he was at the creek again, but up-
stream where the crossing—about twelve feet here and so shallow he could see the stony bottom—was laid across with boards.
He sat down and lashed the sole of his shoe to its top with his
black string tie, then walked across the homemade bridge. The
woods on the other side had a pathway.

Milkman began to shake with hunger. Real hunger, not the
less than top-full feeling he was accustomed to, the nervous desire to taste something good. Real hunger. He believed if he
didn't get something to eat that instant he would pass out. He
examined the bushes, the branches, the ground for a berry, a
nut, anything. But he didn't know what to look for, nor how
they grew. Trembling, his stomach in a spasm, he tore off a few
leaves and put them in his mouth. They were as bitter as gall,
but he chewed them anyway, spit them out, and got others. He
thought of the breakfast food Mrs. Cooper had put before him,
which had disgusted him then. Fried eggs covered with grease,
fresh-squeezed orange juice with seed and pulp floating in it,
thick hand-cut bacon, a white-hot mound of grits and biscuits. It
was her best effort, he knew, but perhaps because of the whiskey he'd drunk the night before, he could only bring himself to
drink two cups of black coffee and eat two biscuits. The rest
had nauseated him, and what he did eat he had left at Circe's
door.

Some brush closed in on him and when he swept it angrily
aside, he saw a stile and the road in front of him. Macadam,
automobiles, fence posts, civilization. He looked at the sky to
gauge the hour. The sun was a quarter of the way down from
what even he knew was high noon. About one o'clock, he
guessed. Nephew would have come and gone. He felt in his
back pocket for his wallet. It was discolored at the edges from
the water, but the contents were dry. Five hundred dollars, his
driver's license, phone numbers on slips of paper, social security

card, airline ticket stub, cleaners receipts. He looked up and down the road. He had to get food, and started walking south, where he believed Danville lay, hoping to hitch as soon as a car came by. He was not only ravenous; his feet hurt. The third car to pass stopped—a 1954 Chevrolet—and the driver, a black man, showed the same interest in Milkman's clothes that Nephew had shown. He seemed not to notice or care about the rip at the knee or under the arm, the tie-tied shoe, the leaves in Milkman's hair, or the dirt all over the suit.

"Where you headed, partner?"

"Danville. As close as I can get."

"Hop on in, then. Little out my way. I cut over to Buford, but I'll get you closer than you was."

" 'Preciate it," answered Milkman. He loved the car seat, loved it. And sank his weary back into its nylon and sighed.

"Good cut of suit," the man said. "I guess you ain't from here'bouts."

"No. Michigan."

"Sure 'nough? Had a aunt move out there. Flint. You know Flint?"

"Yeah. I know Flint." Milkman's feet were singing, the tender skin of the ball louder than the heels. He dared not spread his toes, lest the singing never stop.

"What kinda place is it, Flint?"

"Jive. No place you'd want to go to."

"Thought so. Name sounds good, but I thought it'd be like that."

Milkman had noticed a six-bottle carton of Coca-Cola on the back seat when he got in the car. It was on his mind.

"Could I buy one of those Coca-Colas from you? I'm kinda thirsty."

"It's warm," said the man.

"Long as it's wet."

"Help yourself."

Milkman reached around and pulled a bottle out of its case.

"Got a bottle opener?"

The man took the bottle from him and put its head in his mouth and slowly pried the top off. Foam shot all over his chin and his lap before Milkman could take it from him.

"Hot." The man laughed and wiped himself with a navy-and-white handkerchief.

Milkman gulped the Coke, foam and all, in three or four seconds.

"Like another?"

He did but he said no. Just a cigarette.

"Don't smoke," said the man.

"Oh," said Milkman, and struggled against and lost to a long belch.


"Bus station's right around the bend there." They were just outside Danville. "You can make it easy."

"I really do thank you." Milkman opened the door. "What do I owe you? For the Coke and all?"

The man was smiling, but his face changed now. "My name's Garnett, Fred Garnett. I ain't got much, but I can afford a Coke and a lift now and then."

"I didn't mean . . . I . . ."

But Mr. Garnett had reached over and closed the door. Milkman could see him shaking his head as he drove off.

Milkman's feet hurt him so, he could have cried, but he made it to the diner/bus station and looked for the man behind the counter. He wasn't there, but a woman offered to help. There followed a long discussion in which he discovered that the bag was not there, the man was not there, she didn't know if a colored boy had picked it up or not, they didn't have a checkroom and she was mighty sorry but he could look at the stationmaster's if the boy didn't have it, and was there anything else she could do?

"Hamburgers," he said. "Give me some hamburgers and a cup of coffee."

"Yes, sir. How many?"

"Six," he said, but his stomach cramped on the fourth and bent him double with a pain that lasted off and on all the way to Roanoke. But before he left, he telephoned Reverend Cooper. His wife answered and told him that her husband was still at the freightyard and he could catch him there if he hurried. Milkman thanked her and hung up. Walking like a pimp in delicate shoes, he managed to get to the yard, which was fairly close to the bus station. He entered the gate and asked the first man he saw if Reverend Cooper was still there.

"Coop?" the man said. "I think he went on over to the station house. See it? Right over there."

Milkman followed his finger, and hobbled over the gravel and ties to the station house.

It was empty save for an old man dragging a crate.

"Excuse me," Milkman said. "Is Rev—is Coop still here?"

"Just left. If you run you can catch him," the man said. He wiped the sweat of exertion from his forehead.

Milkman thought about running anywhere on his tender feet and said, "Oh, well. I'll try to catch him another time." He turned to go.

"Say," said the man. "If you ain't gonna try to catch him, could you give me a hand with this?" He pointed down to the huge crate at his feet. Too tired to say no or explain, Milkman nodded. The two of them grunted and groaned over the box, and finally got it up on a dolly, where they could push it to the weighing platform. Milkman slumped over the crate and caught his breath, barely able to nod to the old man's thank yous. Then he went out of the station into the street.

He was tired now. Really tired. He didn't want to see Reverend Cooper and his success-starved friends again. And he certainly didn't want to explain anything to his father or Guitar just yet. So he hobbled back to the bus station and asked for the next bus leaving that was going south. It had to be south. And it had to be Virginia. Because now he thought he knew how to find out what had happened to the gold.

Full of hamburgers, sore of foot, sick to his stomach, but at least sitting down, he couldn't even feel the disappointment that lay in the pit in the cave. He slept heavily for several hours on the bus, woke and daydreamed, napped a little more, woke again at a rest stop and ate a bowl of pea soup. He went into a drugstore and replaced the shaving equipment and toilet articles he'd left at Reverend Cooper's, and decided to wait and get his shoe fixed (it was sealed with chewing gum now), his suit mended, and a new shirt in Virginia.

The Greyhound bus made a sound like the hum of the Weimaraners as it sped down the road, and Milkman shivered a little, the way he had when Circe glanced at them, sitting in the "last room," wondering if she would outlive them. But there were over thirty of them and reproducing all the time.

The low hills in the distance were no longer scenery to him. They were real places that could split your thirty-dollar shoes. More than anything in the world he'd wanted it to be there, for row upon row of those little bags to turn their fat pigeon chests up to his hands. He thought he wanted it in the name of Macon Dead's Georgia peaches, in the name of Circe and her golden-eyed dogs, and especially in the name of Reverend Cooper and his old-timey friends who began to die before their facial hair was out when they saw what happened to a black man like them—"ignorant as a hammer and broke as a convict"—who had made it anyway. He also thought he wanted it in the name of Guitar, to erase what looked like doubt in his face when Milkman left, the "I-know-you-gonna-fuck-up" look. There wasn't any gold, but now he knew that all the fine reasons for wanting it didn't mean a thing. The fact was he wanted the gold because it was gold and he wanted to own it. Free. As he had sat chomping the hamburgers in the bus station, imagining what going home would be like now—not only to have to say there was no gold, but also to know he was trapped there—his mind had begun to function clearly.

Circe said that Macon and Sing had boarded that wagon in Virginia, where they both came from. She also said Macon's body rose up from the ground at the first heavy rain, and that the Butlers, or somebody, dumped it in the hunters' cave one summer night. One summer night. And it was a body, a corpse, when they hauled it away, because they recognized him as a Negro. Yet Pilate said it was winter when she was there, and there were only bones. She said she went to see Circe and visited the cave four years later, in the snow, and took the white man's bones. Why didn't she see her father's bones? There should have been two skeletons. Did she step over one and collect the other? Surely Circe had told her the same thing she told him—that her father's body was in the cave. Did Pilate tell Circe that they had killed a man in there? Probably not, since Circe didn't mention it. Pilate said she took the white man's bones and didn't even look for the gold. But she lied. She had not mentioned the second skeleton because it wasn't there when she got to the cave. She didn't come back four years later—or if she did, it was her *second* trip. She came back *before* they dumped the Negro they found in the cave. She took the bones, all right; Milkman had seen them on the table in the jailhouse. But that's not all she took. She took the gold. To Virginia. And maybe somebody in Virginia would know.

Milkman followed in her tracks.

# Chapter 11

The women's hands were empty. No pocketbook, no change
purse, no wallet, no keys, no small paper bag, no comb, no
handkerchief. They carried nothing. Milkman had never in his
life seen a woman on the street without a purse slung over her
shoulder, pressed under her arm, or dangling from her clenched
fingers. These women walked as if they were going somewhere,
but they carried nothing in their hands. It was enough to let him
know he was really in the backwoods of Virginia, an area the
signs kept telling him was the Blue Ridge Mountains. Danville,
with its diner/bus station and its post office on the main street
was a thriving metropolis compared to this no-name hamlet, a
place so small nothing financed by state funds or private enter-
prise reared a brick there. In Roanoke, Petersburg, Culpeper
he'd asked for a town named Charlemagne. Nobody knew. The
coast, some said. Tidewater. A valley town, said others. He
ended up at an AAA office, and after a while they discovered it
and its correct name: Shalimar. How do I get there? Well, you
can't walk it, that's for sure. Buses go there? Trains? No. Well,

not very near. There is one bus, but it just goes to . . . He ended up buying a fifty-dollar car for seventy-five dollars out of a young man's yard. It broke down before he could get to the gas station and fill the tank. And when he got pushed to the station, he spent $132 on a fan belt, brake lining, oil filter, gas line filter, two retreads, and a brand-new oil pan, which he didn't need but bought before the mechanic told him the gasket was broken. It was a hard and bitter price to pay. Not because it wasn't worth it, and not because it had to be in cash since the garage owner looked at his Standard Oil credit card like it was a three-dollar bill, but because he had got used to prices in the South: socks two pairs for a quarter, resoled shoes thirty cents, shirt $1.98, and the two Tommys needed to know that he got a shave *and* a haircut for fifty cents.

By the time he bought the car, his morale had soared and he was beginning to enjoy the trip: his ability to get information and help from strangers, their attraction to him, their generosity (Need a place to stay? Want a good place to eat?). All that business about southern hospitality was for real. He wondered why black people ever left the South. Where he went, there wasn't a white face around, and the Negroes were as pleasant, wide-spirited, and self-contained as could be. He earned the rewards he got here. None of the pleasantness was directed at him because of his father, as it was back home, or his grandfather's memory, as it was in Danville. And now, sitting behind a steering wheel, he felt even better. He was his own director—relieving himself when he wanted to, stopping for cold beer when he was thirsty, and even in a seventy-five-dollar car the sense of power was strong.

He'd had to pay close attention to signs and landmarks, because Shalimar was not on the Texaco map he had, and the AAA office couldn't give a nonmember a charted course—just the map and some general information. Even at that, watching as carefully as he could, he wouldn't have known he had arrived if the fan belt hadn't broken again right in front of Solomon's General Store, which turned out to be the heart and soul of Shalimar, Virginia.

He headed for the store, nodding at the four men sitting out-side on the porch, and side-stepping the white hens that were strolling about. Three more men were inside, in addition to the man behind the counter, who he assumed was Mr. Solomon himself. Milkman asked him for a cold bottle of Red Cap, please.

"No beer for sale on Sunday," the man said. He was a light-skinned Negro with red hair turning white.

"Oh. I forgot what day it was." Milkman smiled. "Pop, then. I mean soda. Got any on ice?"

"Cherry smash. That suit you?"

"Fine. Suit me fine."

The man walked over to the side of the store and slid open the door of an ancient cooler. The floor was worn and wavy with years of footsteps. Cans of goods on the shelf were sparse, but the sacks, trays, and cartons of perishables and semiperishables were plentiful. The man pulled a bottle of red liquid from the cooler and wiped it dry on his apron before handing it to Milkman.

"A nickel if you drink it here. Seven cents if you don't."

"I'll drink it here."

"Just get in?"

"Yeah. Car broke down. Is there a garage nearby?"

"Naw. Five miles yonder is one, though."

"Five miles?"

"Yep. What's the trouble? Mebbe one a us can fix it. Where you headed?"

"Shalimar."

"You standin in it."

"Right here? This is Shalimar?"

"Yes, suh. Shalimar." The man pronounced it *Shalleemone*.

"Good thing I broke down. I would have missed it for sure." Milkman laughed.

"Your friend almost missed it too."

"My friend? What friend?"

"The one lookin for you. Drove in here early this mornin and axed for ya."

"Asked for me by name?"

"No. He never mentioned your name."

"Then how do you know he was looking for me?"

"Said he was lookin for his friend in a three-piece beige suit. Like that." He pointed to Milkman's chest.

"What'd he look like?"

"Dark-skinned man. 'Bout your complexion. Tall. Thin. What's a matter? Y'all get your wires crossed?"

"Yeah. No. I mean . . . what was his name?"

"Didn't say. Just asked for you. He come a long way to meet you, though. I know that. Drove a Ford with Michigan tags."

"Michigan? You sure Michigan?"

"Sure I'm sure. Was he supposed to meet you in Roanoke?" When Milkman looked wild-eyed, the man said, "I seen your tags."

Milkman sighed with relief. And then said, "I wasn't sure where we were going to meet up. And he didn't say his name?"

"Naw. Just said to give you some good-luck message if I was to see you. Lemme see . . ."

"Good luck?"

"Yeah. Said to tell you your day was sure coming or your day . . . something like that . . . your day is here. But I know it had a day in it. But I ain't sure if he said it was comin or was already here." He chuckled. "Wish mine was here. Been waitin fifty-seven years and it ain't come yet."

The other men in the store laughed congenially, while Milkman stood frozen, everything in him quiet but his heart. There was no mistaking the message. Or the messenger. Guitar was looking for him, was following him, and for professional reasons. Unless . . . Would Guitar joke about that phrase? That special secret word the Seven Days whispered to their victims?

"The drink abuse you?" Mr. Solomon was looking at him. "Sweet soda water don't agree with me."

Milkman shook his head and swallowed the rest hurriedly. "No," he said. "I'm just . . . car weary. I think I'll sit outside awhile." He started toward the door.

"You want me to see 'bout your car for you?" Mr. Solomon sounded slightly offended.

"In a minute. I'll be right back."

Milkman pushed the screen door and stepped outside on the porch. The sun was blazing. He took off his jacket and held it on his forefinger over his shoulder. He gazed up and down the dusty road. Shotgun houses with wide spaces between them, a few dogs, chickens, children, and the women with nothing in their hands. They sat on porches, and walked in the road swaying their hips under cotton dresses, bare-legged, their unstraightened hair braided or pulled straight back into a ball. He wanted one of them bad. To curl up in a cot in that one's arms, or that one, or that. That's the way Pilate must have looked as a girl, looked even now, but out of place in the big northern city she had come to. Wide sleepy eyes that tilted up at the corners, high cheekbones, full lips blacker than their skin, berry-stained, and long long necks. There must be a lot of intermarriage in this place, he thought. All the women looked alike, and except for some light-skinned red-headed men (like Mr. Solomon), the men looked very much like the women. Visitors to Shalimar must be rare, and new blood that settled here nonexistent.

Milkman stepped off the porch, scattering the hens, and walked down the road toward a clump of trees near a building that looked like a church or clubhouse of some sort. Children were playing behind the trees. Spreading his jacket on the burnt grass, he sat down and lit a cigarette.

Guitar was here. Had asked for him. But why was he afraid? They were friends, close friends. So close he had told him all about the Seven Days. There was no trust heavier than that. Milkman was a confidant, almost an accomplice. So why was he afraid? It was senseless. Guitar must have left that particular message so Milkman could know who was looking for him without his giving his name. Something must have happened back home. Guitar must be running, from the police, maybe, and decided to run toward his friend—the only one other than the Days who would know what it was all about and whom he could trust. Guitar needed to find Milkman and he needed help. That was it. But if Guitar knew Milkman was headed for Shalimar, he must have found that out in Roanoke, or Culpeper—or maybe even in Danville. And if he knew that, why didn't he wait? Where was he now? Trouble. Guitar was in trouble.

Behind him the children were singing a kind of ring-around-the-rosy or Little Sally Walker game. Milkman turned to watch. About eight or nine boys and girls were standing in a circle. A boy in the middle, his arms outstretched, turned around like an airplane, while the others sang some meaningless rhyme:

> *Jay the only son of Solomon*
> *Come booba yalle, come booba tambee*
> *Whirl about and touch the sun*
> *Come booba yalle, come booba tambee . . .*

They went on with several verses, the boy in the middle doing his imitation of an airplane. The climax of the game was a rapid shouting of nonsense words accompanied by more rapid twirling: "Solomon rye balaly *shoo*; yaraba medina hamlet *too*"—until the last line. "Twenty-one children the last one *Jay!*" At which point the boy crashed to earth and the others screamed.

Milkman watched the children. He'd never played like that as a child. As soon as he got up off his knees at the window sill, grieving because he could not fly, and went off to school, his velvet suit separated him from the other children. White and black thought he was a riot and went out of their way to laugh at him and see to it that he had no lunch to eat, nor any crayons, nor ever got through the line to the toilet or the water fountain. His mother finally surrendered to his begging for corduroy knickers or straights, which helped a little, but he was never asked to play those circle games, those singing games, to join in anything, until Guitar pulled those four boys off him. Milkman smiled, remembering how Guitar grinned and whooped as the four boys turned on him. It was the first time Milkman saw anybody really enjoy a fight. Afterward Guitar had taken off his baseball cap and handed it to Milkman, telling him to wipe the blood from his nose. Milkman bloodied the cap, returned it, and Guitar slapped it back on his head.

Remembering those days now, Milkman was ashamed of having been frightened or suspicious of Guitar's message. When he turned up, he would explain everything and Milkman would do what he could to help. He stood up and brushed his jacket. A black rooster strutted by, its blood-red comb draped forward like a wicked brow.

Milkman walked back toward Solomon's store. He needed a place to stay, some information, and a woman, not necessarily in that order. He would begin wherever the beginning was. In a way it was good Guitar had asked for him. Along with waiting for him and waiting for some way to get a new fan belt, he had a legitimate reason to dawdle. Hens and cats gave up their places on the steps as he approached them.

"Feelin better, are ya?" asked Mr. Solomon.

"Much better. Just needed a stretch, I guess." He jutted his chin toward the window. "Nice around here. Peaceful. Pretty women too."

A young man sitting on a chair tilted to the wall pushed his hat back from his forehead and let the front legs of the chair hit the floor. His lips were open, exposing the absence of four front teeth. The other men moved their feet. Mr. Solomon smiled but didn't say anything. Milkman sensed that he'd struck a wrong note. About the women, he guessed. What kind of place was this where a man couldn't even ask for a woman?

He changed the subject. "If my friend, the one who stopped by this morning, was going to wait for me here, where would he be likely to find a place to stay? Any rooming houses around here?"

"Rooming houses?"

"Yeah. Where a man can spend the night."

Mr. Solomon shook his head. "Nothin like that here."

Milkman was getting annoyed. What was all the hostility for? He looked at the men sitting around the store. "You think maybe one of them could help with the car?" he asked Mr. Solomon. "Maybe get another belt somewhere?"

Mr. Solomon kept his eyes on the counter. "Guess I could ask them." His voice was soft; he spoke as if he was embarrassed about something. There was none of the earlier chattiness he'd been full of when Milkman arrived.

"If they can't find one, let me know right away. I may have to buy another car to get back home."

Every one of the faces of the men turned to look at him, and Milkman knew he had said something else wrong, although he didn't know what. He only knew that they behaved as if they'd been insulted.

In fact they had been. They looked with hatred at the city Negro who could buy a car as if it were a bottle of whiskey because the one he had was broken. And what's more, who had said so in front of them. He hadn't bothered to say his name, nor ask theirs, had called them "them," and would certainly despise their days, which should have been spent harvesting their own crops, instead of waiting around the general store hoping a truck would come looking for mill hands or tobacco pickers in the flatlands that belonged to somebody else. His manner, his clothes were reminders that they had no crops of their own and no land to speak of either. Just vegetable gardens, which the women took care of, and chickens and pigs that the children took care of. He was telling them that they weren't men, that they relied on women and children for their food. And that the lint and tobacco in their pants pockets where dollar bills should have been was the measure. That thin shoes and suits with vests and smooth smooth hands were the measure. That eyes that had seen big cities and the inside of airplanes were the measure. They had seen him watching their women and rubbing his fly as he stood on the steps. They had also seen him lock his car as soon as he got out of it in a place where there couldn't be more than two keys twenty-five miles around. He hadn't found them fit enough or good enough to want to know their names, and believed himself too good to tell them his. They looked at his skin and saw it was as black as theirs, but they knew he had the heart of the white men who came to pick them up in the trucks when they needed anonymous, faceless laborers.

Now one of them spoke to the Negro with the Virginia license and the northern accent.

"Big money up North, eh?"

"Some," Milkman answered.

"Some? I hear tell everybody up North got big money."

"Lotta people up North got nothing." Milkman made his voice pleasant, but he knew something was developing.

"That's hard to believe. Why would anybody want to stay there if they ain't no big money?"

"The sights, I guess." Another man answered the first. "The sights and the women."

"You kiddin," said the first man in mock dismay. "You mean to tell me pussy different up North?"

"Naw," said the second. "Pussy the same everywhere. Smell like the ocean; taste like the sea."

"Can't be," said a third. "Got to be different."

"Maybe the pricks is different." The first man spoke again.

"Reckon?" asked the second man.

"So I hear tell," said the first man.

"How different?" asked the second man.

"Wee little," said the first man. "Wee, wee little."

"Naw!" said the second man.

"So they tell me. That's why they pants so tight. That true?" The first man looked at Milkman for an answer.

"I wouldn't know," said Milkman. "I never spent much time smacking my lips over another man's dick." Everybody smiled, including Milkman. It was about to begin.

"What about his ass hole? Ever smack your lips over that?"

"Once," said Milkman. "When a little young nigger made me mad and I had to jam a Coke bottle up his ass."

"What'd you use a bottle for? Your cock wouldn't fill it?"

"It did. After I took the Coke bottle out. Filled his mouth too."

"Prefer mouth, do you?"

"If it's big enough, and ugly enough, and belongs to a ignorant motherfucker who is about to get the livin shit whipped out of him."

The knife glittered.

Milkman laughed. "I ain't seen one of those since I was fourteen. Where I come from *boys* play with knives—if they scared they gonna lose, that is."

The first man smiled. "That's me, motherfucker. Scared to death I'm gonna lose."

Milkman did the best he could with a broken bottle, but his face got slit, so did his left hand, and so did his pretty beige suit, and he probably would have had his throat cut if two women hadn't come running in screaming, "Saul! Saul!"

The store was full of people by then and the women couldn't get through. The men tried to shush them, but they kept on screaming and provided enough lull for Mr. Solomon to interrupt the fight.

"All right. All right. That's enough of that."

"Shut your mouth, Solomon."

"Get them women outta here."

"Stick him, Saul, stick that cocksucker."

But Saul had a jagged cut over his eye and the blood pouring from it made it hard to see. It was difficult but not impossible for Mr. Solomon to pull him away. He left cursing Milkman, but his fervor was gone.

Milkman backed up against the counter, waiting to see if anybody else was going to jump him. When it looked as if no one was, and when the people were drifting outside to watch Saul scuffling and cursing at the men pulling him away, he slumped a little and wiped his face. When the entire store save for the owner was empty, Milkman hurled the broken bottle into a corner. It careened by the cooler and bounced off the wall before splintering on the floor. He walked outside, still panting, and looked around. Four older men still sat on the porch, as though nothing had happened. Blood was streaming down Milkman's face, but it had dried on his hand. He kicked at a white hen and sat down on the top step, wiping the blood with his handkerchief. Three young women with nothing in their hands stood in the road looking at him. Their eyes were wide but noncommittal. Children joined them, circling the women like birds. Nobody said anything. Even the four men on the porch were quiet. Nobody came toward him, offered him a cigarette or a glass of water. Only the children and the hens walked around. Under the hot sun, Milkman was frozen with anger. If he'd had a weapon, he would have slaughtered everybody in sight.

"You pretty good with a bottle. How you with a shotgun?" One of the older men had sidled up to him. The smile on his face was faint. It was as though now that the young men had had their chance, with unsatisfactory results, the older men would take over. Their style, of course, would be different. No name-calling toilet contest for them. No knives either, or hot breath and knotted neck muscles. They would test him, match and beat him, probably, on some other ground.

"Best shot there is," Milkman lied.

"That so?"

"Yeah, it's so."

"Some of us is going huntin later on. Care to join us?"

"That toothless motherfucker going too?"

"Saul? No."

"Cause I might have to knock the rest of them out."

The man laughed. "Sheriff took the others—with the butt of a gun."

"Yeah? Good."

"Well, you comin?"

"Sure I'm coming. Just get me the gun."

He laughed again. "Name's Omar."

"Macon Dead."

Omar blinked at the name, but didn't comment on it. He merely told him to come by King Walker's, a gas station about two miles up the road, right around sundown. "It's straight up yonder. Ain't no way in the world you can miss it."

"I won't miss it." Milkman stood up and walked to his car. He fumbled for the car keys, opened the door, and slid into the seat. He rolled down all four windows, found a towel in the back seat, and stretched out, using his jacket for a pillow and the towel as a bandage for his face. His feet stuck out the open door. Fuck 'em. Who were all these people roaming the world trying to kill him? His own father had tried while he was still in his mother's stomach. But he'd lived. And he had lived the last year dodging a woman who came every month to kill him, and he had lain just like this, with his arm over his eyes, wide open to whatever she had in her hand. He'd lived through that too. Then a witch had stepped out of his childhood nightmares to grab him, and he'd lived through that. Some bats had driven him out of a cave—and he'd lived through that. And at no time did he have a weapon. Now he walked into a store and asked if somebody could fix his car and a nigger pulled a knife on him. And he still wasn't dead. Now what did these black Neanderthals think they were going to do? Fuck 'em. My name's Macon; I'm already dead. He had thought this place, this Shalimar, was going to be home. His original home. His people came from here, his grandfather and his grandmother. All the way down South people had been nice to him, generous, helpful. In Danville they had made him the object of hero worship. In his own home town his name spelled dread and grudging respect. But here, in his "home," he was unknown, unloved, and damn near killed. These were some of the meanest unhung niggers in the world.

He slept, unmolested by everything and everybody except a dream in which he thought he saw Guitar looking down on him. When he woke he bought two cans of pineapple and a box of crackers from Mr. Solomon. He ate on the porch with the hens. The men were gone, and the sun was leaving. Only the children stayed to watch him eat. When he poured the last of the pineapple juice down his throat, one of the children stepped forward to ask, "Can we have your can, mister?" He held it out and they snatched the can and ran off to fashion some game out of it.

He started out for King Walker's. Even if he could have come up with a way to get out of the hunt, he wouldn't have taken it, in spite of the fact that he had never handled a firearm in his life. He had stopped evading things, sliding through, over, and around difficulties. Before he had taken risks only with Guitar. Now he took them alone. Not only had he let Hagar stab him; he had let the nightmare witch catch him and kiss him. To a man surviving that, anything else was a joke.

King Walker was nothing like his name suggested. He was a small man, bald, with a left cheek bulging with tobacco. Years ago he'd been a star pitcher in one of the black baseball leagues and the history of his career was nailed and pasted all over his shop. They had not lied when they said no garage or mechanic on duty was nearer than five miles. King Walker's station had obviously gone broke a long time ago. The pumps were dry; there wasn't even a can of oil in the place. Now it seemed to be used as a kind of clubhouse for the men and Walker lived in the back of the station. In addition to King Walker, who wasn't going, there was Omar and another man who had also been on the porch and who introduced himself as Luther Solomon—no relation to the grocery store Solomon. They were waiting for some others, who came soon after Milkman got there, driving an old Chevy. Omar introduced them as Calvin Breakstone and Small Boy.

Calvin seemed to be the most congenial of them, and followed the introductions with a command to King Walker to "get this city boy some shoes for his feet." King rummaged around, spitting tobacco, and came up with some mud-caked brogans. They outfitted Milkman completely, laughing all the while at his underwear, fingering his vest—Small Boy tried to get his wrestler's arms into Milkman's jacket—and wondering what had happened to his feet. Bits of skin still peeled from his toes because of the two days he had spent in wet shoes and socks. King Walker made him sprinkle Arm & Hammer soda on them before he put on the thick socks they gave him. When Milkman was dressed in World War II army fatigues with a knit cap on his head, they opened some Falstaff beer and began to talk about guns. At which point the revelry mixed with meanness abated and King Walker handed Milkman his Winchester .22.

"Ever use a twenty-two?"

"Not in a good while," Milkman said.

The five men piled into the Chevy and drove off into the lessening light. From what Milkman could tell, after fifteen minutes or so they were going up to high ground. As the car swerved through narrow roads, the conversation picked up again and they talked about other trips, game, kills, misses. Soon the only light came from the moon and it was getting cool enough for Milkman to be grateful for his knit cap. The car pulled ahead and around some sharp bends. In the rear-view mirror Milkman thought he glimpsed the headlights of another car and wondered briefly if they were being met by others. The sky was dark enough now for stars.

"Better make time, Calvin. Coon be done ate and gone on home."

Calvin pulled over and stopped the car.

"Let 'em rip," he said, and handed the car keys to Small Boy, who walked around to the back and unlocked the trunk. Three hounds leaped out, sniffing and wagging their tails. But they didn't make a sound.

"You brought Becky?" asked Luther. "Oh, man! We gonna get some coon tonight!"

The dogs' nervousness, their eagerness to hear the signal that would allow them to race off into the trees, made Milkman jittery. What was he supposed to do? Two feet in any direction from the headlights was black night.

Omar and Small Boy hauled equipment from the trunk: four lamps, one flashlight, rope, shells, and a pint bottle of liquor. When all four lamps were ablaze, they asked Milkman if he wanted to use a lamp or a flashlight. He hesitated, and Calvin said, "He can run with me. Give him the torch."

Milkman put it in his back pocket.

"Take that change out your pocket," said Calvin. "Makes too much noise."

Milkman did as he was told and took King's shotgun, a piece of rope, and a deep swig from the bottle they were passing around.

The dogs padded about, silent, panting, almost faint with excitement. But still they made no sound. Calvin and Omar both loaded their double-gauge shotguns with .22 shells in one barrel and buckshot in the other. Small Boy clapped his hands once, and the three hounds sped screaming into the night. The men didn't take off after them at once, as Milkman had supposed they would. Instead they stood quietly and listened for a while. Small Boy laughed lightly, shaking his head. "Becky's leadin. Let's go. Calvin, you and Macon go off to the right. We'll head this a way, and circle over by the gulch. Don't shoot no bears, now."

"Shoot him if I see him," said Calvin as he and Milkman moved away.

As they left the Chevy, the car that Milkman had noticed sped past them. Obviously, there were no others in the hunting party. Calvin was ahead, the burning lamp swinging low from his hand. Milkman flicked on his flashlight.

"Better save it," said Calvin. "You don't need it now."

They plodded on in a direction that may have been toward the screaming dogs, but Milkman couldn't tell.

"Any bears out here?" he asked in what he hoped was an interested but not anxious voice.

"Just us, and we got the guns." Calvin laughed and was suddenly swallowed up by the dark, only the low swinging lamp marking his path. Milkman watched the lamp until he realized that focusing on it kept him from seeing anything else. If he was to grow accustomed to the dark, he would have to look at what it was possible to see. A long moan sailed up through the trees somewhere to the left of where they were. It sounded like a woman's voice, sobbing, and mingling with the dogs' yelps and the men's shouts. A few minutes later, the distant screaming of the dogs and the calls of the three men stopped. There was only the soughing wind and his and Calvin's footsteps. It took Milkman a while to figure out how to pick up his feet and miss the roots and stones; to distinguish a tree from a shadow; to keep his head down and away from the branches that swept back from Calvin's hand into his face. They were walking upland. Every now and then Calvin stopped, threw his lamplight on a tree, and examined it closely from about three feet off the ground to up as far as his arm could go. Other times he lowered the lamp over the ground, and squatting down on his haunches, peered into the dirt. Each time he seemed to be whispering. Whatever he discovered he kept to himself and Milkman didn't ask him. All he wanted to do was keep up, be ready to shoot whatever the game was when it appeared, and look out for an attempt any of them might make on his life. Within an hour after arriving in Shalimar, a young man had tried to kill him in public. What these older men, under cover of night, were capable of he could only guess.

He heard the sound of the sobbing woman again and asked Calvin, "What the hell is that?"

"Echo," he said. "Ryna's Gulch is up ahead. It makes that sound when the wind hits a certain way."

"Sounds like a woman crying," said Milkman.

"Ryna. Folks say a woman name Ryna is cryin in there. That's how it got the name."

Calvin stopped, but so suddenly that Milkman, deep in thought about Ryna, bumped into him. "Hush!" Calvin closed his eyes and tilted his head into the wind. All Milkman could hear was the dogs again, yelping, but more rapidly, he thought, than before. Calvin whistled. A faint whistle came back to them.

"Son of a fuckin bitch!" Calvin's voice broke with agitation. "Bobcat! Come on, man!" He literally sprang away and Milkman did the same. Now they moved at double time, still on land that sloped upward. It was the longest trek Milkman had ever made in his life. Miles, he thought; we must be covering miles. And hours; it must be two hours now since he whistled. On they walked, and Calvin never broke his stride for anything except an occasional shout and an occasional pause to listen to the sound that came back.

The light was changing and Milkman was getting very tired. The distance between himself and Calvin's lamp was getting wider and wider. He was twenty years younger than Calvin, but found himself unable to keep up the pace. And he was getting clumsy—stepping over big stones rather than around them, dragging his feet and catching them in humped roots, and now that Calvin was not directly in front, he had to push the branches away from his face himself. The doubling down and under branches and pushing things out of his way were as exhausting as the walk. His breath was coming in shorter and shorter gasps and he wanted to sit down more than anything in the world. He believed they were circling now, for it seemed to him that this was the third time he had seen that double-humped rock in the distance. Should they be circling? he wondered. Then he thought he remembered hearing that certain prey circled when it was being stalked. Did bobcat? He didn't even know what a bobcat looked like.

At last he surrendered to his fatigue and made the mistake of sitting down instead of slowing down, for when he got up again, the rest had given his feet an opportunity to hurt him and the pain in his short leg was so great he began to limp and hobble. Soon it wasn't possible for him to walk longer than five minutes at a time without pausing to lean against a sweet gum tree. Calvin was a pinpoint of light bobbing ahead in and out of the trees. Finally Milkman could take no more; he had to rest. At the next tree he sank down to the ground and put his head back on its bark. Let them laugh if they wanted to; he would not move until his heart left from under his chin and went back down into his chest where it belonged. He spread his legs, pulled the flashlight out of his hip pocket, and put his Winchester down near his right leg. At rest now, he could feel the blood pulsing in his temple and the cut on his face stinging in the night wind from the leaf juice and tree sap the branches had smeared on it.

When he was breathing almost normally, he began to wonder what he was doing sitting in the middle of a woods in Blue Ridge country. He had come here to find traces of Pilate's journey, to find relatives she might have visited, to find anything he could that would either lead him to the gold or convince him that it no longer existed. How had he got himself involved in a hunt, involved in a knife-and-broken-bottle fight in the first place? Ignorance, he thought, and vanity. He hadn't been alert early enough, hadn't seen the signs jutting out everywhere around him. Maybe this was a mean bunch of black folk, but he should have guessed it, sensed it, and part of the reason he hadn't was the easy, good treatment he had received elsewhere. Or had he? Maybe the glow of hero worship (twice removed) that had bathed him in Danville had also blinded him. Perhaps the eyes of the men in Roanoke, Petersburg, Newport News, had not been bright with welcome and admiration. Maybe they were just curious or amused. He hadn't stayed in any place long enough to find out. A meal here, gas there—the one real contact was the buying of the car, and the seller needing a buyer would naturally be friendly under those circumstances. The same thing held when he'd had to have those elaborate repairs. What kind of savages were these people? Suspicious. Hot-tempered. Eager to find fault and despise any outsider. Touchy. Devious, jealous, traitorous, and evil. He had done nothing to deserve their contempt. Nothing to deserve the explosive hostility that engulfed him when he said he might have to buy a car. Why didn't they respond the way the man in Roanoke did when he bought the car? Because in Roanoke he did not have a car. Here he had one and wanted another, and perhaps it was that that upset them. Furthermore, he hadn't even suggested that he would trade the old one in. He had hinted that he would abandon the "broken" one and just get another. But so what? What business was it of theirs what he did with his money? He didn't deserve . . .

It sounded old. *Deserve*. Old and tired and beaten to death. Deserve. Now it seemed to him that he was always saying or thinking that he didn't deserve some bad luck, or some bad treatment from others. He'd told Guitar that he didn't "deserve" his family's dependence, hatred, or whatever. That he didn't even "deserve" to hear all the misery and mutual accusations his parents unloaded on him. Nor did he "deserve" Hagar's vengeance. But why shouldn't his parents tell him their personal problems? If not him, then who? And if a stranger could try to kill him, surely Hagar, who knew him and whom he'd thrown away like a wad of chewing gum after the flavor was gone—she had a right to try to kill him too.

Apparently he thought he deserved only to be loved—from a distance, though—and given what he wanted. And in return he would be . . . what? Pleasant? Generous? Maybe all he was really saying was: I am not responsible for your pain; share your happiness with me but not your unhappiness.

They were troublesome thoughts, but they wouldn't go away. Under the moon, on the ground, alone, with not even the sound of baying dogs to remind him that he was with other people, his self—the cocoon that was "personality"—gave way. He could barely see his own hand, and couldn't see his feet. He was only his breath, coming slower now, and his thoughts. The rest of him had disappeared. So the thoughts came, unobstructed by other people, by things, even by the sight of himself. There was nothing here to help him—not his money, his car, his father's reputation, his suit, or his shoes. In fact they hampered him. Except for his broken watch, and his wallet with about two hundred dollars, all he had started out with on his journey was gone: his suitcase with the Scotch, the shirts, and the space for bags of gold; his snap-brim hat, his tie, his shirt, his three-piece suit, his socks, and his shoes. His watch and his two hundred dollars would be of no help out here, where all a man had was what he was born with, or had learned to use. And endurance. Eyes, ears, nose, taste, touch—and some other sense that he knew he did not have: an ability to separate out, of all the things there were to sense, the one that life itself might depend on. What did Calvin see on the bark? On the ground? What was he saying? What did he hear that made him know something unexpected had happened some two miles—perhaps more—away, and that that something was a different kind of prey, a bobcat? He could still hear them—the way they had sounded the last few hours. Signaling one another. What were they saying? "Wait up?" "Over here?" Little by little it fell into place. The dogs, the men—none was just hollering, just signaling location or pace. The men and the dogs were talking to each other. In distinctive voices they were saying distinctive, complicated things. That long *yah* sound was followed by a specific kind of howl from one of the dogs. The low *howm howm* that sounded like a string bass imitating a bassoon meant something the dogs understood and executed. And the dogs spoke to the men: single-shot barks—evenly spaced and widely spaced—one every three or four minutes, that might go on for twenty minutes. A sort of radar that indicated to the men where they were and what they saw and what they wanted to do about it. And the men agreed or told them to change direction or to come back. All those shrieks, those rapid tumbling barks, the long sustained yells, the tuba sounds, the drumbeat sounds, the low liquid *howm howm*, the reedy whistles, the thin *eeeee*'s of a cornet, the *unh unh unh* bass chords. It was all language. An extension of the click people made in their cheeks back home when they wanted a dog to follow them. No, it was not language; it was what there was before language. Before things were written down. Language in the time when men and animals did talk to one another, when a man could sit down with an ape and the two converse; when a tiger and a man could share the same tree, and each understood the other; when men ran *with* wolves, not from or after them. And he was hearing it in the Blue Ridge Mountains under a sweet gum tree. And if they could talk to animals, and the animals could talk to them, what didn't they know about human beings? Or the earth itself, for that matter. It was more than tracks Calvin was looking for—he whispered to the trees, whispered to the ground, touched them, as a blind man caresses a page of Braille, pulling meaning through his fingers.

Milkman rubbed the back of his head against the bark. This was what Guitar had missed about the South—the woods, hunters, killing. But something had maimed him, scarred him like Reverend Cooper's knot, like Saul's missing teeth, and like his own father. He felt a sudden rush of affection for them all, and out there under the sweet gum tree, within the sound of men tracking a bobcat, he thought he understood Guitar now. Really understood him.

Down either side of his thighs he felt the sweet gum's surface roots cradling him like the rough but maternal hands of a grandfather. Feeling both tense and relaxed, he sank his fingers into the grass. He tried to listen with his fingertips, to hear what, if anything, the earth had to say, and it told him quickly that someone was standing behind him and he had just enough time to raise one hand to his neck and catch the wire that fastened around his throat. It cut like a razor into his fingers, tore into the skin so deeply he had to let go. The wire pressed into his neck then and took his breath. He thought he heard himself gurgling and saw a burst of many-colored lights dancing before his eyes. When the music followed the colored lights, he knew he had just drawn the last sweet air left for him in the world. Exactly the way he'd heard it would be, his life flashed before him, but it consisted of only one image: Hagar bending over him in perfect love, in the most intimate sexual gesture imaginable. In the midst of that picture he heard the voice of the someone holding the wire say, "Your Day has come," and it filled him with such sadness to be dying, leaving this world at the fingertips of his friend, that he relaxed and in the instant it took to surrender to the overwhelming melancholy he felt the cords of his struggling neck muscles relax too and there was a piece of a second in which the wire left him room enough to gasp, to take another breath. But it was a living breath this time, not a dying one. Hagar, the lights, the music, disappeared, and Milkman grabbed the Winchester at his side, cocked it, and pulled the trigger, shooting into the trees in front of him. The blast startled Guitar, and the wire slipped again. Guitar pulled it back, but Milkman knew his friend would need both hands to keep it that way. He turned the shotgun backward as far as he could and managed awkwardly, to pull the trigger again, hitting only branches and dirt. He was wondering if there was another blast in the gun when he heard right up close the wild, wonderful sound of three baying dogs who he knew had treed a bobcat. The wire dropped and he heard Guitar breaking into a fast run through the trees. Milkman stood up and grabbed his flashlight, pointing it in the direction of the sound of running feet. He saw nothing but branches resettling themselves. Rubbing his neck, he moved toward the sound of the dogs. Guitar did not have a gun, otherwise he would have used it, so Milkman felt secure heading for the dogs with the gun in his hand even though it had no more shot. He didn't miss; his sense of direction was accurate and he came upon Calvin, Small Boy, Luther, and Omar crouching on the ground a few feet away from the dogs and the glistening night eyes of a bobcat in a tree.

The dogs were trying their best to get up into the tree, and the men were considering whether to shoot the bobcat down, shoot a limb and make him jump down and fight the dogs, or what. They decided to try and kill the cat where he lay. Omar stood up and took his lamp over to the left. The cat crept a little ways out, following the light. Then Small Boy took aim and put a bullet just under the left foreleg and the bobcat dropped through the branches into the jaws of Becky and her companions.

There was a lot of life in the cat; he fought well until Calvin hollered the dogs away and shot it again, and once more, and then it was still.

They held the lamps over the carcass and groaned with pleasure at the size, the ferocity, the stillness of it. All four got down on their knees, pulling rope and knives, cutting a branch the width of a wrist, tying it and binding it for the long walk back.

They were so pleased with themselves it was some time before anybody remembered to ask Milkman what he was shooting at back there. Milkman hoisted the stake he was carrying a little higher and said, "I dropped the gun. I tripped and it went off. Then when I picked it up it went off again."

They burst into laughter. "Tripped? What'd you have the safety off for? Was you scared?"

"Scared to death," said Milkman. "Scared to death."

They hooted and laughed all the way back to the car, teasing Milkman, egging him on to tell more about how scared he was. And he told them. Laughing too, hard, loud, and long. Really laughing, and he found himself exhilarated by simply walking the earth. Walking it like he belonged on it; like his legs were stalks, tree trunks, a part of his body that extended down down down into the rock and soil, and were comfortable there—on the earth and on the place where he walked. And he did not limp.

They met dawn in King Walker's gas station for a rehash of the night they had spent. Milkman was the butt of their humor, but it was good-humored humor, quite unlike the laughter the trip had begun with. "Lucky to be alive. Cat wasn't the problem; this here nigger was the problem. Blastin away at us while we got a mean cat gettin ready to chew us and the dogs up both. Shootin all through the woods. Could have blown his own head off. Don't you city boys know how to handle yourself?"

"You country niggers got it all over us," Milkman answered.

Omar and Small Boy slapped him on the shoulders. Calvin hollered to Luther, "Go get Vernell. Tell her to get breakfast ready. Soon's we skin this cat, we comin in there with a appetite and she better be ready to meet it!"

Milkman went with them to the back of the station, where, on a small cemented area covered by a corrugated tin roof, the dead bobcat lay. Milkman's neck had swollen so it was difficult for him to lower his chin without pain.

Omar sliced through the rope that bound the bobcat's feet. He and Calvin turned it over on its back. The legs fell open. Such thin delicate ankles.

*"Everybody wants a black man's life."*

Calvin held the forefeet open and up while Omar pierced the curling hair at the point where the sternum lay. Then he sliced all the way down to the genitals. His knife pointed upward for a cleaner, neater incision.

*"Not his dead life; I mean his living life."*

When he reached the genitals he cut them off, but left the scrotum intact.

*"It's the condition our condition is in."*

Omar cut around the legs and the neck. Then he pulled the hide off.

*"What good is a man's life if he can't even choose what to die for?"*

The transparent underskin tore like gossamer under his fingers.

*"Everybody wants the life of a black man."*

Now Small Boy knelt down and slit the flesh from the scrotum to the jaw.

*"Fair is one more thing I've given up."*

Luther came back and, while the others rested, carved out the rectal tube with the deft motions of a man coring an apple.

*"I hope I never have to ask myself that question."*

Luther reached into the paunch and lifted the entrails. He dug under the rib cage to the diaphragm and carefully cut around it until it was free.

*"It is about love. What else but love? Can't I love what I criticize?"*

Then he grabbed the windpipe and the gullet, eased them back, and severed them with one stroke of his little knife.

*"It is about love. What else?"*

They turned to Milkman. "You want the heart?" they asked him. Quickly, before any thought could paralyze him, Milkman plunged both hands into the rib cage. "Don't get the lungs, now. Get the heart."

*"What else?"*

He found it and pulled. The heart fell away from the chest as easily as yolk slips out of its shell.

*"What else? What else? What else?"*

Now Luther went back into the stomach cavity and yanked the entrails out altogether. They sucked up like a vacuum through the hole that was made at the rectum. He slipped the entrails into a paper bag while the others began cleaning up, hosing down, salting, packing, straightening, and then they turned the cat over to let the blood drain down on its own hide.

"What are you going to do with it?" asked Milkman.

"Eat him!"

A peacock soared away and lit on the hood of a blue Buick.

Milkman looked at the bobcat's head. The tongue lay in its mouth as harmless as a sandwich. Only the eyes held the menace of the night.

Hungry as he was, he couldn't eat much of Vernell's breakfast, so he pushed the scrambled eggs, hominy, fried apples around in the plate, gulped coffee and talked a lot. And, somehow, he had to get around to the purpose of his visit to Shalimar.

"You know, my grandfather came from somewhere near here. My grandmother too."

"Did? From around here? What's their name?"

"I don't know her maiden name, but her first name was Sing. Any of you ever know anybody with a name like that?"

They shook their heads. "Sing? No. Never heard of nobody name that."

"I had an aunt live down this way too. Name of Pilate. Pilate Dead. Ever hear of her?"

"Ha! Sound like a newspaper headline: Pilot Dead. She do any flying?"

"No. *P-i-l-a-t-e*, Pilate."

"*P-i-l-a-t-e*. That spell *Pie-late*," Small Boy said.

"Naw, nigger. Not no *Pie-late*. Pilate like in the Bible, dummy."

"He don't read the Bible."

"He don't read nothin."

"He can't read nothin."

They teased Small Boy until Vernell interrupted them. "You all hush. You say Sing?" she asked Milkman.

"Yeah. Sing."

"I believe that was the name of a girl my gran used to play with. I remember the name cause it sounded so pretty. Gran used to talk about her all the time. Seem like her folks didn't like her to play with the colored children from over this way, so her and my gran used to sneak off and go fishin and berry-pickin. You know what I mean? She'd have to meet her in secret." Vernell eyed Milkman carefully. "This Sing girl was light-skinned, with straight black hair."

"That's her!" Milkman said. "She was mixed or Indian, one."

Vernell nodded. "Indian. One of old Heddy's children. Heddy was all right, but she didn't like her girl playin with coloreds. She was a Byrd."

"A what?"

"A Byrd. Belonged to the Byrd family over by the ridge. Near Solomon's Leap."

"Oh, yeah?" said one of the men. "One of Susan Byrd's people?"

"That's right. One of them. They never was too crazy 'bout colored folks. Susan either."

"Do they still live there?" asked Milkman.

"Susan do. Right behind the ridge. Only house back in there with a brick front. She by herself now. All the others moved out so they could pass."

"Can I walk it?" he asked.

"Most folks could, I reckon," said Omar. "But after last night I don't recommend it for you." He laughed.

"Can you drive a car through?"

"Part of the way you can. But the road is narrow and messy back up in there," said Vernell. "Horse, maybe, but not no car."

"I'll make it. Might take me a week, but I'll make it," said Milkman.

"Just don't carry no guns"—Calvin cooled his coffee in his saucer—"and you'll be all right." They all laughed again.

Milkman thought about that. Guitar was out there someplace, and since he seemed to know everything Milkman was doing or getting ready to do, he'd also know he was going out to some ridge. He touched his swollen neck. He didn't want to go anywhere alone without a gun.

"You ought to have a rest before you go trottin off anywhere," Omar said, looking at him. "There's a nice lady up the road a ways. She'd be proud to take you in." The look in his eyes was unmistakable. "Pretty woman too. Real pretty." Vernell grunted and Milkman smiled. Hope she's got a gun, he thought.

She didn't, but she had indoor plumbing and her smile was just like her name, Sweet, as she nodded her head to Milkman's query about whether he could take a bath. The tub was the newest feature in the tiny shotgun house and Milkman sank gratefully into the steaming water. Sweet brought him soap and a boar's-bristle brush and knelt to bathe him. What she did for his sore feet, his cut face, his back, his neck, his thighs, and the palms of his hands was so delicious he couldn't imagine that the lovemaking to follow would be anything but anticlimactic. If this bath and this woman, he thought, are all that come out of this trip, I will rest easy and do my duty to God, country, and the Brotherhood of Elks for the rest of my life. I will walk hot coals with a quart of kerosene in my hand for this. I will walk every railroad tie from here to Cheyenne and back for this. But when the lovemaking came, he decided he would crawl.

Afterward he offered to bathe her. She said he couldn't because the tank was small and there wasn't enough water for another hot bath.

"Then let me give you a cool one," he said. He soaped and rubbed her until her skin squeaked and glistened like onyx. She put salve on his face. He washed her hair. She sprinkled talcum on his feet. He straddled her behind and massaged her back. She put witch hazel on his swollen neck. He made up the bed. She gave him gumbo to eat. He washed the dishes. She washed his clothes and hung them out to dry. He scoured her tub. She ironed his shirt and pants. He gave her fifty dollars. She kissed his mouth. He touched her face. She said please come back. He said I'll see you tonight.

# Chapter 12

At four o'clock he knocked on the door of the only house back of the ridge with a brick front. Fresh and shining in the army fatigues Sweet had washed and pressed, he had tramped along feeling ready for anything. But he didn't think Guitar would jump him in the daytime on a winding path (which they called a road) that cut through hilly land that was nevertheless tilled and had a smattering of houses and people. If he did confront him (with anything other than a gun) Milkman was sure he could take him, but it would be best to get back before nightfall. He didn't know what was on Guitar's mind, but he knew it had something to do with the gold. If he knows I'm here and where I have been and what I did in each place, then he must know that I'm trying to get it, doing just what I said I would do. Why would he try to kill me before I got it or even found out what happened to it? Most of it was a total mystery to him, but the part that was clear was enough to keep him alert and jittery all the way.

The Byrd house sat on a neat lawn separated by a white picket fence from the field grass on either side of the property. A child's swing dangled from a cedar tree; four little steps painted blue led up to the porch, and from the window, between fluttering curtains, came the smell of gingerbread baking.

A woman who looked to be about his mother's age answered the door.

"Miss Byrd?" Milkman asked her.

"Yes?"

"How are you? My name is, uh, Macon, and I'm visiting here for a few days. I'm from Michigan and I think some of my people lived here a long time ago. I was hoping you'd be able to help me."

"Help you what?" She sounded arch and Milkman had the distinct impression that this lady did not like the color of his skin.

"Find them. I mean find out about them. We're all split up, my family, and some folks in town thought you might know some of them."

"Who's that, Susan?" Another woman's voice came from behind her.

"Somebody to see *me*, Grace."

"Well, why don't you ask him in? Don't make him state his business on the steps."

Miss Byrd sighed. "Please come in, Mr. Macon."

Milkman followed her into a pleasant living room full up with sunshine. "Excuse me," she said. "I didn't mean to be rude. Please have a seat." She motioned to a gray velvet wing-back chair. A woman in a two-piece print dress came into the room, clutching a paper napkin in her hand and chewing on something.

"Who'd you say?" She addressed her question to Miss Byrd, but ran inquisitive eyes over Milkman.

Miss Byrd held out a hand. "This is a friend of mine—Miss Long. Grace Long—Mr. . . ."

"How do you do?" Grace held out her hand to him.

"Fine, thank you."

"Mr. Macon, is it?"

"Yes."

"Susan, perhaps Mr. Macon would like some refreshment." Miss Long smiled and sat on the sofa facing the gray chair.

"Well, he just stepped foot in the door, Grace. Give me time." Miss Byrd turned to Milkman. "Would you like a cup of coffee or some tea?"

"Sure. Thanks."

"Which one?"

"Coffee's all right."

"You've got butter cookies, Susan. Give him some of those butter cookies."

Miss Byrd gave her friend a tired frown. "I'll just be a minute," she said to Milkman, and left the room.

"Yes, well. Did I hear you say you were visiting in these parts? We don't see too many visitors." Grace crossed her ankles. Like Susan Byrd, she wore black laced shoes and cotton stockings. As she made herself comfortable, she inched her dress up a little.

"Yes, visiting."

"You in the service?"

"Ma'am? Oh, no. I was hunting last night. Some friends lent me these." He smoothed the seam Sweet had made in the fatigues.

"Hunting? Oh, Lord, don't tell me you're one of them. I can't stand those hunting people. They make me sick, always prowling round other people's property. Day and night they're shooting up the world. I tell my students—I'm a schoolteacher, you know, I teach over at the normal school. Have you seen it yet?"

"No, not yet."

"Well, there's nothing to see, really. Just a school, like any other. But you're welcome to stop by. We'd be pleased to have you. Where you from again?"

"Michigan."

"I thought so. Susan!" She turned around. "He's from up North." Then back to Milkman: "Where are you staying?"

"Well, nowhere yet. I just met a few people in town and . . .'"

Susan Byrd came in with a tray of coffee cups and a plate of wide pale cookies.

"He's from Michigan," said Grace.

"I heard him. How do you take your coffee?"

"Black."

"Black? No cream or sugar at all?" asked Grace. "Wish I could do that; maybe I could get back into a twelve. But it's never going to happen now." She pressed one hand on her hip and smiled at Milkman.

"What did you want to see me about?" Susan Byrd placed a mild but clear stress on the word "me."

"I'm trying to locate anybody who might have known my grandmother. Her name was Sing."

Grace clapped her hands to her mouth and gave a little squeal. "Relatives! You all are relatives!" Milkman put his cup down.

"Well, I'll be!" Grace's eyes were lit and dancing.

"You've come to the right place," said Susan, "but I doubt if I can help you any."

"What are you talking about, Susan? Your mother was named Sing, wasn't she?"

"No, she wasn't, Grace, and if you let me finish a sentence you might learn something you don't know too."

"I thought you said—"

"My mother's name was Mary. *M-a-r-y*, Mary."

"Well, excuse *me*."

Susan turned to Milkman. "My father, Crowell Byrd, had a sister named Sing."

"That must be her! My grandmother! Sing. Did she marry a man named—"

"I knew there was somebody in your family named Sing!"

"She didn't marry anybody that I know of." Susan interrupted them both.

"Oh, this is really something. A stranger walks right into your house and he's your own . . . what? Cousin? I hate to say it, but this is a small world. Isn't it? You have got to visit my class, Mr. Macon."

Milkman joined Susan Byrd in ignoring Grace Long. "Where did she live?" he asked her.

"The last time my father saw her, she was on a wagon headed for Massachusetts to a private school up there. A Quaker school."

"Your people Quakers? You never told me that. See, Mr. Macon, what your friends hide from you? I bet she'd hide you too."

"And she never married?" Milkman couldn't take the time to acknowledge Grace's attentions.

"Not anybody we heard of. After she went to that Quaker school they lost track of her. I believe they tried to locate her, mostly because my grandmother—her name was Heddy—she was so torn up about it. I always believed the same thing my father believed: that she didn't want to be found after she left that school."

"You know darn well she didn't," said Grace. "She probably started passing like the rest of 'em, that's what." She leaned toward Milkman. "There used to be a lot of that. A lot of it. Not so much nowadays, but there used to be a lot of 'em did it—if they could." She shot a glance at Susan. "Like your cousins, Susan. They're passing now. Lilah, John. I know John is, and he knows I know he is."

"Everybody knows that, Grace."

"Mr. Macon doesn't know it. I saw John on the street in Mayville—"

"Mr. Macon doesn't need to know it. He's not even interested."

"How do you know he's not?"

"Because he said the woman he's looking for was his grandmother, and if she's his grandmother she'd be too dark to . . ." Susan Byrd hesitated. "Well, too dark to pass. Wouldn't she?" She flushed a little.

Milkman ignored the question. "And you say she lived in Massachusetts, right?"

"Yes. Boston."

"I see." It looked like a dead end, so he decided to follow another line. "Did you ever know or hear of a woman around here named Pilate?"

"Pilate. No. Never. Have you, Grace?"

Grace shook her head. "No, and I've been here most of my life."

"I've been here *all* of mine," said Susan. "Both my parents were born here and so was I. Never been farther away than St. Phillips County. I have people in South Carolina, but I've never even been to visit them."

"That's because they're passing too. Just like John. You couldn't visit them if you wanted to." Grace leaned over the plate of cookies and selected one.

"They're not the only family I have left." Susan was indignant.

"I hope not. It's a sad thing, Mr. Macon, when you're left without any people to claim you. I keep up with my family. I'm not married, you know, not yet anyway, but my family is *very* close." She gave him a meaningful look. Milkman turned his wrist and looked down to see what time it was.

"Oh, look at that." Grace pointed to his hand. "What a good-looking watch. May I see it?" Milkman stood up to hand it to her and remained standing. "Look, Susan, it doesn't have a single number on it. Just dots. Now, how can anybody figure out what time it is from those dots?"

Susan rose too. "You ever been down here before, Mr. Macon?"

"No. This is my first visit."

"Well, I hope it won't be your last. How long will you be here?"

"Oh, I think I'll get on back tonight or tomorrow at the latest." He looked out the window. The sun was dropping.

"That soon?" asked Grace. "Why don't you give him something to take with him, Susan? Would you like to take some butter cookies with you, Mr. Macon?"

"No, thank you."

"You'll be happy to have them later." The woman was wearing him down. He smiled, though, and said, "If you like."

"I'll fix a little package for you. Okay, Susan?" She fled from the room.

Susan managed a small smile. "Wish you could stay and visit with us awhile." Her words were as mechanical as her smile.

"So do I," he said, "but, well, maybe I'll be back."

"That'd be nice. Sorry I couldn't be of any help to you."

"You have been."

"Have I?"

"Oh, sure. You have to know what's wrong before you can find what's right."

She smiled a genuine smile then. "It's important to you, is it, to find your people?"

Milkman thought about it. "No. Not really. I was just passing through, and it was just—just an idea. It's not important."

Grace returned with a little parcel wrapped in white paper napkins. "Here you are," she said. "You'll appreciate this later on."

"Thank you. Thank you both."

"Nice meeting you."

"And you."

He left the house feeling tired and off center. I'll spend one more night here and then leave, he thought. The car should be fixed by now. There's nothing here to know, no gold or any traces of it. Pilate lived in Virginia, but not in this part of the state. Nobody at all has heard of her. And the Sing that lived here went to Boston, not Danville, Pennsylvania, and passed for white. His grandmother would have been "too dark to pass." She had actually blushed. As though she'd discovered something shameful about him. He was both angry and amused and wondered what Omar and Sweet and Vernell thought of Miss Susan Byrd.

He was curious about these people. He didn't feel close to

them, but he did feel connected, as though there was some cord or pulse or information they shared. Back home he had never felt that way, as though he belonged to anyplace or anybody. He'd always considered himself the outsider in his family, only vaguely involved with his friends, and except for Guitar, there was no one whose opinion of himself he cared about. Once, long ago, he had cared what Pilate and Hagar thought of him, but having conquered Hagar and having disregarded Pilate enough to steal from her, all that was gone. But there was something he felt now—here in Shalimar, and earlier in Danville—that reminded him of how he used to feel in Pilate's house. Sitting in Susan Byrd's living room, lying with Sweet, eating with those men at Vernell's table, he didn't have to get over, to turn on, or up, or even out.

And there was something more. It wasn't true what he'd said to Susan Byrd: that it wasn't important to find his people. Ever since Danville, his interest in his own people, not just the ones he met, had been growing. Macon Dead, also known as Jake somebody. Sing. Who were they, and what were they like? The man who sat for five nights on a fence with a gun, waiting. Who named his baby girl Pilate, who tore a farm out of a wilderness. The man who ate pecans on a wagon going North. Did he have brothers or sisters whom he left behind? Who was his mother, his father? And his wife. Was she the Boston Sing? If so, what was she doing on a wagon? Why would she go off to a northern private school on a wagon? Not a carriage or a train, but a wagon—full of ex-slaves. Maybe she never got to Boston. Maybe she didn't pass. She could have changed her mind about school and run off with the boy she ate pecans with. And whoever she was, why did she want her husband to keep that awful name? To wipe out the past? What past? Slavery? She was never a slave. *His* slave past? And why didn't his own father, and Pilate, know any of their own relatives? Wasn't there any family to notify when the father died? Macon didn't ever try to get to Virginia. Pilate headed straight for it.

Milkman opened the parcel Grace had fixed for him and took

out a cookie. A little piece of paper fluttered to the ground. He picked it up and read: "Grace Long 40 Route 2 three houses down from the Normal School." He smiled. That's why it took her so long to wrap up four cookies. He bit into one of them and sauntered along, crumpling the napkins and Grace's invitation into a wad. The questions about his family still knocked around in his head like billiard balls. If his grandfather, this Jake, was born in the same place his wife was, in Shalimar, why did he tell the Yankee he was born in Macon, thereby providing him with the raw material for the misnaming? And if he and his wife were born in the same place, why did Pilate and his father and Circe all say they "met" on that wagon? And why did the ghost tell Pilate to sing? Milkman chuckled to himself. That wasn't what he was telling her at all; maybe the ghost was just repeating his wife's name, Sing, and Pilate didn't know it because she never knew her mother's name. After she died Macon Dead wouldn't let anybody say it aloud. That was funny. He wouldn't speak it after she died, and after he died that's all he ever said—her name.

Jesus! Here he was walking around in the middle of the twentieth century trying to explain what a ghost had done. But why not? he thought. One fact was certain: Pilate did not have a navel. Since that was true, anything could be, and why not ghosts as well?

He was near the road leading to the town now, and it was getting dark. He lifted his wrist to look at his watch and remembered that Grace had not given it back to him. "Damn," he murmured aloud. "I'm losing everything." He stood still, trying to make up his mind whether to go back for it now or later. If he went now, he'd be forced to return in deep darkness. Totally defenseless before a hit from Guitar. But it would be a real bother to have to come all the way back here—where no car could make it—tomorrow when he was going to leave. But Guitar might be—

"I can't let him direct and determine what I do, where I go or when. If I do that now I'll do it all my life and he'll run me off the earth."

He didn't know what to do, but decided finally that a watch was not worth worrying about. All it could do was tell him the time of day and he really wasn't interested. Wiping cookie crumbs from his mustache, he turned into the main road, and there, outlined in cobalt blue, stood Guitar. Leaned, rather, against a persimmon tree. Milkman stopped, surprised at the calm, steady beat of his heart—the complete absence of fear. But then, Guitar was cleaning his fingernails with a harmless match stick. Any weapon he had would have to be hidden in his denim jacket or pants.

They looked at each other for a minute. No, less. Just long enough for the heart of each man to adjust its throb to the downbeat of the other. Guitar spoke first.

"My man."

Milkman ignored the greeting. "Why, Guitar? Just tell me why."

"You took the gold."

"What gold? There wasn't any gold."

"You took the gold."

"The cave was empty, man. I got down on my stomach and looked in that pit. I put my hands—"

"You took the gold."

"You're crazy, Guitar."

"Angry. Never crazy."

"There wasn't any gold!" Milkman tried hard not to shout.

"I saw you, motherfucker."

"Saw me what?"

"Take the gold."

"Where?"

"In Danville."

"You saw me with gold in Danville?"

"I saw you with gold in Danville."

"You've got to be kidding. What was I doing with it?"

"Shipping it."

"Shipping it?"

"Yeah. Why the game, man? You just greedy, like your old

man? Or what?" Guitar's eyes rested on the last butter cookie in Milkman's hand. He frowned and began to breathe through his lips.

"Guitar, I didn't ship no gold. There wasn't any gold to ship. You couldn't have seen me."

"I saw you, baby. I was in the station."

"What fuckin station?"

"The freight station in Danville."

Milkman remembered then, going to look for Reverend Cooper, looking all over for him. Then going into the station house to see if he'd gone, and there helping a man lift a huge crate onto the weighing platform. He started to laugh. "Oh, shit. Guitar, that wasn't no gold. I was just helping that man lift a crate. He asked me to help him. Help him lift a big old crate. I did and then I split."

Guitar looked at the cookie again, then back into Milkman's eyes. Nothing changed in his face. Milkman knew it sounded lame. It was the truth, but it sounded like a lie. A weak lie too. He also knew that in all his life, Guitar had never seen Milkman give anybody a hand, especially a stranger; he also knew that they'd even discussed it, starting with Milkman's not coming to his mother's rescue in a dream he had. Guitar had accused him of selfishness and indifference; told him he wasn't serious, and didn't have any fellow feeling—none whatsoever. Now he was standing there saying that he willingly, spontaneously, had helped an old white man lift a huge, heavy crate. But it was true. It was true. And he'd prove it.

"Guitar, why am I here? If I was shipping gold back home, why am I here dressed like this? Would I be roaming around in the country like a fool with a crate of gold off somewhere? Would I? What the fuck would I do that for and then come here?"

"Maybe you shipped the gold *here*, you jive-ass."

"What the fuck are you talking about?"

"I looked! I saw it! You hear me? I drove down there, followed you there, because I had a funny feeling that you were pulling a fast one. I wasn't sure, but I felt it. If I was wrong, I'd help you get it. But I wasn't wrong. I got into Danville that afternoon. I drove right past the freight depot and there you were in your little beige suit. I parked and followed you into the station. When I got there I saw you shipping it. Giving it to the man. I waited until you left, and I went back in and asked the cracker if my friend"—he slurred the word—"had shipped a crate to Michigan. The man said no. Just one crate on the load, he said. Just one crate. And when I asked him where it was going, all he could remember was Virginia." Guitar smiled. "The bus you caught wasn't headed for Michigan. It was headed for Virginia. And here you are."

Milkman felt whipped. There was nothing to do but let it play.

"Was my name on the crate?"

"I didn't look."

"Would I send a crate of gold to Virginia—*gold*, man."

"You might. You did."

"Is that why you tried to kill me?"

"Yes."

"Because I ripped you off?"

"Because you ripped *us* off! You are fuckin with our work!"

"You're wrong. Dead wrong."

"The 'dead' part is you."

Milkman looked down at the cookie in his hand. It looked foolish and he started to throw it away, but changed his mind. "So my Day has come?"

"Your Day has come, but on *my* schedule. And believe it: I will run you as long as there is ground. Your name is Macon, but you ain't dead yet."

"Tell me something. When you saw me in the station, with the crate, why did you back off and hide? Why didn't you just walk up to me? It could have been settled there."

"I told you. I had this funny funny feeling."

"That I was going to cut you out?"

"Cut *us* out. Yes."

"And you believe I did?"

"Yes."

"Back there in the woods you were angry."

"Yes."

"Now you're going to wait till the gold comes."

"Yes."

"And I pick it up."

"You won't be able to pick it up."

"Do me a favor. When it gets here. Check it first to see if there's gold in it."

"First?"

"Or last. But before you haul it all the way back home."

"Don't worry yourself about it."

"One more thing. Why the message? Why'd you warn me with a message at the store?"

"You're my friend. It's the least I could do for a friend."

"My man. I want to thank you."

"You're welcome, baby."

Milkman slipped into Sweet's bed and slept the night in her perfect arms. It was a warm dreamy sleep all about flying, about sailing high over the earth. But not with arms stretched out like airplane wings, nor shot forward like Superman in a horizontal dive, but floating, cruising, in the relaxed position of a man lying on a couch reading a newspaper. Part of his flight was over the dark sea, but it didn't frighten him because he knew he could not fall. He was alone in the sky, but somebody was applauding him, watching him and applauding. He couldn't see who it was.

When he awoke the next morning and set about seeing to the repair of his car, he couldn't shake the dream, and didn't really want to. In Solomon's store he found Omar and Solomon shaking sacks of okra into peck baskets and he still felt the sense of lightness and power that flying had given him.

"Got a belt for your car," said Omar. "Ain't new, but it ought to fit."

"Hey, that's good. Thanks, Omar."

"You leavin us right away?"

"Yeah, I have to get on back."

"You see that Byrd woman all right?"

"Yeah, I saw her."

"She help you any?" Omar wiped the okra fuzz from his hands onto his trousers.

"No. Not much."

"Well, King Walker say he be down this morning and put the belt on. You probably ought to get a good checkup on that car once you get on the road."

"I plan to."

"Sweet give you any breakfast?" asked Solomon.

"She tried, but I wanted to get over here early to see about the car."

"What about a cup a coffee; there's a full pot in back."

"No, thanks. I think I'll walk around a little till he comes."

It was six-thirty in the morning and the town was bustling as though it were high noon. Life and business began early in the South so the coolest part of the day could be taken advantage of. People had already eaten, women had already washed clothes and were spreading them on bushes, and in a few days, when the school in the next town opened, children at this hour would already be walking, running over the roads and fields to class. Now they were sauntering about, doing chores, teasing cats, throwing bread to stray chickens, and some of them were playing their endless round games. Milkman could hear them singing and wandered off toward them and the huge cedar that reared up over their heads. Again their sweet voices reminded him of the gap in his own childhood, as he leaned against the cedar to watch them. The boy in the middle of the circle (it seemed always to be a boy) spun around with his eyes closed and his arm stretched out, pointing. Round and round he went until the song ended with a shout and he stopped, his finger pointing at a child Milkman could not see. Then they all dropped to their knees and he was surprised to hear them begin another song at this point, one he had heard off and on all his life. That old blues song Pilate sang all the time: "O Sugarman don't leave me here," except the children sang, "Solomon don't leave me here."

Milkman smiled, remembering Pilate. Hundreds of miles away, he was homesick for her, for her house, for the very people he had been hell-bent to leave. His mother's quiet, crooked, apologetic smile. Her hopeless helplessness in the kitchen. The best years of her life, from age twenty to forty, had been celibate, and aside from the consummation that began his own life, the rest of her life had been the same. He hadn't thought much of it when she'd told him, but now it seemed to him that such sexual deprivation would affect her, hurt her in precisely the way it would affect and hurt him. If it were possible for somebody to force him to live that way, to tell him, "You may walk and live among women, you may even lust after them, but you will not make love for the next twenty years," how would he feel? What would he do? Would he continue as he was? And suppose he were married and his wife refused him for fifteen years. His mother had been able to live through that by a long nursing of her son, some occasional visits to a grave-yard. What might she have been like had her husband loved her?

And his father. An old man now, who acquired things and used people to acquire more things. As the son of Macon Dead the first, he paid homage to his own father's life and death by loving what that father had loved: property, good solid prop-erty, the bountifulness of life. He loved these things to excess because he loved his father to excess. Owning, building, acquir-ing—that was his life, his future, his present, and all the history he knew. That he distorted life, bent it, for the sake of gain, was a measure of his loss at his father's death.

As Milkman watched the children, he began to feel uncom-fortable. Hating his parents, his sisters, seemed silly now. And the skim of shame that he had rinsed away in the bathwater after having stolen from Pilate returned. But now it was as thick and as tight as a caul. How could he have broken into that house—

the only one he knew that achieved comfort without one article of comfort in it. No soft worn-down chair, not a cushion or a pillow. No light switch, no water running free and clear after a turn of a tap handle. No napkins, no tablecloth. No fluted plates or flowered cups, no circle of blue flame burning in a stove eye. But peace was there, energy, singing, and now his own remembrances.

His mind turned to Hagar and how he had treated her at the end. Why did he never sit her down and talk to her? Honestly. And what ugly thing was it he said to her the last time she tried to kill him? And God, how hollow her eyes had looked. He was never frightened of her; he never actually believed that she would succeed in killing him, or that she really wanted to. Her weapons, the complete lack of cunning or intelligence even of conviction, in her attacks were enough to drain away any fear. Oh, she could have accidentally hurt him, but he could have stopped her in any number of ways. But he hadn't wanted to. He had used her—her love, her craziness—and most of all he had used her skulking, bitter vengeance. It made him a star, a celebrity in the Blood Bank; it told men and other women that he was one bad dude, that he had the power to drive a woman out of her mind, to destroy her, and not because she hated him, or because he had done some unforgivable thing to her, but because he had fucked her and she was driven wild by the absence of his magnificent joint. His hog's gut, Lena had called it. Even the last time, he used her. Used her imminent arrival and feeble attempt at murder as an exercise of his will against hers—an ultimatum to the universe. "Die, Hagar, die." Either this bitch dies or I do. And she stood there like a puppet strung up by a puppet master who had gone off to some other hobby.

*O Solomon don't leave me here.*

The children were starting the round again. Milkman rubbed the back of his neck. Suddenly he was tired, although the morning was still new. He pushed himself away from the cedar and sank to his haunches.

*Jay the only son of Solomon*
*Come booba yalle, come . . .*

Everybody in this town is named Solomon, he thought wearily. Solomon's General Store, Luther Solomon (no relation), Solomon's Leap, and now the children were singing "*Solomon* don't leave me" instead of "*Sugarman*." Even the name of the town sounded like Solomon: Shalimar, which Mr. Solomon and everybody else pronounced *Shalleemone*.

Milkman's scalp began to tingle. Jay the only son of Solomon? Was that *Jake* the only son of Solomon? Jake. He strained to hear the children. That was one of the people he was looking for. A man named Jake who lived in Shalimar, as did his wife, Sing.

He sat up and waited for the children to begin the verse again. "Come booba yalle, come booba tambee," it sounded like, and didn't make sense. But another line—"Black lady fell down on the ground"—was clear enough. There was another string of nonsense words, then "Threw her body all around." Now the child in the center began whirling, spinning to lyrics sung in a different, faster tempo: "Solomon 'n' Reiner Belali Shalut . . ."

Solomon again, and Reiner? Ryna? Why did the second name sound so familiar? Solomon and Ryna. The woods. The hunt. Solomon's Leap and Ryna's Gulch, places they went to or passed by that night they shot the bobcat. The gulch was where he heard that noise that sounded like a woman crying, which Calvin said came from Ryna's Gulch, that there was an echo there that folks said was "a woman name Ryna" crying. You could hear her when the wind was right.

But what was the rest: Belali . . . Shalut . . . Yaruba? If Solomon and Ryna were names of people, the others might be also. The verse ended in another clear line. "Twenty-one children, the last one *Jake!*" And it was at the shout of *Jake* (who was also, apparently, "the only son of Solomon") that the twirling boy stopped. Now Milkman understood that if the child's finger pointed at nobody, missed, they started up again. But if it pointed directly to another child, that was when they fell to their knees and sang Pilate's song.

Milkman took out his wallet and pulled from it his airplane ticket stub, but he had no pencil to write with, and his pen was in his suit. He would just have to listen and memorize it. He closed his eyes and concentrated while the children, inexhaustible in their willingness to repeat a rhythmic, rhyming action game, performed the round over and over again. And Milkman memorized all of what they sang.

> *Jake the only son of Solomon*
> *Come booba yalle, come booba tambee*
> *Whirled about and touched the sun*
> *Come konka yalle, come konka tambee*
>
> *Left that baby in a white man's house*
> *Come booba yalle, come booba tambee*
> *Heddy took him to a red man's house*
> *Come konka yalle, come konka tambee*
>
> *Black lady fell down on the ground*
> *Come booba yalle, come booba tambee*
> *Threw her body all around*
> *Come konka yalle, come konka tambee*
>
> *Solomon and Ryna Belali Shalut*
> *Yaruba Medina Muhammet too.*
> *Nestor Kalina Saraka cake.*
> *Twenty-one children, the last one Jake!*
>
> *O Solomon don't leave me here*
> *Cotton balls to choke me*
> *O Solomon don't leave me here*
> *Buckra's arms to yoke me*
>
> *Solomon done fly, Solomon done gone*
> *Solomon cut across the sky, Solomon gone home.*

He almost shouted when he heard "Heddy took him to a red man's house." Heddy was Susan Byrd's grandmother on her father's side, and therefore Sing's mother too. And "red man's house" must be a reference to the Byrds as Indians. Of course! Sing was an Indian or part Indian and her name was Sing Byrd or, more likely, Sing Bird. No—Singing Bird! That must have been her name originally—Singing Bird. And her brother, Crowell Byrd, was probably Crow Bird, or just Crow. They had mixed their Indian names with American-sounding names. Milkman had four people now that he could recognize in the song: Solomon, Jake, Ryna and Heddy, and a veiled reference to Heddy's Indianness. All of which seemed to put Jake and Sing together in Shalimar, just as Circe had said they were. He couldn't be mistaken. These children were singing a story about his own people! He hummed and chuckled as he did his best to put it all together.

Jake's father was Solomon. Did Jake whirl about and touch the sun? Did Jake leave a baby in a white man's house? No. If the "Solomon don't leave me" line was right, Solomon was the one who left, who "flew away"—meaning died or ran off—not Jake. Maybe it was the baby, or Jake himself, who was begging him to stay. But who was the "black lady" who fell down on the ground? Why did she throw her body all around? It sounded like she was having a fit. Was it because somebody took her baby first to a white man's house, then to an Indian's house? Ryna? Was Ryna the black lady still crying in the gulch? Was Ryna Solomon's daughter? Maybe she had an illegitimate child, and her father— No. It's Solomon she is crying for, not a baby. "Solomon don't leave me." He must have been her lover.

Milkman was getting confused, but he was as excited as a child confronted with boxes and boxes of presents under the skirt of a Christmas tree. Somewhere in the pile was a gift for him.

Yet there were many many missing pieces. Susan Byrd, he thought—she would have to know more than she had told him. Besides, he had to get his watch back.

He ran back to Solomon's store and caught a glimpse of himself in the plate-glass window. He was grinning. His eyes were shining. He was as eager and happy as he had ever been in his life.

# Chapter 13

It was a long time after he left, that warm September morning, that she was able to relax enough to drop the knife. When it clattered to the linoleum, she brought her arms down, oh, so slowly, and cradled her breasts as though they were two mangoes thumbed over in the marketplace and pushed aside. She stood that way in the little rented room with the sunshine pouring in until Guitar came home. He could not get her to speak or move, so he picked her up in his arms and carried her downstairs. He sat her on the bottom step while he went to borrow a car to drive her home.

Terrible as he thought the whole business was, and repelled as he was by mindlessness in love, he could not keep the deep wave of sorrow from engulfing him as he looked at this really rather pretty woman sitting straight as a pole, holding her breasts, and staring in front of her out of hollow eyes.

The engine of the old car he'd borrowed roared, but Guitar spoke softly to her. "You think because he doesn't love you that you are worthless. You think because he doesn't want you anymore that he is right—that his judgment and opinion of you are correct. If he throws you out, then you are garbage. You think he belongs to you because you want to belong to him. Hagar, don't. It's a bad word, 'belong.' Especially when you put it with somebody you love. Love shouldn't be like that. Did you ever see the way the clouds love a mountain? They circle all around it; sometimes you can't even see the mountain for the clouds. But you know what? You go up top and what do you see? His head. The clouds never cover the head. His head pokes through, because the clouds let him; they don't wrap him up. They let him keep his head up high, free, with nothing to hide him or bind him. Hear me, Hagar?" He spoke to her as he would to a very young child. "You can't own a human being. You can't lose what you don't own. Suppose you did own him. Could you really love somebody who was absolutely nobody without you? You really want somebody like that? Somebody who falls apart when you walk out the door? You don't, do you? And neither does he. You're turning over your whole life to him. Your whole life, girl. And if it means so little to you that you can just give it away, hand it to him, then why should it mean any more to him? He can't value you more than you value yourself." He stopped. She did not move or give any sign that she had heard him.

Pretty woman, he thought. Pretty little black-skinned woman. Who wanted to kill for love, die for love. The pride, the conceit of these doormat women amazed him. They were always women who had been spoiled children. Whose whims had been taken seriously by adults and who grew up to be the stingiest, greediest people on earth and out of their stinginess grew their stingy little love that ate everything in sight. They could not believe or accept the fact that they were unloved; they believed that the world itself was off balance when it appeared as though they were not loved. Why did they think they were so lovable? Why did they think their brand of love was better than, or even as good as, anybody else's? But they did. And they loved their love so much they would kill anybody who got in its way.

He looked at her again. Pretty. Pretty little black girl. Pretty little black-skinned girl. What had Pilate done to her? Hadn't anybody told her the things she ought to know? He thought of his two sisters, grown women now who could deal, and the litany of their growing up. Where's your daddy? Your mama know you out here in the street? Put something on your head. You gonna catch your death a cold. Ain't you hot? Ain't you cold? Ain't you scared you gonna get wet? Uncross your legs. Pull up your socks. I thought you was goin to the Junior Choir. Your slip is showin. Your hem is out. Come back in here and iron that collar. Hush your mouth. Comb your head. Get up from there and make that bed. Put on the meat. Take out the trash. Vaseline get rid of that ash.

Neither Pilate nor Reba knew that Hagar was not like them. Not strong enough, like Pilate, nor simple enough, like Reba, to make up her life as they had. She needed what most colored girls needed: a chorus of mamas, grandmamas, aunts, cousins, sisters, neighbors, Sunday school teachers, best girl friends, and what all to give her the strength life demanded of her—and the humor with which to live it.

Still, he thought, to have the object of your love, worthy or not, despise you, or leave you . . .

"You know what, Hagar? Everything I ever loved in my life left me. My father died when I was four. That was the first leaving I knew and the hardest. Then my mother. There were four of us and she just couldn't cut it when my father died. She ran away. Just ran away. My aunt took care of us until my grandmother could get there. Then my grandmother took care of us. Then Uncle Billy came. They're both close to dead now. So it was hard for me to latch on to a woman. Because I thought if I loved anything it would die. But I did latch on. Once. But I guess once is all you can manage." Guitar thought about it and said, "But I never wanted to kill her. *Him*, yeah. But not her." He smiled, but Hagar wasn't looking, wasn't even listening, and when he led her out of the car into Reba's arms her eyes were still empty.

All they knew to do was love her and since she would not speak, they brought things to please her. For the first time in life Reba *tried* to win things. And, also for the first time, couldn't. Except for a portable television set, which they couldn't connect because they had no electricity, Reba won nothing. No raffle ticket, no Bingo, no policy slip, no clearing-house number, no magazine sweepstakes, no, nor any unpierced carnival balloon succumbed to her magic. It wore her down. Puzzled and luckless, she dragged herself home clutching stalks of anything that blossomed along the edges of lots and other people's gardens. These she presented to her daughter, who sat in a chair by the window or lay in bed fingering, fingering her hair.

They cooked special things for her; searched for gifts that they hoped would break the spell. Nothing helped. Pilate's lips were still and Reba's eyes full of panic. They brought her lipstick and chocolate milk, a pink nylon sweater and a fuchsia bed jacket. Reba even investigated the mysteries of making jello, both red and green. Hagar didn't even look at it.

One day Pilate sat down on Hagar's bed and held a compact before her granddaughter's face. It was trimmed in a goldlike metal and had a pink plastic lid.

"Look, baby. See here?" Pilate turned it all around to show it off and pressed in the catch. The lid sprang open and Hagar saw a tiny part of her face reflected in the mirror. She took the compact then and stared into the mirror for a long while.

"No wonder," she said at last. "Look at that. No wonder. No wonder."

Pilate was thrilled at the sound of Hagar's voice. "It's yours, baby," she said. "Ain't it pretty?"

"No wonder," said Hagar. "No wonder."

"No wonder what?" asked Pilate.

"Look at how I look. I look awful. No wonder he didn't want me. I look terrible." Her voice was calm and reasonable, as though the last few days hadn't been lived through at all. "I need to get up from here and fix myself up. No *wonder!*" Hagar threw back the bedcover and stood up. "Ohhh. I smell too. Mama, heat me some water. I need a bath. A long one. We got any bath salts left? Oh, Lord, my head. Look at that." She peered into the compact mirror again. "I look like a ground hog. Where's the comb?"

Pilate called Reba and together they flew through the house to find the comb, but when they found it Hagar couldn't get the teeth through her roped and matted hair.

"Wash it," said Reba. "Wash it and we'll comb it while it's wet."

"I need shampoo, then. Real shampoo. I can't use Mama's soap."

"I'll go get some." Reba was trembling a little. "What kind?"

"Oh, any kind. And get some hair oil, Reba. Posner's, and some . . . Oh, never mind. Just that. Mama? Have you seen my . . . Oh, my God. No wonder. No wonder."

Pilate pulled a piece of string from Hagar's bedspread and put it in her mouth. "I'll heat up the water," she said.

When Reba got back she washed Hagar's hair, brushed it, and combed it gently.

"Just make me two braids, Reba. I'm going to have to go to the beauty shop. Today. Oh, and I need something to wear." Hagar stood at the door of the little cardboard closet, running her hands over the shoulders of dresses. "Everything's a mess in here. A mess. All wrinkled . . ."

"Water's hot. Where you want the tub?"

"Bring it in here."

"You think you should be taking a bath so soon?" Reba asked. "You just got up."

"Hush, Reba," said Pilate. "Let the child take care of herself."

"But she's been in the bed three days."

"All the more reason."

"I can't put these things on. Everything's a mess." Hagar was almost in tears.

Reba looked at Pilate. "I hope you right. I don't approve of getting up too fast and jumping right in some water."

"Help me with this tub and stop grumbling."

"All wrinkled. What am I going to wear?"

"That ain't enough water to cover her feet."

"It'll grow when she sits down."

"Where's my yellow dress? The one that buttons all the way down?"

"Somewhere in there, I reckon."

"Find it for me and press it, would you? I know it's a mess. Everything's a mess."

Reba found and pressed the yellow dress. Pilate helped Hagar bathe. Finally a clean and clothed Hagar stood before the two women and said, "I have to buy some clothes. New clothes. Everything I have is a mess."

They looked at each other. "What you need?" asked Pilate.

"I need everything," she said, and everything is what she got. She shopped for everything a woman could wear from the skin out, with the money from Reba's diamond. They had seventy-five cents between them when Hagar declared her needs, and six dollars owed to them from customers. So the two-thousand-dollar two-carat diamond went to a pawnshop, where Reba traded it for thirty dollars at first and then, accompanied by a storming Pilate, she went back and got one hundred and seventy more for it. Hagar stuffed two hundred dollars and seventy-five cents into her purse and headed downtown, still whispering to herself every now and then, "No wonder."

She bought a Playtex garter belt, I. Miller No Color hose, Fruit of the Loom panties, and two nylon slips—one white, one pink—one pair of Joyce Fancy Free and one of Con Brio ("Thank heaven for little Joyce heels"). She carried an armful of skirts and an Evan-Picone two-piece number into the fitting room. Her little yellow dress that buttoned all the way down lay on the floor as she slipped a skirt over her head and shoulders, down to her waist. But the placket would not close. She sucked in her stomach and pulled the fabric as far as possible, but the teeth of the zipper would not join. A light sheen broke out on her forehead as she huffed and puffed. She was convinced that her whole life depended on whether or not those aluminum teeth would meet. The nail of her forefinger split and the balls of her thumbs ached as she struggled with the placket. Dampness became sweat and her breath came in gasps. She was about to weep when the saleswoman poked her head through the curtain and said brightly, "How are you doing?" But when she saw Hagar's gnarled and frightened face, the smile froze.

"Oh, my," she said, and reached for the tag hanging from the skirt's waist. "This is a five. Don't force it. You need, oh, a nine or eleven, I should think. Please. Don't force it. Let me see if I have that size."

She waited until Hagar let the plaid skirt fall down to her ankles before disappearing. Hagar easily drew on the skirt the woman brought back, and without further search, said she would take it and the little two-piece Evan-Picone.

She bought a white blouse next and a nightgown—fawn trimmed in sea foam. Now all she needed was make-up.

The cosmetics department enfolded her in perfume, and she read hungrily the labels and the promise. Myurgia for primeval woman who creates for him a world of tender privacy where the only occupant is you, mixed with Nina Ricci's L'Air du Temps. Yardley's Flair with Tuvaché's Nectaroma and D'Orsay's Intoxication. Robert Piguet's Fracas, and Calypso and Visa and Bandit. Houbigant's Chantilly. Caron's Fleurs de Rocaille and Bellodgia. Hagar breathed deeply the sweet air that hung over the glass counters. Like a smiling sleepwalker she circled. Round and round the diamond-clear counters covered with bottles, wafer-thin disks, round boxes, tubes, and phials. Lipsticks in soft white hands darted out of their sheaths like the shiny red penises of puppies. Peachy powders and milky lotions were grouped in front of poster after cardboard poster of gorgeous grinning faces. Faces in ecstasy. Faces somber with achieved seduction. Hagar believed she could spend her life there among the cut glass, shimmering in peaches and cream, in satin. In opulence. In luxe. In love.

It was five-thirty when Hagar left the store with two shopping bags full of smaller bags gripped in her hands. And she didn't put them down until she reached Lilly's Beauty Parlor.

"No more heads, honey." Lilly looked up from the sink as Hagar came in.

Hagar stared. "I have to get my hair done. I have to hurry," she said.

Lilly looked over at Marcelline. It was Marcelline who kept the shop prosperous. She was younger, more recently trained, and could do a light press that lasted. Lilly was still using red-hot irons and an ounce of oil on every head. Her customers were loyal but dissatisfied. Now she spoke to Marcelline. "Can you take her? I can't, I know."

Marcelline peered deeply into her customer's scalp. "Hadn't planned on any late work. I got two more coming. This is my eighth today."

No one spoke. Hagar stared.

"Well," said Marcelline. "Since it's you, come on back at eight-thirty. Is it washed already?"

Hagar nodded.

"Okay," said Marcelline. "Eight-thirty. But don't expect nothing fancy."

"I'm surprised at you," Lilly chuckled when Hagar left. "You just sent two people away."

"Yeah, well, I don't feel like it, but I don't want no trouble with that girl Hagar. No telling what she might do. She jump that cousin of hers, no telling what she might do to me."

"That the one going with Macon Dead's boy?" Lilly's customer lifted her head away from the sink.

"That's her. Ought to be shamed, the two of them. *Cousins.*"

"Must not be working out if she's trying to kill him."

"I thought he left town."

"Wouldn't you?"

"Well, I know I don't want to truck with her. Not me."

"She don't bother nobody but him."

"Well, Pilate, then. Pilate know I turned her down, she wouldn't like it. They spoil that child something awful."

"Didn't you order fish from next door?"

"All that hair. I hope she don't expect nothing fancy."

"Call him up again. I'm getting hungry."

"Be just like her. No appointment. No nothing. Come in here all late and wrong and want something fancy."


She probably meant to wait somewhere. Or go home and return to Lilly's at eight-thirty. Yet the momentum of the thing held her—it was all of a piece. From the moment she looked into the mirror in the little pink compact she could not stop. It was as though she held her breath and could not let it go until the energy and busyness culminated in a beauty that would dazzle him. That was why, when she left Lilly's, she looked neither right nor left but walked on and on, oblivious of other people, street lights, automobiles, and a thunderous sky. She was thoroughly soaked before she realized it was raining and then only because one of the shopping bags split. When she looked down, her Evan-Picone white-with-a-band-of-color skirt was lying in a neat half fold on the shoulder of the road, and she was far far from home. She put down both bags, picked the skirt up and brushed away the crumbs of gravel that stuck to it. Quickly she refolded it, but when she tried to tuck it back into the shopping bag, the bag collapsed altogether. Rain soaked her hair and poured down her neck as she stooped to repair the damage. She pulled out the box of Con Brios, a smaller package of Van Raalte gloves, and another containing her fawn-trimmed-in-sea-foam shortie nightgown. These she stuffed into the other bag. Retracing her steps, she found herself unable to carry the heavier bag in one hand, so she hoisted it up to her stomach and hugged it with both arms. She had gone hardly ten yards when the bottom fell out of it. Hagar tripped on Jungle Red (Sculptura) and Youth Blend, and to her great dismay, saw her box of Sunny Glow toppling into a puddle. She collected Jungle Red and Youth Blend safely, but Sunny Glow, which had tipped completely over and lost its protective disk, exploded in light peach puffs under the weight of the raindrops. Hagar scraped up as much of it as she could and pressed the wilted cellophane disk back into the box.

Twice before she got to Darling Street she had to stop to retrieve her purchases from the ground. Finally she stood in Pilate's doorway, limp, wet, and confused, clutching her bundles in whatever way she could. Reba was so relieved to see her that she grabbed her, knocking Chantilly and Bandit to the floor. Hagar stiffened and pulled away from her mother.

"I have to hurry," she whispered. "I have to hurry."

Loafers sluicing, hair dripping, holding her purchases in her arms, she made it into the bedroom and shut the door. Pilate and Reba made no move to follow her.

Hagar stripped herself naked there, and without taking time to dry her face or hair or feet, she dressed herself up in the white-with-a-band-of-color skirt and matching bolero, the Maidenform brassiere, the Fruit of the Loom panties, the no color hose, the Playtex garter belt and the Joyce con brios. Then she sat down to attend to her face. She drew charcoal gray for the young round eye through her brows, after which she rubbed mango tango on her cheeks. Then she patted sunny glow all over her face. Mango tango disappeared under it and she had to put it on again. She pushed out her lips and spread jungle red over them. She put baby clear sky light to outwit the day light on her eyelids and touched bandit to her throat, earlobes, and wrists. Finally she poured a little youth blend into her palm and smoothed it over her face.

At last she opened the door and presented herself to Pilate and Reba. And it was in their eyes that she saw what she had not seen before in the mirror: the wet ripped hose, the soiled white dress, the sticky, lumpy face powder, the streaked rouge, and the wild wet shoals of hair. All this she saw in their eyes, and the sight filled her own with water warmer and much older than the rain. Water that lasted for hours, until the fever came, and then it stopped. The fever dried her eyes up as well as her mouth.

She lay in her little Goldilocks'-choice bed, her eyes sand dry and as quiet as glass. Pilate and Reba, seated beside the bed, bent over her like two divi-divi trees beaten forward by a wind always blowing from the same direction. Like the trees, they offered her all they had: love murmurs and a protective shade.

"Mama." Hagar floated up into an even higher fever.

"Hmmm?"

"Why don't he like my hair?"

"Who, baby? Who don't like your hair?"

"Milkman."

"Milkman does too like your hair," said Reba.

"No. He don't. But I can't figure out why. Why he never liked my hair."

"Of course he likes it. How can he not like it?" asked Pilate.

"He likes silky hair." Hagar was murmuring so low they had to bend down to hear her.

"Silky hair? Milkman?"

"He don't like hair like mine."

"Hush, Hagar."

"Silky hair the color of a penny."

"Don't talk, baby."

"Curly, wavy, silky hair. He don't like mine."

Pilate put her hand on Hagar's head and trailed her fingers through her granddaughter's soft damp wool. "How can he not love your hair? It's the same hair that grows out of his own armpits. The same hair that crawls up out his crotch on up his stomach. All over his chest. The very same. It grows out of his nose, over his lips, and if he ever lost his razor it would grow all over his face. It's all over his head, Hagar. It's his hair too. He got to love it."

"He don't love it at all. He hates it."

"No he don't. He don't know what he loves, but he'll come around, honey, one of these days. How can he love himself and hate your hair?"

"He loves silky hair."

"Hush, Hagar."

"Penny-colored hair."

"Please, honey."
"And lemon-colored skin."
"Shhh."
"And gray-blue eyes."
"Hush now, hush."
"And thin nose."
"Hush, girl, hush."
"He's never going to like my hair."
"Hush. Hush. Hush, girl, hush."

The neighbors took up a collection because Pilate and Reba had spent everything getting Hagar the things needed to fix herself up. It didn't amount to much, though, and it was touch and go whether she'd have a decent funeral until Ruth walked down to Sonny's Shop and stared at Macon without blinking. He reached into his cash drawer and pulled out two twenty-dollar bills and put them down on the desk. Ruth didn't stretch out her hand to pick them up, or even shift her feet. Macon hesitated, then wheeled around in his chair and began fiddling with the combination to his safe. Ruth waited. Macon dipped into the safe three separate times before Ruth unclasped her hands and reached for the money. "Thank you," she said, and marched off to Linden Chapel Funeral Home to make the fastest arrangements possible.

Two days later, halfway through the service, it seemed as though Ruth was going to be the lone member of the bereaved family there. A female quartet from Linden Baptist Church had already sung "Abide with Me"; the wife of the mortician had read the condolence cards and the minister had launched into his "Naked came ye into this life and naked shall ye depart" sermon, which he had always believed suitable for the death of a young woman; and the winos in the vestibule who came to pay their respects to "Pilate's girl," but who dared not enter, had begun to sob, when the door swung open and Pilate burst in, shouting, "Mercy!" as though it were a command. A young man stood up and moved toward her. She flung out her right arm and almost knocked him down. "I want mercy!" she shouted, and began walking toward the coffin, shaking her head from side to side as though somebody had asked her a question and her answer was no.

Halfway up the aisle she stopped, lifted a finger, and pointed. Then slowly, although her breathing was fast and shallow, she lowered her hand to her side. It was strange, the languorous, limp hand coming to rest at her side while her breathing was coming so quick and fast. "Mercy," she said again, but she whispered it now. The mortician scurried toward her and touched her elbow. She moved away from him and went right up to the bier. She tilted her head and looked down. Her earring grazed her shoulder. Out of the total blackness of her clothes it blazed like a star. The mortician tried to approach her again, and moved closer, but when he saw her inky, berry-black lips, her cloudy, rainy eyes, the wonderful brass box hanging from her ear, he stepped back and looked at the floor.

"Mercy?" Now she was asking a question. "Mercy?"

It was not enough. The word needed a bottom, a frame. She straightened up, held her head high, and transformed the plea into a note. In a clear bluebell voice she sang it out—the one word held so long it became a sentence—and before the last syllable had died in the corners of the room, she was answered in a sweet soprano: "I hear you."

The people turned around. Reba had entered and was singing too. Pilate neither acknowledged her entrance nor missed a beat. She simply repeated the word "Mercy," and Reba replied. The daughter standing at the back of the chapel, the mother up front, they sang.

> *In the nighttime.*
> *Mercy.*
> *In the darkness.*
> *Mercy.*
> *In the morning.*
> *Mercy.*

*At my bedside.*
*Mercy.*
*On my knees now.*
*Mercy. Mercy. Mercy. Mercy.*

They stopped at the same time in a high silence. Pilate reached out her hand and placed three fingers on the edge of the coffin. Now she addressed her words to the woman bordered in gray satin who lay before her. Softly, privately, she sang to Hagar the very same reassurance she had promised her when she was a little girl.

*Who's been botherin my sweet sugar lumpkin?*
*Who's been botherin my baby?*
*Who's been botherin my sweet sugar lumpkin?*
*Who's been botherin my baby girl?*

*Somebody's been botherin my sweet sugar lumpkin.*
*Somebody's been botherin my baby.*
*Somebody's been botherin my sweet sugar lumpkin.*
*Somebody's been botherin my baby girl.*

*I'll find who's botherin my sweet sugar lumpkin.*
*I'll find who's botherin my baby.*
*I'll find who's botherin my sweet sugar lumpkin.*
*I'll find who's botherin my baby girl.*

"My baby girl." The three words were still pumping in her throat as she turned away from the coffin. Looking about at the faces of the people seated in the pews, she fastened on the first pair of eyes that were directed toward her. She nodded at the face and said, "My baby girl." She looked for another pair of eyes and told him also, "My baby girl." Moving back down the aisle, she told each face turned toward her the same piece of news. "My baby girl. That's my baby girl. My baby girl. My baby girl. My baby girl."

Conversationally she spoke, identifying Hagar, selecting her away from everybody else in the world who had died. First she spoke to the ones who had the courage to look at her, shake their heads, and say, "Amen." Then she spoke to those whose nerve failed them, whose glance would climb no higher than the long black fingers at her side. Toward them especially she leaned a little, telling in three words the full story of the stumped life in the coffin behind her. "My baby girl." Words tossed like stones into a silent canyon.

Suddenly, like an elephant who has just found his anger and lifts his trunk over the heads of the little men who want his teeth or his hide or his flesh or his amazing strength, Pilate trumpeted for the sky itself to hear, "And she was *loved!*"

It startled one of the sympathetic winos in the vestibule and he dropped his bottle, spurting emerald glass and jungle-red wine everywhere.

# Chapter 14

Perhaps it was because the sun had hit the rim of the horizon, but Susan Byrd's house looked different. The cedar tree was a silvery gray and its bark crinkled all the way up. It looked to Milkman like the leg of an ancient elephant. And now he noticed that the ropes that held the swing were frayed and the picket fence that had looked so bright and perky before was really flaked, peeling, even leaning to the left. The blue steps leading to the porch were faded into a watery gray. In fact the whole house looked seedy.

He lifted his hand to knock on the door and noticed the doorbell. He rang it and Susan Byrd opened the door.

"Hello again," he said.

"Well," she said, "you're as good as your word."

"I'd like to talk to you some more, if you don't mind. About Sing. May I come in?"

"Of course." She stood back from the door and the odor of another batch of gingerbread wafted out. Again they sat in the living room he in the gray wing-back chair, she on the sofa this time. Miss Long was nowhere in sight.

"I know you don't know who Sing married or if she married, but I was wondering—"

"Of course I know who she married. That is if they *did* marry. She married Jake, that black boy her mother took care of."

Milkman felt dizzy. Everybody kept changing right in front of him. "But yesterday you said nobody heard from her after she left."

"Nobody did. But they knew who she left with!"

"Jake?"

"Jake. Black Jake. Black as coal."

"Where—where did they live? Boston?"

"I don't know where they ended up. North, I guess. We never heard."

"I thought you said she went to a private school in Boston."

She dismissed the whole notion with a wave of her hand. "I just said that in front of *her*, Grace. She talks so much, you know. Carries tales all over the county. It's true she was supposed to go to some school, but she didn't. She left on that double-team wagon with that black boy, Jake. A whole lot of slaves got together. Jake was driving. Can you imagine it? Riding off with a wagonload of slaves?"

"What was Jake's last name? Can you tell me?"

She shrugged. "I don't think he had one. He was one of those flying African children. They must all be dead a long time now."

"Flying African children?"

"Um hm, one of Solomon's children. Or Shalimar. Papa said Heddy always called him Shalimar."

"And Heddy was . . ."

"My grandmother. Sing's mother and Papa's too. An Indian woman. She was the one who took care of Jake when his father left them all. She found him and took him home and raised him. She didn't have any boy children then. My father, Crowell, came later." She leaned forward and whispered, "She didn't have a husband, Heddy. I didn't want to go into all of that with Grace. You can imagine what she'd do with that information.

You're a stranger, so it doesn't matter. But Grace . . ." Susan Byrd looked pleadingly at the ceiling. "This Jake was a baby she found, and he and Sing grew up together, and I guess rather than be packed off to some Quaker school, she ran away with him. You know colored people and Indians mixed a lot, but sometimes, well, some Indians didn't like it—the marrying, I mean. But neither one of them knew their own father, Jake nor Sing. And my own father didn't know his. Heddy never said. I don't know to this day if he was white, red, or—well—*what*. Sing's name was Singing Bird. And my father's name was Crow at first. Later he changed it to Crowell Byrd. After he took off his buckskin." She smiled.

"Why did you call Solomon a flying African?"

"Oh, that's just some old folks' lie they tell around here. Some of those Africans they brought over here as slaves could fly. A lot of them flew back to Africa. The one around here who did was this same Solomon, or Shalimar—I never knew which was right. He had a slew of children, all over the place. You may have noticed that everybody around here claims kin to him. Must be over forty families spread in these hills calling themselves Solomon something or other. I guess he must have been hot stuff." She laughed. "But anyway, hot stuff or not, he disappeared and left everybody. Wife, everybody, including some twenty-one children. And they say they all saw him go. The wife saw him and the children saw him. They were all working in the fields. They used to try to grow cotton here. Can you imagine? In these hills? But cotton was king then. Everybody grew it until the land went bad. It was cotton even when I was a girl. Well, back to this Jake boy. He was supposed to be one of Solomon's original twenty-one—all boys and all of them with the same mother. Jake was the baby. The baby and the wife were right next to him when he flew off."

"When you say 'flew off' you mean he ran away, don't you? Escaped?"

"No, I mean flew. Oh, it's just foolishness, you know, but according to the story he wasn't running away. He was flying.

He flew. You know, like a bird. Just stood up in the fields one day, ran up some hill, spun around a couple of times, and was lifted up in the air. Went right on back to wherever it was he came from. There's a big double-headed rock over the valley named for him. It like to killed the woman, the wife. I guess you could say 'wife.' Anyway she's supposed to have screamed out loud for days. And there's a ravine near here they call Ryna's Gulch, and sometimes you can hear this funny sound by it that the wind makes. People say it's the wife, Solomon's wife, crying. Her name was Ryna. They say she screamed and screamed, lost her mind completely. You don't hear about women like that anymore, but there used to be more—the kind of woman who couldn't live without a particular man. And when the man left, they lost their minds, or died or something. Love, I guess. But I always thought it was trying to take care of children by themselves, you know what I mean?"

She talked on and on while Milkman sat back and listened to gossip, stories, legends, speculations. His mind was ahead of hers, behind hers, with hers, and bit by bit, with what she said, what he knew, and what he guessed, he put it all together.

Sing had said she was going to a Quaker school, but she joined Jake on his wagonful of ex-slaves heading for Boston or somewhere. They must have dropped their passengers all along the way. And then Jake, at the reins, took a wrong turn, because he couldn't read, and they ended up in Pennsylvania.

"But there's a children's game they play around here. And in the game they sing, 'Jake the *only* son of Solomon.' *Only*." He looked at her, hoping she wouldn't mind the interruption.

"Well, they're wrong. He wasn't the only son. There were twenty others. But he was the only one Solomon tried to take with him. Maybe that's what it means. He lifted him up, but dropped him near the porch of the big house. That's where Heddy found him. She used to come over there and help with the soapmaking and the candlemaking. She wasn't a slave, but she worked over at the big house certain times of year. She was melting tallow when she looked up and saw this man holding a baby and flying toward the ridge. He brushed too close to a tree and the baby slipped out of his arms and fell through the branches to the ground. He was unconscious, but the trees saved him from dying. Heddy ran over and picked him up. She didn't have any male children, like I said, just a little bitty girl, and this one just dropped out of the sky almost in her lap. She never named him anything different; she was afraid to do that. She found out the baby was Ryna's, but Ryna was out of her mind. Heddy lived a good ways off from the place Solomon and them others worked on. She tried to keep the girl away from that place too. And you can imagine how she felt when both of them ran off. Just my father was left."

"Did Jake have to register at the Freedmen's Bureau before he left the state?"

"Everybody did. Everybody who had been slaves, that is. Whether they left the state or not. But we were never slaves, so—"

"You told me that. Weren't any of Jake's brothers registering too?"

"I couldn't say. Those must have been some times, back then. Some bad times. It's a wonder anybody knows who anybody is."

"You've helped me a lot, Miss Byrd. I'm grateful." He thought then about asking her if she had a photo album. He wanted to see Sing, Crowell, even Heddy. But he decided against it. She might start asking him questions, and he didn't want to trouble her with a new-found relative who was as black as Jake.

"Now, that's not the woman you're looking for, is it? Pilate?"

"No," he said. "Couldn't be." He made motions of departure and then remembered his watch.

"By the way, did I leave my watch here? I'd like it back."

"Watch?"

"Yes. Your friend wanted to see it. Miss Long. I handed it to her but I forgot—" Milkman stopped. Susan Byrd was laughing out loud.

"Well, you can say goodbye to it, Mr. Macon. Grace will go to dinner all over the county telling people about the watch you gave her."

"What?"

"Well, you know. She doesn't mean any real harm, but it's a quiet place. We don't have many visitors, especially young men who wear gold watches and have northern accents. I'll get it back for you."

"Never mind. Never mind."

"You'll just have to forgive her otherwise. This is a dull place, Mr. Macon. There's absolutely nothing in the world going on here. Not a thing."

# Chapter 15

The fan belt didn't last long enough for him to get to the next gasoline station. It broke on the edge of a little town called Jistann, the needle trembling at H. Milkman sold it to the tow-truck man for twenty dollars and caught the first bus out. It was probably best that way, for over the humming wheels, his legs folded in the little space in front of his seat, he had time to come down from the incredible high that had begun as soon as he slammed the Byrd woman's door.

He couldn't get back to Shalimar fast enough, and when he did get there, dusty and dirty from the run, he leaped into the car and drove to Sweet's house. He almost broke her door down. "I want to swim!" he shouted. "Come on, let's go swimming. I'm dirty and I want waaaaater!"

Sweet smiled and said she'd give him a bath.

"Bath! You think I'd put myself in that tight little porcelain box? I need the sea! The whole goddam sea!" Laughing, hollering, he ran over to her and picked her up at the knees and ran around the room with her over his shoulder. "The sea! I have to swim in the sea. Don't give me no itty bitty teeny tiny tub, girl. I need the whole entire complete deep blue sea!"

He stood her on her feet. "Don't you all swim around here?"

"Over at the quarry is where the kids go sometimes."

"Quarry? You all don't have no sea? No ocean?"

"Naw; this hill country."

"Hill country. Mountain country. Flying country."

"A man was here to see you."

"Oh, yeah? That would be Mr. Guitar Bains."

"He didn't give his name."

"He don't have to! He's Guitar Bains. Gitar, Gitar, Gitar Bains!" Milkman did a little dance and Sweet covered her mouth, laughing.

"Come on, Sweet, tell me where the sea is."

"They some water comin down below the ridge on the other side. Real deep; wide too."

"Then let's go! Come on!" He grabbed her arm and pulled her out to the car. He sang all the way: " 'Solomon 'n Ryna Belali Shalut . . .' "

"Where you learn that?" she asked him. "That's a game we used to play when we was little."

"Of course you did. Everybody did. Everybody but me. But I can play it now. It's my game now."

The river in the valley was wide and green. Milkman took off his clothes, climbed a tree and dived into the water. He surfaced like a bullet, iridescent, grinning, splashing water. "Come on. Take them clothes off and come on in here."

"Naw. I don't wanna swim."

"Come in here, girl!"

"Water moccasins in there."

"Fuck 'em. Get in here. Hurry up!"

She stepped out of her shoes, pulled her dress over her head and was ready. Milkman reached up for her as she came timidly down the bank, slipping, stumbling, laughing at her own awkwardness, then squealing as the cold river water danced up her legs, her hips, her waist. Milkman pulled her close and kissed her mouth, ending the kiss with a determined effort to pull her under the water. She fought him. "Oh, my hair! My hair's gonna get wet."

"No it ain't," he said, and poured a handful right in the middle of her scalp. Wiping her eyes, spluttering water, she turned to wade out, shrieking all the way. "Okay, okay," he bellowed. "Leave me. Leave me in here by myself. I don't care. I'll play with the water moccasins." And he began to whoop and dive and splash and turn. "He could fly! You hear me? My great-granddaddy could fly! Goddam!" He whipped the water with his fists, then jumped straight up as though he too could take off, and landed on his back and sank down, his mouth and eyes full of water. Up again. Still pounding, leaping, diving. "The son of a bitch could fly! You hear me, Sweet? That motherfucker could fly! Could fly! He didn't need no airplane. Didn't need no fuckin tee double you ay. He could fly his own self!"

"Who you talkin 'bout?" Sweet was lying on her side, her cheek cupped in her hand.

"Solomon, that's who."

"Oh, him." She laughed. "You belong to that tribe of niggers?" She thought he was drunk.

"Yeah. That tribe. That flyin motherfuckin tribe. Oh, man! He didn't need no airplane. He just took off; got fed up. *All the way up!* No more cotton! No more bales! No more orders! No more shit! He flew, baby. Lifted his beautiful black ass up in the sky and flew on home. Can you dig it? Jesus God, that must have been something to see. And you know what else? He tried to take his baby boy with him. My grandfather. Wow! Woooee! Guitar! You hear that? Guitar, my great-granddaddy could flyyyyyy and the whole damn town is named after him. Tell him, Sweet. Tell him my great-granddaddy could fly."

"Where'd he go, Macon?"

"Back to Africa. Tell Guitar he went back to Africa."

"Who'd he leave behind?"

"Everybody! He left everybody down on the ground and he sailed on off like a black eagle. 'O-o-o-o-o-o Solomon done fly,

Solomon done gone /Solomon cut across the sky, Solomon gone home!' "

He could hardly wait to get home. To tell his father, Pilate; and he would love to see Reverend Cooper and his friends. "You think Macon Dead was something? Huh. Let me tell you about *his* daddy. You ain't heard nothin yet."

Milkman turned in his seat and tried to stretch his legs. It was morning. He'd changed buses three times and was now speeding home on the last leg of his trip. He looked out the window. Far away from Virginia, fall had already come. Ohio, Indiana, Michigan were dressed up like the Indian warriors from whom their names came. Blood red and yellow, ocher and ice blue.

He read the road signs with interest now, wondering what lay beneath the names. The Algonquins had named the territory he lived in Great Water, *michi gami*. How many dead lives and fading memories were buried in and beneath the names of the places in this country. Under the recorded names were other names, just as "Macon Dead," recorded for all time in some dusty file, hid from view the real names of people, places, and things. Names that had meaning. No wonder Pilate put hers in her ear. When you know your name, you should hang on to it, for unless it is noted down and remembered, it will die when you do. Like the street he lived on, recorded as Mains Avenue, but called Not Doctor Street by the Negroes in memory of his grandfather, who was the first colored man of consequence in that city. Never mind that he probably didn't deserve their honor—they knew what kind of man he was: arrogant, color-struck, snobbish. They didn't care about that. They were paying their respect to whatever it was that made him *be* a doctor in the first place, when the odds were that he'd be a yardman all of his life. So they named a street after him. Pilate had taken a rock from every state she had lived in—because she *had* lived there. And having lived there, it was hers—and his, and his father's, his grandfather's, his grandmother's. Not Doctor Street, Solomon's Leap, Ryna's Gulch, Shalimar, Virginia.

He closed his eyes and thought of the black men in Shalimar, Roanoke, Petersburg, Newport News, Danville, in the Blood Bank, on Darling Street, in the pool halls, the barbershops. Their names. Names they got from yearnings, gestures, flaws, events, mistakes, weaknesses. Names that bore witness. Macon Dead, Sing Byrd, Crowell Byrd, Pilate, Reba, Hagar, Magdalene, First Corinthians, Milkman, Guitar, Railroad Tommy, Hospital Tommy, Empire State (he just stood around and swayed), Small Boy, Sweet, Circe, Moon, Nero, Humpty-Dumpty, Blue Boy, Scandinavia, Quack-Quack, Jericho, Spoonbread, Ice Man, Dough Belly, Rocky River, Gray Eye, Cock-a-Doodle-Doo, Cool Breeze, Muddy Waters, Pinetop, Jelly Roll, Fats, Leadbelly, Bo Diddley, Cat-Iron, Peg-Leg, Son, Shortstuff, Smoky Babe, Funny Papa, Bukka, Pink, Bull Moose, B.B., T-Bone, Black Ace, Lemon, Washboard, Gatemouth, Cleanhead, Tampa Red, Juke Boy, Shine, Staggerlee, Jim the Devil, Fuck-Up, and *Dat* Nigger.

Angling out from these thoughts of names was one more—the one that whispered in the spinning wheels of the bus: "Guitar is biding his time. Guitar is biding his time. Your day has come. Your day has come. Guitar is biding his time. Guitar is a very good Day. Guitar is a very good Day. A very good Day, a very good Day, and biding, biding his time."

In the seventy-five-dollar car, and here on the big Greyhound, Milkman felt safe. But there were days and days ahead. Maybe if Guitar was back in the city now, among familiar surroundings, Milkman could defuse him. And certainly, in time, he would discover his foolishness. There was no gold. And although things would never be the same between them, at least the man-hunt would be over.

Even as he phrased the thought in his mind, Milkman knew it was not so. Either Guitar's disappointment with the gold that was not there was so deep it had deranged him, or his "work" had done it. Or maybe he simply allowed himself to feel about

Milkman what he had always felt about Macon Dead and the Honoré crowd. In any case, he had snatched the first straw, limp and wet as it was, to prove to himself the need to kill Milkman. The Sunday-school girls deserved better than to be avenged by that hawk-headed raven-skinned Sunday man who included in his blood sweep four innocent white girls and one innocent black man.

Perhaps that's what all human relationships boiled down to: Would you save my life? or would you take it?

"Everybody wants a black man's life."

Yeah. And black men were not excluded. With two exceptions, everybody he was close to seemed to prefer him out of this life. And the two exceptions were both women, both black, both old. From the beginning, his mother and Pilate had fought for his life, and he had never so much as made either of them a cup of tea.

Would you save my life or would you take it? Guitar was exceptional. To both questions he could answer yes.


"Should I go home first, or go to Pilate's first?" Out in the street, late at night with autumn air blowing cold off the lake, he tried to make up his mind. He was so eager for the sight of Pilate's face when he told her what he knew, he decided to see her first. He'd have a long time at his own house. He took a taxi to Darling Street, paid the driver, and bounded up the stairs. He pushed the door open and saw her standing over a tub of water, rinsing out the green bottles she used for her wine.

"Pilate!" he shouted. "Have I got stuff to tell you!"

She turned around. Milkman opened his arms wide so he could hold all of her in a warm embrace. "Come here, sweetheart," he said, grinning. She came and broke a wet green bottle over his head.

When he came to, he was lying on his side in the cellar. He opened one eye and considered the option of not coming to for a little while more. For a long time now he knew that anything could appear to be something else, and probably was. Nothing could be taken for granted. Women who loved you tried to cut your throat, while women who didn't even know your name scrubbed your back. Witches could sound like Katharine Hepburn and your best friend could try to strangle you. Smack in the middle of an orchid there might be a blob of jello and inside a Mickey Mouse doll, a fixed and radiant star.

So he lay on the cool damp floor of the cellar and tried to figure out what he was doing there. What did Pilate knock him out for? About the theft of her sack of bones? No. She'd come to his rescue immediately. What could it be, what else could he have done that would turn her against him? Then he knew. Hagar. Something had happened to Hagar. Where was she? Had she run off? Was she sick or . . . Hagar was dead. The cords of his neck tightened. How? In Guitar's room, did she . . . ?

What difference did it make? He had hurt her, left her, and now she was dead—he was certain of it. He had left her. While he dreamt of flying, Hagar was dying. Sweet's silvery voice came back to him: "Who'd he leave behind?" He left Ryna behind and twenty children. Twenty-one, since he dropped the one he tried to take with him. And Ryna had thrown herself all over the ground, lost her mind, and was still crying in a ditch. Who looked after those twenty children? Jesus Christ, he left twenty-one children! Guitar and the Days chose never to have children. Shalimar left his, but it was the children who sang about it and kept the story of his leaving alive.

Milkman rolled his head back and forth on the cellar floor. It was his fault, and Pilate knew it. She had thrown him in the cellar. What, he wondered, did she plan to do with him? Then he knew that too. Knew what Pilate's version of punishment was when somebody took another person's life. Hagar. Something of Hagar's must be nearby. Pilate would put him someplace near something that remained of the life he had taken, so he could *have* it. She would abide by this commandment from her father herself, and make him do it too. "You just can't fly on off and leave a body."

Suddenly Milkman began to laugh. Curled up like a Polish sausage, a rope cutting his wrists, he laughed.

"Pilate!" he called. "Pilate! That's not what he meant. Pilate! He didn't mean that. He wasn't talking about the man in the cave. Pilate! He was talking about himself. His own father flew away. He was the 'body.' The body you shouldn't fly off and leave. Pilate! Pilate! Come here. Let me tell you what your father said. Pilate, he didn't even tell you to sing, Pilate. He was calling for his wife—your mother. Pilate! Get me out of here!"

Light exploded in his face. The cellar door opened over his head. Pilate's feet appeared on the stone steps, and paused.

"Pilate," said Milkman, softly now, "that's not what he meant. I know what he meant. Come, let me tell you. And Pilate, those bones. They're not that white man's bones. He probably didn't even die. I went there. I saw. He wasn't there and the gold wasn't there either. Somebody found it and found him too. They must have, Pilate. Long before you got there. But, Pilate . . ."

She descended a few steps.

"Pilate?"

She came all the way down and he looked in her eyes and at her still mouth. "Pilate, your father's body floated up out of the grave you all dug for him. One month later it floated up. The Butlers, somebody, put his body in the cave. Wolves didn't drag the white man to the front of the cave and prop him on a rock. That was your father you found. You've been carrying your father's bones—all this time."

"Papa?" she whispered.

"Yes. And, Pilate, you have to bury him. He wants you to bury him. Back where he belongs. On Solomon's Leap."

"Papa?" she asked again.

Milkman did not speak; he watched her long fingers travel up her dress, to rest like the wing of a starling on her face. "I've been carryin Papa?" Pilate moved toward Milkman, stopped and looked at him for a while. Then her eyes turned to a rickety wooden table that stood against the stone wall of the cellar. It was in a part of the room so dark he had not even seen it. She walked over to the table and lifted from it a green-and-white shoe box, its cover held down with a rubber band. "Joyce," it said on the box. "Thank heaven for little Joyce heels."

"If I bury Papa, I guess I ought to bury this too—somewhere." She looked back at Milkman.

"No," he said. "No. Give it here."

When he went home that evening, he walked into the house on Not Doctor Street with almost none of the things he'd taken with him. But he returned with a box of Hagar's hair.

She wouldn't set foot on an airplane, so he drove. She seemed happy now. Her lips mobile again, she sat next to him in Macon's Buick, a mink stole Reba had won wrapped around her shoulders over her old black dress. The knit cap was pulled down on her forehead and her shoes still had no laces. Every now and then she glanced at the back seat to check on the sack. Peace circled her.

Milkman felt it too. His return to Not Doctor Street was not the triumph he'd hoped it would be, but there was relief in his mother's crooked smile. And Lena, though unforgiving as ever, was civil to him, since Corinthians had moved to a small house in Southside, which she shared with Porter. The Seven Days, Milkman guessed, would be looking for a new recruit, as they had to when Robert Smith jumped off the roof of Mercy. But there were long rambling talks with his father, who could not hear it enough—the "boys" who remembered him in Danville; his mother's running off with his father; the story about his father and his grandfather. He wasn't a bit interested in the flying part, but he liked the story and the fact that places were named for his people. Milkman softened his description of Circe, saying simply that she was alive, and taking care of the dogs.

"I ought maybe to take me a trip down there," said Macon.

"Virginia?" Milkman asked him.

"Danville. I ought to go by and see some of those boys before these legs stop moving. Let Freddie pick up the rents, maybe."

It was nice. No reconciliation took place between Pilate and Macon (although he seemed pleased to know that they were going to bury their father in Virginia), and relations between Ruth and Macon were the same and would always be. Just as the consequences of Milkman's own stupidity would remain, and regret would always outweigh the things he was proud of having done. Hagar was dead and he had not loved her one bit. And Guitar was . . . somewhere.

In Shalimar there was general merriment at his quick return, and Pilate blended into the population like a stick of butter in a churn. They stayed with Omar's family, and on the second and last evening, Milkman and Pilate walked up the road to the path that led to Solomon's Leap. It was the higher of two outcroppings of rock. Both flat-headed, both looking over a deep valley. Pilate carried the sack, Milkman a small shovel. It was a long way to the top, but neither stopped for breath. At the very top, on the plateau, the trees that could stand the wind at that height were few. They looked a long time for an area of earth among the rock faces large enough for the interment. When they found one, Pilate squatted down and opened the sack while Milkman dug. A deep sigh escaped from the sack and the wind turned chill. Ginger, a spicy sugared ginger smell, enveloped them. Pilate laid the bones carefully into the small grave. Milkman heaped dirt over them and packed it down with the back of his shovel.

"Should we put a rock or a cross on it?" Milkman asked.

Pilate shook her head. She reached up and yanked her earring from her ear, splitting the lobe. Then she made a little hole with her fingers and placed in it Sing's snuffbox with the single word Jake ever wrote. She stood up then, and it seemed to Milkman that he heard the shot after she fell. He dropped to his knees and cradled her lolling head in the crook of his arm, barking at her, "You hurt? You hurt, Pilate?"

She laughed softly and he knew right away that she was reminded of the day he first met her and said the most stupid thing there was to say.

The twilight had thickened and all around them it was getting dark. Milkman moved his hand over her chest and stomach, trying to find the place where she might be hit. "Pilate? You okay?" He couldn't make out her eyes. His hand under her head was sweating like a fountain. "Pilate?"

She sighed. "Watch Reba for me." And then, "I wish I'd a knowed more people. I would of loved 'em all. If I'd a knowed more, I would a loved more."

Milkman bent low to see her face and saw darkness staining his hand. Not sweat, but blood oozing from her neck down into his cupped hand. He pressed his fingers against the skin as if to force the life back in her, back into the place it was escaping from. But that only made it flow faster. Frantically he thought of tourniquets and could even hear the rip of cloth he should have been tearing. He shifted his weight and was about to lay her down, the better to wrap her wound, when she spoke again.

"Sing," she said. "Sing a little somethin for me."

Milkman knew no songs, and had no singing voice that anybody would want to hear, but he couldn't ignore the urgency in her voice. Speaking the words without the least bit of a tune, he sang for the lady. "Sugargirl don't leave me here/ Cotton balls to choke me/Sugargirl don't leave me here/ Buckra's arms to yoke me." The blood was not pulsing out any longer and there was something black and bubbly in her mouth. Yet when she moved her head a little to gaze at something behind his shoulder, it took a while for him to realize that she was dead. And when he did, he could not stop the worn old words from coming, louder and louder as though sheer volume would wake her. He woke only the birds, who shuddered off into the air. Milkman laid her head down on the rock. Two of the birds circled round them. One dived into the new grave and scooped something shiny in its beak before it flew away.

Now he knew why he loved her so. Without ever leaving the ground, she could fly. "There must be another one like you," he whispered to her. "There's got to be at least one more woman like you."

Even as he knelt over her, he knew there wouldn't be another mistake; that the minute he stood up Guitar would try to blow his head off. He stood up.

"Guitar!" he shouted.

*Tar tar tar*, said the hills.

"Over here, brother man! Can you see me?" Milkman cupped his mouth with one hand and waved the other over his head. "Here I am!"

*Am am am am*, said the rocks.

"You want me? Huh? You want my life?"

*Life life life life.*

Squatting on the edge of the other flat-headed rock with only the night to cover him, Guitar smiled over the barrel of his rifle. "My man," he murmured to himself. "My main man." He put the rifle on the ground and stood up.

Milkman stopped waving and narrowed his eyes. He could just make out Guitar's head and shoulders in the dark. "You want my life?" Milkman was not shouting now. "You need it? Here." Without wiping away the tears, taking a deep breath, or even bending his knees—he leaped. As fleet and bright as a lodestar he wheeled toward Guitar and it did not matter which one of them would give up his ghost in the killing arms of his brother. For now he knew what Shalimar knew: If you surrendered to the air, you could *ride* it.